HOME RULE

HOME RULE

Clare Boylan

HAMISH HAMILTON • LONDON

For Noeleen

HAMISH HAMILTON LTD
Published by the Penguin Group
Penguin Books Ltd, 27 Wrights Lane, London W8 5TZ, England
Penguin Books USA Inc., 375 Hudson Street, New York, New York, 10014, USA
Penguin Books Australia Ltd, Ringwood, Victoria, Australia
Penguin Books Canada Ltd, 10 Alcorn Avenue, Toronto, Ontario, Canada M4V 3B2
Penguin Books (NZ) Ltd, 182–190 Wairau Road, Auckland 10, New Zealand

Penguin Books Ltd, Registered Offices: Harmondsworth, Middlesex, England

First published 1992

1 3 5 7 9 10 8 6 4 2

Filmset in Monophoto Bembo
Printed in England by Clays Ltd, St Ives plc

A CIP catalogue record for this book is available from the British Library
ISBN 0-241-13208-8

Chapter 1

ALL through June Daisy had been looking forward to the holy-days when she would have Will and Tom and Janey and Essie and Beth and Weenie to herself. For the rest of the year there was only Lena and Bertie at home and Lena was busy with housework all day. She had been taken out of school for this purpose. Mama considered seven years of books more than enough for a girl.

At last the children were released. The little sealed house, with its smell of baked dust and stewed food, was shaken to its rafters by so much bustle and clutter. There was always someone boxing or bawling or singing or sewing. Mama retreated to her drawing room with her dolls. Daisy ran in and out of the house after her brothers and sisters, her unused legs shaky in their thunderous wake. They made forbidden excursions to Granny Devlin's or looked for bodies in the canal. They went to Gloucester Street to see the fallen women at the Magdalen Institute. Daisy followed them everywhere. Then she realized they did not want her. She was six and they had grown-up preoccupations which could not include her. The girls played games of Amateur Reprehensibles in the garden. This was Janey's adaptation of a game called Amateur Representations which mama had played in her youth and described as a parlour game. In Janey's version the children dramatized gruesome crimes reported in the newspapers.

'Why can't I come with you?' she asked Will, who at thirteen, was not expected to stay with the girls and went over Clarke's Bridge with Tom to Ballybough with its fields and pig farms, or to Middle Arch, the swimming place close to the Sloblands.

'I'll tell you tomorrow,' he said kindly.

But when the next day came and she asked again, he pointed out: 'This is today. I said I'd tell you tomorrow.'

Janey was the only one whose company she did not seek. In the ten-year-old's murderous games Daisy was always the first to die and she had to lie still on the ground while the others ran off and left her. It was a good method of getting rid of infant nuisances. She was even meaner in the dark. The heavy purple nights, canopied by city smells of drains, were rendered sleepless anyway by having to sleep three to a bed and six to the tiny room. 'Are yis awake?' Janey would give Daisy a pinch to make sure she was. 'I can't sleep. I'll tell yis a story.'

In the city of Paris that summer a reservoir burst its banks and washed away a graveyard. Hundreds of decomposing bodies were floated into houses and gardens and some lingered there for weeks. Janey described the rush of water, the freakish waves which stripped the corpses of their flesh and hurtled them into polished hallways and then for days, and worse – nights – the greenish figures danced gently on the flood, the remains of their eyes staring in speechless apology at their helpless hosts while the worms, unperturbed, dined and drifted.

Just when Lena had comforted them by telling them that Paris was hundreds of miles away in France and that no one had ever been there except mama, Janey would walk her fingers up Daisy's back and whisper in her ear: 'I hear tramp, tramp, tramp. And there's no one there.'

Daisy took to spending the days of August alone in the bedroom watching out the window for pa. When he rounded the corner she ran out to meet him. 'How's my oul' cod?' He would swing her into his arms. 'How's my figarious fairy?' And then seeing her miserable face he asked, 'Are you all right?'

'Yes, pa,' she would answer quickly, even though she was not.

Whenever pa asked the children how they were, he was disappointed if they said they were all right. He watched them for signs of hot skin, of high colour or running noses; for furred tongue, significant, he had read, of a variety of morbid disorders, or spots or slouching or dullness of eye. He spied on their comings and goings to the shed to gauge their regularity.

The city was riddled with slums, its languid air fogged with infection. The wide streets, arranged for views of domes and spires smelled of blood from its abattoirs, of beer from Guinness's brewery, of the putrefying stench of the River Liffey. People still reeled from the small, subsidiary fevers that drifted in the wake of the great cholera epidemic of 1849 and horses fell dead in the street, poisoned by the reek of makeshift coffins. Country folk who had crept away from the famine forty years ago lived in mud cabins with poisonous open drains. The starving fed at soup kitchens where the spoons, attached by chains, carried the afflictions of previous diners.

Nearly all the city children had a wan look and runny noses, but not pa's. It was mama's good blood. She frequently reminded them of this, as if they did not deserve it and might waste it. In any case, even if they had been at death's door they would have feigned good health, for pa's remedies were worse than ordinary ailments. While Lena boiled up the wash or some scraps of mutton, pa mixed his potions beside her at the stove – a calf's foot, still with the hair on it, sulphur, sulphate of iron, castor oil, oil of turpentine, sulphide of calcium, a pinch of Gregory's Powder, a tincture of Mindererus Spirit. He also had boundless faith in patent remedies and liked to read out advertisements for these during meals.

'Magneto-electricity – the great remedy for rheumatism, lumbago, sciatica, gout, kidney disease, epilepsy, paralysis, indigestion, constipation, bronchitis, pulmonary afflictions, colds, neuralgia, consumption, asthma, female disorders.'

Upon the last pronouncement he would gaze with gratitude at his large brood of female dependants. The younger children pierced him with their curiosity and Lena, who was the only one old enough to qualify, would flee to stove or sink. Now and again he would reach out and pat one of his offspring and ask them how they were and the child squirmed away from the questing fingers. 'Well, thank you, pa.'

On the day of the cats Daisy was minding Bertie in the yard. A torpid atmosphere had sent mama to lie on her bed and the boys had gone down to the canal to commence digging a monster hole. The bedroom had been taken over by the twins, who wanted to cut out some new chemises, and Lena was made irritable by that curious disorder defined only by her sex.

Janey rolled around the grass in the yard making terrible faces and groaning hideously. 'I have sinned beyond forgiveness!' she wailed, 'and I am riddled with the pox!' Weenie wrung her hands and implored her to make her last confession to a priest. Janey was playing her favourite game with Weenie, employing as their subject the Bayswater Suicide, who was reported to have purchased aconite, saying she had neuralgia. She swallowed it and died after an hour and a half of great agony. Before she expired she confessed that she had sinned beyond forgiveness, and had an assortment of diseases.

Daisy was not allowed to join in. She had been told to keep the baby happy, but Bertie, seeing the state of his older sister, leaned out of his pram and began to grizzle. To make him quiet Daisy hauled him out of the pram and left him to crawl about the grass. She lay on her stomach to watch the sun painting stripes of whiteness on to Lena's grey wash on the line and to dream of her future when she would be loved and beautiful and famous.

Bertie forgot Janey's antics and turned his attention to a large cat, prowling on top of the wall. They stared at one another until the animal opened its furry jowls and stuck out its tongue. Disturbed, the baby turned away. For a time he found amusement in the ashes and peelings on the compost heap. He even discovered the bone of a mutton chop to chew. Then he was tired and wanted to get into his pram and smell his blanket. He crawled towards it and pulled himself up by the wheels, rocking the vehicle to make it squeak and draw attention to himself. When he looked inside he saw that his place had been taken. The cat had climbed down off the wall and now occupied his pram, stretched to full length to convey that there was no room for any other creature. The shock was so considerable that the infant pulled himself up higher yet and perched on unstable toes, clinging to the edge of the pram with the tips of his fingers. The animal yawned hugely, showing a trap of pointed fangs. The whiteness of this circular trap, coming out of nowhere in the dappled garden, so terrified the child that he began to scream. It was a serious male bellow of despair and it frightened Janey and Weenie out of their drama and brought mama in a fury to her bedroom window.

Everyone blamed Daisy. Janey threw her out of the garden and mama instructed her not to set foot in the house. She got bored and lonely sitting on the doorstep and went off to meet pa. She had not been further than Edward Street on her own before. Sometimes the children took a left-hand turning for the city and sometimes they went to the right. It depended. Uncertainly she turned right past the five lamps. She walked quickly, imagining herself as a child genius playing the piano, alone on the stage of a concert hall with a huge orchestra. After five minutes or so she noticed that there was a strange silence in the air, and a queer dead reek. She got the sense of being watched. Someone laughed and she slowly looked up at a young woman who seemed to have shrunk inside her rags so that her waxy skin was loose and puckered. She had no teeth. She stopped

dead and peered around her. Gaunt, half-dead creatures stared at
her from every rotten doorway, and barefoot children with sores on
their faces and the pinprick marks of vermin bites on their arms.
Their wretched faces were stretched in grins. They were laughing at
her good dress, her boots, her long shiny hair. She had taken the
wrong turning. She was in the slums of Killarney Street, which led to
crumbling Gloucester Street and to the unspeakable horror of Monto
– Montgomery Street – where poor women sold their bodies to men.
She remembered now why they sometimes turned to the right. It was
when Janey was with them, so that they could go and look for fallen
women. What did the men do with the women's bodies? 'They eat
them,' Janey told her. 'They boil them until they're nice and gluey
like the pigs' feet in the crubeen shop and then they eat them up,
although they prefer a child to eat when they can get one.' Daisy
began to run. She prayed furiously, pursued by taunts of toothless,
mirth, and some saving instinct guided her into Buckingham Street
from which she emerged on to respectable Great Britain Street with
its shops and traffic and terraces of good dwellings. Waiting on the
corner at the Old Maids' Home she tried to hum a tune. Its notes
came without thought and drifted on the air like smoke. It was a
strange, haunting air and began to draw people, who were summoned
by its mysterious power. At first she sensed it as a thickening in the
rhythm of horses' hooves on the cobbles. She looked down the street
and saw carts and carriages charging in her direction with bicycles
dangerously weaving in between. The crisp, querying clops were
joined by more hurrying vehicles until it made a typist's busy patter.
A rush of pedestrians hurried towards her with strained, eager faces.
More horses came and more, until the blows of hoof on stone
slithered into one another and the creak and clatter of wheel and the
snap of whip and the snarl of bell and the gasp of hems pitched
together, curdled into that slush and hue of rush-hour sound. The
urgent throng and herd that was drawn mesmerically towards Daisy
then fled on past her without a pause, but she only saw them coming
and did not notice when they passed her by. After half an hour the
city had spewed out the greater part of its daily workers and the
traffic began to thin out and slow down, and then along came pa.

'Are you all right?' he asked her and she told him that she was.

'Well, what are you doing out here all alone in the path of horses
and hooligans?'

'They threw me out,' she said. 'Nobody wants me.'

'We'll see about that.' He picked her up and carried her all the way back, past Summerhill and Summerhill Parade, past Edward Street and round the corner into the recently erected splendour of St Lucy's Church. 'Look!' He pointed to the domed ceiling, mosaicked with stars, at the flower-decked altar with its elaborately engraved little golden hutch where God was captive like a pampered bird. 'Isn't this a grand place all the same? Wouldn't it put you in mind of a palace? Do you know that Dublin Castle isn't a real castle at all, but only a class of a barracks where the queen's unemployables hold hooleys and the crown jewels are kept there so she can't put them in the hock?' He sauntered down the aisle whistling a tune under his moustache. 'Who do you think owns this gaff?' He did not wait for her to answer. Anyway, she was not sure if it belonged to God or the parish priest or the pope. 'You do!' pa said. 'This is your house.' He showed her a beautiful stained-glass window on which were engraved the romantic phrases 'Lily of Israel', 'Rose of Sharon', 'Tower of Ivory', 'House of Gold'. 'Did you ever wonder who your woman is, Lily of Israel? It's yourself! That is your name in heaven. It was put in that window for Daisy Devlin.'

When they got back to Edward Street she did not want to go in. 'It's all right, pettie,' he soothed. 'You're all right with me. I am the man of the house.' Inside he recklessly inquired of mama if there was a bottle of stout on the go.

'There is a bottle of filth in the press,' she told him softly.

He laughed uneasily and the five Es ran to get him his porter. The five eldest girls were known as the five Es. Mama had named her first daughter, Elinore, after herself, although she was never known by any name but Lena. When the births of her beloved boys, Tom and Will, were followed by four more girls, imagination failed her and interest too, and she could only think of more names that commenced with E – Eugenia and Elizabeth and Esther and Edwina. Eugenia called herself Janey as soon as she could speak. The twins, Elizabeth and Esther, were shortened to Essie and Beth, and Edwina, because of her diminutive size, earned the abbreviation of Weenie, which she hated. Only mama employed their formal names.

When pa was settled with his stout and Lena was serving the tea, he read out an important announcement from the newspaper. 'Something frightful!' All eyes were on Lena to see that they got equal portions of her variable fourteen-year-old's cooking. He waited until they each had their share of bread and onions and proceeded: 'A testimonial for Clarke's blood mixture!' Mama sent him a warning glare and he beamed in appreciation. She waved Lena's pot away and gave herself some thin bread and butter.

'"I cannot neglect giving you the particulars of an extra-ordinary cure"' – pa made extraordinary into two words, in the fashion of Dubliners – '"for I feel that it is a duty."' He scrubbed his plate with bread and washed it down with tea, keeping them in suspense. '"My life was a misery to me due to the terrible suffering arising from eleven dreadful abscesses on my chest and side, the discharge from them being something frightful. From the first box of Clarke's Mixture, the effect was beneficial. I am now perfectly cured."'

'And that,' he announced, 'is from Mr Thomas Kent.'

'As if it were a sonnet by Mr Shakespeare,' said mama.

'From Fiskerton, near Lincoln.'

Mama put out an impatient hand for her paper but he held on to it long enough to memorize the address of the sufferer. He would write to Mr Thomas Kent, send him a bottle of his own sulphur mix. 'Should I mention,' he wondered aloud, 'that Fellows' Syrup of Hypophosphites is useful when a chronic discharge has lowered the tone of the system?'

'Tell him you have remedies for everything,' mama said grimly, 'except this!' She jerked a dismissive profile towards the crowding of heads at the table.

'Ah, now!' Pa was shocked. 'Which of them would you be without?'

There was an anxious moment while she looked over them, considering. 'Anyway,' pa grinned proudly, 'there is no remedy for that.'

'What about the bolster?' mama demanded.

This was an episode from history, from years ago, that would never be forgotten. Once, when there were only eight of them, she had come back from the city with what looked like yet another infant but swaddled in brown paper and tied about with string. 'Look!' she summoned pa. Her fingers shook with nervous excitement and all the children pressed around. When the string and paper came away they were looking at a sausage of fabric upholstered in mattress ticking.

'It's a bolster,' Lena guessed. 'I think you put it under your head.'

'I have been to France,' mama said, claiming her superiority. She addressed herself again to pa. 'Placed lengthwise along the bed it prevents accidental contact.'

'Contraception! That's a mortal sin against the Catholic Church,' pa protested. The children crouched around, intent and uncomprehending. They did not understand, but were excited by the flamboyant word which sounded like a bold Spanish woman who did as she liked. Pa had never been to France. He examined the bolster's discouraging length and declared it a queer class of a gazebo before throwing it in the bin. When mama went to retrieve it, it was gone and she could never find out where. Daisy had taken it and placed it lengthwise along her own bed to prevent accidental contact with Janey, who was a devil in human form.

Mama calmed down as she read from the paper the pieces that she liked. Cookman's Hair Salon was taking orders for the coming fancy balls and Court Hairdressing. Pa stuffed his pipe with Violet Smoking Mixture and held out his cup for a refill. He had once known a woman, he remarked, who lost an eye through an unattended abscess.

'They are specializing in diamond and fancy powdering,' mama argued strongly. A boil, mused pa, could be anything from the size of a pinhead to a carbuncle containing a pint of matter. 'A peculiar phenomenon – putrefaction of the living flesh.'

'Listen!' mama implored. She read out the next announcement as if all of their lives depended upon it. 'The Lord Lieutenant will hold a levee at Dublin Castle on the 31st at one o'clock.'

'Come here to me. Is that a break on your skin?' Pa leaned forward with sudden alertness and touched Essie's arm. It wasn't that he wanted his children to fail. He loved them. He loved them with such a passion that he wanted to save them. They were so different from him that he felt he could only enter their lives in a heroic role. 'I'm all right.' Essie nursed the unfortunate limb which she had grazed in a fall and which had suffered a mild infection. 'No,' pa sighed. 'You look all right, but you're delicate.' He rose from the table, clutching his pipe in his teeth.

'Something frightful,' Janey chanted in delight. 'He's gone to get you something frightful.'

That night Janey found a new way to taunt Daisy, who was an obsessively modest child and would not undress in front of anyone, so that when they went to the sea she bathed in all her clothes. 'I've got hair growing down there.' Janey pointed to her navy-blue drawers. 'And you've got none, because you're only a rotten oul' herring.'

A wall collapsed in a house in the Liberties, which was backed by an abattoir. Janey described the tide of putrid blood and maggots that swept into the house, flooding it to a depth of several inches. It foamed over the ankles of householders as they waded to their rooms. Blood-red rats swam for their lives and a small girl tripped and fell and was choked to death. In the dark she made a gurgling noise which so terrified Daisy that she slipped out of bed and ran down the stairs.

Pa was asleep in his chair by the stove. After the episode of the bolster, mama had locked him from her bedroom and he slept in the kitchen, although on rare occasions, when he had taken porter, he climbed up the drainpipe and in her bedroom window. When Daisy touched him he woke at once and speechlessly took her into his arms. As she fell asleep on his lap she had a dream. 'Ah, you are so beautiful. No one loves you more than me,' he sighed. 'Ah, little pretty one.' He kissed and kissed her. 'Mustn't. Mustn't. Sure there's no harm, pettie. This is our little secret. I only need a little love.' And then she woke to find that she had not been dreaming. For the first time she did not feel safe with pa. She struggled to be free but he was so intent he seemed to have forgotten her. He was like someone looking for something he had lost. Quite suddenly he sighed and fell asleep. She scrambled unnoticed off his knee. She could not go back to bed because of Janey. Stealthily she turned the knob of the kitchen door and slipped out into the warm night. A big moon painted the yard so that the washing on the line and the bristly grass and the rubbish in the corner were dyed to the bruised blue of sugar bags. She remembered the pram and wondered what had happened to the cat that had got in. She clambered underneath the dripping clothes, and there, stretched out on Bertie's blanket, was a blue cat. In spite of her confusion she gave an impetuous cry of joy. Stretched along the cat like neatly rolled socks were six, tiny, new-born kittens.

Chapter 2

ON days when no one noticed her, Daisy took to wheeling her cats through the city. After the incident in the garden, Bertie had walked away from his pram with stiff-toed dignity. He had not walked before and would not let himself be wheeled again. The heavy carriage which had trundled nine children now boasted six sets of baleful yellow eyes glaring out of frills. Daisy had dressed the kittens in the ruffled bonnets and frocks which mama had made for Bertie, and which he hated.

'The Marchioness of Londonderry will be holding a drawing room at the Castle next week,' she informed Mrs Boake, imparting the vital news that mama had read out from the *Irish Times*. She jiggled the handle of the pram and the kittens bickered and boxed and tremulously yelped, dismayed by the rolling transport. Mrs Boake's little gravy-coloured eyes grew studious and she rummaged in a pocket for a pin. She removed a yellowing napkin from her naked breast where she had left it for airing and skewered it on to a boiled-looking boy. 'Holding a drawing room? She must have arms like an ox.'

She went on down to the grass verge of the canal where boys loitered to watch the freight train clattering past. A gurrier plucked one of the cats from the pram and threw it into the water, where it drowned. She ran with her remaining charges until she had left behind the familiar neighbouring streets and was out in the wide world of Summerhill. This was a mile-long stretch of seething life, of shops and houses and tenements, of chandlers, pawnbrokers, hay merchants, which led to Great Britain Street and Sackville Street. She walked on the cobbled road, for the pavements were dangerous with angry women and drunk men and thieving beggars. People looked into the perambulator but showed no surprise. Strange sights were common in the city – performing dogs and monkeys and bears, beggars who coyly displayed hideous deformities to tease people into parting with their money.

Close to Sackville Street, the thoroughfare grew refined. Daisy

10

held her breath as she turned into North Great George's Street, where every one of the tall terraced houses had its own carriage house and the roads were cleared by private sweepers. She stopped and listened to the mutinous clumping of scales being practised by a child. The noise stopped and an adult took over. A flight of little dainty notes was muffled behind lace curtains.

Pa said that the small families in the big houses were supplemented by scullions and cooks and nannies and maids and visiting medical men, bishops, nobs and music teachers. He maintained that the men kept a third eye of glass on a rope of chain for looking at women's ankles and that the ladies produced their babies by coughing behind a hanky. Both sexes feasted off cuts of meat so tender you could chew them with the cheeks of your arse while the hapless infants dined in dread of dim-witted wet nurses who were frequently seized with a mania for suffocating their charges. Mama had a different version and probably more correct since she had grown up in such a house, but when Daisy spied on the long windows at the softly lit rooms with their mirrors and pictures, she would have loved to see a lady coughing up a large pink infant into a little square of lace.

No such remarkable thing happened, but a voice beside her asked, 'May I have one of your cats?' She looked up and there was a lady, beautiful as a tower of ivory and smelling of scent. With her was a little girl of eight or nine. The girl had golden hair like her mother and in every way seemed more to resemble a very small woman than a child. She wore a dress of blue organza, tight in the waist, and cut so low in front that nearly the whole of her chest was bare. Underneath the short skirt of her gown could be seen the legs of her gossamer drawers and she had thin stockings and little boots so flimsy they might successfully have adorned mama's mantelpiece. When she saw Daisy staring at her the child tossed her curls and looked away. She showed only the coolest interest in the kittens.

'What pretty kittens!' The lady drew back Daisy's attention. 'Won't you let me buy one?' She picked out a white kitten whose face was marked by black and orange in the pattern of a pansy. It hung on her wrist like a muff. Daisy speechlessly studied the two lovely apparitions, which seemed composed of layer after layer of luxurious stuff, of silk and organza and silky skin and hair. The woman opened a little brocaded purse and took out half a crown. 'Is that enough?'

'I can't sell it,' Daisy blurted out. 'It isn't mine.'

11

'Then whom does it belong to?' The lady bent down and her beautiful pink gown touched the mud of the street. She held the kitten up to her face. The silver in her purse made dull, intoxicating bells.

'To a white cat on the wall,' Daisy whispered, numbed by a surfeit of opportunity.

'Well, then.' She put the kitten back in the pram where it squawked in disappointment. 'I suppose it must go where it belongs. We all must be where we belong.' All the way back her heart pounded with jealousy. Why could she not live in such a beautiful house and have a blue dress and her mama all to herself? She imagined the disagreeable little girl dead of typhoid and herself adopted by the lady who would buy her from mama with the contents of her purse. Passing by Great Portland Street a starving dog sprang out of an alley and leaped upon the pram full of cats. An ossified soldier rambled into the obstruction and swung a fist at the animal, which reeled back, showing foaming fangs. Daisy ran, wanting nothing but the safety of 11 Edward Street.

When she got home she related her adventure to mama, who peered into the pram. 'Now you shall have the trouble of drowning the lot,' she ruefully observed.

The fourteen small houses on Edward Street marked the edge of the city. The country – Ballybough, whose Georgian terraces gradually gave way to fields and farms and backward natives – was kept at bay by Clarke's Bridge and the milky margin of the canal. Edward Street had houses on one side only. Built opposite were a school for boys and an institution for orphan females, which preserved the calm of the terrace as well as cutting out all its light. The dwellings themselves were of a curiously distorted nature, as if the builders had expected the residents to make a tableau within, instead of moving from room to room. Narrow stairs commenced within a foot of the front door, there being no hall. This left the drawing room as the only route to a hell-hole of a scullery which served as living room, dining room, bathroom, study, nursery and kitchen. There was no side passage to protect the best room from muddy feet. At the back, a small yard was shadowed by high walls, bound by clothes-lines and shackled by a sanitary shed. On the 'good' end of the street the yard was long enough to support a patch of grass and call itself a garden. These stretches diminished house by house until at the bad end the yard was no more than a description of measurement. Upstairs were two small rooms, poorly partitioned, in which a family of four might have lain in constricted comfort. There was scarcely an address on Edward Street with less than a dozen inhabitants. Accommodation in the four-roomed houses was further limited by the conversion of the front rooms. These had been turned into a makeshift shop in all but number 11, which faced the street with an exquisite little drawing room, where mama defended herself against her nine children and the calamity of family life.

Mama's parlour was an oddity on the street. It marked them off as if they were Jews or had come up from the country. They were an oddity anyway, for the children wore shoes all the time. In the day, with the light blocked off by the bulk of the orphanage, it could have been just another shop, although better set up than the others. At dusk, when the rest of the women covered their windows with newspaper, mama lit a little lamp with a pink glass shade. Then the room, bathed in flamingo light, showed a composition so fantastic that people stopped in the street to look in and wistful fingerprints were left on the glass with its underwear and overwear of lace and velvet with bobbles. Once mama heard a poor woman remark to her children: 'Nobody hereabouts lives like that. Sure it's only a painted window.' She had stifled a smile and sat very still, enjoying the joke. None of the children was allowed in the drawing room, which was awkward since they had to pass through it to get to the kitchen or out into the street. Like anyone else, they had to view it through the window and they had developed a habit of pausing to glance enviously in before entering their house.

Mama's parlour had a wallpaper, Chinese gold, with a tiny pattern of mauve flowers. The floor was heaped with Turkey carpets, overlapping so that they patterned the entire area in colours as subtle as a pot-pourri. A little sofa covered in rose brocade was smothered in beaded and embroidered cushions. There were two small ebony chairs with striped silk seats and a wine table with ornaments and a silver dish of sweets. More ornaments crowded the mantelpiece – a lantern from Japan, a Venice bud-holder with a necklace of beads woven into its primrose stem and two white china dogs which laughed at each other across a clutter of small boxes. She had a collection of dolls imprisoned behind the glass doors of a walnut cupboard. Cloth roses, fans, boas, silk parasols, a fan, a Spanish shawl, hung and draped and poked out of corners. There was even a small piano with a silk scarf on its lid and silver-framed photographs of the boys as babies and other people whom pa and the children had never seen.

Mama was different from the rest of them. She had come from Kensington. She had once been to France. Her ascendancy – although she had little to do with the children, apart from the boys whom, voluptuously, she loved – in turn made them different from other children on the street. The boys she preserved from the influence of the city as from some noxious infection. She refined their speech and ordered their hair until they were taunted by neighbourhood bullies. They went to the High School in Harcourt Street instead of the Christian Brothers like their father. Pa, mystified and respectful, kept a distance from them and called them the Cod and the Card. She made the girls use dress holders to keep their hems free from the mud of the street, although Janey said it caused strange men to look at their legs. When any of the girls had to pass through the drawing room mama always had a special remark for them, about the state of their stockings or their hair, their want of washing or manners, their muteness or fatness, so that from trepidation they had educated themselves and looked better and spoke better than their neighbours.

They did not mind. The untouchable room was an enchanted place. The whole of the city was theirs and Edward Street was their refuge. For all of them, their greatest fear was the loss of their home. It was a common anxiety. Other families vanished in the night, evading the rent man, aided by the special night transport carts that were available for that purpose.

Pa promised them that no such thing could ever happen, for fate had held this residence especially for them, had cleared the decks by roasting the breast of a winkle-seller with a passion for a wall-eyed bint called Aggie Fossett.

Mr Talbot Jutton polished his hair with Trotter's Oil and bought a complete new set of teeth for a guinea. He foamed away the breath of ocean at the Nassau Place baths. Then he offered himself to Aggie Fossett. All Edward Street was there for the proposal due to his mode of transport which was a sidecar and attracted a rim of gougers, hanging on and falling off. He asked Aggie would she chance it and she said no. As a testimony to his character he added that he had donated a box of herrings to the Penny Dinners. No, Aggie parried, not if she was carrying a Chinee.

Mr Jutton declared that he would end it so. He bought soot and arsenic in a pharmacy and went into a public house to drink his courage. After the event his courage took a different form, for he returned to Edward Street and issued an ultimatum. Aggie had withdrawn and covered her shop with a newspaper, but he made his announcement anyway to her door and to the entire street – that if she would not marry him he would sport Minnie Harrington an oyster and stout dinner at Reece's Hotel and take her to see the performing dogs and monkeys at the Queens.

Women crept out from their little shops and lurked in doorways with infants parcelled in their shawls and old-fashioned young ones rolled into their skirts. The horse sighed, tormented by boys, and slapped the cobbles with her hoof. A drunk man rambled on the path and the white faces of orphans clung like snow to the high windows of the asylum. Washing dripped from window poles at the bad end of the street. After an eternal moment Aggie called out could her mother come too and because he was mouldy the fishmonger said yes.

'What became of the arsenic?' the children pestered.

He savoured their attention, scratching his head with pleasure, thinking it would soon be time to have another, for Bertie was beginning to turn into a person and as soon as they could speak you took them for granted and ceased to be astonished by their existence. 'He tipped the arsenic into a bottle of ink, and used it to write poison-pen letters.'

'Why would Aggie be carrying a Chinee?' They pictured his pyjama-clad legs fastened around her neck, his yellow face grinning beneath a coolie hat. A comfortable torpor held them, in which suspense took up the slack. Pa said that Aggie Fossett was a well-known pox bottle who took her pleasure from assorted sailors, bowsies and militia. Mama gave him a scorching look and the children backed away from a cantankerous mystery.

In any case, that was how they came to live on 11 Edward Street, so said pa. That they should end up there, instead of any other place – any castle or cottage or villa – was due to the luck of God and the whim of Aggie Fossett who gave in to the galdy oul' fishmonger. 'What luck!' whispered mama through clenched teeth.

Chapter 3

MAMA was late (late for what, since she never went anywhere?). She announced this bitterly over breakfast. Pa, absurdly, beamed. 'Isn't it high time, now, and Bertie gone four years of age?' Late or not, mama made no effort to move. The children too seemed transfixed. Catching the curious sea-green gaze of nine pairs of eyes she let out a warning cry. She plucked Bertie from the brood and held him to her while Lena herded the others through the delicate objects of the drawing room. 'Ten and two is twelve,' pa mused delightedly. 'The baker's dozen!' Mama's voice rose on a chilling note. 'I wish that I was old, that I had a blank space between my legs.'

With the backs of their minds busy with the odd idea of the space between mama's legs, the remaining children flooded noisily on to the street. 'Reprehensibles!' shouted Janey. They played Janey's game on the way to school, improvising upon the Eustace Street Tragedy in which a man shot himself and his book-keeper in a frenzy brought on by tippling. This was followed by the Basin Lane Butchery where drunk soldiers set upon a man with swords and 'cut him to griskins'.

It was 1896 and Daisy was ten. She went to school with the others now. At first it had been a shock to share a classroom with poor children almost faint with hunger and blue with cold from having no proper food or clothes, but she was the nuns' favourite, being the cleanest and prettiest child in her class, the one who was not dull with malnutrition.

After school the girls decided to stay out of mama's way by going to Granny Devlin's. They were forbidden by their mother to visit the slum in Fishamble Street where pa's mother lived, but sometimes they needed her.

'Our mama's late,' Weenie told their granny when they were at her fire with Boozy the cat. At the mention of mama the old woman reached beneath her and commenced a frowning hunt in the pile of rags that protected her backside from broken springs. A black clump was brought out, greasily garnished with pink. She beat it about until it became a hat with a trellis of roses. 'Now I'm fit for the queen of Nova Scotia, me oul' segocia,' she said happily. 'And why is that one comin' here?'

'She's not coming here. It's a different kind of late. Give us a biscuit, granny,' Janey bargained. She recounted the events of the morning while the old woman, between little gasps of mirth, rooted in bags and boxes. She handed a fractured Boudoir Finger to Janey as a reward. The younger children waited anxiously for information and broken biscuits as their grandmother settled herself back at the fire. 'Now youse girls listen carefully to me for that ma of yours will tell you nothing useful except how to bow and scrape to the Lord Lieutenant. The minute you get married, have your teeth took out. That always sets a man off the boil.' She opened her mouth to install a chip of wafer biscuit and the children peered into a dark, glistening pit devoid of dental apparatus. 'And when you grow to women, count each month for seven days after the last drop of blood and then ate an onion raw every day for five days. The trouble with your ma is she looks too particular. Dainty ways is for gettin' a husband, not for normal married life.'

Oh, the horror of it, blood and teeth and onions. The children ate their broken biscuits and shuddered comfortably. Granny Devlin had only one child, their pa, yet her store of legend and experience was as vile and raw and mysterious as the very guts that were hidden underneath their bones and bodices.

'Did I ever tell yis about Little Ma?'

The girls felt quite faint with suspense in the nauseating gloom. There wasn't a curtain on the window but a filthy petticoat draped across it day and night. All the tenement dwellers used rags to keep the sun at bay, but it fought through the holes and fray, making a burning, incandescent dusk.

'After her twenty-second child was born she refused ever to speak again.' Granny Devlin spoke lightly of death but birth was a fear-some combat. Little Ma was her mother, revered by her many sons and daughters into a hushed senility. Her protest, which commenced with her twenty-second confinement, became a feat, so that, mutely, she delivered herself of that last huge boy: 'Three days and nights. A wall of blood rose up before her eyes and never a peep did she make. And when they all began to die on her, still she held her whisht. One child shuddered through the smallpox, and another fell into the

17

convulsions of scarletina. She saw the rice-water diarrhoea of cholera on a third. The pink tongue of an infant girl dried up and went brown like a leaf – the terrible mark of typhoid. She lived in one room in a wreck in the Liberties with a varmint for a landlord, who took shillins' offa poor people, but never put nail nor pane in the building. Once a wall fell out, killing all the cattle in the yard next door. Little Ma woke to see mattresses full of her children flyin' across the floor towards the sky.' Granny Devlin left the fire and the speechless little girls and went to look for some other interesting treat. She found a bag with scraps of bacon and cut them into the pan with bits of bread broken in for a fry-up. In spite of her filthy living conditions she always had delicacies. On one memorable occasion she had made Janey a port wine jelly. 'Two more of her young ones were mangled amid the crazed beasts.' She crunched fried bread as she finished her story. 'Did she squeal? Never a squeak!' She laughed in admiration of her mother's defiance.

Walking home through the Liberties in the stench of the street market and the reek from little mouldy houses, it was possible to believe all their grandmother's awful tales. The pavements were strewn with rotting refuse and small barefoot children crouched and darted, stuffing cabbage stalks and mouldering potatoes and bits of stinking offal into sacks. Here and there mounds of rubbish had accumulated. Starving dogs clawed at them and the shadows of rats bulged and vanished like dusty bubbles. Over everything hung the sweetish smell of old death. It came from the flat baskets spread out on stalls upon which were heaped up the poor people's meat; stale cows' feet, tripe, intestines, skins and the dull-eyed heads of sheep. Flies crept over bright, flabby bits of veal. Weenie paid for fourpence worth of tripe which Lena had requested and they walked, more quickly now, past the curious stare of crabbed and louse-bitten children. Women with sunken eyes and rough, drunken men watched them sourly from houses falling down and oozing the dirt of decades.

Shortly after they had left this most decaying part of Dublin, they came to its most splendid area, Dublin Castle, the seat of the Lord Lieutenant, of the wonderful crown jewels, of mama's hopes and dreams. They stood outside and waited, for ladies and dandies and gentlemen in uniform constantly came and went in handsome carriages.

'Go on in! I dare you,' Janey said to Daisy.

'I will. Some day I'll go in there and meet the king.'

'The king is dead. Ya oul' herrin'! Oul' eejit. You know nothing.'

Of all the children, Daisy was most influenced by her mother's urgent messages of social style and standards, just as Janey was most at home with her grandmother's earthy life. Daisy believed that she was destined for greatness while poor mama maintained that she had been snatched from such a destiny. 'To have come to this from leafy Kensington,' mama sometimes said as she gazed helplessly around her seething household. It was a phrase from legend like the lovely phrases in the litany to the Blessed Virgin. Tower of Ivory. House of God. Leafy Kensington. Mama never bothered to give them a detailed picture of her past nor seemed to imagine how she could have avoided her fate. Daisy waited for someone to pluck her into her future.

They went the long way home past College Green where the people gathered to watch the splendid spectacle of the Changing of the Guards, so that they could walk over Carlisle Bridge and along the glittering stretch of Sackville Street. This was the most elegant street in the whole world, pa said, with its cigar importers, silk mercers, tea rooms, the Pioneer Teeth Institute, Camille Fauvin's Continental Restaurant, the Hammam Hotel and Turkish Bath, the Edinburgh Temperance Hotel, the Irish Mission to the Jews, the Sackville Club, Thwaite's Mineral and Medicinal Water Company. Here was a permanent parade of fashion, where men and women alike wore satin and feathers and diamonds and perfumes. There were also cripples and beggars and thieves and dwarves and Janey played a terrible trick, running ahead, darting between the gentry pleading, 'Penny for me sisters, deaf and dumb.'

As they neared Edward Street Daisy said cautiously, 'Janey – do you really know why mama was cross this morning?'

'She was late.' Janey twirled round in front of Daisy. 'Late for her rags – only you don't know what I'm talking about because you're only a rotten oul' eejit.' She put her face down close to Daisy's so that the smaller child was forced to look into those burning black eyes that made her think of a devil.

But she did know. Lena and Janey and Weenie were almost women now and they whispered about women's matters in the night. Daisy not only understood but felt she was to blame. Over the past few years pa had come to expect her night-time visits to the kitchen. When first he had begun this queer feverish stroking (as if he was trying to iron out lumps with his fingers, she thought) she resolved to get used to it. She would pretend not to notice, as he afterwards pretended not to remember. It was later, when she went to school and the priest talked mysteriously of the evils of the flesh, that she knew she had led her pa into temptation. He had done no more than touch her but it was an awful sin. The sin of touch. After that she did not go downstairs in the night, except once when she needed the lav. Pa was waiting for her. She tried to get away. 'I'm a good girl, pa.' He told her he loved her. Afterwards he wept. 'You are a good little girl. I am no use to anyone,' he said. 'It would be better if I was dead.' She hated to see him cry. She felt sorry for him but some strange cold voice spoke out of her mouth. 'I wish you were dead.' His arms fell away from her. For a minute he was unable to speak or move and then he said in a very small voice, 'Go back to bed, pettie, before you get cold.'

After that he climbed up the drainpipe and in the window to mama.

Edward Street was in darkness. Mama was nowhere to be seen. The door was flung open and Lena's face appeared, her skin white as starch. 'Don't go in!'

'I want me tea,' Janey protested.

'You're to go straight up to bed.' Lena burst into tears.

The doors of neighbouring houses were sprung from their catches as women on the street caught wind of a catastrophe. Strange moans came from the kitchen. 'It's mama,' Lena said. 'She's after making me give her a bath in boiling water.'

The younger girls crept upstairs and listened to poor mama's gasps of pain as she tried to boil herself to death.

Chapter 4

FROM the bedroom the children heard a shout as Lena poured scalding water in the tub. 'God damn and blast you, Emily Brontë!'

After this outburst mama lay so still in the bath that Lena thought she had extinguished her with the boiling flood. Still holding the empty vessel she bent over the limp pink figure until at last she discerned some movement, although it was only a fevered murmur from her lips. '"Marry me," Danny Devlin said, "and you'll never be bored." You should have seen him then! He was dark and exciting. I had just read *Wuthering Heights*. I was only eighteen.'

'*What* heights, mama?' Lena's homely face frowned over the humid torture chamber. Mama shuddered. The luxury of boredom was the right of every well-bred woman. For years she had borne it bravely. She could bear no more and least of all the thought that her mother had been right. She sat up suddenly, as if revived by her bath instead of half killed by it. 'He was different from the other young men I had known. He seemed so spirited – as I myself was then. "Whatever our souls are made of, yours and mine are the same," I told him.' She gave a sour laugh. 'Do you know what he said? "Are you a Catholic too?"'

'My mother warned me. She told me that if I married an Irishman he would give me ten children and leave me destitute. After that she did not speak to me at all.' Mama's mouth twisted bitterly and she signalled Lena to refill her bath. Lena sobbed as she tilted the pan towards the tub, for her mother's terrible screams were renewed. Afterwards she seemed to expire again. There was no sound in the little room except Lena's jittering cries until mama recovered enough to resume her ramblings. 'I ran away with him. Girls are such fools. To think I saw it as an escape – this little horror of an island. The family was at a funeral. I packed my few things and had them shipped. They were mine, I had every right to take them! God knows I had need of them. We came back to this filthy city. Imagine, I thought it would be all lakes and mountains! We were married in the corner of a church by a Roman priest and there a sort of miracle took place – ' She mocked herself again with her miserable laugh; 'My Heathcliffe turned into a strange youth, amiable and rather common. He placed a cheap band on my finger and took me home to this dreadful little house.'

'Then . . .' She looked into Lena's round, anxious face, as empty of experience as hers had once been, and fell silent. Then, when she was taking off her hat, weary and suddenly overcome with the disappointment that there was no bathroom, that she could never again take a proper bath, he fell upon her.

'What are you doing? No! Oh, yes, well, kiss me if you wish. Oh, *no!*'

He had seemed in pain yet utterly absorbed and at the same time curiously unaware of her presence. She recalled that he was like a man trying to kill something that would not die. She had come to marriage knowing nothing except the suffocating joy of desire, the mystifying thrill of being held against a man's jacket and hearing his breath rasp. Yet she understood absolutely that this is what she had accepted in the church in front of the priest when she said 'I do'. She seemed to wilt again. With a cry of distress Lena fetched a cloth and wrung it out in cold water and dashed it in her mother's face. Mama slapped it back at her daughter. 'There was no privacy,' she complained, eyeing the girl sourly as if her presence now were to blame. 'I had to wash in a tin bath and excuse myself to a shed in the yard. When I looked out the bedroom window the eye of an orphan looked back from a window of the girls' asylum.' Catching her daughter's mild, puzzled eye, she snapped, 'It is all very well for you. You have never known anything else. I was used to a better way of life.' She began to cry, a soft mewling whinge, like a baby. 'Such sights! I had never dreamed to see such sights!'

When at first she had peered, with a girl's curiosity, into the dim front parlours on Edward Street, the shock was horrible. Her eye engaged with an area like a dirty basement, in which was piled up wilting cabbages, musty turnips and bad potatoes. She hurried on, as if to escape from a nightmare, and was drawn by the extraordinary domestic setting in the adjacent window, of two sides of rancid bacon with an army of insects in attendance. Bad vegetables and rotting bacon in the drawing room! These alarms by far superseded any others. It was like lifting the coverlet of one's bed and finding the ocean underneath. She moved with hideous curiosity to the next address where she found herself staring at piles of dirty clothes heaped up in wooden boxes which lounged against the front window. Remembering her own drawing room at home where she sewed while the young men stood with their backs to the fire taking tea and little sandwiches, she felt her way along the dull brick wall until she met another window crammed with bales of wax candles, and in the next the entirety of the drawing room had surrendered to louse-crawling sods of turf. In the adjoining house there was something which resembled the contents of a normal living room, but one which had been caught up in an earthquake. Heaped up together in any fashion were piles of broken china, chairs and clocks that disgorged their inner parts, rusty curtains collapsed as in a faint.

She was gazing at this calamity when a woman came to the door of the house. As if to crown the base mockery, the woman's feet and breasts were bare.

'Are you lookin' or buyin'?'

Her imperious teenage face hid none of its emotion. She extended a hand, conscious of the rebuke in its white glove. 'Elinore Dubois Devlin,' she introduced herself. The naked savage appeared to be weak in the brain for she merely stood where she was, gazing Elinore up and down while a hell's babble of babies filled in the silence from some interior part of the house. 'Ellen-or-Dubious-Devlin,' said the creature, and she laughed. 'Good luck to you, now. Either we'll get used to you or you'll get used to us. I'd better get back to the shop.'

'All of the parlours had been turned into shops,' mama instructed Lena, although Lena knew that a shop in the front room was the normality and that their house, with its preserved front room, was the oddity. 'Everything they sold was old and dirty. None of them sold soap, or chloride of lime or any cleansing agent, although all the people and their houses were in want of it.' Mama began to scrub at herself with the little scented bar she kept for her own use. 'This water is half cold,' she complained, and Lena hurried to replenish it with hot. She howled at the temperature and the girl backed away. 'Go on!' Mama's voice was faint but impatient and with a cry of anguish Lena pitched in the rest of the boiling cauldron. 'Kill me!' mama murmured with grim satisfaction.

And again Lena thought she had. She studied the gaunt face for signs of death but then she detected larger drops among the beads of moisture and she knew her mother was only crying.

In the early days of her marriage, which came as a surprise, she could not imagine how so many children arrived when there was so little space for them. She wanted a son. A woman was nothing unless she had a son. 'I did not mind, Lena, when you were born. It was useful to have an eldest daughter. William came next.' She smiled, remembering that joy. It seemed to make it all worth while. She believed she was adapting to her life. Her husband adored her. She liked not having to compete with her brothers and sisters, not having to obey her parents. To her astonishment, her body ceased to resist what she looked on as Danny's spells, although she could wish they were less frequent. She secretly believed it was this acceptance that had enabled her to conceive a son.

After William, Tom appeared so quickly that they might have been twins. She was happy again. There! She had two sons and she was not yet twenty-one. The little house was quite full up. She did not know much about such things but imagined that children were given by God to fill the space available for them. Quite the opposite proved true. The big handsome houses in Fitzwilliam Square scarcely ever emitted a pram whereas the pitiful dwellings on Edward Street were choked with children. When Eugenia or Janey came, Elinore Dubois Devlin had no doubt that the corridors of a Catholic heaven were still filled with children greedily waiting to claim her body.

She opened a plaintive eye and it was as shocking to Lena as if the eye of a corpse had suddenly flown apart. 'All that my mother warned me about Catholics proved true! The men were uncommonly active in their marital duties and doggedly faithful to their wives. After Janey was born I did what I had to. There was nothing else for me to do.'

'You left us!' Lena remembered. 'I was only five. We thought you were never coming back.'

'You would have been perfectly all right. Irish families can always absorb more children.'

It had been so simple. She had packed her few good clothes and her dolls and taken a cab to Kingstown. No one questioned her when she purchased her ticket for the boat. She went on deck and watched, beneath her parasol, a flock of gulls rocking upon the oily waves. By tilting the umbrella's edge she could see groups of men who eyed her keenly. Breathing in the sea air, she had felt an enormous, overwhelming relief at having surpassed the episode of family life. By a single thrust of will she was restored to girlhood. She would start off her life again, unhampered by ignorance or an appetite for adventure. Quite without warning panic assailed her. It was a feeling that some vital part of her luggage was missing. 'No! Oh, no!' She had left Will behind. She had forgotten her darling first-born little boy. As the boat was not far from Kingstown and the pier was still in view, two gentlemen had to restrain her from flinging herself into the water. She came home the following day and would say nothing of the incident. Pa was delighted. 'Post-parturient hysteria!' he declared, consulting his books. He put her to bed with a bromide of potassium and a solution of Mindererus Spirit.

For years she lived on the edge of panic. Until Lena was old enough to take over, she felt like someone set upon by a mob. The tiny house seemed to crack and seep at the seams with the noise and flow of infants. Her husband proved yet another child, uncouth and irresponsible. He irritated her beyond belief. Nine children came in fifteen years! She was only thirty-six. Her lovely little waistline lost its tension and her bladder grew weak so that she had to keep a po beneath her bed. They were obliged to open up the attic to make her boys a bedroom where they could not stand up without hitting their heads on the ceiling. All she could do was to guard her few small possessions in the drawing room. No matter what happened she protected her good pieces. She took some pride in that.

The traffic of birth was so congested on the street that its control was a permanent topic among the women, although they bore no resentment towards their numerous offspring. They tried to give advice to Miss Snotty-Ellen, as they called her, but Elinore was repelled by the notion of feeding her children from the breast like a common wet nurse or worse, the curious variations on the curious act of marriage that they crudely conveyed. It was only desperation that had driven her to this desperate measure, and it had not worked. 'You may turn out the stove,' she said grimly to her daughter. 'The little fiend means to have its life.'

'I'm glad.' Lena knelt and threw her arms around her mother's wet shoulders. 'I'll take care of it. You'll have nothing to do.'

'That is not the point.' Her mother shook her off. 'You don't understand. This will be the tenth child, the one which will prove my mother's prediction. I cannot bear that.'

'It might be a boy,' Lena tried to cheer her. 'You would have four boys.'

'Fate does not seem disposed to favour me.' Mama gave her frightening little laugh again. 'Lena! Do you know what those hags on the street say concerning the sex of their children? No, of course you don't. Have you noticed that they all have boys? Boys and boys and boys. They claim it is because of their appetite for ... give me a towel.' She stepped out of the bath. Lena marvelled at how rosy she looked, as if she had had a health treatment, while she herself was bedraggled and blotched. Her knees trembled from the ordeal.

'Even my own mother could not call a woman with four sons a failure!' mama reflected. She damped her hot skin with rosewater and finished her dressing. 'Lena! Do the nuns at school teach you when a child develops its soul and its sex?'

'A baby born before its term cannot be baptized because it has not yet got a soul,' Lena instructed her. 'I don't know when its sex is decided.'

Bertie had begun to grow in her body after a wedding party in Summerhill, where stout and cider made her head spin and she did not mind her husband's advances. If she could once more subdue her distaste, the thing inside her might turn out a boy. She reached for the garments her daughter held, but instead explored the girl's moist cheek. 'You are to go to Findlaters and buy two nice chops, a good piece of cheese and half a bottle of port.' She produced from her purse the enormous sum of five shillings. 'When you have brought them back take all the children to a concert.'

'Why, mama?'

'I must be alone.'

'Oh, why, mama?' Lena began to cry, fearing worse than the boiling bath.

'Does it never occur to you that I might wish to be alone with your father?' mama said.

'No, mama.'

Her eyes widened as mama's little birdlike hand sailed through the air and struck her face in a stinging slap. She said no more but she was still confused as she completed the errand and then assembled the other children. 'Where are we going?' demanded Essie and Beth. 'I don't know,' Lena said miserably. Janey had an idea. 'The Cinématographe!' she cried. The others waited with interest and trepidation to see if this was some fresh subject for Amateur Reprehensibles or a horror story for the night. But it turned out to be a new invention, a radical advance on the Wheel of Life, which had already supplanted the Magic Lantern. 'It's the very first week of the Cinématographe. They are showing it with the variety in Dan

Lowry's Theatre!' If Janey was to be believed, photographs could walk off a screen and live the lives of men and women.

That night, while pa cautiously savoured beef chops and port as rare and red as blood, the children took their places in the cheapest wooden seats in 'the gods'. Lena and Will were scarcely children any more, she having passed seventeen and he being almost sixteen and a scholarship student at St Andrew's College. They watched the screen light up with jerky lettering and then the pictures appeared. Ghost-like, they released themselves from the dead image of the printed picture and began to move. Like balloons cut from their strings, the children were freed from the anchor that bound them to reality. They watched a short film called *The Waves*, in which the ocean threatened to plunge out of the screen and flood the theatre and those in the front seats panicked and screamed. This was followed by an animation of a contortionist act, and then a film called *Boxing Cats* and *A Scene in a Barber's Shop*. Afterwards there was a live performance by Miss Bessie Hinton, the Champion Lady Whistler of the World, but nothing could match up to the magic of pictures come to life.

'We shall have an early night,' mama declared. 'An early night will do us good. Come and join me in my room.' It was only nine o'clock but she had been nice to him all evening and pa had no wish to damage her mood. He was undoing his braces, with his back turned for modesty, when the little hand that had struck Lena's cheek reached out from the bed and touched him. The slender fingers fluttered between his legs and he groaned loudly. Then, realizing that she must have been looking in her book and was summoning him for some other service, a glass of water or a ribbon to mark her page, he coughed and moved aside. The fingers followed with voluptuous greed and the whole business almost ended there and then. He reared before her sculptor's touch and bellowed like a beast in slaughter.

Embarrassed, he gave a little cough of apology. She had not spoken to him all week, except to wish him or herself dead. She had never, lady that she was, touched him in such a manner before. She must have been trying to punish him in some special way. Abashed in the face of her innocence he moved away to finish his toilet and buttoned himself into pyjamas before sheepishly climbing into bed. Her eyes were closed and her face gave no warning that she would take his hand and draw it to her female part which to his petrifying astonishment was entirely exposed. She wore no gown. The tips of his fingers were warm and wet and he pulled his hand away with a shout as if it had been dipped in blood. The excitement, like finding the vaults of a bank flung open as one passed, was such that his first instinct was to shut the doors again and sound the alarm. Was she suffering a fever? Should he dose her with a syrup of chloral?

His trembling hands, seeking a pulse, found a strange hot creature who was not his wife and he had to remind himself that he was in the company of a superior. 'My Queen,' he breathed. She made queer, endearing little noises that incited him beyond measure and her body writhed like a cat.

Mama shuddered. She had embarked upon this humiliating business, a bit intoxicated but quite cool in the brain and only determined to overcome the aversion that had turned the sons in her into women. When she touched him, as she never had before, she was dismayed by the pleasure her fingers absorbed from that shape, the small triumph of bringing it to life. This arousal was unlike the passive pleasure she had once known, and she had to remind herself of its proper function before flinging herself into a voyage towards unknown excitement. 'My little boy,' she huskily murmured.

Pa was overcome by this rare tenderness. 'God, ah, God,' he gasped in glorious awe. Mama waited. Her heart thundered and her innards clamoured. She touched him in a manner between a caress and an impatient push. A groaning snore drained out of his weight. The sudden cooling of their mingled perspiration was like the lights going down in the theatre where the children still sat transfixed by the memory of *The Waves*. Mama, her interesting journey cut short, felt herself falling through space with a feeling of chill and ashes.

Chapter 5

SHE tried everything, even loathsome gin. Once she paid a visit
to St Lucy's Church. On a single other occasion – her wedding
day – she had been inside a Catholic church. Then, as now, she was
astonished by such ornament in the midst of so much poverty. It
might have been a bawdy-house but for the drabness of the poor
women gabbling on their knees. As furtive as if she had been putting
money on a horse, she slid a florin from her purse and dropped it
into a sort of brass coffin. She lit a candle beneath the feet of a
whey-faced saint. 'Make something happen,' she said tersely.

After that she did nothing except sit on her sofa with poor Bertie,
staring at the panic-stricken porcelain face of her favourite doll.
Four months had passed and she could only wait out the nightmare.
The traffic on the street – of horses, of children playing, of
neighbours calling to each other – was so close that she might have
heard it in a shell clamped to her ear, but she had learnt not to
notice it and soon she and Bertie were asleep on the sofa. She did
not even hear the knock upon the door. Bertie woke with a start
when the knock became a pounding and mama rose like one in a
dream to admit a common, working-class boy who tortured his cap
with bashful fingers.

'I have news, ma'am.' He glanced up at her and then away, for a
brief amazed glimpse into her drawing room.

'What do you want?' mama said.

'There was an accident, ma'am. Your husband ...' He fixed his
elderly child's eye on the scandalous red lips of the doll. Mama's
face had gone as white as her toy. She pushed him on the shoulder
to make him continue.

'We was bringin' stale loaves to the workhouse and a brawl broke
out in the street. There was a man swingin' a woman by the hair and
a little girl got in between them. The horse took fright and the girl
fell in his path. Your husband, ma'am, leapt into the street to take
the reins and the beast tramped him down.'

Mama trembled and clasped the doll to her breast.

'He looks perfect,' the lad consoled. 'There's nothing, only a cut above his eye. The horse is now remorseful. I think he will be shot.' The boy gave his cap a last desperate wrench and burst into tears although it was not clear if he wept for the hurt man or the condemned beast.

'My husband . . .' Mama scraped together words from the dust of her breath. 'You have not said if he is alive or dead.'

'Oh, poor missus, he is no more!'

'No more . . .?' she appealed to him.

'He is dead!' the boy shouted. 'Dead as the Christmas goose!' She was briefly amused by this image, for it was almost Christmas. The boy fled bawling into the street.

She crept back on to her sofa and sat there to let the news sink into herself. 'No more,' she whispered to her porcelain doll. She took Bertie out into the kitchen and made him some bread and sugar. There was no one else in the house. Lena had that morning taken Daisy and the twins to the dental hospital, where children sat in line on a bench listening to screams and waiting to have teeth extracted and dropped into a metal bucket filled with teeth and blood. She returned to the sofa to sit and rock herself and murmur. 'No more.' She did not move until the children came home from school and tiptoed past her to the kitchen where the breakfast dishes still cluttered the table. With an effort she summoned them. 'Elinore! Thomas! Eugenia, Esther . . . Elizabeth.' She rested and continued on a little mew. 'William, Daisy. Bertrand.' She kissed her youngest child, who was sleeping again on her knee, and then touched her stomach with a frown. 'No more!'

As she waited for the children to assemble she composed a telegram in her mind. 'Regret terrible news stop Daniel dead in accident stop coming home stop Elinore.'

'Stop!' she told herself. She had an urge to change her clothes; a trimmed bodice or a tea gown. In her parents' house everyone dressed nicely at all times of the day.

The children squeezed into the parlour. They saw at once it was bad news. Mama took the boys into her arms and gently told the girls that they were orphans. The impact of the announcement was damaged by Lena falling in a faint. Reaching out to save herself she clutched at one of the little white laughing dogs which fell with her to its doom. Again there was a pounding on the door. The boys helped Lena into a chair and the girls nervously darted to answer the knock.

A man entered the house backwards, groaning from some heavy burden so that his moustaches shifted. The startled children ran forwards and then surged back, up the stairs, down the stairs, into the parlour, backwards towards the scullery. The bearer had now entered the parlour, for there was nowhere else for him to go, and it could be seen that, with the baker's lad who had broken the bad news, he carried poor pa's corpse.

'The Departed,' they announced, and stood panting with their luggage while the children condensed themselves into a mass of dismay.

He did not look departed. He looked like a man who had got drunk and been in a fight – quite relaxed although dishevelled and with a dash of blood across his left eye. Out of respect the men had removed their caps and placed them on the hill of the dead man's stomach. Almost, one expected them to rise and fall.

'Where will we put him?' gasped the lad, who appeared to be suffering under his burden.

'I don't know.' Mama shook her head fearfully. She continued to shake her head as she looked around her little room, as if someone had asked her to take delivery of an elephant and howdah. Various neighbours had begun to poke their nose around the door. Their poor smell seeped in and mama put a hankie to her nose. The room, she thought, now looked like the grand finale of a musical comedy. 'Put him in the bedroom!' ordered Gladys Fadden.

'No!' mama weakly cried. How could she rest with a corpse for company?

Norah Boake, a baby taking noisy nourishment from her left breast and a shawl precariously flung across its bald head and the bald contour of her right breast, suggested the kitchen table. 'The children have not had their tea,' mama feebly protested.

'Where did ye put him when he was alive?' Bridget Mulvaney wondered. Mama looked around in perplexity. She could not imagine where he used to be. Reluctantly she got up from her rose-coloured sofa. 'Put him there.' The moustached man and the bakery youth stood guard beside the sofa. Did they expect to be tipped? The neighbouring women fell to weeping. They pushed each other forward to pay their respects. Small ornaments fell back with a sound of snapping bones and lay on their polished surfaces, staring at the ceiling. There was a smell of smouldering on the clothes of these people from the turf they burned in their grates. They began to organize, to talk about priests and porter. Their red hands touched her treasures. Through some chink in this mob she perceived a fresh assault. The children were pressing forward to gape at their dead father. She squeezed her eyes shut in an effort at self-control but a little word slipped out. '*Doucement!*' she pleaded softly.

At once the room grew still. People began to back away on tiptoe. Mama stood over her husband, guarding his repose, her fingers resting on the arm of the sofa as if they were posing for a portrait. She studied him with care, inspecting all his features. When she married him he had been a handsome tree of a man. Over eighteen years he had run to paunch. His body, she thought, looked as if he, and not she, had borne the brunt of multiple childbirth.

The children, observing this exclusive tableau, withdrew. They helped Lena to the kitchen and put her into pa's chair. 'What should we do with her?' the twins pondered.

'Pa would know,' Weenie said and then she drew in her breath and they all looked at one another in fear. Pa wasn't there any more. They began to weep. Will could not stand to see the girls cry for he was close to tears himself. 'It's all right. I will see to things now,' he said. 'What will we do?' The girls turned their great dismal eyes to him and he had to clench his fists and look away. Grief always made him feel violent but his gentle personality had no outlet for fury. Tom, who understood his brother better than anyone, said quickly, 'We never finished our monster hole. Years ago, it was our project. We ought to see it through.'

'We're too big now.' Will impatiently pushed tears from his face.

'We'll do it for pa,' Tom said quietly. He put a hand on his brother's shoulders. 'We have to do something for pa.'

The girls got mama and Lena to bed and said a prayer over the remains of their father and then they followed their brothers down to the canal with spades and shovels and every kind of utensil. Will and Tom were already at work, their sleeves rolled up, their features twisted with pain and effort. Scalps of grassy mud flew into the air and the hole became a shallow basin. Deeper their spades foraged. They moved closer to the centre of the cavity, their faces grim and their breath coming out in panting cries. Soon they were covered in mud. It spattered their hair and faces and filled their mouths. Still their spades flew and denser muck, related to the river bed, spun up into the air and daubed the faces of the girls and a growing audience of boys.

All the boys on the street had gathered round. 'Their da's dead,' they told each other in respect. Even the rough youths who had tormented Will and Tom as children were awed by the enterprise. The brothers were waist-deep in the earth when a little rush of water from the canal began to fill up the bottom of the hole. They sweated and dug. They panted and they cried. By now they themselves seemed rooted within the earth. Each uplifting of the spade pulled them from their natural element, tearing with agony through their shoulders and arms. With shouts they carried on. The observers crouched, tense with sympathetic understanding.

At last only the mud- and tear-stained faces of the boys remained above the earth and they flung away their spades and sat down in the watery depth of the hole. There they stayed quite silent down below and up above the watchers loitered, looking down at them sitting there.

Devlin's Pit, as it was afterwards named (or Devil's Pit to the superstitious), became a historic landmark. Neighbouring tribes of boys fought battles for its possession. Whenever a grown-up passed by and peered down, it was always occupied by a group of boys sitting in perfect silence in the pool of water at its bottom. After several months a drunk man fell in and broke his leg and corporation workers threw in some stones and put up a sign that said 'Danger'.

Chapter 6

'I SHALL need a travelling gown, a tea gown, a cape, several pairs of shoes, a silk umbrella and a holdall . . .' Mama, absorbed in her list, was spared the stupefied looks of her brood. 'There will be a maid for my use so I must make sure my undergarments are not a topic for kitchen gossip. Six chemise tops and drawers trimmed with lace – machine lace, I wonder, for the sake of economy!'

'A maid?' Essie and Beth said in unison. 'At a funeral?'

'A funeral?' Mama noticed for the first time that all the children had pieces of crape tied on their arms, hideous, like dirty bandages. They had a drab and bruised look and wore dark clothing which ill-suited their complexions. Thank goodness little Bertie was fair. 'No, don't be ridiculous – after the funeral. I shall be making a journey.'

All the plain clothes that year were lavishly adorned with lace and trimmings. Wings and whole birds, silk asters were sold by the dozen at Kelletts. Her face remained grave but a tiny smile seemed to shimmer around it like a halo. Lena's shocked hand unsettled the tea as she handed it to her mother. 'Where do you mean to go?'

Mama, still as stone, stared into some distance that was greater even than that over which pa had travelled. She had once been to France. 'Home,' she said.

'To leafy Kensington,' Daisy recited beneath her breath.

Even those who did not normally admire mama had to weep for her courage. How still she sat, how perfectly straight, holding the hands of her two eldest boys in the church to which she did not belong. Only the trembling of a bright little bird pinned on her black hat betrayed the state of her mind. The children shivered, seemed amazed, but would not be parted from their feelings. Something seemed to sustain them, some secret unknown to ordinary people.

'You shall have a bath,' mama had told them. 'You can get one for sixpence at the Iveagh – any temperature. You are each to buy a pair of good used boots and some clean gloves. To have good gloves and

34

shoes is to be well dressed.' There was a great silence in which poor mama had to wonder yet again if she spoke a different language and then Will said in an amazed tone, 'Are we to come with you?'

Mama's plan was unfolded in the kitchen while the undertaker's men came and put pa in a box and tied his feet with tape. Discreetly, they left a leaflet of their charges, which Lena studied while mama explained that they must all present themselves to her family in London. The house was big enough and only one of her sisters remained unmarried. Now that the impediment of an Irish husband was removed, she saw no reason why they should not return to their proper home.

'Four guineas for a hearse and four black horses,' Lena interrupted anxiously. 'Ten and sixpence for the coachman. Then there are the bearers and horse feathers, the winding sheet and mourners.'

'This is a funeral, not a circus,' mama reminded her gently. 'We have better things to spend our money on than half a dozen hired mourners at five shillings a day and their beer. We shall mourn very nicely ourselves.'

Lena got the tin box on the mantelpiece where the housekeeping money was kept. She upturned it like a dice cup on the kitchen table. A single florin lay on the grain. Mama looked quite pleased. 'That would surely purchase a little bird.' She folded the coin into her hand and then tapped her fist against her chin. She seemed to be in a sort of dream, which was just as well. From the drawing room came a fearful banging and the timorous chatter of glass and china as the men from the undertakers commenced the hammering down of pa's coffin lid.

In the event, pa was richly mourned. All the neighbours bawled. They loved Danny Devlin. He had snatched their children from the jaws of death, swabbed at septic toes, predicted the sex of babies, dosed wormy infants and never taken a penny. People came from Summerhill, Spring Garden Street, King's Row. A thin little widow gripped mama's hand and presented herself as Chrissie Savage. Mama took her hand away. The women wore no glove. 'Times was very bad, missus, and I hanged meself.' Mama and Daisy looked at her in horror. 'The neighbours cut me down an' I was blue. They didn't know whether to get the physician or the mortician so they went for your husband. He saved me life, missus, by pouring hot and cold water on me head, alternately, from a height. Then he did slip me a shilling.'

Mama was furious. Her anger found its focus in a reporter from the *Freeman's Journal*, a gingery-looking fellow who had come to write a piece about pa, referring to him as a working-class hero. He could not understand mama's coolness and asked if she realized that he had not merely given his life to rescue a little girl from trampling, but had once saved a whole street from typhoid. Mama said that she knew nothing of the sort and it was true, none of them did. They were all amazed by pa's celebrity. Mama, being upset, said that he would have done better to think of his own children, who were now left fatherless as a result of his thoughtless action. At this the young man became incensed. His limp red whiskers trembled and his pale complexion grew roseate. 'Madam, why are you wearing the body of a dead bird on your hat?' he said. Mama's hand flew to her pretty trimming. 'I am a naturalist by dedication,' the boy said very loudly, 'and I consider it a crime that because of the vanity of women, thousands of happy, beautiful creatures who would delight us with their song are ruthlessly slaughtered. Songbirds such as goldfinches, thrushes and blackbirds, the beautiful hoopoe and the waxwing! They are shot when in their breeding plumage and the young are left to starve to death while piteously crying out for a parent who never comes.'

At this, the children, who had admirably contained their grief, all burst into tears.

When mama had rested for a day or two she summoned Will into the drawing room and handed him his father's watch. He took the plump golden disc with great solemnity and crunched the thick chain in his hand. 'Is it to be mine?'

'I hope so – one day.' She reached out and patted his hair. 'In the meantime you are to take it to Ellen M'Guinness in Upper Gardiner Street. Make sure you get five shillings.'

'No!' Will backed away. His face went very pink and his voice came out a whisper. He had no temper and anger always took the form of embarrassment. 'I won't pawn pa's watch.'

'If there were any other way . . .' Mama spread her hands to demonstrate at once their emptiness and their uselessness. 'Our whole future depends on it.'

'Pa's estate . . .!'

'This very day I shall go to College Green and have a meeting with the bank manager,' mama promised. 'Then I shall go directly to the bakery and find out what we are due in the way of insurance money or a pension. In the meantime we have nothing – no money for food. You are to have baths and new boots. There is no time to waste. So much has already been lost. I appeal to you, Will. You are now the man of the house.'

Will hung his head. He knew the battle was lost. 'This room!' He growled against the threat of tears. 'It's crammed with stuff. Sell some of this.'

'Through all our hardships I have held on to our parlour. It is our standard.'

'Yes, but pa's watch! Just because he's dead, we can't forget him.'

She gave him a long look in which appeal outweighed reproach. 'As if I could do such a thing' – she laid her hand very gently across her front – 'when he has left me a widow with a child still to bring into the world.' This bombshell made Will feel as if his chest was bursting inside. He plunged his hands into his pockets, squeezing the watch very tight in his fist, to stop himself from sweeping the ornaments from every surface on to the floor. He felt betrayed by everyone – by his father for leaving his mother at such a disadvantage and by mama for claiming her advantage in this inarguable way. 'Six bob,' he said gruffly over his shoulder as he swaggered out into the street. 'I'll stick out for six bob.'

While mama was in town on her business the children went to Francis Street for their baths. They did not take Daisy with them, for, as Janey said, it was a waste of money to have a proper bath if she would not take off her clothes. They returned looking wonderfully scrubbed. The shabby, dislocated look left behind by pa's death seemed to have been washed away from them.

'Dirty little scut!' Janey teased Daisy. 'Never had a bath in your life!'

'Be quiet, you damn hooligan,' said Will in a shocked voice. 'Those baths cost us my watch. It should have been mine. I should have had the watch of a hero.'

'Whose watch. What hero?' said Daisy.

'See here!' Tom pushed the others aside and drew Daisy over to the table where a copy of the *Freeman's Journal* was spread out. 'On our way to the baths we went to see Granny Devlin and she had a copy of this kept for us.'

'Death of a humble hero!' Daisy read out.

37

There followed an account of how their pa, in 1864, as a youth of fifteen, had saved an entire street from an epidemic of typhoid.

A little girl, Nellie Gann, died of the disease in a tenement house and her parents laid her out for all the neighbours to see. Young Danny Devlin, an avid reader of medical books, knew that the dead girl was bait for an epidemic. He wrapped her tightly in a bed sheet and ran with her in his arms to the infirmary. People thought he was insane when he then rushed back to the house, threw the misfortunate family's possessions into the street, covered them with a lake of paraffin and set them on fire. After that he nailed up the doors of their room, placed flowers of sulphide over boiling water and threw a live coal on top, filling the quarters with their purifying steam. People outside, seeing smoke through the window, thought he was in league with the devil.

'The hero is rarely honoured in his own country,' Daisy finished reading this in a flood of tears.

'It's the prophet,' Beth remarked, 'who isn't honoured.'

'So it is,' agreed Essie.

'I killed him. I wished him dead,' Daisy sobbed, as mama arrived home in a Hackney cab, paid for by Mr Muldowney at the bakery.

'There were two guineas in Mr Devlin's account,' she announced at once. 'I withdrew it all.' She took the money from her purse and put it on the table in a defiant way, watching the silver coins with a baleful eye. She gave a little mirthful bark. 'The estate!'

'What about the pension?' Lena said. 'The insurance money?'

Her mother gave her a pitying look as if it were to be known all along that no such schemes existed. 'Vesty Muldowney was kind enough to suggest that there might be jobs for my boys at the bakery. I told him he had already killed my husband for me. I did not bring three boys into the world to have their heads kicked in by horses.'

'There is the house!' Will said. 'We could always sell the house.'

'After the house is sold we shall have recourse to the poorhouse,' mama said, 'for I have learned from the bank manager that we are only rent-paying tenants. 11 Edward Street is no more ours than Dublin Castle.'

Vesty Muldowney sent them a present of a goose for Christmas, thinking they might be missing this treat with the absence of a provider in their lives. In fact they had never eaten goose before. Pa always got a cut of pork in the Liberties on Christmas Eve. Grief made the children morbidly hungry and they devoured the greasy bird, along with a bread pudding made by Lena. On Christmas night Mr Muldowney came around with a bottle of port for mama and sweets for the children. He patted little Bertie on the head. 'Well, old man,' he said, 'did you enjoy the goose?'

'I don't know,' Bertie growled, anxious at pa's long absence, alarmed to be mistaken for an old man. 'I only got a claw.'

Chapter 7

'OUR baths are wearing off,' Janey lamented. She pulled the blankets from her sleeping sisters. In the curtained morning light they had a sea-bed look, greenish and translucent, the fronds of their hair drifting as their nests were disturbed. They grunted and pulled their knees to their chins. Essie and Beth inspected and picked at one another with a married familiarity.

'Sacred hour!' Janey was gazing at the bed where Weenie lay trussed in hair, locked in dreams. 'Daisy's gone!'

After mama went to England they struggled against a rising tide of disorder. There seemed to be so much hair to brush and so few stockings to put on. Without their mother's biting encouragement, neatness was difficult to achieve. There wasn't even any reason to keep the house. Their life in Edward Street was at an end.

Mama had to travel alone. There was no money for the rest of them. She hadn't even the price of nice new underwear. She looked on forlornly as the girls beat at her fur muff with fig dust and freshened her black cape with dabs of benzine. Her old woollen travelling gown was unpicked on the kitchen table and washed by Lena, piece by piece, in a solution of shaved soap.

When she waved goodbye, Daisy felt that she was never going to come back. She had been unable to suppress a little smile as she tipped Lena ten shillings for their expenses. A week passed. The sisters bickered and the boys grew hungry and morose. The house which was not theirs began to slide into an abandoned state. Waiting behind the drooping curtains with their opulent scent of dust and damask rose, Daisy watched the business of the street – the horses and the housewives, the daily alligator of the orphans with their bustling parentage of nuns. No one knew they were all alone in there. No neighbour would notice their mother's absence since mama had nothing to do with them. She began to envy the orphans whose loveless state was recognized whereas she had merely been forgotten.

She watched from the window until the first of the crocodile appeared through the heavy brown doors. Every morning at seven the nuns took the orphans for an airing and then to mass before they returned for breakfast and their lessons. Daisy sometimes ran errands for the sisters. The orphanage seemed a wonderful place, spotlessly clean, with all the girls identically dressed in starched white collars and navy blue pinafores. The lives of the orphans were secure. And there was no Janey. First came a pair of nuns with their butterfly head-dress and after that a line of big girls. Then two more nuns led a long troupe of younger charges. When the sisters had gone ahead Daisy ran across the road to join the procession. At first the orphans studied her in the silent, sniffing manner of stray dogs and then a voice beside her said, 'Have you got any tobacco?' Daisy turned to a small child of nine or ten with grey skin and dull brown hair, cut very short. She was skinny and had bright, burning eyes.

'I don't smoke tobacco.' Daisy was shocked. 'I'm only ten.'

'I don't neither,' the girl sighed. 'But I have to start soon. Have you any snuff?'

Daisy shook her head. They passed a tenement house where part of the wall had collapsed and through the gaping hole a poor family could be seen living their lives. 'What's your name? Why do you have to smoke?'

'Because I'm going to hell,' the girl grinned. 'My name is Ellen. You can call me Nellie.'

Nellie explained that she was going to hell because of The Stain. The nuns told them they carried the stain of their parents' sin. 'Hell's full of sinners. I don't want to turn up there without any sins.'

'Have you got any yet?'

'Yes, I steal.' She put her hand in her pocket and drew out some coins, a pencil and a mint. 'Here, you can have the mint.' Daisy sucked on the humbug and allowed a meagre arm to link hers. 'So tell us,' Nellie said. 'Have you The Stain?'

'I don't know.'

'Were your parents married before you were born?'

'Yes!'

'Then you can't be an orphan.' Nellie rejected her from their exclusive society.

'My father's dead.'

'Where's your mother?'

'In London. She has gone to plead for us with her parents.'

'They won't let you in,' Nellie decided. 'You're not a proper orphan.'

'How will they know?'

'You ain't got no uniform. All orphans wear a uniform. Here! You can have my hat.' Nellie crammed her navy hat over Daisy's long hair. Then she cackled, 'Now you'll have nits. I've terrible nits.'

Daisy took the hat off quickly. 'Are they the same as lice? Mama always warned us about lice. She said not to mix with the common children or we would get them. Do you really have them?' Nellie shook her head. 'I can't tell you. I have to tell lies as well as steal.' Daisy examined the hat carefully. It was a bit worn on the inside but seemed to have no animate grime. Warily she perched it back on her head and was rewarded, after mass, by being able to slide in with the seventy or so girls through the orphanage door. She found herself in a strange, dark, polished silence where the girls' boots struck echoes like the early morning horses on the cobbles. Pity streamed down from the outstretched hands of saints perched high on plaster brackets. She followed the children into a long hall where they sat on benches at a table set with pitchers of cocoa and trays piled high with wedges of bread. No one seemed to notice her so she poured herself cocoa and spread dripping on bread from a huge bowl that was passed around.

'What if there aren't enough cups?' Daisy whispered to Nellie.

Nellie shrugged. 'There be's nearly always some extra from those children that do be sick. Quite a lot die.'

Daisy began to feel uneasy. 'Die from what?'

'Diseases.' Nellie piled up slices of bread on her plate and chewed like a savage. 'Or sadness. We get looked after here, but we don't get loved. Some just fade away from lack of use.'

'What do you mean, lack of use?' Daisy cautiously wiped her mug on her sleeve.

'We're not allowed to play in the street like ordinary children. We can't climb trees or lamp-posts. We're not ever allowed to scream, not even when they beat us on the legs.'

'They beat you?'

'Like carpets! That's the motto here – spare the rod and spoil the broth!'

Daisy looked up and down the long line of orphans seated at the table. Their hair was neat, their faces composed and white. She thought of motherly Lena and the kindly teasing of Will and Tom. 'I have to go now,' she said to Nellie.

'Well, you can't,' Nellie replied. 'You're an orphan now. You're stuck here like the rest of us. Do you think we'd be here if we had any choice?'

'I'm not really an orphan,' Daisy said anxiously. 'My mother is still alive.'

'How do you know?' Nellie began to eat the bread on Daisy's plate. 'She might have been murdered by a madman. Probably never got to England – fell overboard from her ship.'

'I'm Daisy Dubois Devlin,' Daisy said firmly. 'I live at number 11 Edward Street.' She repeated this, louder and with a faint edge of hysteria, until various sisters gathered round and tried to silence her by clapping their hands in her face and then one went to fetch the reverend mother.

'Who is this child?' Mother Agnes said.

'I'm Daisy Dubois Devlin. I live at number 11 . . .'

'Well, of course you do,' the nun said at once. 'The house with the drawing room.' Daisy almost wept with relief. Mother Agnes brought her to the door herself. She stood behind the child with her hands on her shoulders and pointed her at her address. 'Never lose sight of your good fortune,' she said. 'You are a very lucky little girl to have such a home. We watch it in the evenings from our window.' She seemed now to be talking to herself. 'It is a glimpse of heaven. Just to know that such order exists is a comfort.'

Nellie had followed Daisy to the door. 'Take me with you,' she whispered.

'I can't,' Daisy said uncomfortably. 'There are too many of us at home.'

'But your pa is dead.'

'Yes, but there is another baby coming. We can be friends, though.'

This seemed to present some difficulty to Nellie. She frowned, considering the offer. 'I can't be friends with the likes of youse. I know me station. You could be my friend if you like. You could lower your sights. Don't forget!' the grey little girl urged. Daisy nodded, but as soon as she was out in the street she forgot everything except the heavenly vision of mama's parlour. All the children were waiting. 'Where were you, you oul' herrin'? I'll swing for you,' Janey threatened, but Will picked her up and put her on his shoulders and carried her indoors where they had toast and jam and tea. It was too late for school. 'Let's go to the sea!' Janey took out a shilling which Granny Devlin had given her.

'We should clean the house,' Lena said. 'Mama might be home.'

'The sea! The sea!' Bertie began to chant in a high, urgent voice, his hands bunched into little fists. He had never been to the sea, although the city was surrounded by ocean. It formed a blue band like Our Lady's girdle all around the capital, fringing out into beaches on either side. To the south was Sandymount and on the north of the city a storm of gulls barked above the twin excitements of Dollymount Strand and a vast municipal dump called the Sloblands. Because of this sinister attraction, all the children preferred Dollymount.

With Granny Devlin's shilling to squander they took a tram from Nelson's Pillar. Lena carried the towels and a change of dress for Daisy, and Essie and Beth looked after the picnic of jam sandwiches and cold milk. They travelled on top of the tram, which had no roof. A warm wind brushed their skin and tangled their hair. Bertie, reprieved from his frills and dressed in a dull blue pinafore that once had belonged to Daisy, wore an expression of dangerous male bliss. Relieved of mama's constantly caressing and rearranging hands he was tearing through the air with Janey at his side teaching him a new phrase to speak.

Up there the dull blanket of grief that pa's death had flung about them was blown away. Mama's rules and criticisms were forgotten. They felt that breathless sense of power that children sometimes experience when they touch the world and it moves under their hands. Lena, freed from housework, allowed herself to think of skating at the Rathmines rink with a fur muff and, perhaps, a boy. Will imagined tall, leafy trees where he could perch with his books and not be tormented by other boys and Tom thought of painting, just for pleasure, for there was no money to train him for such nonsense. He had his paintbox in his pocket and a little bottle of water and a school jotter. He was going to make a picture of the sea. The twins dreamed of a cottage in the country, with a hen and a goat, maybe a horse. Janey wanted to be an actress. Weenie saw herself as a married woman with a husband to admire her hair and servants to rule. Daisy pictured herself in London with mama, dressed in a low-cut gown of blue organza. Only Bertie was without ambition for he could imagine no more than this – to be dirty and on his way to the sea.

Suddenly, all the children unleashed a wave of noise. The ocean had come into view. The flat, grey expanse, distantly piped with a

44

frill of Howth's hills, was the end of the ordinary world. Here rules ceased. Primitive cries were torn from their centre as they tumbled down the tram steps and raced each other to the beach. Bertie stood transfixed on the grainy dampness. 'The waves!' he breathed in astonishment. He crept forward cautiously with hands extended to feel the screen which harboured this illusion, until murky wetness swarmed over his feet. The rest of them ran into the freezing water in their drawers. None had any bathing costumes. Daisy would not take off her dress, and waded in fully clothed. Tom and Will had learned to swim in the canal. The girls stayed close to the edge, splashing each other with shallow waves and chasing one another with slimy fronds of seaweed. Bertie, with a bullish look, staggered in deeper, deeper, until the water dabbled about his chest. He raised his fists, faintly blue, and shouted out the phrase that Janey had taught him. 'I'm a blooming gouger!' With arms rigid he continued his progress into the deep until the words came out as bubbles and Will and Tom had to race back to rescue him.

Dollymount is a long flat beach with a sluggish tide, not much favoured by lovers for there are no concealing places. Children like it because you can see all the vastness at once. Boys and men like to poke beneath the wet sand for slow unpleasant creatures to eat. The children stopped to stare at an old man who had collected cockles in a bucket and was boiling them over a fire made with driftwood. He gave them tea from a billycan and let them sit by his fire to dry their hair. He put the cockles between bread and gave them each a sandwich. 'Why are these called sandwiches?' He winked at Tom. 'Because they're full of sand!' They were full of sand which rasped uneasily beneath the teeth and Janey said the cockles looked like nose-pickings, but all the same they ate them.

To the unease of the boys the old man then told the girls to sit quite still and he decorated them with shells, adorning their hair which had been turned to vapour by wind and spray. 'God bless ya,' he said. 'You're like creatures from a harem.' Will and Tom were forced to see their sisters differently, not just as sisters. Tom jumped up as if something in the sand alarmed him. 'Race you down the beach!' he said in a high, uncertain voice. Janey scrambled after him but in a minute she lost interest and started to dance. Dressed only in her drawers and chemise she spun around on her bare toes, her long black hair swirling around her. The old man began to whistle a charmer's tune. The children looked on, admiring and appalled, and

Tom stopped running and panted in a hopeless way. She ended the dance in a mood, dropping her arms to her sides. 'I'm bet!' The old man spat in the sand to clear his mouth of music. 'That there is a magnificent specimen of the female sex,' he said. 'She is like a houri!' She glared at him and stamped away over the sand. Reluctantly, the others gathered up their clothes. 'Dirty oul' blackguard.' Janey kicked at ridges in the sand and brushed away the dress that Lena tried to offer her. 'That's a desperate dirty name he's after calling me.' Bad-temperedly she began to pull on her clothes. 'Come on. We're going. Let's go to the dump.'

Janey's moods were unpredictable. She sang a song as they commenced the three-mile walk back to the Sloblands. She turned to the others with a wild smile. 'We are like creatures from a harem. We've been washed clean by the sea. Think what we'll be like when we live in London and have baths every day!'

The Sloblands was a sinister place, where bands of shabby men and boys wandered among reeking dunes and mounds of refuse. It was not merely queer and dangerous. It was a world. The path that led to the dumping ground crackled with broken glass. The place had its own silence – a thick stillness, drilled by the murmur of flies and shattered at intervals by screaming gulls. Apart from the scavenging birds and rats and the rotting corpses of horses, dogs and cats, it had its own population which laboured silently beneath the wrenching smell, like a burial crew in a plague. Small boys and starving widows with their children clawed at the heaps of filth, looking for things to sell. There were eccentric men called picaroons who lived upon the pickings of the dump and had set up shacks there and existed in quiet contentment under the pall of stench. The children were forbidden excursions to the rubbish dump but they were fascinated by it and went all the same.

'If I found anything good,' said Will, 'I could sell it and get back pa's watch.' Tom was looking for a bicycle. He began energetically to haul at wheels which poked out from under old mattresses and rags, but they disappointingly came away with no vehicle attached. Weenie found a green necklace with a broken clasp and Janey vigorously dug about in the dirt hoping for money or more jewellery. Lena and the twins located a very good chair with only some strings undone in its cane backing, which would make a surprise present for mama when she got home. Bertie rolled about in the rubbish with a surprised and happy look, shouting, 'I'm a blooming gouger. I'm a desperate filthy blooming gouger!'

Daisy wandered off alone. After the clean and salty sea she did not wish to get dirty again. She was thinking of something mama had once said, how in polite society soup was eaten from the outside of the plate. She pictured herself with her spoon held external to the dish, scraping at its side up as far as the brim, but she could not imagine how to get at the soup. Perhaps one could tilt the plate. With her mind pleasantly in quest of the unreachable soup she was taken by surprise when a push from behind sent her sailing through the air into a festering pile of waste. Awful things got into her mouth. She held herself in a lump as the hand pulled her round to face a youth of thirteen or fourteen with a wicked, elderly face and foul-smelling clothes. 'Will!' Her scream seemed to come out as a whisper.

The boy roughly pinned her hands to the ground and lay on top of her, glaring into her face. Seconds passed. She could feel the weight of his bones and he smelled of decay. 'Pretty, ain't you?' he said. 'I could make you cry.'

'I don't cry,' she said.

He bent his face and kissed her. It was not nice. It seemed to search for something beyond itself. When Will and Tom ran in answer to her cry she could feel them pause, utterly shocked, before they flung themselves on the vagabond youth. Although the boy was younger than her brothers he was bigger and stronger and he kicked and punched them as they feebly beat back. 'Now I'm all dirty,' Daisy thought furiously. She felt nothing but rage. It was a hot, restless energy that replaced her normal lethargy and her eyes darted around for some means of revenge. She found a brick and raised it high up over her head and then brought it forward with all her might on the strange boy's nose. He let go of Will and Tom to clutch at his face. It was very clean blood that gushed over his dirty skin. She admired this for a moment before her brothers each took her by a hand and they all ran for their lives.

Silent, dishevelled, screamed-out, they walked the long walk home. Sodden and sated with adventure, they carefully carried their experiences and their treasures. Their pockets were weighted down with shells. Beth had found a hair comb, missing scarcely any teeth, and Janey wore in her hair a funeral wreath of artificial flowers.

The last mile seemed endless, especially for Will, who carried Bertie, and Tom, who was bearing Lena's chair with its back all unravelled and awry. They were relieved when they got back to

Edward Street to see the welcoming pink light of mama's parlour. Bertie struggled out of Will's arms. 'Mama! Mama!' It took a moment for the others to realize the significance of the light and then they all broke into a run, fighting back tears because none of them had really believed that she would come back to them.

Mama's confinement was beginning to be visible. She looked pinched. Her face was hard and shadowed. As the old gown was wrestled from within, she gave something of the appearance of a small man in a woman's dress.

'Oh, mama,' said Lena, 'you are home!'

'To be greeted by a pack of savages!' Mama viewed them with regret.

'I'm a blooming gouger,' Bertie murmured contentedly, before pitching himself on to his mother's lap and falling into heavy snores. Lena quickly seized the baby. 'We did not expect you back.'

'That is very clear! The state of the place!'

'We brought something for you.' Tom proudly dragged in the chair. It did not compete well with the marvels of the parlour. When he saw mama's face he lugged it through to the kitchen and flung it out in the yard. Lena quickly washed her hands and face. She made up a tray and brought in some tea. 'Mama, how did you get on in London? Is everything settled?' she said eagerly.

'Yes, it's done,' mama sighed.

'So when are we to leave?' said Will.

She tasted her tea with a sour expression. 'The smell of you. I could not think of nourishment with such a smell.' She wanted to lie down and asked Lena to unpack her case. 'There are some things in a bag there that have come from my family.' She motioned a light portmanteau which had been added to her luggage.

'Presents!' Janey headed for the bag the moment mama was out the door. Their mother seemed too tired or dispirited to climb the stairs. She paused and glanced back bleakly into her room. 'London?' she spoke in a querulous little voice. 'As if I could ever go back home with such a troupe of vagabonds. It is all hopeless.'

Heat rose from their fear and they stood in utter silence smelling the dump revived on their anxious skin. On tiptoe, they crept out of the parlour and began to clean the house. They cleaned fiercely and silently, washing heaps of dishes and clothes, scouring the floor and even the window and when they had finished the kitchen they boiled up more water and scrubbed themselves.

'Hey, look!' Janey was first to lose interest in the housework. She was bent over mama's bag. Something about her transfixed obstinacy drew the others and they peered in at an extraordinary collection of exquisite shoes.

'Perhaps mama wanted to make up for the boots we were meant to have for our trip to London,' Beth said.

'They're not children's shoes. They're women's shoes.' Lena longingly stroked a lovely primrose satin slipper with a matching ribbon bow. The shoes were not new but they looked experienced more than worn. 'I expect we are to practise walking in them,' suggested Weenie, 'so that we won't look like clodhoppers when we are presented to the cream of London society.'

'But mama said we aren't going.' Will and Tom looked utterly perplexed. It had been an exhausting, challenging, growing-up day.

'She was tired and she was angry,' Lena said. 'Of course we must go to London. What else can we do?'

The primrose slipper was not in a pair. To Daisy's delight it did not fit any of the other girls. Although she was only ten it seemed to have been made for her. When she put it on she felt that she had half stepped into her future. The others divided up among them the glacé kids and patent leathers, with adornments of rosettes and ribbons, with gilt beads and waisted heels and little bud-like buttons. Freshly washed, the six girls caught curve and shimmer from the room's beguiling glow, their impending womanhood borrowed from the shoes' disabling daintiness. Hitching up their skirts, they minced and blundered through the precious clutter. Mother Agnes, peering wistfully from her window at the orphanage, had the extraordinary notion that the heavenly heart of the Protestant woman's home had been transformed into a house of ill-fame.

Chapter 8

MAMA rested on her little sofa, pale and faintly petulant, like a saint in a shrine. 'In the restaurants of Mayfair grapes are served on platters lined with ivy leaves painted gold,' she instructed them. 'That primrose slipper! It danced with Lord Percy Jermyn.' She waved a hand towards the exotic shoe which had been caged in the unused fireplace, the toe poised upon the gilt fender. 'It belonged to my sister Ada. It is far from dancing that Ada is now.' She smiled coyly. 'I took her shoes. She has no more use of them.'

No one asked about her real mission in London. The scraps of conversation tossed aimlessly about must sooner or later strike at the truth. Tensely the children observed this progress and wondered when to mention that their money had run out. She was like a teasing girl with a secret in her pocket. She allowed them startling glimpses of what might have been a frog or an emerald, a marble or an eye. The shoe on the fender preened with victorious history; unknown Aunt Ada snaring Lord Percy Jermyn.

'Is she dead?' Essie whispered.

'Worse than dead,' said mama indifferently.

The post brought in error a hotel bill for a week's accommodation at five pounds. Its postmark reminded mama of a costly dinner house where the men ate asparagus with their fingers, butter dripping into their cuffs.

'Who can it be meant for? Where did they get your name?' Lena could not let alone the dull matter of the invoice.

Mama said, 'It is mine.'

Lena kept staring at it, at the sum on the bottom. 'We have no money,' she said.

'It is good of you to think up such original news to cheer me!' She took the piece of paper away.

'But why should they send the bill to us? We do not stay in hotels,' Will said.

Mama covered her face with her hands and spoke through the spire of her fingers with her eyes perched above, very woeful. 'All that has happened since I left home as a girl, and no one told me. My sister, Ada, is paralysed with a wasting disease. Myself, I think it is only idleness, so I took away her shoes. My father has spent all his money on her medical bills. They have been forced to take in lodgers.'

'Had they no room for you?' Beth said.

Mama shook her head.

'Then they will have no room for us,' Essie concluded.

'So they won't,' nodded Beth.

'Well done,' sighed mama without looking up.

'What are we to do for money?' Lena persisted. Mama took her hands from her face to look at her with distaste. 'We shall borrow.' She said it sharply, as if it were the obvious thing and only a fool would not have thought of it.

The children toyed stupidly with this solution. 'All the people we know are poor. Who would lend us money?'

'Vesty Muldowney!' Will brightened. 'He said to call on him if we needed anything.'

'As if I would go to a man!' mama rebuked.

'Mrs Cohen still advances!' she warned them sharply from behind her newspaper a day or two later. 'Sums from three pounds upwards at low interest, easy repayments.' And then, as if to clinch the matter, 'Established 1876!'

Mrs Cohen gave them five pounds to pay the hotel bill and the same sum again to cover household expenses. Mama bought herself a new gown with room in it for the baby from Mrs Dashper of Baggot Street, Court Dressmaker. Afterwards, she ordered cheese and bacon and butter and treacle and eggs and biscuits and toffee from Findlaters and for days on end there was plenty to eat and the treacherous feeling that their standard of living had risen since pa's departure. She even bought some grapes. The children had never eaten grapes before and were so pleased by the bursting, nestling look of them that they were reluctant to eat them. They went out to look for ivy leaves to arrange beneath them. On the wall of the Jewish cemetery in Ballybough the leathery green leaves sagged in abundance. Out of respect they stayed to look at the gravestones and wondered about Mr Ritz Rothschild, who had claimed the largest monument. The Jews had come to Dublin in the middle of the century and settled in nearby Annadale and after a generation they vanished again, summoned to migrate or nestled like grapes amid the ivy. Tom's paintbox had no gold paint but they selected other exotic colours for the solemn foliage – burnt umber, cerulean, yellow lake.

Somehow, the enormous sum of money ran out. Lena did her best to budget and then, tactfully, they tried to stop eating. In due course two men were sent by Mrs Cohen. They were not rough but went away with the surviving twin of the laughing china dogs, and the silver bon-bon dish and the Venice bud-holder. The incident seemed to rob mama mostly of colour and she explained, very white and breathless, that she had succeeded in getting the men to take the smallest items so that with rearrangement their absence might not be noticed. Besides, she added, it was well to have the matter resolved, because now she could borrow again. Bit by bit the pieces began to disappear. The wine table, an ebony chair, a Chinese lamp. With dismay the children found that they could cross the room without any special manoeuvre, that their passage was not pursued by the musical whisper of glass and china. The room lost its gorgeous air of excess, its scent of distant lands, its sense of plunder.

Mama did as she had always done, as she had taught herself to do, removed her mind to some other place. She stayed on her sofa growing larger, more silent, more distant, and held on to Bertie or one of her dolls. Sometimes she did not even notice Bertie and he gratefully slid off her lap to run after the other children in the street. He was very anxious to get away from her and grow up into a boy.

A suitor had begun to call on Lena. His name was James Gorman, and he made deliveries for Findlaters. Janey called him Grange Gorman, which was the name of the criminal lunatic asylum. He was a serious boy of seventeen with pink cheeks that blushed even darker when Lena came out. In the evenings they went for walks by the canal and when she came back she seemed wrapped in clouds. Lena had always looked after them but there was no point in asking her about the drawing room now because she no longer appeared to see the things they saw. Her eye was on a different future.

'What will we do?' The rest of the children gathered round the kitchen table trying to think of something. Tom wondered if anyone would buy his sketches and Essie and Beth talked of taking in mending. They paused to nibble at the strange new food mama ordered with the borrowed money – cheese and marzipan, fish paste and fruit cake. Daisy decided to sell her cats. They had all turned out to be tom cats, so there were no more kittens. They were no longer pretty and fluffy as when new. Four years on, they had grown fat and tough, so she put them on special offer. 'Cats – were 2/6. One day sale 1/–!' she wrote on a piece of cardboard.

She wheeled the pram up and down the city streets. One woman seemed to consider a purchase. 'You can get a rabbit for tuppence and you can ate it!' she decided. Daisy wrote out a fresh sign on the other side of the board. 'Thoroughly trained Ratters who Know their Business!' A day was spent parading the smelly markets of the Liberties, until two of the cats demonstrated their worth by leaping out of the pram and vanishing under the meat stalls after a squalling pair of rats. Half an hour later, and much intimidated by crawling about in the filth of the street, she resigned herself to their independence.

Of the three cats remaining, one had been the kitten with the pansy-patterned face that had once moved a rich woman to open her purse. Apprehensive but excited, she returned to the big house in North Great George's Street. The door was opened by a country maid who let out a yelp when she saw the child with the pram. 'Jaysus! Cats! Get them whiskery divils outa here!' And she aimed a thickly booted foot at child and carriage. In the long hall where a fountain of glass drops drizzled from the ceiling, a young woman loitered. She stared at Daisy with disdainful curiosity. When they had gazed at one another at sufficient length, the other retreated into a room. She wasn't a woman at all. She was only a girl, twelve or thirteen. It was the child in the blue dress whom Daisy had so envied when she was six. She had peered at Daisy as if she was a common beggar. 'What do I look like?' Daisy wondered fearfully. She wanted to run into the house after her, to pull at her coiled hair and tell her that they had a drawing room just like hers, but the maid slammed the door in her face.

There seemed an acre of space in the tiny parlour when she got home. She gazed around the room to where mama was marooned on her sofa, sipping a glass of the port which had come with the grocer's most recent order. 'Has the cat got your tongue?' she greeted Daisy. A cat began to slide, snail-like, out of the carriage and mama let out a gulp of mirth. 'Why, there is now room to swing a cat. Why don't you?' She gave a little giggle.

'The piano!' Daisy breathed.

'No doubt you will sorely miss it. Pity. I had great ambitions of you as a concert pianist.'

Daisy whispered, 'What next?'

Mama shrugged. Her regretful little smile had a crooked edge to it. 'I can scarcely think! I am spoilt for choice.' A splash of laughter fell untidily from her jaws and Daisy took in her breath, sensing that loosening of hinges that sometimes followed adult refreshment. 'I shall let them start removing items around the edges until I am marooned on the Turkey rug and then . . . then, when it is all gone, please God, I too shall vanish.'

Daisy backed her pram out into the street. She dawdled there, composed and dreamy, her body pounding with panic, while the cats fastidiously plucked their paws from the blanket and stuck their heads out for a look-out vantage of the world, but they had grown used to portage and subsided like invalids. When she could manage her fear she took her pram to St Lucy's Church. There she offered up a cat to St Anthony. 'Don't let her vanish,' she said. 'Save her and I'll be a nun.' She suspended the animal from a brown-clad plaster arm. The saint retained its rapt inattention.

She knew where mama had got the money. She had taken the two youngest children with her to help her plead her case. North Brunswick Street lay close to Sackville and Dorset streets and it was part of the children's familiar trail. She knocked on the door and waited in the dark until blackness was relieved by a brick-coloured wig and beneath it a woman with a bust like a ship's masthead. The woman took a cat from the pram and laid it on her bosom and stroked it and the creature stretched out its chin and extruded a low, groaning purr. 'Follow me,' she said. Daisy was brought into a large room with black-and-white engravings on the wall and a desk in the corner and arranged in between were mama's bits of furniture, her ornaments and her piano. Mrs Cohen advanced with a glass of milk and an iced biscuit on a tray. A cat sat on her shoulder, its orange fur raucous against the terracotta wig. Daisy drank her milk. 'Why have you got mama's drawing room here?'

'It's mine,' Mrs Cohen said.

'Your men came and took our things.'

Mrs Cohen patted the child's knee. 'Is just business,' she said. 'I am like your mother – a poor woman alone in the world. I cannot be soft in the heart. The heart is like a pet, my pet. It is a luxury which we women love to spoil, but when times is hard, we cannot afford to have a heart.'

'What happened to your husband?' Daisy said.

'My late husband ...' Mrs Cohen cradled her knees and made a rueful face. 'My late husband – he was so late he never caught me!' She made a cackle like a hen. 'I have no husband. I don't want no husband, eating my food and lying on me in the night when I want some sleep.'

Daisy remained thoughtful. 'If you are a poor woman, why did you not sell mama's things to get your money back?'

'Because your mama, she have something that money cannot buy. She have style. I too have style. Do you like my hair?' Daisy was about to say that she could not see it beneath the wig but then the woman added, 'I have it done by Monsieur Mathias Grieveldinger Prost of St Stephen's Green. I am poor woman but I must have style.'

'We need our drawing room.' Daisy plucked her cat from the woman's shoulder. 'Our pa is dead. When the parlour is gone mama will vanish too. We are in a fix. Soon all our things will be taken.' Gazing into the child's troubled green eyes Mrs Cohen suffered an uncomfortable pressure beneath the uppermost rib of her corset. To relieve it she cleared her throat in a rumbling way. 'Your mama send you here to make soft my heart,' she charged. 'Go now or you put me in the workhouse.'

'Mama doesn't know I'm here. She is ill with her lying up.'

Mrs Cohen looked forlorn. 'Women's lives!' She sharpened her gaze for Daisy. 'What you want I should do?'

'Talk to her, please. She has no one else. There is only us children.'

'What you give me for my trouble?'

'You can have a cat.' Daisy held out the creature that had adorned the woman's bosom.

Mrs Cohen hardened her heart. 'I want the two of them.'

The arrival of the money-lender in Edward Street was an event like the visit of Talbot Jutton. She drove in a carriage, which was followed by a trail of boys. All the neighbours were drawn to their doors and watched as the brick-coloured wig emerged and two cheeks, very rouged for the outing. She wore a gown of velvet eau-de-Nil with a rust-coloured boa and carried a carpet bag, slightly opened for the two cats to look out. Mama threw the children out in the street to talk to the visitor. Daisy stayed close to the house, looking in the window. Mama had Bertie on her knee and was holding him like a shield and Mrs Cohen was making some strong point, tapping her palm with Aunt Ada's primrose slipper, which she held in her left hand and coveted with her eye. Mama looked miserable and kept shaking her head. The other woman's face was lit up and she used her arms, stretching them out like a swimmer to describe some imagined scene. The satin slipper, imprisoned and forgotten in her grasp, vaguely pawed the air with its strand of ribbon.

The sky began to darken and the women faded into dusky shadow. The drawing room glowed with its rosy light and in spite of the bare patches and the meagre furnishings it projected an image of a warmer, better life. Mama's head began to nod unhappily. For some reason Daisy now felt a violent unease. She wanted to burst in and tell the money-lender to go away, to give her back her cats, to leave them all alone. Mrs Cohen settled and began to write on paper and mama paid unwilling heed. As the two women's heads drew together and the little neighbouring shops began to shut down, Daisy felt lonely and excluded. She left Edward Street and headed for Summerhill where the shops stayed open later and the streets were full of bustle. In the busier thoroughfare her mood improved. 'I have turned the hand of fate,' she thought as she watched poor women clutching monkey-faced babies under their shawls and drunk men arguing with their flailing feet. 'Whatever happens next will be because of what I have done.' She felt full of power, like Aggie Fossett, accepting on a whim the fishmonger, determining the address of the entire Devlin family.

'It is for the best,' mama murmured to herself as if rehearsing part of an important speech she had to deliver. 'It is best done quickly.'

She had to tell Lena to sit down. The girl was making her nervous, her swift movements touched with grace as she went about the dull business of the meal. 'Be still, can't you? Let Weenie do it for a change.'

'I'm used to it,' she smiled, and whipped a pancake batter almost to a soufflé. Charged by love, she could not be still. 'Besides, Weenie is only twelve.'

'So much the better,' said mama. 'If there must be bustle, better that of a child than a woman.' She paused to consider something. 'I will tell you,' she uttered in a confidential way to her eldest daughter, 'I cannot stand the smell of another woman in my house.' Mortified, Lena sank into a chair. While the other little girls got on with the tea, mama suggested to her eldest that it was time she went out to work. 'Mrs Cohen has advised me that I must no longer view my children as a burden, but as a resource. It is only that with the new baby coming there will not be space for all of you and even a very small wage would be a help. I think I have found a way for us to keep our heads above water.'

A job, Lena thought, would give her freedom. Maids got a half-day off every week. She and James could go skating at the rink. They might make an excursion to the Strawberry Beds. Oh, she would miss the children, but it was well for them to learn to do without her for soon she would be married.

'There is no need to sit there sulking like a martyr boiled in oil,' said mama. 'We shall all have to make sacrifices and mine will be far greater than yours.'

'I don't mind,' Lena said eagerly. I'll get a job – anything at all! A maid!'

Mama muttered in exasperation as Beth put a burnt pancake on her plate. 'A maid! Sometimes I feel that all my efforts are for nothing.'

'What else can I do?' pleaded Lena.

'You could work in a good house as a lady help. It is not at all the same thing as a kitchen drudge. You would assist with the children and do some light sewing. It is the proper work for ladies in reduced circumstances and is very popular in remote parts of the country where companionship is valued as much as labour.'

They sat before their plates but did not eat. They sensed that some contest was going on, which they could not understand. As yet it was no more than a shadow on the wall, and such things are often in the imagination, but Lena had shrunk down in her chair and mama had the air of one who has just dined well, although a corner of her eye continued to criticize at a distance the charred batter on her plate. 'Of course such work does not normally go to Catholic girls, but I believe that the Dubois name will make the difference. I may already have found you a position. Say your prayers or cross your fingers or whatever you people do and with luck you may soon be lording it over the kitchen staff at Balmullet House in County Louth.'

She sat back and waited. She even ate a little centre piece of the pancake, busying herself over it in that way she had, which was so neat that it made her chewing seem more like sewing. Of course, they realized now, she had known all along about James Gorman. Lena remained quite still, until the feelings she struggled to hide burst up in her face and her cheeks got a bludgeoned look and her lips began to tremble. Mama looked up with faint disapproval as she ran from the room. 'I shall say that she is a very good girl but in need of excellent influences.'

'Who'd have you as a lady help?' Janey tried to stop Lena's sobbing in bed that night. 'You're only a scrawny oul' hen.' It was not a serious hope. Mama's pretty handwriting, with French phrases thrown in, easily conquered Balmullet. 'Run you eejit,' Janey urged. 'You and Grange Gorman! Get on the boat – go to England. You're old enough for work. Mama won't find you.'

Meekly Lena let herself be led to Madame Laurie's shop for left-off clothes in Kildare Street, where she was fitted out with some respectable used gowns. 'I daresay you would like to be tricked out in frills, flaps, doublers, danglers, flounces and dragglers and all the other deceits of fashion, but unremarkable dress is the mark of the successful subordinate,' mama explained as she selected several durable dresses in brown and grey and navy blue. Lena frowned distantly at her image in the mirror. Up to now she had worn loose pinafores like the children, with her long hair slightly frizzed around her shoulders, and the effect was rosy and kind. Now she looked stiff and matronly. The last of her softness vanished when she was plunged into a Sparrows' extra-strong grey corset.

Bertie would not come to her. 'Bones,' he growled sadly when she lifted him on to her hard new lap. Even the older children were constrained in her company, for she seemed like some different, more mature relation. Mama was delighted. She insisted that Lena adopt her new outfits and hairstyle immediately for practice, and when next James Gorman called to the door she greeted him herself and invited him through to the kitchen to witness the transformation. The boy stood at a distance and looked uneasily at the sudden woman, with her forbidding bust and iron waves nailed on to her skull. He had been proud, at seventeen, to be her protector. He felt all at sea now, a youth in the daunting face of maturity. Fear made Lena look cold.

'She is a young woman now,' mama exulted. 'Kiss her if you like.' His feet seemed soldered to lead. Her frozen cheeks defied his advance. In the end he could only extend an awkward hand. Lena turned her face and then the whole of her stiff body away.

Out in the narrow hall, mama had a talk with him. For decency, he tried to press himself into the wall or up the stairs, for there wasn't room for the two of them. He held his breath, suffocated by her closeness, her mix of bulk and frailty, her childlike innocence and the engulfing sweetness of her rose-water. 'As you can see, the girl is not well. I have lost my husband. If anything should happen to Lena . . .' She turned her head aside to hide her emotion and it was almost pressed to his shoulder. She seemed, suddenly, to have grown younger than Lena. The scent of her rose-water made him feel ill and excited and gallant. 'As it is . . .' her sigh was warm on his cheek; 'she must not be upset. I am sending her to the country. You ought not to see her again.'

The boy looked so miserable that mama patted his shoulder. 'Oh, it is a pity. I am all on your side, you know. Lena is not strong. She needs a man who will marry and take care of her. Perhaps . . .!' For a moment hope smoothed her anxious look. 'If you were in a position now to take on marriage and children. If you could get a little house and look after Lena until she was well. One or two of her sisters could come and stay to keep her company, for we are so very short of space here. Oh, I am sure that would make her happy. Could we hope for that?'

'No!' he almost shouted and mama nodded sadly. 'You are young but I can see that you are sensible.'

He left with conflicting feelings – of pride that she had confided in him, of tenderness for her frailty and naivety. Only afterwards he thought of Lena and was miserable, but he had given his word to mama and there was nothing he could do.

All of this took attention away from the other development. Items continued to disappear from the drawing room. Some vanished and were never seen again and as if to hurry up the destruction of that exquisite little showpiece, mama had begun to squirrel away pieces in her bedroom. Every day Daisy went in to count the remaining contents and accustom herself to each new loss: the ebony chairs, the fringed lamp, the breakfront cabinet. Before she allowed that to be taken mama had removed all the dolls and heaped them up on her dressing table, where they looked like a murdered wedding party. One morning, bringing her mother a cup of tea, Daisy was unsettled to observe that the room had reproduced itself. The mountainous green quilt, the clutter of jars and brushes on the dressing table, the intrusive wardrobe, even the rearing red face of the orphanage, were flung back upon their own image. She saw then the second bedroom was suspended in a speckled haze and held aloft by angels. Mama had attached the large gilded overmantel with the cherub candle-holders to the wall above her bed and the confusion of her small room was reflected there. She stared too long for mama told her to be off to school. 'I shall need the perambulator,' she added. 'I hope you have got rid of those wretched cats.'

Daisy's heart skipped. 'The baby!'

'Don't remind me!' hissed mama.

She was going to have her baby. When Bertie was born Daisy was considered too young to wheel him out, but now she was ten. At last she would have a baby of her own to show off. After school she went to the church to pray for the infant's safe delivery. 'And please let it be a boy,' she added, 'for poor mama has had so many girls.' Rat-like, through the aisles skirmished St Anthony's cat. In due course it returned to Daisy and folded up like a plump fur hat on the bench beside her, inconspicuous but for its great noisy rumblings of relief. She picked her cat up and went home. Although it was almost dark the drawing room was not yet lit, but as usual she paused to look in the window. The first thing she saw was lakes of shadow on a gleam of skin, like Janey undressing in the dark, like church lilies gulping dusk into their creamy cores. It was Aunt Ada's satin slipper. Someone had set it up in the window. It stood on tiptoe on the rosewood table, propped up by some lumpy object concealed beneath a nest of black velvet. Ranged around in more passive poses were the rest of the crippled woman's shoes: grey dance shoes with beads of gilt and steel, waist-heeled shoes in scarlet kid with a big bow flattened on the instep, a pair in blue glacé kid with a ribbon rosette.

'Oh mama!' Daisy breathed. Something really big must have gone, so that she had to draw the eye away by filling up the window. She stood on her toes for a better look. The dark would not defy her for she knew the shape and sheen of the remaining pieces. For a few seconds the objects prowled and gyrated in the grainy gloom until her adjusting eyes forced them to settle to their identities. Daisy's mouth worked in silence as she sought a scream but all that came out was a little grunt. The whole of her mother's room had been taken over by boots – women's boots, men's boots, cork-soles, waterproofs, heeled boots, buttoned boots, gaitered boots, kid boots, kids' boots. Some were glossy and only faintly wrinkled like the skin of rich women. Others carried within them the burdened warp of a haulier's plodding. There were children's boots with so much wear in them that little feet must have been broken before they outgrew them.

She squeezed her eyes shut and held them tight until she thought the nightmare might have passed. When she opened them the boots were still there but it seemed to her they had advanced a little bit, they were creeping forward. She strained to see but could determine only that every single one of her mother's treasures was gone, vanquished by this ghost army. Inside the dainty shell of the drawing room, wrapped around by the pretty Chinese wallpaper, the dusty toes shuffled in silence. She ran away, pursued by an echo of Janey's teasing menace: 'I hear tramp, tramp, tramp, and there's no one there.'

At the canal bank she threw herself down and watched the elastic frieze of the little white cottages on the opposite side, which flexed and shivered in the dark water. Nothing was substantial, nothing constant. On the way back she bumped into Norah Boake, who stood in her doorway with a baby at her breast. 'You look as if you seen a ghost eatin' toast, halfway up the lamp-post,' the woman commented.

'Mama's room,' Daisy gasped and shuddered. 'It's gone. There's nothing there now but dirty old boots.'

'It's all right,' the kindly neighbour soothed. 'Your mammy's after opening a little shop, the same as the rest of us. You're the same as the rest of us now.'

Chapter 9

ONE day when Will was being pasted by Scut Mulvey, he spotted, as he fell to earth, a ten-bob note in the gutter. He allowed the blows to rain about his ears as his knuckles closed around the fortune and he clawed it up into his cuff. The effect of the prickle of paper upon his wrist was of a total anaesthetic. He felt no more pain. He felt nothing but the thunderous flooding of awe to his heart.

The first thing he did was to buy back pa's watch from the hock. It cost him seven shillings because of interest. The remaining three bob he gave to Tom and together they went to Charles Yore, scrap merchant, and asked if he had a cycle for three shillings. Yore led them to a rusting tangle of iron skeletons with which they spent a good hour before hauling out a brilliant Centaur with no brakes.

Up and down the hilly streets they rode, using their feet for restraint. When this failed they rang the bell, which still, miraculously, coughed up its throaty, gurgling alarm. The tyres, which were smooth as wet stones, whistled in the path of horses or shrieking nursemaids with baby cars. Pedestrians waved their canes at them, policemen blew their whistles. Whenever they slowed down Will took the watch from his pocket and consulted the time. The smell of his father's Violet Smoking Mixture was still comforting inside the case. The large, arrow-headed golden hands seemed to slip around in a swaggering, deliberate manner, offering a more leisured sort of time, a time in which skies might clear of rain, in which a clothy flap of wings might raise a lid on nests of eggs. Before putting it back in his pocket he wrapped it in his handkerchief, for they frequently fell off the Centaur. Blood dripped from muddy gashes and pa's watch, a man's watch, beat steadily against the unsteady joy in Will's chest. It was a glorious day, a day they would never forget as long as they lived.

Unforgettable too was the day on which the child was born. It was May and the sky was of that pitiless blue that singes black at its edges when you look at it. That was how Weenie was engaged, dreaming of romance as she sat on the canal's sunlit bank, the sky rippling darkly in her absent gaze while Bertie played at the water's edge and birds screamed overhead.

On the day of the Centaur, this was still in the future, months away, a heavy parcel in the post. Mama was working in her shop. Daisy was enjoying school. There were girls who linked her arms and slipped scraps beneath her textbooks. To please the nuns she prayed for mama's conversion and was a great favourite among the less murderous sisters. After school each day Tom wheeled Bertie's pram from house to house around the city, looking for worn footwear to buy. He saw many strange sights. A woman in a corset lay on a bed drinking gin from a bottle while a drunk man attacked a chair with great violence and personal enmity. In a house that had been rented by country people, there was a horse in the hall. He learned in time to stay away from the poor parts of the city, where people wore their shoes until they fell in tatters from their feet, and to avoid bedrooms for formality was eroded there and men and women might show you any part of their person or their personal lives.

Mama's shop was more than a success. It became a landmark. The hostile envy she had inspired in the neighbours was boiled down to admiration of a resourceful widow and they subscribed to her penny-a-week savings scheme for cast-off children's boots. Within a three-month, little blue feet became a rarity on Edward Street. All the neighbouring children were soon as well shod as the orphans. Mama frequently served in the shop, wrapped in a lacy shawl to disguise her maternal girth. Now that she was without a husband men were constantly calling on the pretext of browsing and she sent them off with a pair of boots they did not want, purchased at outrageous cost. There was another side to the business which almost compensated for the loss of the room. Aunt Ada's slipper, naturally, did not sell. It served the function of a wedding cake in a bread shop window. It enhanced necessity. It was a conversation piece. The conversation, which spread from neighbour to tradesman, from downstairs maid to upstairs mistress, in due course drew a surreptitious visitor from the region of Merrion Square. The lady, who had concealed herself in a veiled bonnet, carried a pair of blue dance slippers wrapped in brown paper as if they were a fish. She had worn them twice, she said, once to the Castle, and she could not appear in them again. And they had been so expensive. Mama, enthralled by the company, still managed to stay cool as ice. She was not in the fashion business, she said, but would take the slippers for their ornamental value. She offered a shilling. 'Only a token but I can afford no more and of course you will be donating the sum to charity.' The lady very pinkly put away her shilling and mama took the shoes.

The cream of society sold to mama. The full fat professional wives came and squeezed their feet into pods of silk and kid to kick up their heels at suppers and sing-songs. Mama had one wall shelved from floor to ceiling and here she arranged the utility boots, with a ladder propped up, for men or children to scramble for dusty bargains stored beneath the ceiling. The good shoes were placed on tables backed by mirrors so that the twinkling fripperies, reflected and reflected, danced off into infinity. She would have liked to keep them but they made a better living than the boots, and their trade enriched her life with desirable company. She returned the pink brocade sofa to the front room and customers of a better type rested on this while refreshments were brought in by the girls.

Mama had a special flair for business, which is to say, the turning of a profit infused in her a tiny spark of pure joy. She discovered that the biggest impediment to an impulse buy was the dull imagination of well-off wives. She could have told them that for pure style one should cut a dash in some striking contrast, but she knew that what they wanted was a bonnet and bag and gloves and shoes matched in every detail so that they resembled a cloth doll with stitched extremities in pink or blue or green poking out from every exit in their apparel. The joke was so tempting that she took Essie and Beth from their books to help her out by making up accessories. The twins stitched beautifully and no woman who congratulated herself on having saved her husband the price of a new pair of shoes could forbear to celebrate with a really quite modestly priced little scarf or bag or bow or gloves.

Daisy often dreamed about the drawing room. In her dream it was as it had been, filled with pretty pieces. When she came home from school she avoided looking in the window but hurried through the shop into the kitchen where St Anthony's cat slept beside the stove. They were all lonely for Lena but there were letters every week. At first they would race each other for the post but her letters were so polite and distant, so lacking in any information that she became, after a while, a shadowy figure like a distant cousin. They missed pa, but there was no denying that mama seemed less guarded since the threat of his virility was removed. Only Bertie knew that this was not the case. Still clutched to mama's bosom, he was weekly edged further out on her lap towards her knees. Sometimes when she held him close the unknown opponent within boxed him stealthily and Bertie responded with a furtive elbow into mama's massive stomach. When she gasped with dismay he assumed a look of cunning innocence. The rest of them, busy with work or school, gave scarcely a thought to the coming infant, and mama, well and pretty in spite of her size, dressed so cleverly that she could fool even herself into forgetfulness. She looked as surprised as if someone had spiked her coffee with arsenic one morning when some internal assault made her drop her cup and swoop down to seize the edges of the table.

All day, mama's screams, in the hot, dark little bedroom, were scattered over with flakes of song. Children from the orphanage walked in a May procession to St Lucy's Church with communion wreaths on their heads and hard brown boots on their feet, singing hymns to Our Lady.

'No!' Mama cried. 'No! Oh, no!' When at last the baby came and its feet were unlocked to show pink petals folded over nothing, she showed no interest at all but continued to howl into some tormented space as if she could see what Weenie could not.

Weenie had been kept back from school to take Bertie out of the house. She played with him on the canal bank for a while and then she grew sleepy in the sun and fell back on her elbows to warm her face and dream into the sky. Bertie saw a duck upon the water and, improvising a word of welcome, he sped towards it with crab-like efficiency. Unwise to the treacherous textural variety of the elements, he did not pause as he reached the edge. 'I'm a blooming gouger,' he murmured in happy memory of his one day at the seaside as he lost his balance and slipped comically through the slimy reeds into the porter-like depths of the canal. Three times his astonished head and hands appeared above the water while Weenie woke and screamed and housewives, lumbered by their shape, ran awkwardly from their houses and reached the grassy bank too late.

Ba spent the start of her life in the pram in the kitchen wrapped in damp blankets and rescued from starvation by indifferent hands that fished her out and stuffed a feeding bottle in her mouth. Her first taste was not of breast or milk but of a ribbon of black crape that someone had tied about her arm. She sucked on it and it tasted dusty. She did not see her mother at all. No one gave her a name. Even the girls blamed her for having taken Bertie's place.

In the front room, the dance shoes dimmed under a cloak of dust. The shop, which had promised them prosperity and social connection, declined into a dirty little huckster premises like any other on the street, where the poor loitered over a penny purchase and deterred superior custom. Mama had taken to her bed. It was frightening to see her lying so still, barely eating or moving. She was not even able to reproach Weenie, but merely touched the stunned girl's beautiful hair. 'You are as you were made,' she sighed. 'I suppose we had better make you as you are.' With a listless gesture she reached out towards her side table for a long, dagger-nosed pair of sewing shears. She glanced at it a moment as if it were not the thing she expected to find in her hand but anyway it made no matter, and then with a sleep-walker's unpremeditated rashness she sawed through Weenie's hair, just below the skull. The gesture seemed to cost her the last of her strength for she then lay back, mute as a board. Weenie flew to the mirror and screeched. The little rasping lick of the scissors, like a cat's tongue on a kitten's fur, would stay in her head as long as she lived. As for mama, she no longer lived at all but only imposed upon the air a frugal rent of breath.

The twins brought up treats of beef tea and chocolate porridge to try and tempt her back to vitality, but there was no spirit there and they did not know if all the life had been taken from her by the one child which struggled out of her body or the other who so meekly went beneath the earth. Privately, they blamed Janey.

At first mama had seemed to manage after Bertie's death. She had a purpose that was still connected to her little boy. She would not stay in bed but dressed herself and oversaw his laying out. He was perfect. He had only been killed by water. A table in the room was cleared of dance shoes and decked with scented flowers and there she dressed him in a tiny bride's gown of lace and muslin stitched by nuns, and packed him into a white box like a jewel case. For two days she would not move but crouched above his docile body which had grown wise with the passing of reckless life. To her own body, exhausted and still bleeding from childbirth, she paid no heed. In an effort to make useful her maternal role she sought to unite herself to him in patience. Only the odd, staggering collapse of a rose with its tiny whisper and attendant belch of worldly scent intruded on the suspense.

66

In the kitchen, the children tried to keep the infant quiet and one by one, on tiptoe, they visited the room. They did not cry for fear of disturbing mama although Janey shouted out, 'Ah, for God's sake' – as if the horror was far more than she had imagined – and ran from the room, slamming the door. At any rate mama seemed scarcely to notice. She did not react to anything at all until the men came to hammer down the coffin lid and then she flung herself at them and tried to claw them asunder with her hands.

Bertie was buried in the Protestant cemetery. Defying convention mama had saved the boys for her own faith. The coffin was carried by the boys. More roses had been heaped on the lid and it looked like a cake. Everyone seemed petrified by grief except Janey, who suddenly ran forward and began to tear the roses from the coffin. 'No!' mama gasped. 'Stop her!' The other girls scrambled for the fragments of blossom and tried to put them back but they were all broken and it was this that finally broke mama. She cried in the way that a child does, loudly and without depth, and kept sifting through the petals. Even as the coffin was lowered into the ground she knelt down and tried to reach with her arm to find an unharmed bloom. Janey was shocked by what she had caused. She touched her mother on the shoulder. Mama looked up with a face dark with loathing. 'Don't ever let me see you again,' she said.

'You're always in trouble, ain't you?' Granny Devlin said when Janey turned up in Fishamble Street with her clothes in a bag.

'I couldn't stand what she done to him.' In her grandmother's company Janey reverted from the refined speech imposed by her mother to the Dublin vernacular.

'She did love him.' Granny Devlin swiped the cat from a chair and sat the child down by a consuming turf fire which pitted its might against the sun's invading force. Old food and newspapers warped in the torpid air and enfeebled flies droned behind the window panes. 'Even if she never loved no one else.'

'No!' Janey buried her head against her grandmother's chest. 'She turned him into a blooming doll. She wouldn't let him be a boy. That was all he wanted.' Bertie had been Janey's weakness. She had taught him how to box – a skill which he could never hope to learn from his brothers – and imparted to him all the rough words of the street. On one memorable occasion she had been woken by her little brother jumping up and down in his night-shirt on the bed singing an improvised song of all his newly acquired swearwords. 'He didn't want to be buried in a girl's dress with shagging roses,' Janey mourned. 'He would have liked to be buried with a catapult.'

'Go to bed.' Granny Devlin stroked the girl's thick hair. 'When you wake up I'll make you something nice. I've a tin of desiccated red soup.' Janey threw her clothes on the floor and the old woman felt a seducer's triumph when she saw that the fourteen-year-old had developed a beautiful woman's figure, as if she had done it to spite the ha'p'orth-o'-dates Englishwoman with the airs. Janey was hers now. As the girl had bestowed on her poor little brother the gift of profanity, so she would lead her favourite grand-daughter into womanhood. She would teach her to hold her porter like a man.

Whenever Will was upset he would take out his father's watch and study the golden hands' unhurried progress. He had noticed that when a hand reached the minute or the hour, it seemed to hesitate, as if reluctant to leave the pleasant familiarity of the now. He understood this feeling. As time slid past, snatching the parent or the brother or the shilling you thought you would keep, you squeezed your eyes shut and tried to hold it back. In the end you made the leap because you had to know. You were the key to time unknown.

After Bertie's death there was a suspended interlude in which they felt they could not carry on. They should have gone with him and not sent him off alone. But already they were in a new time, rustling with questions.

'It's Lena,' Daisy said doubtfully, and frowned at the strange young woman in the doorway. Then she began to jump up and down, her body accepting what her eyes still could not. 'Lena! Lena!'

She had come home for Bertie's funeral but an error in the telegram made her miss it by a day. Daisy's cry brought all the children running. She had to drop her bags for there were so many hands to hold, so many wet faces and noses to wipe. 'Lena! Oh, Lena, how are you?' They could not wait for her to say for there was so much they needed her to hear.

She did not resemble their Lena, not even the one that mama had corseted and clad in iron-grey. In four months she had grown thinner and looked like a lady of twenty-two or -three. She had lost that sleep-walking grace that all of the girls had. She had grown nervous, with a habit of starting her head like a hen when anyone called her. She wore fine, decrepit clothes – not the utility dresses chosen by mama – but gowns with lace at the wrist and spots of mildew in the folds, clothes that might have waited in a dead person's wardrobe.

Underneath she was still their Lena. Half an hour after her arrival the kitchen was in order, the fire was lit and tea and sandwiches had been made. The house took warmth and comfort from her return. She picked up Ba and the infant rigidly submitted to the strange sensation of affection. Even so, they found themselves watching her warily. She used her knife and fork in a finicky manner like mama now. She never seemed to relax or join in with the family. When the ordinary work was done she would move away into a corner to daintily devour a cold pudding. The only one with whom she seemed entirely at home was Ba and she carried her everywhere, even to bed as she used to with Bertie.

The result of this luxury was that Ba no longer cried at night. Instead, the girls woke to hear sad, frightening sniffs from their eldest sister. She seemed so far removed from them in maturity that they did not like to disturb her, any more than one interferes with a grown-up who is crying, but one night Beth slipped out of bed and went up the ladder to the attic for Will.

'Is it Grange Gorman, Lena?' Will had grown tall. His new height filled the room up to the ceiling and in the dark he assumed a sort of authority. Lena rubbed her face with her hands. She shook her head.

'I could get a message to him. I'll go on Tom's bike tomorrow.'

'No, Will. That's past. Too much has happened since.'

'What's the matter with you, Lena?' Beth said in fright. 'You look half starved.'

'So you do!' Essie said vehemently.

'So I am.' Lena tried to smile.

At last she told them about her job as lady help. She was kept in a position of virtual slavery. There were no other staff in the house and no children. She worked for two unmarried sisters as cook and kitchen maid and dairymaid, as well as having to do all the ironing and sewing. For this she received no payment except old clothes and her food which she ate alone in the attic room where she slept. 'The Misses Grizzard take no notice of me. I've been dying of loneliness,' she said.

'Oh, Lena! Why didn't you say?' They all sat around her and patted her and stroked her hair, except the boys who were too old for that sort of thing. 'Why didn't you tell us when you wrote?'

'How could I when mama was in such straits? I had no money to send but at least I was one less mouth to feed. And I knew it made her happy thinking of me living the life of a lady. I did write to James once. I never heard from him. I think he had become afraid of me. That doesn't matter so much. It's my family I want. I just want all of us, the way we were.'

'You're not going back,' Will said. 'I won't let you. I am the man of the house now. I'll talk to mama.'

'We need you here,' Beth agreed. 'Mama is not well enough to run the shop and Essie and I can't afford to miss any more school for the nuns say we stand a chance of a scholarship to secondary.' They were all talking at once. 'She cut my hair off,' Weenie said. 'She treats me like a drudge.'

'I thought you didn't need me any more,' Lena wept. All the girls climbed into bed to comfort her. With her hair down and her corsets off, she felt like the old Lena. The boys, although they felt a pang, said goodnight and went back to their room.

When they tried to get mama's attention she made a little moan of protest as if they had tried to pull her hair. 'Lena is to stay at home, mama,' Will attempted an imposing man's voice. 'We need her here.'

'You are all against me,' mama said. 'I don't know what to do. I have six daughters – seven!' She wept bitterly when she remembered this misfortune. Lena soothed her and settled her more comfortably on her pillows. 'You don't have to worry about anything now. I am here to take care of you all.' This was a temptation even mama could not resist.

After she had settled her mother with a scented sachet and the curtains drawn against the sun Lena got into one of her old gowns and gave the house a vigorous spring-clean. Before she made the tea she tidied up the shop and had the children polish the boots on the shelves. When the work was done she baked a jam tart for their tea. 'After school tomorrow you are to go to Granny Devlin's and tell Janey to come here on Saturday,' she announced as they licked the jam from its hot biscuity base. 'We are all going on a picnic to the Furry Glen.'

'Oh, why tell Janey?' Weenie said. 'Let's just go on our own. Janey always makes trouble.'

Lena was firm. 'We are a family. We must all stick together. Until you've been taken away from your family you don't know how much you need them.'

That evening she wrote to the Grizzard sisters at Balmullet explaining that she could not return. The following day she set out to buy fancy biscuits and cordial to take on their picnic and a pound of pig's kidneys to fry up with bread and dripping for their tea. As she wheeled out the baby in the pram they lifted their faces as if they had not seen a sunny sky before. The heat of summer curdled in drains, shimmered on church spires, seeped into thin alley-cats so that they squatted down on the pavement and licked their legs with as much pleasure as a child with an ice. Lena sighed with contentment. She no longer thought about romance. At eighteen she had left all that behind. She felt like an older woman now, who took her pride and pleasure in her children.

There was a visitor at the house when she got back. Her first thought was of relief that the house was clean, but then she said to Ba, 'Now who do we know that owns a brake?' It took her just a moment more to recognize the carriage from Balmullet.

Because they were gentry, mama had offered them the sofa as she did her best customers. She herself was standing. She had put the embroidered Spanish shawl over her night-gown and looked young and pale. When Lena came in she linked her arm in a sisterly way. 'Darling,' she whispered, 'we are all confusion here. The Misses Grizzard have had a letter from you. They think you are not coming back to them.'

Lena's fright made her graceless. 'I'm not going back. Excuse me, ma'am,' she said to Miss Alice. 'I've got to feed the baby.'

'Unlike you, the baby has the manners to wait,' snapped mama. 'Miss Alice and Miss Alma are very upset to think that you would walk out on them when they have taken trouble to train you.' Lena tried to back away with the pram but the sisterly arm gripped her very firmly. 'I worked like a dog, mama. They paid me no wage.'

'Well, I hope you worked like a dog for you have the manners of one,' mama said. 'Of course they did not pay you when you were merely an apprentice. From now on you are to receive a little allowance.'

'I can't go! I'm needed here.'

'Needed to play the fool with grocery boys!'

'The children have to go to school.'

'There is no law that says so!' She spread out her arms and the silk shawl gave a curious strong rustle like a swan's wings. Then, realizing that an episode of combat was being enacted before the visitors, she extended her outstretched hand to Miss Alma Grizzard and smiled

71

in apology. 'Young girls! Was ever a generation so headstrong? In our day we obeyed our parents.' In her day she had eloped with Danny Devlin but she did not look on that as a wilful act but some subversion of her will that had made her powerless. 'Make us tea now like a good girl,' she said to Lena. 'We do not wish to be all business. What have you there – biscuits? We might take a biscuit.'

That year there wasn't a summer. The brown bodies of urchin boys tumbling into the canal like the propeller seed-pods of poplars, the warm splatter of summer rain like men urinating in an alley, were sounds and pictures that floated past somewhere outside of them, like fragments of a dream. They stayed in the heavy mourning clothes they had put on for pa and kept on for Bertie. The school holidays came but there was no sense of release. They remained inside the house feeling drugged and irresolute. The rooms were dirty, the shop neglected. The baby whined. At last mama had to withdraw from the privacy of her grieving to organize the household once more. Her first move was to put Weenie permanently in charge of the housework.

'I'm only twelve,' Weenie reminded her.

'Old enough for a kitchen maid.' Mama fetched the scissors and gave her hair a good sharp trim to the bone. 'If you do not yet feel up to the job I shall send you outside to train.'

'No!' Weenie said quickly, for mama did not waste breath on idle threats. 'I can do it.'

'I'm only twelve,' Weenie told the kitchen. The greenish glow of gas lent a watching air so that objects seemed to graze sullenly like some very low form of life. Grease drifted in a vapour over the neglected surfaces. Dishes lay heaped up in the stone sink and on the table. There was a tub of clothes left soaking for the wash and more heaped up that would not fit in the tub. Something had burnt dry upon the stove with a smell of tortured flesh. She lifted the smouldering pot with a cloth and peered into two other vessels. In one, an ox heart blew a froth of blood from its amputated tubes. There were cloths simmering in another pot – babies' napkins or women's rags – she would not look. 'Even if I start now,' she thought, 'there'll be more dishes by tea-time and then a meal to cook and after that the washing and clothes on the line to iron. It's going to take me the whole rest of my life.'

By the time school resumed in September mama had come a little back to life. What peace she might have had, she said, was ruined with a fool like Weenie to run the house but she was better pleased with her second appointment. Beth was to remain at home to look after the shop. Some nuns came to plead for her to be left on at school but mama sent them off with a flea in their ear, telling them they knew nothing of the realities of life and could have her as long as they were prepared to pay for the support of the household. Beth read and sewed while she waited for custom. She did not have mama's impelling personality and the second-hand shoe shop never recovered the breathless air of a salon, but there was a steady business and quite good people often came in. Within a year one of these – a Polish *émigrée* called Madame Pawelczcyk – had snatched Beth from the shop to do fine bead-work on the dresses she made at her home in Howth. Loath to have the girl's working hours wasted in travelling, she took Beth to live with her there. Essie begged to go too but mama declared that since she had clearly lost interest in her schooling she could instead replace Beth in the shop. The twins looked so alike that no one outside of the house could tell that one more girl was gone from the house.

Ba became Daisy's job. She had to wash and change and feed her and wheel her out after school. For a time she was squeamish about the more practical parts of the task, but Ba, starved of affection, responded eagerly to any attention. She held out her hands to Daisy and had little words only for her. Like Bertie, she had fair hair and grew into a thin and pretty child whom mama detested. Daisy would comfort her with a spoon or ribbon or a string of beads. From the earliest days Ba did not play with these toys but hid them very carefully. As soon as she was old enough to walk she selected her own treasures and spent most of her time devising hiding-places where they would never be found.

Small items went missing – a brooch, a hat pin, a beaded purse – but since the house was never quite tidy in Weenie's management there was always the feeling that one day they would give the place a proper shake-out and the vanished items would reappear.

Chapter 10

JANEY stayed away from home. No one considered it odd, for children of large families frequently boarded out with relatives. Nor was it thought amiss that her mother did not come to see her. Poor widows had more to think of than parental sentiment and she had her sisters and brothers to keep in touch. The others were torn between envy and unease. Janey had a pampered air and always seemed to have some new bow or comb but she wore her hair hanging loose like a tinker and her dresses were too bright to be respectable. She was very good-looking and the old woman liked to boast that it was only a matter of time before her residence would be haunted by whoremongers. 'An' it's me who'll quench their fires!' She wielded a chamber-pot to demonstrate how this would be achieved.

Janey turned out a wild young woman. Tom had the humiliation of having to run away and hide when he saw her being kissed by Scut Mulvey's brother, Weasel. Her grandmother did not believe in discipline and was proud of the girl's conquests. Nuns at school sent warning notes to mama who dropped them in the fire, proclaiming that Janey was on the road to ruin. This route took an unforeseen turning when Granny Devlin fell ill. Janey left school (where she had never, in any case, wasted much of her time) and came home to look after her. No one could believe how well she took to this protective role. She washed and fed the old woman. She even braved the grizzled nest of her hair with soap and a comb and put talcum powder on her face. When the other children came to visit they were astonished to see light coming through the window, which for once had been washed, and to find that they no longer had to suspend their breath for fear of stifling odours. Janey had become the spoiling elder of an adored charge. She bought her grandmother sweets and small bottles of whiskey. The visiting nurse did not approve. 'What is this?' She would point a warning finger. 'It's holy wather!' Granny Devlin would snatch back the vessel and anoint her throat, which she said was perished with the thirst.

Apart from Ba they had all grown out of childhood. Now that Granny Devlin's flat was habitable they liked to gather there to talk about their lives. Janey seemed so strong in her new role that they came to rely on her although they could not quite decide if her wilfulness was a threat to decency or an example of independence. She still had her sharp, teasing tongue and they feared the way in which she said rude things, like her grandmother, just for the pleasure of it.

Mama had a bit of money put by and she had developed a new obsession – to send Will to a military academy in England. She eked out her income to pay for riding lessons and smiled encouragement from a hard chair in a corner of Miss Higgins's Academy as he endured the agony of dance instruction. She herself tutored him in elocution. Tom anxiously observed the changes that would take his protector away from him. He could not imagine surviving the rough youths of the neighbourhood without the companionship and jokes of his elder brother. Already they had seen the cruel suffering of Essie and Beth. Each twin had been like half a person since their separation and they talked of little except ways in which they might be together again. Their fears and hopes were nothing compared with the strength of mama's sacrifice. Coal and food rationed and a round of humiliating social calls initiated to introduce Will to members of the petty gentry who had visited the shop in its finer days. With infinite patience and iron intent, mama moulded her chosen son into a gentleman. Armed with this pretence, Will went to England and was enrolled as an officer cadet. The same year Tom left school and became an apprentice printer.

For two years, while the house on Edward Street grew larger through absences, the girls became familiar with the dark, rat-infested stairway to the neat room where Granny Devlin was kept by Janey like a withered doll. The old woman, used to hardship, fared badly in a soft climate. Her mind began to wander. She grew hostile to sleep and she took to wandering the streets to fulfil an earlier threat. 'Take that, ya whoor's drawers, ya!' With a defiant cry she would empty her chamber-pot over passing men. Janey tried to avoid going out. She was getting a thin and strained look. Her grandmother surprised an old neighbour in his bed and set fire to the tassel of his night-cap, declaring afterwards that he was an oul' wax candle and she had only lit his wick. Finally, being tired of old age, she went back to her youth. Along with the other virtues of girlhood she had lost restraint and she importuned a man upon the stairs, telling him of all he could have for sixpence. Since the man was that evening on his way to visit a girl of twelve, the lewd apparition with whiskers and a dribble of tobacco on her chin seemed like a visitation of his self-disgust. At first he stepped back and then he struck out with all his might. She fell down the stairs, shouting that the man that was in it now had neither micky nor manners, and landed at the bottom with a small exclamation of dismay and a fracture to her spine.

There was no longer any possibility of caring for her at home. The doctor advised transferring her as quickly as possible to the workhouse. 'Her mind is all but gone,' he promised. 'She will know no difference.'

'She knows me,' Janey said, 'and she knows I'd never sell her down the river.'

For the first time since Bertie's funeral four years ago she paid a visit to Edward Street to ask mama for a loan of money. Mama was astounded. 'After all I have done and that has been done to me, I am to part with my little hard-earned savings so that old hag can live in the lap of luxury?'

'She's goin' to die on me. If I have no money she'll die in the poorhouse.'

'It is as good as she is used to. It is where people of her sort expect to end their days.'

'She's our family.'

Mama gave a little shudder. 'Not my family.'

'Ah, go to hell! She's my family and I'll find a way to pay for her.'

Mama quailed before the big woman her daughter had become, with her working-class bosom. 'I have been there,' she said in a piteous little voice. 'Now you can find out what it's like to have your youth go sour as mine did while you expend yourself on people who cannot possibly appreciate it. I tell you only because you are my child, if you give that old drunkard a chance she will live forever.'

'What will you do?' The other children ran after Janey into Edward Street. 'Spit in her eye.' Janey surprised them with a grin. She began to sing. It was what she always did when she felt angry or threatened.

She went to see the money-lender, Mrs Cohen. 'I don't want money,' she told her, 'for I have no means of paying it back.' For her immediate needs she found a kind benefactor in Vesty Muldowney, the owner of the bakery where pa had worked. From the money-lender, she wanted the kind of advice that had once saved mama. Mrs Cohen, who liked to feel that her service was, in spirit, a charitable one, agreed to help. She made Janey take off her outer wear and turned her this way and that, appraising her figure. She asked her if she liked men, and what were her special talents and pleasures. She believed she knew a gentleman who could help her to a more profitable occupation.

Granny Devlin went into a retirement home for genteel ladies and enriched their vocabulary and broadened their vision of life and Janey was launched on a new career. 'I've got work!' She sat on the floor in her grandmother's room, spearing sequins on to a bodice with a hasty needle. She grinned at her brother and sisters and bit the thread with her teeth.

'What kind of work?' Essie rescued the bodice and daintily continued with the application of little silver discs.

'Easy work! The kind where it matters less where you come from than what you've got.' She spread her hands on her hips. 'There's still a few corners of this world where it's an advantage to be a woman.' They looked worried. It had never occurred to any of them that there might be advantage to being a woman. They began to sense something dangerous in Janey's good humour, a shifting of their brittle ground, as if Janey's independence, which might redeem them from mama's authority, would also undermine their small sense of social superiority, taken like air from their mother's breath.

'Don't do anything you'd be ashamed of.' Tom tried to look stern.

'I'm not ashamed of anything,' she said, and when she told them what she meant to do it was clear she meant it.

If ever mama might have found forgiveness for Janey, its pursuit was now ended. She had disgraced the family. The only small comfort was that she had changed her name. She called herself Janey Lorraine. Mama swore that the rest of the children would never see her again. All the same they did, using the threepenny bits that Janey had handed out to each of them for the purpose.

They sat in the dark eating oranges and swept by excitement and dismay as Janey showed her bosom in the low-cut sequinned bodice and sang a vulgar song about love on the music-hall stage of Dan Lowry. All around men whistled and grinned as if she wore no clothes at all. Daisy felt consumed by shame. She folded her arms over her chest and tried to make herself invisible. For the others, alarm was mixed with admiration. Janey had a good voice and a clever sense of comedy. It was awful the way she stuck out her top half as if it was for sale, but she was more than just a pretty girl making herself cheap. She knew how to entertain. Women as well as men laughed and looked up at her with shining eyes and none shone brighter than Ba's. She sat on Weenie's lap with eyes and mouth wide open, a forgotten moon of orange seeping stickily through her fist as the world she knew did an astonishing twirl to reveal a glorious layer of female existence concealed beneath its suffocating skirts.

'I don't like it,' Daisy confided to Sister Cecil.

'What are you frightened of, childie?' The nun took her hand and Daisy's heart did a skip. She had a crush on this mild-faced nun whose voice never rose above a whisper.

'Growing up. I'm thirteen. I'll soon be fourteen. I'm the same but bits of me keep changing.'

Stepping into her drawers one morning. Daisy was dismayed to see hair growing down there, the awful hair about which Janey used to tease her. She looked anxiously at her reflection and saw that her whole image had been accentuated. Her eyes had grown larger, her lips fuller, her eyebrows heavier. Ignoring the stays that had recently been bought for her she quickly got into her shift so as not to have to notice that the rest of herself seemed intent on advertisement. She plaited her hair into long, tight braids and convinced herself that she still looked a child.

Sister Cecil bestowed her placid gaze on the good little girl. 'It is God's plan for you to grow up to be a woman. You will be a beautiful woman, Daisy, in every sense. In due course a good man will fall in love with you and marry you. He will find you. You need think no more on the matter of adult life at all.'

'I try not to but I feel I am being watched. My mama watches me. She considers me prim.'

'Prim?' The nun pushed her hair back from her face. Her touch was cool and slightly distant. 'What do you mean?'

'Modest.' Daisy produced the word shyly.

'Oh, child of grace, modesty is beautiful. It is all the protection you need from whatever might harm you. As long as you are good and pure, you are always safe.'

She still got a feeling she was being watched, especially when she caught her own large and wary eye in the mirror. All the same she took Sister Cecil's advice and threw herself into adolescent virtue with a fervour that made her mother feel ill. She was at an age when a cultivated young girl would be taking an interest in romantic poetry, in fashion and dancing and French. Mama could not like girls but there was something touching about the awakening of vanity, the comic mimicry of the rites of womanhood. She surprised Daisy one day with a present of a little oval brooch she had. Daisy was delighted and put it away in a box.

'Aren't you going to wear it?'

'Where? To school?' Daisy smiled.

Mama did not like to be smiled at. 'You girls seem to spend your whole lives at school, yet I cannot see that you are learning any accomplishments,' she said sharply.

'We learn sums and history and geography. We are taught to cook and sew.'

'What year is this?' Mama demanded.

'It is 1900,' Daisy answered in surprise.

'It is the Jubilee Year of our Queen Victoria. Are you aware, even, that our queen is coming to honour this country with a visit, that she has organized a picnic free of charge in the Phoenix Park for ungrateful children such as yourself?'

'May I go?' Daisy said at once. 'Can I take Ba?'

'You may not. Ba is too young and you are far too old. Thirteen and you have not a word of French!'

'I can't think where I would use it.'

'Are you being impudent? Every well-mannered person makes use of French. It is the language of discretion. It is the only way to hold private conversations before servants.'

'We have no servants,' Daisy pointed out. In fact the girl's directness reminded mama of servant girls they had had at home who could never understand that when questioned they were required not to answer. 'Why do you refuse to accept me as your model? Can you not at least put your hair up and look like a passable member of your sex?'

'I'm not a member of my sex,' Daisy protested. 'I'm only a girl.'

Mama pondered this revelation. Beneath the perfect mask of her composure a fleeting shadow passed, like a well-mannered diner in that moment before she sets her resolute fork in a snail. 'I see. There are certain matters I would prefer not to discuss, and if necessary then I would far rather do so in French, but I realize that you have

79

chosen not to understand me unless I respond to your bluntness in kind. Beneath those unattractive garments you are entirely a mystery to me, but am I wrong in assuming that you have women's breasts growing there? Do you not, like any other woman ... once a month ...?'

Daisy could not bear it. 'I'm not a woman yet! Sister Cecil said I need not think about it.'

'So! *Mon Dieu!*' Mama shuddered. 'Already the nuns have got to you. You have no excitement at all in the thought of growing up?' Daisy could only shake her head. 'With a face like that and heaven knows what figure, you want to stay a child?'

'I am a child.'

'Well, I have had enough of children,' her mother said.

Daisy did not move. She wanted to explain that she would love to be a lady as mama was. To grow up in Edward Street was only to be a woman.

'Go!' Mama would no longer look at her. 'If you are a child then you can at least obey your elders.' To see the prettiest of her daughters in this gauche state of denial was almost as disappointing as seeing another flaunting her body in vulgar entertainments. The trouble with mama was that she had no real vagueness. In so far as she knew how and lacking any sympathy, she did her best for her children. All she could do for Daisy was release her from the source of her mawkish suspension and she set about this with energy and dedication, although she could not but smile at the unconscious humour in her solution.

'I have a job for you.' Mama was writing on an envelope.

Daisy held out her hand to take the letter to the post. Mama looked up with a vague frown. 'This is not for the post. It is for your nuns. Take it when you go to school tomorrow.'

'What's in it? I work hard in school and always do my homework.'

'You need not bother any more with homework. This letter is to explain to the sisters that you will not be returning to school after the holidays. You are going out to work in a job.'

There was a long silence in which Daisy seemed to wilt, very slowly, like a cut flower before a fire. Her head drooped and her face flushed. Inside, her heart seemed to skate around her chest. 'No, mama.' Her voice hardly came out at all. No one could have guessed at her feelings. She only looked sullen and disagreeable.

'A nice little job – surely yes!'

'Not yet. Please, mama, I . . .' She was going to say she was not ready for the world. She was unripe. She could not continue because her voice came out in a whinge.

'Something any child could do. I chose it. Something to delight the heart of a little child.' In her head Daisy protested passionately but no words came. 'There! I knew I could appeal to your curiosity.' Mama was relieved. 'Now see how well I try to please you. You are to work in a sweet factory.'

'A factory! I won't be able to come to school any more!' Daisy broke the awful news to Sister Cecil. To her disappointment the nun remained impassive. She folded the letter and returned it to its envelope. 'Making a few little sweets will never kill you.' She seemed amused. 'It is your mother's will. It is God's will.'

'Have I no will of my own?' Daisy wondered as she set out for her first day's work at the Sweeteries in Capel Street. She knew she had not. When Sister Cecil would not help her she realized that the lives of women were ruled by fate as crops are by weather. But no one could make her change herself. To mama's ire, she would not alter her hair or her dress for her new life but set upon her plaits an old wool hat that she had knitted years ago.

The first choking breath of hot caramel, of vanilla and sugar and cocoa, of essence of clove and of lemon, convinced her that nothing could survive in such air. Clutching her bag of lunch she gazed in trepidation at her workmates. They were coarse, noisy young women and poor pregnant housewives whom the cloying smell affected with nausea. When she cautiously drew closer she found that the smell of skin and clothing offered an alarming challenge to the sickly sweetness. Most of that morning was spent weeping into an assortment of boiled sweets until her employer took pity or lost patience and sent her on an errand to the General Post Office. Daisy ran all the way to Sackville Street, gulping in the summer air, sucking on the sweet that the kindly man had given her. When she got to the centre of the city she could not get through for the streets were choked with children. Thousands upon thousands of city urchins cheered and jostled. Their dirty bare feet skipped excitedly on the cobbles, their thin white arms waved green branches. When Daisy tried to pass she was stopped by an exceptionally tall and beautiful woman. She too seemed in a state of high excitement. 'We have twenty-five thousand loyal children here. Do you wish to join our picnic? There will be sweets and buns and oranges for everyone in the park.'

It was the queen. Daisy had been singled out by the queen. Shaking with excitement she accepted the placard she was given to carry. It said, 'Irish Patriotic Children's Treat – No Flunkeyism Here!' Laughing and singing and waving her placard, she marched along with all the rough children of the city. The sun shone gloriously. The children followed horse-drawn vans piled high with casks of ginger beer and buns and sandwiches. They poured into the park. Their screams sheared off into the air. Released from the ageing burden of penury they ran and chased and leaped and screamed until it seemed that they might swoop like a vast flock of birds into the spotless sky. Daisy ran with them until she could play no more and fell down exhausted on the trampled grass to eat an orange. Soon all the other children were carrying off armloads of food and settling in groups on the ground for their picnic. Some were so unused to the exotic fare that they stowed it away and took it home like geological specimens to prove its existence to their parents. Others silently devoured the golden fruits, the spicy, fizzy drinks and the sugar-frosted buns, freckled with raisins. For Daisy the day offered a different sort of luxury. She was savouring the last day of her childhood.

'Mama! I met the queen. She is the most beautiful lady I have ever seen. She spoke to me. She asked me on her picnic.' Her excitement spilled over when she got home.

'What are you talking about? Queen Victoria is not beautiful. What are you carrying? Why were you not at work?'

Daisy had brought home her placard as a souvenir of the wonderful day. When mama inspected it, her face drained of colour. 'Where did you get this?'

'From the beautiful lady – from the queen.'

'This is the very last straw,' mama hissed, although in truth her life seemed a veritable stable of such substances. 'Do you know who that woman was? It was that traitorous blackguard Maud Gonne, who set out to thwart the queen's patronage by diverting the city's children to a different picnic – a different park too, for all your lessons in geography. You have betrayed your mother and your mother country.'

Her employer was more forgiving. He accepted her excuse that she had been taken ill and patted her on the head. 'You will get used to the work,' he said so kindly that it brought tears to her eyes. She came to realize that there was kindness too in the rough humour of the factory girls who made jokes to forget the hardship of their lives. Compared with others, Daisy had an easy life.

After a year mama gave her back a small allowance from her wage and she saved up for a used cycle. In the evenings after work she went on long excursions to the sea or the country with Tom on his Centaur. On Sundays, after mass, she visited Sister Cecil. She no longer had a childish crush on the nun but she found her easier to talk to than other women. If it was not the life she had dreamed of, nor was it as bad as she had feared. She found reassurance in the routine work. She grew to like the sweet smell and developed a lifelong fondness for caramel sweets. Occasionally she glanced up from her work in case her perfect husband might be there, but when she only saw poor girls and women, she said to herself, 'Some day, something will happen.'

When it did, it was not to Daisy. Essie vanished out of their house on the arm of Art Mulrooney, a skin, hide and feather merchant from Red Cow Lane. He was forty years of age and had a complexion like a kipper. He had no jokes and there was a contained brooding-ness about him that made the house fall silent when he came to call. Where had he come from? There had been no lengthy courtship, no letters to Essie except from Beth. Essie seemed mesmerized, but it was not a lover's trance. She had about her a resolutely sacrificial air.

'Where did you meet him?' Tom demanded. 'When did he ask you to marry him?'

'He didn't ask me,' Essie said.

'Of course not! He asked me on Essie's behalf,' said mama. 'He may not be a gentleman, but he has manners. He also has means. I wish the rest of you girls would follow Essie's example. She has always been good. She has kept herself neat and obedient and now she has her proper reward and the best a girl can hope for — a good husband with a solid income who will care for her properly for life. I hope you will all do as well.'

'You don't have to marry the oul' savage, sis,' Janey said. 'Think of him lying on you like a sack of hammers in the night. You're to come and live here with me. Tom can go on the bike for Beth and we'll sort out between us what's to be done but don't go back to Edward Street or she'll have you hoodwinked.'

'I mean to marry him.' Essie spoke like a sleep-walker. 'I wish you would offer me congratulations and leave me alone.'

'Well, I won't,' Janey said. 'You may be soft in the head but you're my sister.'

'I am not in love with him,' Essie admitted, 'but he's my only hope. He has made me a promise. When we are married, he's going to fetch Beth to come and live with us.'

'You're weak!' Janey was angry. 'If you put your mind to it you could manage without Mulrooney. We should only rely on ourselves and each other. Don't trust no one else.'

Mulrooney's large family crowded into the little kitchen at Edward Street for the wedding, drinking the crates of stout they had brought. First they sang songs and then they fought and swung their fists at one another. Essie, white and silent, sat with her twin in the beautiful beaded gown that Beth had made her. The rest of the family tried to be cheerful until Mulrooney lurched into the yard to relieve himself and returned looking addled, with half his clothes undone.

'Look at him!' Janey said to mama. 'No better than a farmyard beast! How can Essie go to the likes of him? She knows nothing about men. Have you no pity? How could you even think of such a thing?'

'What else is there for women?' mama snapped. 'And certainly I do not think about it. No lady does.'

Mulrooney took his bride away. The house yawned and footsteps echoed. With Daisy and Tom at work and Ba at school there was only mama and Weenie in the house all day. Mama took over the running of the shop again. She had not remembered the work so hard and it tired her and made her sharp. 'Why do I have to be shut away with an imbecile?' she pondered as she sheared her timid daughter's hair back to a penitent's crop. Weenie's shoulders heaved with despair. Mama would have liked to stick a fork into the big wet lump of misery.

Weenie hardly ever went anywhere, so when she was resolved upon an expedition, she got thoroughly decked out. She wore a hat with fruit on it which she had had for Essie's wedding. With her nose powdered and her neck damped with violet water she guiltily hid her workworn hands in mama's fur muff and hurried down to the canal. She should have done it years ago. It was the way mama might forgive her. As she looked into the muddy black water, she briefly resented life for ignoring her so completely when she had wanted so little from it. She was the only one of the girls who had seen nothing the matter with Art Mulrooney. He was a man. He was willing to be a husband. He had got Essie away from mama. He would give her children and the enviable position of wife. Well, if she could not get any pleasure from life, then she would treat herself to the relief of an early death. Her eyes filled with tears as she pictured her small, lifeless form borne away from home to be discovered by strangers. Oh, it was too bad her hair was still kept cut to a stubble by mama for she would have made a lovely corpse with that shimmering fleece drifting out behind her. Those who found her would have thought her beautiful and tragic. As it was, she would be just another of the women who were frequently found in the canal, upon whom tragedy was speculated but about whom nothing interesting was ever discovered. There wasn't much point in dying when no one cared about you. Nor was there any point when everyone cared the way they had all loved Bertie. She tried to stop the memory of Bertie. Over all the years she had managed to hold it back. In place of the black November sky she saw a harsh spring blue that hurt the eyes and a frivolous sun which sprinkled the water with shavings of light and attracted the heedless joy of a little boy of four. Quite clearly she saw Bertie stagger towards the water's edge. 'No!' she cried, and ran into the engulfing dark.

'No!' The shock of the water was beyond imagining. All of the untenable present was rendered insignificant by that icy seizure and Weenie could do nothing but scream and scream. A man passing on the path above the bank jumped in and fished her out. When he laid her on the grass she seemed to have died on him, so he bent over her and hazarded a kiss of life. Weenie woke from her brief death to find herself in a damp sort of heaven where a man's face was the only scenery and his mouth was on hers. 'I love you,' she tried to say. Since he could get no sense out of her, nor think what else to do, he took her home.

Chapter 11

ONE Saturday, when Daisy cycled out to Howth with Tom, he paused on the cliff path to admire the view, and reaching across as if to touch her shoulder, he snatched from her head the old black tam-o'-shanter and tossed it over the headland into the foaming tide below. 'My hat! What's that for?' she said in annoyance.

'I'm sorry, Day. I've wanted to do that for ages,' he confessed. 'I can't make out why you have to wear such rotten clothes. You're seventeen, Daisy. You're a pretty girl.'

'I dress for comfort,' Daisy said. 'I haven't got money for luxuries. Anyway, who cares what I look like?'

'Lots of people do.'

'Do they?' She was curious.

'Honest to God, Day. I'd love to take you out with my cronies, but you have to start dressing like a proper girl.'

'What cronies?' She leaned her face close into his. Passers-by would have thought them a perfect match with their dark good looks and serious dreamers' faces.

'Des Dillon. Mickser Hogan.'

'Oh, them.' Tom was hurt by the indifference in her voice. He would never understand that her lack of vanity masked a depth of pride that bound her to an ideal lover. The ordinary young Dublin men with whom Tom went to tea-dances or on mountain hikes were as invisible to her as germs in the air.

There had been a pause in Weenie's devotion to her rescuer when she got back after her drowning to discover that her clothes were covered in black marks which proved difficult to wash. She recalled that her saviour had seemed slightly soiled, but there was an explanation for this. Three days after the incident he called at the house to know if she had recovered her health. She observed that he was black from head to foot for the reason, as he apologized, that he made his living as a coal heaver. He was fairly well washed when he took her out for a glass of port on Saturday night. He wanted her to go back to his rooms again but she would not. She had allowed him a kiss on the night of the accident since he had saved her life, but now that she had a suitor she meant to make him marry her and she was not going to give him an opportunity to grow tired of her. The coal heaver was made peevish by her resistance, but the memory of the succulent body he had felt through a blanket while her clothes dried at the fire encouraged him to call another night. Soon the Saturday night glasses of port and the subsequent pleadings and the consoling kiss which let him briefly put his arms around her inflaming bulk became a habit. At last Weenie did consent to come to his digs, for a supper was being arranged by his landlady at which she was to be presented to his mother.

'Weenie is getting married,' mama announced to Daisy.
  'I'm glad! She looks so nice now that she is happy and has begun to grow her hair again.'
  Mama made a rueful face. 'They say that love is blind. Certainly a degree of short-sightedness would be a blessing on both sides.'
  'Oh, mama, they love each other! Looks are not everything.'
  'Weenie would have loved a lamp-post if it had taken her away from me. I hope you will not prove so averse to my company.'
  'Of course not,' Daisy said uneasily.
  'You might change your mind when you have to put up with me all day. I may even live to regret Weenie's absence when forced to enjoy at permanence your girlish charms. Still, it is all for the best. You have never really adjusted to the outside world. At seventeen you still dress like a schoolgirl.'
  'Mama, what are you talking about?'
  'Can you really be as stupid as your sister? Your brilliant career as a factory girl must come to an end. You are to come home and look after your mama.'

Hours she sat in the church. She could not even cry. She was too old to cry. She hated housework and feared mama. To be buried alive in that little house was a prospect too wretched to contemplate. It was cruel to think that if a man had come for her, mama would not have resisted, but because she was independent, she had no independence at all.
  'I can't bear it. Please help me,' she prayed into the candle-lit nothingness. She looked up and there was her bridegroom, perfect

87

and irresistible, waiting for her as he must have been waiting all along.

'I'm going into a convent.'

At first Daisy thought her mother had not heard. She had taken up painting and was at her dressing table with a tiny easel perched beside her dolls, making a still life of imaginary roses. She paused briefly and her brush pointed out into the air. 'To be a nun,' Daisy said.

Mama swabbed her brush and with great concentration coloured in a rose until it was like a boil.

'I have had a calling,' Daisy added.

'To avoid housework.' Mama looked around at last.

Daisy took a deep breath. 'You can't understand. You are not a Catholic. It is more serious than marriage – more than human love.'

Mama wiped her hands fastidiously on a cloth. 'How you dramatize! If you must speak of convent life in terms of love, then it is a harem. The cloisters are full of semi-demented spinsters. You would disgrace your family if you ended up in such a place. The women who go there are women with a past.'

'I am in love,' Daisy said. 'I am in love with God.'

Mama shrugged with distaste. 'You have said nothing about the fasts and penances in these places.'

'I have made up my mind. I have spoken to Sister Cecil. She is my friend and my example.'

'And what am I to do for help in the house when Weenie has left?'

'Mother Agnes would let you have an orphan very cheaply.'

'I have had seven daughters and I am supposed to look to strangers for support.'

'Are you going to try and stop me?' Daisy said.

'No.' She looked at her hideous painting and sighed. She wiped the excess paint from her brush on to the cheeks of a doll, giving it a wanton look. 'I am sick of you. I have done all I can and now I am going to let you do as you wish and wreck your life. But don't expect me to make it easy for you.'

'There is nothing you can do to hurt me now.' Daisy spoke uncertainly. 'I have only to pack my bags and walk out the door and I shall always be safe and happy.'

There was very little to pack. She gave mama's marcasite brooch to

Ba and ten shillings to Weenie. 'Get married as soon as possible,' she urged her. 'Mama respects men.'

'I'm meeting his mother tomorrow.' Weenie was almost speechless with excitement. 'Just think! After tonight we'll never sleep together in the same bed and soon we'll both have left this house forever.' For a moment they could remember nothing but happy times with pa and all the girls and boys, with a pramful of cats and picnics and improvised Christmases and a sense of plenty that came not from money but from the certainty that they were one family and would be together forever.

When the two girls set off the following evening mama could not help a pang. Daisy, who had taken nothing except some spare underwear, a sponge and comb, was scrubbed and plain as if for a career in nursing. Plain Weenie was dressed like a bride. Daisy might have made a good wife for some high-ranking army widower who would be intrigued by her schoolgirl appearance and could afford to protect her from the realities of life. She had hoped that Will, with his military contacts, might in due course furnish such a prospect, but she no longer had the energy to wrestle her daughter's determination. She thought there was something missing in the girl – a component necessary to women – the ability ever to be agreeably surprised by fate.

Daisy, alone in the convent parlour, was terrified. Sister Cecil had said goodbye. She was left with her bridegroom, who was testing her cruelly. She was not to remain in Dublin. In the morning she was leaving on the boat for Liverpool and then by train to Manchester to take up residence in a sister convent of the order, which cared for female orphans.

'I don't like orphans.' Daisy had said this before she could stop herself. 'My vocation is for this convent.'

'One convent is the same as another,' Mother Eustace said. 'Your vocation is for Christ.'

'I came here to be with you, to follow your example,' she pleaded with Sister Cecil. 'You have always been my example.'

'It is because of me that you are being sent so far away.' Her mentor mildly patted her hand. 'Your mama spoke to Mother Eustace and said how happy she was that you had a special friend in the convent, who would look after you like a sister. As you know from school, particular friendships are forbidden in religious life.'

'Mama!' she cried out in bleak fury, and then wondered if it were still not to late for her to go back home.

Weenie rang the door bell. It didn't look like much of a party. The house was dark. When Gussie answered he beckoned her up the stairs. 'Where's your ma?' She followed him. 'My landlady is sick,' he told her. 'We are to take a glass of port with my mother in my room. Then we will go out to a dining room.' He was so nervous she felt sorry for him. 'That's all right,' she said, although she had been looking forward to the formality of the occasion, with two grown women to witness her victory.

She stood in the doorway looking for his mother. 'Would she have gone to the lav?' she asked. She was still politely waiting when he flung himself upon her. His fingers scraped her flesh as he tore away her clothing. 'Shut up!' He cracked her jaw with his fist to stem her shriek of sheer surprise. 'I'll put your half-dollar down for you. Don't let on you mind, for I know you don't. I've had a hoult of you already, an' you owes me, for I saved your life.' Every time she cried out he hit her. She couldn't help it and she wouldn't have minded if he'd said anything nice. Afterwards she wanted to ask him if he loved her but he threw a half-crown coin at her and told her to get out. 'Now I'll have a black eye,' she thought ruefully as the coin struck her in the face.

When she got home she went straight to mama. She did not cry although she looked like a half-slaughtered animal. 'My God!' mama gasped. She drew back when Weenie came towards her. 'What has happened?'

'I've been ruined. By a man.' She waited under the sentimental gloom of the pink lamp until mama could look no more and then she backed out quietly and went to her room. She sat on her bed, her face covered by her hands, and after a long time, beneath this cover, she smiled. She had not sought mama's sympathy. She wanted her to know that whatever had happened, whatever was to follow after this, she was not an old maid. She was a woman of experience.

Chapter 12

THE Manchester convent was a sooty edifice of red brick, as grim as the factories that surrounded it. There was no green place for the nuns to walk, only a concrete yard with outside lavatories for the children. The nuns' cells and even the chapel were invaded by sounds of factory horns and horses' hooves. There were children everywhere all the time, their gruff voices demanding the lav, announcing that their lice were back. One could not speak with God in such a place. Within half an hour He would have stormed out in search of peace.

For months Daisy sought her God and fought her loneliness. She looked for ecstasy in the sacraments, in the sweet, harmonious singing of the nuns, in the lives of the saints, which they read each evening in their recreational hour. The morbid slavery of martyrs was devoid of romance. Alone in her little cell she begged for some emotional solace and, weeping, fell asleep thinking of pa, of Will, of Lena and Ba. She even tried fasting, but she could not last. She was seventeen and she was always hungry. She tried to convince herself, as women do, that such emotional heights as she had envisaged did not exist at all and if they did she was better off without them.

Because she had left school at thirteen, she was given the youngest children to teach. Her arrival was convenient. The convent required a replacement for Mother Anastasia, who was indisposed through having seen a miracle. One day when she was alone in the chapel, this mild-mannered woman in middle years had been summoned by Christ on the cross. When she walked to the altar, the figure held out a hand to her. She reached towards it and it spilled drops of blood on her hand. To witness a vision of Christ was what all the nuns most passionately desired, just as carnal lovers crave the moment when an admirer reveals his need. Yet none but Daisy envied her. The doctor had given her a tabloid of chloride and said that such imaginings were common to women in their later years. The bishop demanded material evidence. Mother Anastasia opened her hand but her fingernails had bitten through the flesh in her

anxiety and her own blood was in her palm. She had become a
beggar, pleading in the chapel for some crumb of proof, deprived of
her beloved orphans, while the children, who called her Mother
Station, were abandoned by the only person who loved them, and
had to make do with Daisy.

The little girls had the look of middle-aged women who had
seen enough of life and whose only ambition was to get through it.
There was not a single fetching one nor any with the light of childhood. They all seemed to be Aggies, Annies, Ethels and Ednas.
Solid, short-legged and sour, they squinted at Daisy as if she was a
sky that might rain on their wash.

'I am new. My name is Sister Teresa. You may ask me anything
you like.' Daisy smiled at them.

A squat hand rose in a gesture of arrest. 'You be'int from
hereabouts.'

'I come from Ireland, the land of saints and scholars.'

This did not seem to please any of them very much. They
exchanged suspicious glances and looked bitterly down at their bitten
fingers, planted on their desks.

'I am here to teach you how to read and write. Today we will read
a poem by Lord Alfred Tennyson.'

A ripple of outrage disturbed the mass of infancy and another
dumpy Eth or Ag lumbered to her feet. 'Mother Station says the
Bible's good enough for us.'

Daisy had picked the piece of verse with care. As a small child she
had loved the pounding rhythm of 'Morte d'Arthur', which was
similar to that of the Bible. She could see now that it was the word
'poem' that upset the children. Poem was a luxury item which their
spartan vanity spurned. 'We don't need no fancy learnin'.' Another
protestant was on her feet. 'Mother Station says we're girls of modest
aspiration.' The rest of the children nodded in gloomy confirmation
as if Daisy was trying to rob them of their rightful status.

'I am sure Mother would wish you to do as I say.' She was
beginning to grow impatient. 'Mother Station?'

'Mother Anna Station,' a sullen dumpling explained. 'She's our
nun.'

'I am in charge now. We will read "Morte d'Arthur" by Alfred
Lord Tennyson. The title is French.' Daisy was astonished at how
like mama she sounded, how, failing to communicate, she affirmed

her superiority. 'It means the death of Arthur, who was king of Camelot.'

'Sister Yuke'll have yer life,' said a small grey wraith with such contempt that Daisy thought she would then turn her head aside and spit.

'Who is Sister Yuke?' Daisy said less bravely.

Sister Yuke, or Eucharist, was a scathing woman with a biting, satiric tongue directed alike at her sisters and her charges. She judged Daisy (astutely) of the sin of pride and recommended that her plaits be cut off, although postulants were usually allowed to keep their hair. Daisy was accused of selfishness at meals, of taking all she wanted from a plate before passing it on to others. If there was truth in this, it was a habit acquired from membership of a large family, for if one did not help oneself there was nothing left at all. She even found fault with the manner in which the new nun ate, informing her that to use a fork with the tines pointing up was a habit tolerated only in Ireland and America. In England people ate with the tines directed down.

Daisy took her grievance to Mother Benedict and confided that Sister Eucharist was making her life unbearable. 'Sister Eucharist is difficult,' the mother superior agreed.

'Why must we put up with her?'

'You sound as if you are about to establish a trade union.' The older woman smiled in trepidation. 'Every convent has a difficult sister. If we did not have one we would have to send out for one. Besides, although harsh, she is very often right. We keep her as our conscience.'

'She's not right,' Daisy protested. 'She's always picking on me. She argues with all that I do and say and gets others to join in against me until I cannot endure it.'

'Then you should simply agree with her. You will spare yourself a great deal of trouble in institutional life if you accept the simple fact that if one person says you are wrong, you probably are, and if two people say so then there is no further question about it. Why should one not be wrong?'

Daisy sighed and went away to her little white room with its narrow bed and black crucifix, which she loved. This room was her consolation. There was no mirror to challenge her and no one to disturb her thoughts and dreams. She also liked the stark black-and-white habit. It was a relief not to have to think about what to wear in the morning and she knew even without a looking glass that it suited her dark skin and huge eyes. She also liked the routine – the classes and prayers and hymns and the reassuring monotony of their meals.

It was a pity this pleasing tedium could not last. Every morning at seven o'clock she had to pay attention to the gruff utilitarian demands of thirty-seven little girls. She could not like the orphans. Their long faces and short limbs oppressed her. They were neat and subdued but they were not appealing. Little girls should be dainty if they were to be anything at all. Daisy had taken directly from mama the belief that the custody of girls was menial work. Boys were the inheritors. The ingratiation of little females was a parody of one's own need to please.

In spite of her aloofness she became a favourite with both nuns and orphans. In the unfair system of life, this was largely due to her looks. Nuns like a pretty sister because it confounds the theory that only plain women enter convents. The lumpy foundlings came to worship her as a maternal surrogate, for in the fantasies of abandoned children their mother is always beautiful.

She kept in touch with a small part of the world through letters with her family. Granny Devlin had passed away and Janey had shocked them all by marrying their old benefactor, the elderly Vesty Muldowney. Essie and Art Mulrooney had moved to a little house in Paradise Row, near Dorset Street. A baby had been born dead and Essie had not recovered her strength. Lena wrote to say that her old ladies at Balmullet had now grown helpless. She could not leave them but she felt sure they would not last for long and then she would come home. Tom and Will were living in England and Tom had taken a printing job on the *Sun* newspaper. 'I have made friends with our "Dubois" relations and have an interesting tale to tell.' From those left at home there was little news. Ba got into trouble at school for stealing a fountain pen.

Daisy was professed when she was twenty. She congratulated herself on having adjusted to convent life. She had controlled those emotions that get women into trouble. Still, on summer evenings she grew dizzy with yearnings, but she held her breath and they went away.

One evening, while quietly reading in the parlour, she was subjected to an emotional attack so strong that she had to leave the room and retire to bed. She had come across a passage in the *Confessions* of St Augustine: 'But yet when I love Thee, what is it that I love? Not the beauty of any body nor the order of time, not the harmony of sweet songs of every kind, not the fragrance of flowers or spices, or aromatical odours, not manna, nor honey, nor limbs delightful to the embrace of flesh and blood. Yet do I love a kind of light, a kind of voice, a kind of odour, a kind of food, a kind of embracing when I love my God who is the light, the voice, the odour, the food, the embracing of the inward man . . .'

She knew she had been cheated. She had never been embraced to her inward self. She had had no light, no fragrance, had heard no voice at all. Her love had been rejected. She, who had given up everything for a singular love, had been offered in return charitable lodgings like an unmarriageable aunt. All of this happened a month after her profession when she was sworn to be wedded to God for life. She had been warned by Mother Benedict that new nuns were often tested with a loss of faith, a lessening of their joy in God's service. But Daisy had never been a radiant bride. She had only been obedient.

As with many a disappointed wife, she continued to smile and pray and waited for her jealous yearnings to subside. At twenty it is easy to believe that ungovernable emotions will settle down, so there seemed no harm in satisfying her most childish impulse, which was curiosity. On the approach of her feast day she wrote to Ba, asking for a mirror. She wept with frustration when she saw that she had become a beauty.

Chapter 13

DAISY hurried along noisy streets that seemed corseted in brick and steel. She had been given an errand by Mother Benedict, a letter to post. It was the first time she had been outside the convent in three years. On a reckless impulse she turned left instead of right so that she had to circle a full block of buildings, passing shops and coffee houses before reaching the post-box. She paused in front of one of the big fashion houses to gaze with avid curiosity at a summer day dress of striped cotton trimmed with white cotton embroidery, which a notice proclaimed as 'Broderie Anglaise! New for 1906!'.

A group of factory girls came towards her and she delayed to watch them. Just a few years ago, in another lifetime, she had been one of them. They were ill-made young women, being either bulky or bony from lack of nourishment, but every man that passed appraised them and they made the most of it, whispering and vulgarly laughing among themselves. 'Look at me!' Daisy silently implored. She challenged one man with a glare and he touched his hat with a guilty nod. 'I have become invisible,' she thought in panic. 'I am no longer a woman, no longer a person.' In the convent she was frequently reminded of what she was, a consecrated virgin. It was meant to be a source of pride, but the word 'consecrated' had a mummified sound. She believed that God did not want her, for he had allowed her no joy. She wondered if it was because of the way she had thrown herself at Him, 'cheapened her affections' as mama used to say of girls like Janey. What had she become? A woman set apart by lack of love, a creature dressed from head to toe in black, like a widow.

'God help me,' she prayed. Immediately she felt a burning shame. Was she asking Him to conspire in her faithlessness? 'God help me, God help me, God help me!' Ahead of her rolled the light of His furious refusal. He was an old husband for a young girl.

The sight of the pillar-box cheered her. Every smell and fixture in England seemed to carry a world-weary sophistication that was different from the gentle resignation of home. Letter-boxes in Ireland were for bills and bad news but this one might be filled with invitations to balls and correspondence of romance. In twenty years she had never written or received such a letter. What did one say to a man? How did people make their interest known without betraying the whole of their longing, the unsatisfactoriness of life as it was lived without the other?

She had no idea how long she stood there, but long enough to make a man behind her impatient. He had grown weary of waiting and reached in front of her to deliver his letter. Disturbed from her fantasy she turned around. At first all she saw was a brown hand and then a strong, straight body in a white uniform braided in gold. She looked up and found herself gazing into slanting eyes of a most astonishing blue. Two years in India had tanned his complexion to the colour of wheat and bleached his hair to a rough, bright gold. He was not tall but his body seemed immensely strong.

What he saw was an oval of golden-skinned face, framed in white, dominated by green eyes and dark lips that were parted in surprise. Something in a forest, he thought, sensing danger, but compelled by curiosity to peer out of its lair. Her lack of any sexual advantage enchanted him. She was neither flirtatious nor coy. He was glorified in her gaze. She watched him with naked adoration. The encounter so dismayed them that both their looks seemed fierce. He felt exhausted and saved by her green eyes. 'What colour is your hair?' he demanded roughly. Her hands flew to her veil, thinking of the stubble that was underneath. 'It's brown, but not a plain sort of brown.'

'You're Irish!' He noted her accent. 'I have to see you.'

'You can't.' Her voice shook with disappointment. 'I'm a nun. You can't see a nun.'

'You're only a girl,' he said in contempt.

'I can't see you.'

'Marry me, then.'

'Oh, no! I couldn't!' She could not take her eyes off him. He was the very image she had given herself of God. She had no choice but to worship him. 'When?' He clicked his tongue, showing teeth that were very white. She loved this intimacy. The sharing of a momentary mood was like a picnic. 'I'm on my way to rejoin my unit now. Tomorrow we leave for India. New Delhi. We're out there to keep the buggers in order. Oh, Jesus Christ, I shouldn't be swearing in front of a nun.'

'When will you be back?'

'I'll write. Where can I write to you?'

97

She was going to give him the name of the convent, but that part of her life must now be over. 'Write to me in Dublin, at 11 Edward Street.'

'I don't know your name.'

'Sister Teresa of the Ecstasies.'

He laughed at her. 'That sounds like a tart.'

'Daisy,' she said quickly. 'My name is Daisy Devlin.'

'That's not much of a name for a girl like you.' He was only a boy – he could not be more than nineteen – yet he had a faintly mocking way of claiming authority over her. 'Everyone calls me Daisy,' she said. 'I was christened as Margaret – Margaret Dubois Devlin.'

He reached out a brown finger and touched her mouth. He thought it had the texture of an orchid. 'Lick my finger.' He just found himself saying it. 'What?' Her lips moved slightly beneath his touch and both of them trembled. 'Let me tell you something.' He spoke very softly. 'There's a kind of daisy that's called a marguerite. It's like both your names together. That's what you will be to me – Marguerite. Shake hands, Marguerite.' He had a harsh voice that was slightly nasal but now it was altered to a husky murmur. He had made himself gentle for her. She put out a gloved hand.

'Will you take off your glove? Oh, please?'

'No. No!' His touch seem to encircle the whole of her. Her hand went faint inside his grasp. When he let her go she could only feel relief. She smiled at him, grateful for an opportunity to compose herself. 'Margaret Daisy Dubois Devlin,' he said and she could tell from his playful tone that he was teasing her. She almost cried out when he took her hand again and roughly stripped away the glove. The black fabric departed from her with a slither like a rat. She could not think if she was glad or sorry, for she was consumed by the sensation of the rough skin of his fingers moving against hers. She wished he were kinder, that he would give her more time to get used to him. Just as she was ceasing to be afraid of his harsh breathing he seized her hand and brought it to his mouth. She felt his lips, dry on her palm and then soft and slightly moist. In panic she pulled her fingers back from that sweetness and clung to the black wooden cross that swung from her neck on polished beads.

'Your hands are so pale,' he marvelled. 'I must see you.'

'I have to go,' she said.

He watched her intently and then stepped back and gave a military salute. 'Marguerite!'

★

98

Streets and weather transformed their textures so that she existed in some new element composed of swamp and storm. Her legs were weak, she could not move; yet she flew, her feet scarcely touched the ground. Time also seemed deformed. The journey of half a mile back to the house appeared endless yet was achieved in minutes. Her very body had become a mass of contradictions. She was transported on wings but looked like someone in pain – hunched and high-coloured. She felt as if all her bones had been removed. 'I love you, I love you,' her soul sang out. Her heart pounded with fear in case anyone should find out. At intervals she almost collapsed and had to lean against a wall for support.

In the street that housed the convent she stopped and seemed to struggle with herself like a small black insect caught in a web. She had discovered that she was still holding the letter to post. She could not go back to the letter-box for she had already delayed too long, yet she was afraid to return to the convent with the errand undone. With a grunt she stooped and dropped the letter through a grating in the street. There could have been anything in there, money for the missions or the price of coal for the furnace. It might have been a letter responding to some mother's demand to be united with her child. With grim imaginings she watched the envelope drifting down into a black cavern. So might the fate of others be altered as hers had been. 'It is God's will,' she whispered.

People were staring at her. She was no longer invisible. Apart from the touch of his lips on her hand she was still a nun, still untouched, yet some unknown part of her had been touched and she had opened herself to it and she knew it was this exposed part that onlookers saw. To account for her curious position and to hide her burning face she pretended to tie her bootlace. 'All of this will be over in a little while,' she told herself. 'I will be a respectable married woman. I will be Mrs . . . Mrs . . .?' She let out a cry of pain. He had not told her his name. The hem of her robe heaved about her and her hands were clenched into fists as she raced back to where she had found him. She reached the letter-box in a state of madness and it was to no purpose. She no longer had a letter and the man was gone. Going back, she began to weep. Tears splashed about her in a downpour, 'Oh, I wish he had not used bad language,' she sobbed peevishly. The smoke and clamour of the streets, the indifference of its hurrying pedestrians, made her think that every thing and soul in sight was powered by steam and nothing had a heart. When the plain brick face of the convent came into view, she almost howled for rescue. All the sisters were waiting. They seemed very grim. Let them kill her, no smaller punishment would serve her shame. Even the orphans were crammed into the gloomy red-tiled hall. The mass of their pessimism simmered beneath the dim red glow of a Sacred Heart lamp.

'I'm sorry, something happened . . . a man!' Her words kept getting swallowed up in sobs.

Mother Benedict strode forward with an utterance of disgust. Daisy winced and waited to be slapped. 'My poor child!' Instead she was wrapped in compassionate arms.

'Oh, we should never have let her go into town on her own.' Mother Anastasia shook her head. 'She's not used to the ways of the world.'

'Oh, poor Sister Trees,' the orphans chorused dismally.

'A man . . .!' She tried to speak again. 'At the post-box.'

'Don't try to talk about it. Don't even think of it,' Mother Benedict soothed. 'These are terrible times.'

Even Sister Eucharist seemed to soften. 'Put the child to bed,' she ordered.

'I want to go to the chapel,' Daisy protested. 'I have to pray.' She knelt beneath the purple ray of light that came down from the altar window and poured her heart out to the Lamb of God. Chastened and exhausted she sank her head in her hands and awaited forgiveness. She felt stained by the exciting human touch and prayed for the embracement of the inward man which would relieve her of her body.

Something happened which made her pull her hands away from her face. It was a queer feeling, not within but all around – that sensation she had as a child when she was left for dead by her brothers and sisters and they ran off to play without her. The gaunt chapel with its ugly portraits of the holy family, the stumps of candle waving rags of flame beneath shrines of the saints, had the air of a deserted ballroom. Even the little gold vault of the tabernacle seemed tauntingly empty. She was all alone. She had not deserted God. He had abandoned her.

What had happened to poor little Sister Trees? She did not seem the same after the incident at the post-box. She hid herself in unlikely places like the outdoor lavatory that was used by the children. Once, some workmen came to mend the pipes, and one of them having waited a full half-hour for admission to the shed decided his colleague had gone in to smoke a pipe. 'Come out, you bugger.' He attacked the door with his boot. The orphans slowly gathered around – lumpy little girls of five and lumpy women of thirteen. 'Ooh, how low! Ooh, how common,' they mourned.

A doctor was summoned but Daisy would not see him. Her refusal was respected as a gesture of modesty. Sister Rita of the Angels pressed a picture into her hand, of Saint Maria Goretti, who achieved her sainthood at the age of twelve by resisting the advances of a soldier who then killed her. The convent was proud of its quota of martyr nuns who had retained to the death their cancers of the womb rather than be examined by a man. She was seen as a suffering innocent. The children were told to pray for her.

For Daisy the most mauling grief was not the loss of love, nor even of God, but the loss of her privacy. After the feeling of desertion in the chapel she had wanted only to get to bed, to find solitude and sleep. When she lay down between the rough sheets that had always brought such solace, the boy was there. He had been there all along, she could tell, waiting for an unguarded moment in which to claim her. Her lips were touched by his finger. The grainy silence of her curtained room was sawn across by the tremor of his breath. It was the roughest kind of torment for there was no reward to these imaginings, no friendship to remember, no experience to hint at what lay beyond the discomfort of desire, or hope of achieving this dismaying knowledge. The man had been making fun of her. He had not even taken down her address. He had robbed her pride and her composure. To burn forever without respite or resolution – it was hell! She had committed a sin and had been sent to hell. She understood now what had brought such desolation to Mother Anastasia. She had been outcast by solitary witness. She sought refuge in the most unlikely places – the coal shed or the kitchen pantry – but the more alone she was the more she was overwhelmed by his closeness. She came to dread and crave the suffocation of his presence, the wounding penetration by those eyes of piercing blue.

While Daisy was in combat with her relentless ghost, others in the convent battled with their own small concerns. Mother Anastasia, once a robust and practical woman, was now purple-shadowed and peculiar. She continued to spend all her time in the chapel and had taken to punishing herself, to going without food or keeping a nail in her boot. One of the big girls, Ettie Sammon, threw herself out of a window and was killed. She did not fall discreetly into the yard, but out in the street for everyone to see. A note was found in her pocket from another of the orphans, Alice Battle. 'Dear Ettie, yes, I know what that means. If you have blood coming from there it's a sign of the devil.' There was a bout of hysteria among the older girls and Alice Battle had to be locked in isolation, but it did no good for she believed what she had told Ettie, having got this information from a kitchen maid on the staff. The nuns summoned the adolescent girls to talk to them about their bodies. They were told that it was perfectly natural, it was God's curse on Eve. They must keep themselves clean and never mention it as it gave offence.

In the mornings there were prayers and in the evenings song. The sisters bent their heads and prayed to their husband to notice them, jealous of any sign of rapture that might suggest a secret conversation with another. There was approval for Daisy's agitated state. It was deemed proper that God should test His youngest and fairest spouse.

The dumpy little girls had come to love her although she could not understand why. When she walked through the dormitory at night their squat hands reached out and clutched at her robes. 'Tell us about our mothers in heaven.' 'I know nothing of your mothers' – Daisy rescued her garments – 'I don't know if they are alive or dead.' In that long room of cots with its vague smell of salt and earth, the muffled sobs and snuffles faded on the approach of a huskier breath. She turned to the window, resolutely denying the radiant presence with golden skin and hair, with flat cheekbones and entrancing eyes, but his breath was on the back of her neck, his hand passed in front of her breast.

'Please, Sister Trees, have to go to the lav.'

'I been sick on me pillow, Sister Trees.' The stern little voices barely penetrated her reverie. 'Poor Sister Trees,' the children sighed and they coped and, in due course, slept.

Meals went on at the long table with thanks given for porridge and cabbage and bread and herrings and turnips and what the children called skin soup, it being composed of vegetable peelings or the skin and bones of animals donated by charitable butchers. On one such bone a girl called Emily Hodder choked to death at the table. Deaths were frequent among the little girls. At any one time there would be four or five of them in the infirmary infecting one another with their whooping cough or diphtheria. This was a different sort of drama because it happened in front of everyone. Emily had gone blue in the face and gasped for breath for several minutes while two hundred children clutched their spoons and waited and Daisy, who should have been supervising the dinner, was hiding in the shed.

On the day of the funeral there was no school. Nuns and orphans gathered in the church. Mother Station was too ill to appear and the little ones clung to Daisy. So many griefs were there, concentrated on a plain girl whom nobody missed very much. For once her vanished lover did not torment Daisy. When the little girls squeezed her hand for comfort, it was this she felt, and not his lips on her palm. 'Our Father, who art in heaven,' the priest intoned. 'And our mothers,' the little girls grumbled. Daisy allowed them the comfort of a nod.

As there were no parents to mourn or inquire, the tragedy would have been forgotten but for the upsetting aspect of Daisy's negligence. It was not a solitary incident. There were reports of wet sheets in the children's dormitory, of classes left unattended while the young nun shut herself away. When the useful pretext of a letter from home presented itself, Mother Benedict summoned her. 'Are you well, Sister Teresa?'

The question made her think of pa. She thought no one had loved her since pa. 'Yes, thank you.' Her eyes protested behind tears.

'Are you homesick?'

Daisy shook her head.

'It is not a crime for a young woman to miss her mother. Would you like to go home for a little while?'

'Oh, no!' Daisy said.

The older sister nodded. 'Perhaps that is wise. The present pains will soon pass. In due course others in the community will look to you for courage.' The girl looked so bright she seemed transparent. She had a kind of light about her, although one could not tell if it came from the spirit or the blood; anyway, some kind of stored-up passion. She would find life difficult wherever it was lived.

Daisy had got used to her pain. At times she was elated by it. 'I don't mind suffering,' she said. 'It's better than nothing.' The superior gave her an intent look. 'That is true – a hard lesson to learn. God is closer than you think. In the darkest hour there is always comfort.' She reached into the folds of her gown. 'I have a letter for you.' The effect of this very ordinary news on the child was to drain all the blood from her face. She put out a ravenous hand but it shook so much that she had to take it back again. 'Oh,' she said in a little voice. 'Oh.' Mother passed the note across the table and Daisy fell upon it. 'Oh,' she said. This time it was a grieving moan. 'It's from my mother.'

The letter was stuffed into some subterranean pocket in her habit. That evening during the hour of recreation when she grew weary of stitching an altar cloth, she fished it out again. 'Dear child,' mama wrote. 'I do not know how long your sisters and I can sustain the burden of this house with no help from you, either physical or financial. You may still see yourself in the guise of a holy woman with those demented spinsters but in fact you are running away from your duties. And speaking of running away, I am mildly curious to know of your connection to India, from whence the enclosed letter came for you.'

The sight of the two Indian stamps attached to the travel-soiled letter was like two blows to the stomach and she had to rush to the lavatory to be sick. Afterwards, events moved in a manner so swift and systematic that it was as if she had been arrested following a crime. Her secondary impulse was of thunderous joy. She thought of poor Mother Station in the chapel begging for proof. It scarcely mattered what was contained in the letter. He had written to her. She had her proof. She went to her cell to read the letter and immediately made out a reply – not to the man for his message needed no response, but to her mother, with regret for the inconvenience she had caused and to announce that she was coming home. After that she changed her clothes.

To the other sisters and the orphans with their unfailing bad-weather antennae, the sight of a nun walking along the corridor in a cape and hat and long tweed skirt was as shocking as if they had seen her in the nude.

'It's Sister Trees!'

'No it's not, it's a woman!'

'It's Sister Trees. She's after turning into a woman.' Nuns and children backed away as she passed.

Daisy waited a moment in the doorway to allow her superior to get used to her worldly image. When nothing was said she walked to the window and peered out warily as if considering how narrowly their world was defended from the brawling, clattering street below. 'I have to go home,' she said.

The older woman was shocked, not by her announcement or her clothing, but by the change that half a day had wrought in her appearance. She had lost her frailty. 'Sit down,' she urged the restless girl. 'Have you had news from your mother?'

'My mother says she needs my help, but I have had other news.' She moved away from the window but seemed unable to settle. 'I have to leave.'

'You mean to leave the convent? You are part of our community. Tell me, dear little Sister Teresa, what urgent summons you have had?'

'I have fallen in love with a man.' She put her hands on the table. Her voice sounded hoarse and unhealthy. 'I have set him on fire.'

In the buffet car of the train to Liverpool, where she would connect with the steamer to Kingstown, Daisy took out his letter again. 'My dearest Marguerite (on the envelope it was Daisy Dubois Devlin, but inside, in private, he addressed her as Marguerite), 'You have set me on fire.' She had read the letter so many times that the words were engraved on her brain and those on the page had become an echo. She could not imagine a letter more direct, a summons with better authority. It absolved her of responsibility to herself. He wasted no words in wishing her well or describing his voyage back to India. It was instruction and command. 'After we parted I supposed I would forget you but I could not get you out of my mind. I know now there is no peace without you. Swear you will wait for me. Do not look at any other man with those green eyes and keep your pale hands from any other touch. Stay in the convent until I get back because I know you are safe there. Do not forget me. Yours ever, Cecil Cantwell.'

To assist his last direction he had enclosed a photograph. He was in his white uniform, his skin very brown. His handsomeness surpassed both memory and dream. 'Cecil,' she whispered to herself. She found the name uncomfortable in her mouth, but it was the name of her favourite nun, Sister Cecil, who had predicted her perfect lover.

When she told Mother Benedict she did it quickly, to get to her punishment before she had time to dread it. The superior turned her head away and Daisy imagined this as a summoning of wrath. The skipping of her heart caused her wimple to shake.

105

'How well do you know this man?' Mother, in fact, only sounded weary.

'His name is Cecil Cantwell. He is in the army.'

'A childhood sweetheart?'

'I don't know him at all.' Daisy, deprived of combat, flopped down into a chair.

'You've been waiting for it all along, haven't you?'

'Waiting for what?'

'An escape.'

'I never wanted to escape from the convent,' she lied.

'From ordinary life.' The older woman considered the jaded girl. 'I am a middle-aged woman, just as I would be if I had married and had children. I know what any woman knows. There are no escapes. Life is difficult. The love of God is painful and challenging but God never deserts you. It must take great courage to love an ordinary man.'

Daisy was dismayed. She did not like this kind of talk. She felt she had introduced an anarchic element to their calm communal life. 'It was meant,' she said in a shocked voice.

'Yes, but which was meant?' Mother Benedict pursued. 'We who have been called by God believe that outside of religion there is no meaning in anything for us. It is all dust and ashes. This man has awakened your physical desire. There are women in the world who can never adjust to the demands of their bodies – and others who cannot submit to the claims on their bodies. This is very frank talk, but we love you here. We will suffer if you go.'

'Will you let me?'

'You must stay until the bishop grants a dispensation. Perhaps you will change your mind. It may be that God has carved out this special cross for you and we must all accept it.'

'It's not a cross. I love him,' Daisy said forlornly.

In the weeks before she left the convent the younger nuns were like kitchen maids, avid for details of her romance. The children laboured to bind her. There was no crying in the dormitory and by day they struggled to surprise her. One little girl embroidered a sampler with the word 'Marp'. It was meant to be Mary, after the Blessed Virgin, but her stitches ran away with her and the 'y' closed up. Little Edna Moore wrote a poem: 'Dear Sister Teresa young and kind, don't leave your orphan girls behind. If you forsake us for another, please take us with you as our mother.'

She piled up a small trousseau in her room – holy pictures and prayer books, pieces of embroidery. At night she slept in her narrow bed with the picture of Cecil Cantwell. Astonishingly no one stopped her. Candles burned into the night and food was left untouched on plates as different sisters performed novenas and did penances to sway her affections. She herself believed these prescriptions would be effective, that she would be claimed back into the fold, her passion burning on raggedly within her like the chapel's vigilant candles. But the day came when nuns and children were queuing up to say goodbye. She had been allowed to grow her hair in the past month and when she put on her clothes she looked like a girl again. She was afraid. She was walking off into nothing. No lover was coming to claim her. There was just a strange man in India who had written her a letter. She felt exposed. So much of herself was on display. For three years she had become a child again. Now she had to come to terms with her thick eyebrows and dark mouth, her declaring breast. 'Help me, save me,' she wanted to say, but her voice had locked up out of fear. She could only stand there, stiff as the black figures that enfolded her and the children who grunted with grief and tried to hang on to her skirts. The farewell was brisk for it was not seemly for the sisters or orphans to hang about waving into the street. As if she was only going on an errand, the big brown door slithered indifferently into its lock. Behind that door they were going into classrooms to start the lessons of the day. The name of Alfred Lord Tennyson would never be heard again. Mother Station had come back to a weary sort of sanity and resumed charge of her class. In the schoolrooms, the children's heads would stay inclined towards the window, fretting and envying. They would shuffle out for soup at eleven and prayers at four. For every hour of the day they knew what they must do. And God loved them.

Standing on the grey street she felt like a sailor left behind on shore, watching his ship drift away until it is a tiny dot on the horizon with all the real world contained within it. What would she do next? All her life decisions had been made for her. She could not imagine the journey to the train and then the boat and a cab to Edward Street. She had been given money, but she had no idea if it was enough or too much.

'Can I help you, miss?' It was a boy. He had stopped in the street to pick up her bag. He had called her 'miss'. When she turned her lost face to him, he smiled at her. The awful coldness began to dissolve. She was back in the real world. 'Is that your cab, miss?' Of course it was. A cab had been booked to take her to the station. The boy helped her into it and then put in her bag. The driver's eye, watching through the mirror, seemed very pleased with her.

Chapter 14

SEVERAL shocks awaited her at Edward Street. The first, when she glanced into the parlour, was that pilgrim's graveyard, the boot shop. In her mind the drawing-room window still glowed like a jewel, its snowfall of lace and swags of velvet making misty the vision of a tantalizing life within.

The second surprise was mama. She was remarkably altered in three years, still beautiful but somehow reduced. All her beloved boys were gone. Daisy, touched by pity, ran inside. 'Mama! I am home!'

Mama spoke peevishly, as if unwilling to be coaxed out of an old argument that had been interrupted in 1903. 'They have sent you home and now you are to be a burden to your family for the rest of your life.' At least she was not wholly changed. 'A spoilt nun! There are few more unattractive species. They can neither be presented in society nor be kept in useful employment.'

'I have news.' Daisy spoke cautiously.

'What news?' She noted the high colour of her daughter's cheeks, the splinters of light in her eyes. 'What have you been up to?'

'I am to be married.'

Now Daisy got her full attention. 'They have men in these convents?'

'I met him out on an errand. He is an English gentleman. He says he cannot live without me.' She took the letter from her bag and handed it to her mother. Mama sat back behind the table which served as desk and counter. She put on her spectacles – a new acquisition – and addressed herself to the letter. As she unfolded the paper the photograph fluttered from it to land face down amid the boots.

'He is quite good-looking.' She couldn't resist this as mama, her face like stone, reached for the image. 'A common soldier!' She almost spat.

'He is not common! He is an honourable man.' In fact, Cecil Cantwell's accent had a roughish edge and she regretted this.

'Honourable? Have you any idea how soldiers use women. This is an enlisted man. He has no more intention of marrying you than the pope of Rome. You may be sure he has other ideas in mind.'

'He loves me!' Hysterical colour flooded Daisy's face at the memory of his lips upon her hand.

'Look at you!' Mama flung the photograph down in disgust. 'No wonder the convent threw you out. You have no backbone. Of course he will not marry you. No one would.' Daisy began to tremble. How would she survive until he came for her? What if he did not? The door behind her opened and there was Weenie, unkempt and overweight but as full of eagerness as a puppy. She flung herself upon her sister. 'Oh, Day! Tell us everything.' Assured of the most rapt response in the world she began again. 'I have fallen in love.'

She rescued the photograph and risked its perfection to Weenie's flour-stained fingers. 'He wishes to make me his wife.'

She climbed to the small room that smelled of girls growing up – of washed hair and talcum powder and blood. The door was buffered by a weight of girls' dresses hanging behind it. The tiny space was filled with the beads and bottles and shoes of grown-up women and their signals to suitors. She thought with longing of her little white room in the convent, perfumed with wood and soap.

'Do you want to see Janey's clothes?' Weenie pulled back the door and a magician's bouquet of bright garments sprang back – gowns, pelisses, chemises – all with a stubborn spoor of Woolworth scent. 'She's left us her cast-offs now she's married to a wealthy man.'

Three years of convent life had enhanced Daisy's natural modesty. She could not imagine sleeping in this stifling atmosphere. She hated the thought of undressing in front of her sisters. 'You can have a bed to yourself now Essie's gone.' Weenie was anxious to please. 'Ba and I can share.'

'I'd like to see the boys' room.' She sensed Weenie's disappointment as Janey's finery slithered from her grasp. Weenie lived through others now.

Under the low ceiling in the small attic she sniffed the room's smells of socks and dust and earth. Growing up was a lighter business for boys. There were two planks nailed to the wall to serve as shelves and one had books by G. A. Henty and Daniel Defoe, Mr Bram Stoker's horror story, *Dracula*, and a volume called *A Hundred Things for a Boy to Do*. On the other plank was a careful arrangement of stones and shells from Dollymount strand, a little sketch Tom had made of Bertie, the skull of something very small and some marbles in a saucer. She lay down and thought she could smell Will's hair.

'You are in my boys' room!' Mama had come to throw her out.

'Please, mama, I prefer it here. I have grown used to sleeping on my own.'

'Then a nice surprise awaits you when your soldier comes to claim you. Oh, you are a fool! Get back to your room at once.'

'I love him. He loves me.'

Her mother reached out and barely touched the choppy ends of her hair. 'I expect you looked quite fetching as a nun, although I am glad I did not see it. You have such indignant eyes. No man knows how to love a woman. All they want is . . . that. And it brings such unhappiness to women.'

All through tea – an uncomfortable meal in which Weenie blurted out unwise questions which mama did not wish to hear and Daisy could not answer since she knew so little about her lover – she felt a sacrificial glow, thinking of 'that'. She knew nothing. She did not wish to. It gave a heroic dimension to her infatuation to think of submitting to unhappiness for him. The meal was almost over when Ba came in from school. She flung her arms around Daisy and held on tightly. 'Oh, Day,' she said, 'the whole world's changed since you went away. There's electric lighting and telephones. The lord lieutenant's son's got himself married to a widow. And the hats! Wait till you see!' She ran upstairs and came back half hidden under a pale-blue chip hat of Janey's with one blue ostrich feather and a border of white roses. She still had her nervous, waifish air, with a child's silky corn-coloured hair, but her eyes were knowing, almost adult. 'I'm not stopping. I'm off to the Mission with some girls from school.' She gulped a cup of tea and restlessly picked at the crust of a loaf. 'Come with us, Daisy.'

Daisy shook her head. She was very tired.

'You're not going to hang around like an oul' misery until you become an oul' married woman, are you?'

Unlikely rescue came from mama. 'Don't encourage her. She is full of flighty nonsense. It is time she settled down and made herself useful around the house.' Ba gave mama a rebellious look. 'She needs someone to encourage her. She has the looks of a nun and the air of a nun and her clothes are ten years out of date.' Mama remained composed as the door banged after Ba's exit. 'We must get this matter settled,' she said quietly. 'It is a disturbance in the household. Come up to my room, Daisy.'

Mama's room was an accumulation of clutter organized to mimic her old parlour. The gilded mirror with the cherubs had been joined by other looking glasses as well as embroideries, enamel, glass and china and a large, wood-framed screen which hid the bed. The room had the bright, crowded stillness of a cage of tropical birds. Mama moved gracefully amid the jumble and sat at her small dressing table. 'When does he mean to marry you?' She looked very severe in the shadows.

'I don't know. Whenever he can be free.'

'Where do you plan to live? What is his income? What is his religion?'

'We have all our lives to sort out these matters. We have only just found one another.' She wished she could have kept her voice more hopeful. In the dusk there was a swift rasping sound as if a match was being struck, but it was mama striking the roof of her mouth with her tongue in irritation. 'Marriage is a contract, just like any business matter. You must establish a basis.'

'You make it sound cold.'

'Don't be a fool. If you are really content to pitch in your lot with a soldier, then you had better put your mind to it. Men's passions are ruled by whim. Another idiotic girl might flash her eyes at him and you will never hear from him again.'

This touched a genuine chord of fear. 'I will write to him this evening.' She bent to kiss her mother on the cheek. Mama did not move. The shadows turned her to stone. She looked like the sculpted bust of an empress among the ill-assorted pieces.

'My Darling,' Daisy wrote, and she crossed that out with many black lines from her pen, dismayed by her own impudence. She was in the shop, having discovered it to be the only private place in the house.

'Dear Mr Cantwell,' she put down. He did not look old enough to be Mr Cantwell, but he was. For an hour she faced Mr Cantwell with her nib, unable to make any kind of conversation. 'Thank you for your photograph which I shall keep in a frame beside my bed.' The sentences came at last, stiff and unwarmed. 'My mother sends her good wishes and is anxious that you should establish a date for our wedding. You need not fear for my safety. I shall do nothing but wait. I remain, Yours truly, Marguerite (Daisy Dubois Devlin).'

She hated what she had written. It was a schoolgirl's letter, prim and narrow. She wished she knew how to make a joke, or that she could be bold enough to say she loved him. Already she had disobeyed. She had left the convent and she was afraid to tell him. She sacrificed a lock of her meagre hair to fold into the message and then quickly shut it into an envelope. When she lay down she found she was homesick for the convent and wept until she fell asleep.

On Sunday Janey came to tea. Mama treated her with circumspection now that she was grown up, and no longer tried to keep her from the house. Although she had not progressed beyond small parts in theatre, she had the flamboyance of a star. She wore a black voile Russian blouse with a skirt of tussore silk. 'Jaysus tonight!' she greeted Daisy's news. 'You'd think the men would be safe with her locked up in a nunnery. Well, go on, sis, give us a look at the oul' savage.' She took the picture and stared at it with intent black eyes. When she pouted her lips Daisy suffered the horrifying thought that she meant to kiss the image, but she let out a low whistle. 'That's what I call a man. You are a dark horse, Day. I wouldn't kick him out of my bed.'

'Eugenia,' mama warned. She dabbed at her mouth with her napkin, as she often did when someone else's mouth had offended.

'Give it back!' Daisy fearfully took her picture. She felt as if they were back in childhood, with Janey teasing and tormenting her. She made up her mind that when Cecil Cantwell married her they would move as far away as possible – to Manchester, at least. Janey pushed aside her plate and lit a cigarette. 'Stop acting like a reverend mother, Day. You're not a saint and you're not even a nun any more. You're just an ordinary woman like the rest of us.'

Daisy felt pity for Janey's view of life. She still believed that she had been ordained for a singular love. Because of this, the dullness of her days in the shop, her evenings spent with Weenie and mama (for Ba was always out), could be endured. Until he summoned her, life was suspended. There was nothing she had to do except wait.

'Darling Marguerite,' he wrote. 'Your message came to me like a little winged bird. I love you in all your simplicity and purity. You seem like a cool stream in this hellish place. Write to me and let me have a picture of your dear self.' She wrote back at once. 'I have no news for you. Life is very quiet. I exist only for our future together. Let it be soon. Your Marguerite.'

Two months, she told herself, between each post – a month for her letter to travel to India, a month for his to return. Her waiting became so intense that she developed a habit of holding her breath. His letters were terse with passion. For a brief period she would be transported by rapture. Mama mocked her joyful state. 'Look at you! You revel in your unreality. It would suit you well enough if he were never to come for you. You have no nature for the realities of married life. All you want is to worship and be worshipped from afar.'

It wasn't true. She longed for him. Her life without him was a fevered dream. Her only happiness lay in his promise. Waiting for the reassurance of his letters, she grew short of breath and temper. Her sisters were worried. They thought the years of institutional life had affected her. 'Daisy has got herself engaged to a fella she met at the post-box,' Janey wrote to Lena. 'She is wearing old dresses more suited to a girl of ten than a woman of twenty. We are all of the opinion that she went into the convent to avoid the fate of Weenie and wonder did she set her cap at this soldier as a means of escape from the convent? Poor Day! She always was a queer oul' herring and now she has grown queerer than ever but she still thinks she is a cut above the rest of us even though mama makes her life a misery.'

Mama wrote to Will. 'Dear boy, here I am at home with the fatheads of the family, while all my best and dearest ones are far away. I am left with the two virgins on my hands – one desecrated and one consecrated – and I cannot see much prospect of marriage for either, although Daisy has got herself involved with an enlisted man serving in India. I enclose some money for your expenses. In return I would dearly love a joke as the opportunities for wit these days at 11 Edward Street are as good as at any graveside.'

Daisy felt she was caught in some dangerous trap – a maze of emotions with no visible release. She knew none of them believed that Cecil Cantwell would marry her. They did not envy her. They even pitied her. It was three months before a letter came. The trial of waiting, of snatching other bits of post which then turned out to be from Will or Lena or Beth, left her physically weakened. Lena's letter said that the Grizzard sisters were now so frail that she had to care for them night and day. 'I wish them health but fear they cannot last very much longer. Then I will be free and we can all be together again.'

'She doesn't realize,' Ba said bitterly. 'There is no family left –

only the few of us stuck together by circumstance and mad for any escape.'

When finally the postman brought an exotically stamped envelope it was like a nightmare. The shock of relief caused Daisy's legs to weaken and she had to crawl across the remaining space in the shop and into the hall. In the same manner she pulled herself up the stairs to her room under mama's gaze and then she sat on the bed and wept, the fear and misery of waiting too great for any consolation. When she recovered enough to open the envelope, she tore the letter in her haste.

'Dear little Marguerite,' he said. 'I must warn you that our marriage cannot be for a considerable time. For a start, I am only nineteen. Also I am signed up for seven years and with five still to run. Be patient, my dark-eyed girl. You are better off where you are than anywhere else in the world. Pray for all the sins of the world and all its poor. With love, Cecil.'

'Five years!' Her voice came out dry and cracked. 'Years, years, years!' She crumpled up the letter and ran to the window, where a little slice of sky in a chemical shade of pink rested on the orphanage roof. 'How can he say I am better off here than anywhere? I am in hell. What does he know of my life?'

She remembered then that he imagined she was still in the convent. She sat down instantly to pen a reply. Her hand shook and the writing came out haunted and distended. 'My darling, my love, my only hope – you must not make me wait. I need you now. I am older than you – twenty years of age. I can work to earn money. I have left the convent and am living at home as I had broken my vows by intent. My mother hates me. Do not make me live like this.'

Now she knew how other women overwhelmed the discretion of their sex to put such things on paper. They were written not from passion or boldness, but out of despair. She could not believe how quickly the idyll had been twisted into confusing argument. She would do anything to recover the moment when he asked her to marry him, to recapture that confidence. He was hers, he was meant for her. She had not known that she would have to fight to assert her claim. She was only a woman, a girl. All her training was towards submission. She fell on her knees and tried to pray. In a contrary way, praying made her calm. Cecil Cantwell was hers, unlike God, whom she had had to share with every kind of plain and ugly woman, who did not care that she was beautiful but equally loved the unappetizing poor.

Yet it was not so. Her plea dropped off into some infernal void. Parched and hysterical, she awaited the relief of him. He did not answer her. Months that were a decade long twisted into formless corridors of time. As hope died, desire gave way to anger. She could not think how she had liked his nasal voice. His accent was coarse and his language uncouth. She looked forward to telling him so – with mama's indignation. The anger exhausted itself and was replaced by an anguished sort of tenderness. 'Oh, my darling,' she murmured over and over, no longer needing the comfort of his presence, but to comfort him. He was only a boy and he had said he could not live without her. A pain bore down on her chest, so severe it hurt her lungs. She bent over her suffering and moved slowly and carefully. Every day she crept to the door to see if there was post and the little mat below the stairs seemed a hateful, mocking thing. Six months passed. She went to her mother. 'He is dead,' she said. 'My fiancé is dead.'

Mama was relieved. She thought her daughter looked as if she had spent years under a rock. She touched her dull hair and then, as if this act disgusted her, drew back and slapped her on the face. 'Why do you say such a thing? It is a lie. There has been nothing in the post.'

'He is dead,' Daisy said calmly. 'I can feel it. He has been killed in whatever war they are having in India.'

'I have read of no war,' mama said. 'We will write to Will.'

'There is no war.' Mama sounded disappointed. A week had passed and she held a letter. It was from Cecil Cantwell.

'Marguerite. You have disobeyed me. You have left the convent when I wanted you there. Do you realize what swine there are out in the world? I am stuck out in this heathen place and you could not even do one small thing to keep my mind at rest. You have put me in a filthy temper and for that I have had to punish you by sending you no letter. Try not to annoy me, Mags, as I have a hell of a temper and all the fellows here say I am the devil to live with when I am cross. With love, Cecil.'

Daisy let out a cry – harsh, exultant.

'What is the matter?' Mama defended herself with clasped hands.

'We are having our first real quarrel, like an ordinary couple. He is angry with me. He loves me still.'

Her mother force-marched her across the room until they faced the shop's mirrored wall. 'He loves a fool of a girl that he met at a post-box. Look at yourself! You are no longer that girl. What do you think he would make of you now? It is barely a year since you left the convent and already you have the look of a miserable spinster.' Daisy jerked her head evasively but mama pushed it back. 'Who is going to want to look at you when you cannot bear to look at yourself? You have not even begun to live your life. You have been waiting all along for someone to take it over. You do not keep in touch with your brothers and sisters. You have no friends.'

'I love only one man,' Daisy said.

'You have only ever met one,' mama reminded her.

'I have given him my promise.'

'And I can promise you,' said mama grimly, 'that unless you now begin to live the life of a normal girl, I will send you away to employment as I did with Lena and Beth, for I can no longer bear to look on your sick face.'

'Do, then,' Daisy said, although she was afraid. 'He will come and fetch me wherever I am.'

'It is twelve months since you met. In that time he has done nothing to suggest plans for the future. What do you suppose he is up to while you are here, pining and pathetic? Men do not make sacrifices. He will forget about you as quickly and as certainly as if you had never existed on the face of the earth.'

Mama had such power that Daisy thought if she were to wipe her hand over the mirror her very image would disappear. She had a horrid ill feeling that her mother was rummaging about inside her head and pulling out all her own worst fears, for she had already imagined every such thing. 'What do you want me to do?'

'Dress yourself up to look like a woman. Soon you will be twenty-one. What is the matter with you that you refuse to grow up? It is time someone took you in hand. I shall get the family together for your birthday. I would love to see the boys and you need a man to talk some sense into you.' Having dealt with the problem she seemed to lose interest in Daisy and peered at her own reflection in the mirror. A sour beauty looked back at her. 'It is a bad thing to be without a friend,' she told herself, 'someone to whom you can show the bare bones of your heart.'

Daisy didn't want to show anyone the bare bones of her heart but she would have liked a friend. There wasn't an easy exchange between her and Cecil Cantwell. Love was not a friendly thing. She needed and resented sympathy. Throughout her life she would only be able to accept compassion from those who envied her good fortune.

From the outside, the orphanage on Edward Street was entirely unchanged. It was a surprise to discover the inside equally untouched by time. Even the faces of the nuns she remembered seemed not to have aged. There was a new cast of children but they too looked the same, practical and forlorn. As she waited, girls came to peer around the door at her, wondering if she was their mother or some stranger come to adopt them. It gave her a queer sense of claustrophobia, being surrounded once again by orphans, and a curious sense of loss.

'Do you remember a girl called Nellie?' She said to Mother Agnes in the convent parlour.

'We have had more than one Nellie,' the nun reasonably pointed out. 'What is your business with her?'

'It was ten years ago. She would have been nine or ten. She asked me not to forget her.'

'Nellie Hanratty? A wilful girl. We placed her in a good position with a priest but she got into trouble.'

'What sort of trouble?' Daisy could not help a smile, thinking how Nellie had fulfilled her early ambition.

'She made up dreadful lies.'

'Do you know where she is now and what she is doing?' Daisy wondered.

'I wish I did not, but yes I do,' the reverend mother admitted. 'She was arrested in Upper Mount Street for disorderly conduct. She lives near there. I believe she exists by casual domestic work. She is a char.'

From a small, monkey-faced girl, Nellie had grown into a big-boned young woman. Her hair was artificially curled into tight waves and the baby in her arms had developed a slight squint from the fountain of tobacco smoke which erupted constantly from a corner of her mother's mouth. The miserable room in which she lived had neither water nor a fireplace. There is something about squalor that is set and accentuated by cold. Granny Devlin's room, though poor and dirty, had never been mean, because a huge fire always blazed in the hearth. Even though it was summer, Nellie's living quarters were dark and chilly, unwarmed by the narrow fingers of sun that reached between the buildings in her alley. Daisy wished she had worn something other than a summer frock, yet Nellie, sitting with legs crossed on the edge of the bed, a tiny bar of sun poking at the top of her crisp hair, seemed to luxuriate in some private atmosphere of ease. 'There you are,' she smiled affectionately. 'I knew you'd turn up someday unless you were dead or married.'

'I am engaged to be married,' Daisy said. 'My fiancé is in the army, serving with the cavalry in India.' She did not mention to Nellie that she had spent three years as a nun.

'Well, if that ain't the bee's drawers,' Nellie said. 'You're looking dismal, though.'

'I miss him.' She put out a hand and cautiously touched the baby. 'I see that you are married.' Nellie made a face. 'You won't find me at any man's beck and call. You're better off without the oul' scourges. A man's all right for courtin' or treatin' but there's no living with them. I never met a one that didn't have a bug in his bonnet over some figary.'

'But a man could provide for you and your child.' Daisy looked around her wretched surroundings. Nellie laughed. 'It ain't much, but we manage. I only take work where they gives me me dinner. I do feck a bit extra — a few fags or some scraps of meat in a paper bag.'

'What about the baby?' Daisy tried to draw a smile from the child but the stoic infant had not the range for coquetry.

'Gertie's quiet. Mostly I takes her with me but there's them as doesn't like it and then I leave her home.'

Daisy was shocked. 'Anything could happen.' Nellie gave a wry grin. 'Well it hasn't, has it. No good moaning unless you got a pain. Come here to me, though, I'm glad to see you.' She poured tea that she had brewed on a spirit stove. 'I'd give you cake, only I'm a bit short at the moment,' she said in her amused, mocking way. Daisy had not much money of her own but she gave Nellie a shilling. In return, Nellie offered her a cigarette. Daisy put the scandalous white cylinder cautiously between her lips. Smoke flooded her lungs and made her cough. 'It suits you,' Nellie coaxed, 'It'll soon come as easy as puddin'.' In spite of the abominable sensation of suffocation, Daisy found her first tranquillity in a year, concealed within a yellow fog behind a greasy window with this disgraceful woman, her friend.

Chapter 15

FOR a week the family was reunited. Will and Tom travelled from London for Daisy's birthday. Essie and Beth obtained brief, temporary leave from work and marriage. Lena guiltily deserted her ancient dependants. She was now a tranquil woman of twenty-eight in full charge of the house at Balmullet and able to employ a staff to do the work. The old ladies had become like children to her and she was as devoted to them as they were to her. Nurturing was in her nature and she would do it wherever she could. She held on to a harmless fantasy that when the elderly sisters died, Balmullet would be left to her and all the family would come and live there with their husbands or wives and grand parties would be held to please mama. 'There is plenty of money,' she said. 'The poor Misses Grizzard had a miser of a father and were frightened to spend it after he died, but now I am allowed to handle the finances.'

'Don't be daft,' said Janey, who suffered no qualms of conscience at forsaking her husband to celebrate with her siblings. 'They'd ate the house as soon as leave it to you.' Lena only laughed at Janey's bluntness. 'You could be right, but there's no one else except a nephew who lives in Australia and who does not keep in touch. They are fond of me.'

The twins were like creatures under some miserable enchantment. Both still had their childish, secretive look but their beauty was gone. Beth had to wear spectacles because of all the close needlework and kept her hair pulled tightly back from her face. She said very little all evening, contented to hold her sister's hand. Essie was pregnant again. Art Mulrooney was drinking heavily. When he drank he was rough with her, and her arms and neck had a dusty look from old bruises. No one thought to interfere with their situation for they were in someone else's care as was deemed right in the lives of women; nor was there any resentment of the comfortable existence the boys now enjoyed. Will had been made an officer and was in the company of gentlemen who shared interests like his own. He liked his life and said he never had to work hard, but he would love to settle down in the country and run a farm. Tom had a permanent job as printer on the *Sun* newspaper, a position achieved through the influence of his uncle, who was a cartoonist on the paper. He had become friendly with his Kensington relatives. They were all longing for news of them but he kept them in suspense until mama had gone to bed. 'The best of it is that they are not called Dubois at all!' he revealed. 'Their name is Wood. Mama changed hers after a visit to France.'

'What about their house? Is it a mansion?'

'What are they like?' Everyone was speaking at once.

'They live in an ordinary, pleasant terraced house like Mrs Muldowney here!' Tom winked at Janey, who shrieked with delight to think of how her middle-class married quarters must upset her mother. 'They are all terrified of mama and say they never knew peace until she left home.'

'What did she do to them?' Weenie said in awe.

Tom lit his pipe in a leisurely way and Janey blew out his match to make him carry on. 'As a girl she had ideas of grandeur and was always complaining because she could not do a tour or have a season. Her father took her abroad to give the rest of the family some quiet and it was when they came to Ireland that she met pa. The family tried to stop the affair, of course, for they knew how she would hate being married into the working classes. They said they would cut her off if she persisted, and mama, in a temper, ran away, taking with her all the most valuable items from the house. Most of the treasures of our old drawing room belonged to her family – even the dolls. She took her sisters' toys as well as her own. They tried to get in touch but their letters were returned. They believe she thought they were seeking the return of their property.'

'But what of mama's efforts to get help for us in London after pa's death?' Daisy said.

'Her account of that is true in a way. When Aunt Ada became ill they had to take in paying guests to cover the bills, but they would have helped us in what way they could. They have been very kind to Tom and I. Poor Aunt Ada is dead now and there is room there for any of us to go and stay. Daisy, would you like to come to London for a holiday? You used to want to see London and it would be a sort of present for your birthday.'

'Is this something mama has arranged?' Daisy said cautiously.

'Don't be a goose, Daisy dear,' Will rebuked. 'We daren't tell mama that we are in touch with her precious Dubois's. Say you'll come, now.' A silence held around the table so that she knew it was a campaign among her siblings. She had loved the past week with its laughter and warmth. Another three months had passed since she had heard from her lover. To break the tension Will took out pa's watch and commenced a countdown, making everyone laugh. Will brought such ease and lightness to the house. He had grown up a gentleman, but a kind and mild-mannered one. He was a perfect mix of pa and mama. It would be lovely to have him to herself for a week. 'I will come to London,' she decided, 'but only to meet my relations. I have no wish for dances or parties.'

The following morning a telegram came. 'Happy birthday to my own darling Daisy. Cecil.'

She almost danced with joy. 'You must all come for my next birthday too, for of course I cannot leave now. Mama needs me and I promised Cecil I would stay at home.'

The telegram was followed by a letter. 'As you are no longer in the convent there is something you can do for me. Grow your hair long and send me a measurement each time you write. With your dark skin and your hair in plaits you will look like the young Indian girls here, who are so very beautiful.'

This unnerved her but by now her brothers and sisters were gone back to their lives. Will and Tom took Beth to London instead. Everyone was amazed at the ease with which this was achieved after Beth's years of slavery. She was free because a man had freed her. Mama accepted it. Even Madame Pawelczcyk respected the male prerogative. By this accident fate made one of its languid sweeps. Beth was offered a job in a smart London dress-house where her exquisite needlework was properly valued. After a month she wrote to say that she would not be coming back to Dublin. She rented a small flat and waited patiently there for some other fatal contortion that would allow Essie to come and share her good fortune.

When Will went Daisy watched her life go with him. She knew she should have accepted his offer. She would not have another such chance. Instinct told her that the moment of revelation at the post-box would never be repeated. She had been a girl then. Now she was a woman. Such things did not happen to women. Will would have introduced her to well-mannered men like himself. She could have had what other women had, a good husband, a nice home. She went to see Nellie, bringing a carton of cigarettes. 'Next time, take us a sup of gin or whiskey,' Nellie said. 'You can't really go to the bad on a fag.'

'What should I do?' Daisy reluctantly imparted her woeful tale. 'Should I write to my brother and tell him I've changed my mind?'

Nellie shrugged. 'You can't change your mind. You can change your plans but you can't change your mind – do you folly me? Even if you was to go to England and marry the king you'd still be hankering. Your mind'd still be set. That's the class of a creature you are.'

'What is this class of a creature to do?'

'I dunno. I've had fun with men but I never had any luck with them. I suppose you could try axin' him what he wants – although divil a one I met ever wanted anything only to persecute the plucks out of you.'

'Then what will I do if that does not work.'

'I expose you'll die of a broken heart,' Nellie reflected.

Daisy concentrated on growing her hair. Mama no longer bothered to shear back Weenie's locks, so the two girls spent long evenings brushing and measuring their hair while Weenie read aloud from mama's *Lady of the House* magazine a serial story called 'A Tide of Evil'.

> '*He had thrust her away with almost brutal force, sending her staggering against a heavy writing table. But even this Lucie did not resent. She stood there gazing in a curious fashion at the door she had so vehemently closed, a little ripple of satisfied laughter escaping her red, disdainful lips. "Thou art a fool and a craven," she cried mockingly. "But I care not. I love thee still, love thee and thine inheritance . . ."*'

'My hair has grown to eight inches,' Daisy wrote. 'What do you want of me? I fear I have failed you. I would do anything in the world for you if I only knew.'

The boy wrote back to her quite eagerly. 'I am a man. I want what any man wants. I know you are innocent, my dear, but sometimes I fear that you are cold. We have never even had a kiss. Do you know what it takes to keep a girl on a fellow's mind? Please write and let me know that you desire the same things I desire. If you do not know the words, just put it in any language you know.'

Daisy's expression, on reading this letter, was that of a housewife coming upon some overkept item in the larder. She knew and did not know what he was referring to. She understood that men thought more about these things than women but she was dismayed that he should expect it of her. It was the sort of response a man might seek from a woman like Janey.

Janey was surprised by Daisy's visit. She was further startled when her sister asked for a cigarette and a drink of whiskey.

'Aren't you the bad oul' herring?' Janey amiably complied. 'Next thing it'll be men.' Daisy did not smile. She lit her cigarette and puffed upon it.

'Janey,' she frowned, 'how do you write to a man?'

Janey looked amused. 'I don't know. I've never written to a man.' Daisy was embarrassed. She looked around the pretty, overdone room, with its mirrors and pictures and oval table covered with a chenille cloth. Everything seemed soft and sumptuous and spoke of easy living. She had to fight back a sudden seizure of envy that Janey had acquired this comfortable household without effort or desert. Janey came and sat beside her on a red plush sofa. 'What's the trouble, pet?'

'There's no trouble.' She couldn't help the coldness in her voice. 'I have no experience with men. I don't know the phrases.' She fell silent and when she spoke again she only sounded miserable. 'I don't know what they want.'

Janey sighed and stood up. 'Well, it's time you knew.' Daisy flinched but Janey's dark eyes held her. 'Men want whatever they can't have. Until you go to bed with them they want that more than anything in the world, but after that there has to be something else.'

'What else?' Daisy looked almost comically fearful.

'You have to hold a part of yourself back – never let them think they own you completely. You have to make them insecure.'

'That is false and cruel!'

'Don't blame me. The way they are is cruel too. If a man can possess you absolutely, you cease to be of value.'

'But pa wasn't like that. He worshipped mama.'

'Precisely what proves my point!' Janey refilled her glass. 'Mama was always as distant as China. Easy for her, of course. She didn't love him. It's hard all right when you love the buggers, but it's only another discomfort in women's lives – like the curse. Oh, Day!' Janey laughed. 'You've got a face as long as your grandmother's drawers. What's the matter now?'

'If what you say is true, then everything is impossible. One can't even properly write to a man. One can't ... declare oneself.' Her voice almost broke on the pain of this admission.

'Oh, you poor oul' herrin'! It's the soldier!'

'I fear my letters sounded cold. He said so.'

Janey laughed. 'The oul' cod! He wants a micky tickler.'

'A what?'

'Go on! Be a devil! Say that you long to be crushed against his manly form and to feel your lips bruised by his.'

Daisy only crushed out her cigarette. 'That sounds like a penny romance. Our affair is not like that. It is a spiritual, predestined love.'

'You sound like a penny romance yourself, sis. Tell you what. I'll write the letter for you.'

'Janey ... ?'

'I mean I'll ghost-write it. I'll tell you what to put down.'

'What will you say?'

She folded her arms and watched her sister with a sort of exasperated sympathy. 'Maybe you'd be better off not knowing. You just leave me a sample of your writing and I'll copy it. I'm good at that. Well? Do you want him or don't you?' She noted Daisy's disapproving look. Slowly Daisy nodded. She asked Janey for a piece of paper and a pen and wrote a sample note from which her script could be imitated. After she left Janey picked up the page and read what she had written: 'God's will be done.'

'Amen!' said Janey. She gave herself another drink and lit up a cheroot and sat down at Vesty Muldowney's mahogany desk.

In Janey's hands Cecil Cantwell turned into an entirely other creature. He was eager, tender, diffident, warm. Letters came, not just by two-month return of post but sometimes two and three a day. 'I thought you were cold,' he wrote. 'Oh, but you are soft and warm as a kitten. How can I last a single day without my kitten in my arms?' Daisy became his little bird, his adorable darling. As if each endearment was a painter's brush-stroke, she grew daily more radiant, more taut and glowing. She looked glorious. Mama, who knew nothing of the private transaction, was mystified. Once she had to touch her daughter's hair which, out of nowhere, had developed spring and shine. 'Oh, to marry you off in this moment to someone sound,' she said.

Daisy laughed. 'You mean solid, mama. Then he would crush me out of existence, for I am as light as air.'

Anyway, it would not be long. He almost moaned with deprivation. 'I can no longer sleep, I cannot eat. I am ill, my darling. In the hot nights I am caressed and tortured by your words.'

There was more than a lover's gratification in this. It was sweet satisfaction to know that he suffered as he had made her suffer. For the moment he was at the mercy of a heartless woman like Janey, but when his trial of waiting was over it was she, all compassion, who would soothe him. Once a week she paid a visit to Janey. Daisy's childish handwriting was easy to copy and she passed on any ordinary information contained in his letters so that Janey could sustain the conversation. She never asked what Janey wrote. She wasn't even curious. It was a remedy for an ill. One did not analyse the bromide one took for a fever.

At least she believed this until the remedy began to develop side-effects. Midway through a passionate correspondence which made her rapturous with its praise she was halted by a phrase: 'Write and tell me what underwear you are wearing and then describe what is underneath that.' After a momentary shock she dismissed this queer request from her mind. She thought he must be unwell, that he had been affected by the sun. His next letter was harder to ignore: 'I do not mind telling you that I have been hot as any dog since you last wrote. You are driving me insane. I have got to mount you. Will you really wear your nun's habit with nothing underneath? I shall have to get out of this infernal place and find a way to be with you.'

She watched this letter with a mild frown, as if it was in a code or in a foreign language. Certainly he had gone insane. She wondered what kind of fever could pervert a man's mind and how long he would take to recover. Then she began to shake. Janey had seduced him. It was her he wanted now, or the kind of woman she was. As if it was a weapon she picked up her pen and very quickly she wrote: 'Do not ever address such filth or profanity to me again. It has nothing to do with me, do you hear? You have made a very bad mistake.' To Janey she wrote to say that she never wished to see her again.

Contrary Janey came right away. She entered the shop crackling like a firework in her paste and taffeta. Mama and Daisy left at once for their rooms. Weenie rushed in full of delight but Janey, after a quick kiss, pursued Daisy to her refuge. Daisy would not look at her. 'If you've come to apologize, you needn't bother. I don't want anything more to do with you.'

'I amn't sorry.' Janey sat down on the bed beside her sister's rejecting form. 'Listen, you daft oul' herrin', we've almost got the savage. Three months from now you could be married.'

'We've almost got him?' Daisy turned to her a face stiff with fury. 'That's it, isn't it? You've seduced my fiancé and turned him into something that I don't recognize.'

'Oh, you're such an eejit,' Janey groaned. 'I don't want him. I did it for you. If you want to put a noose on a man it's not his heartstrings you have to tug.'

'Stop!'

'You're still the nun, aren't you? Let me write one more letter and then it will all be over. I promise you he'll be here with his flute in his hand before you can whistle 'Hail Mary'. Look, it doesn't even matter if you don't like that sort of thing. It only lasts a little while. As soon as a man is married and has kids he gets as proper as a pope and as wet as a po.'

Daisy began to cry. 'You make everything base,' she wept. 'Why can't you leave me be? I want nothing to do with you.'

Daisy wanted Nellie. In the months of heady courtship she had neglected her friend. She bought a miniature of whiskey and a packet of cigarettes. It was a warm August evening and she was glad of a change of scene. She thought they might go out together. A writer by the name of James Joyce had opened the first-ever picture theatre, the Volta, showing nothing but moving pictures from Italy, and she was curious to see them. Disappointingly, Nellie was not at home. She smoked a cigarette while she waited, nodding at a woman who passed her on the stairs. 'Terrible about poor Nellie Hanratty!' the neighbour greeted.

'What about Nellie?' Daisy's urgency startled the creature so that her features fell back into a snarl. 'They gave her three year for stealing a chicken from the market and her poor little girl got put in the orphanage, if it's anything to you.'

'Where is she?'

Nellie had been locked up in Mountjoy gaol. 'I'll go and see her,' Daisy resolved. 'First thing tomorrow.' But on the following morning there was a letter from Cecil Cantwell. 'My love, I know I promised not to refer in my letters to the things you said to me. You are shy and rightly so. Do not punish me. Do not stop those marvellous letters which bind me to you utterly. I will be careful how I answer.'

She could not think what to say. She felt abject and un-sophisticated. 'Marry me and all that I said will be yours,' she put down recklessly. Her hair, she added, had grown to twelve inches.

This information and her promise failed to ensnare him. She wrote and wrote again. After a long while he got in touch to say that his life had taken a strange turning for which she and her letters were to blame and he was too busy now to correspond. With what was he busy? Oh, how she wished that he was decently dead. As it was, she was left with an absurd picture of him, hot as any dog, craving a woman in fancy dress. Once, with thumping heart, she wrote that her breasts were as white as lilies. No word ever came to say what he made of this.

Essie died of puerperal fever after giving birth to another dead baby. Beth returned from London, beautifully dressed. She did not cry but spoke quietly to her dead twin. 'Wait for me. I will keep myself for you.' She would not allow Essie to be buried in the family plot but bought a new place beneath a tree. The headstone was carved to her order. 'Essie Dubois Devlin Mulrooney, born August 1885, died April 1910, and her twin Beth Dubois Devlin, Died —. Together forever in heaven's garden.'

'Now,' she said, 'Essie will suffer no more and the business of our lives is put in order.'

The following year Ba fell in love with a rosy-cheeked farmer's son called Patsy Macken. She was fifteen and he was twenty and neither had any money, but his parents offered them lodgings on their farm in Ballybough. A week before the wedding this healthy youth confounded them all with a fit of coughing which spattered his handkerchief with blood. 'It's nothing,' he consoled them. 'It's only a bit of consumption. I do get it from time to time.' The wedding was postponed while he went to recover in the chilly sanitorium in Cheeverstown and there, quite quickly, he passed away. Ba did not cry but her childish features seemed more harshly etched and she almost lost her job in M'Birneys for stealing a pair of white buckskin wedding shoes.

Three months later, there was another death, more distant and yet more influential to the family. The Misses Alice and Alma Grizzard died of typhus fever, leaving Balmullet House on 130 acres and a sum of £10,000 to Lena.

Will was coming home. Lena was determined that the house would be his when he married. Mama and Daisy and Weenie and Ba were to live in the big house too. They rented a brake to drive them to Meath for their first visit to Balmullet. Mama was excited as a child. 'For me, it is like a homecoming. You see, I grew up in a house like this.' The girls exchanged secret smiles but mama was too happy to notice. 'I shall keep to my parlour,' she said excitedly. 'I shan't get in the way of Will and his wife.'

Lena had been hard at work to show the dour Georgian house at its best. It was in need of new paint and fabrics but she and the maids had spring-cleaned it from top to bottom and put flowers in all the rooms. She looked feverishly excited and exhausted. 'I cannot begin to spend money until the will has been probated, but all should be ready within eight months. Then we will begin our new lives.'

There were eight bedrooms with lovely views of gentle countryside. The best room was kept for Will and the prettiest for mama and then they each picked out their own apartments. Daisy had a blue bedroom with a long window and a window seat, and a white marble fireplace. There was a view of trees and a stream. Here she would put a desk and there a piano. She would have the maid bring her breakfast in bed every day. In summer there would be parties in the garden and Will would bring his gentleman friends. Her past in the sweet factory and in the convent, the miserable years of waiting for Cecil Cantwell, would be wiped away. She was twenty-five. She had given up dreaming – or at least she had yielded up that painful dream. Now she pictured herself as a well-to-do young matron with pretty children, nicely dressed, playing in a garden. The husband was an image of blank benevolence. She remembered the woman on North Great Georges Street who had wanted to buy a kitten. She would look like that, tranquil and kind and content. She began to think of clothes and to look out for pretty patterns for dresses. She studied the new styles in parasols and hats. Searching in a drawer for a length of trimming she came upon her prayer book from the convent. She picked it up and a piece of paper fluttered out, an old page, a relic of her past.

The leaf-dry note shivered beneath her flattening palm. 'My dearest Marguerite,' she read, 'You have set me on fire.'

A bolt of rage ran through her. The letter was five years old. By now he should be ready to make her his bride. She ought to be awaiting the rapturous fulfilment of half a decade of dull virtue. By such a careless phrase could a man waste a woman's youth. He had not merely imprisoned the girl that she was. He had killed her. She should have married young. She had the kind of looks in which girlhood remained suspended like liquid in a brimming glass but hers had not spilled over into ripe womanhood, rather into a diluted, ageing girlhood. She had learned to accept what she had become. Now his letter had come back to taunt her. It was more than bad. It was bitter. She had found contentment in the prospect of Balmullet. At a stroke it was lost. She felt again that ache that took her breath away and made her want to crouch. The love had been destroyed but the loss still crushed her – the feeling of a child abandoned, that slaughter of self that told her she could not be anything if she could not be loved. All the same she had made herself forget him. She had put him out of her mind. She had only to do so again. 'Mr Cantwell,' she wrote. 'You broke your promise and you have ruined my life. As you will not come to claim what you spoiled I have no choice but to end it.' She put the letter away in her purse. She would never post it. Just to have written it made her feel better.

When next she passed a post-box her wilful fingers plucked the note from her purse and flipped it through the slot. She stood in awe, trembling at this irreversible strike at destiny. Oddly, she could feel no regret. A lightness entered her heart, a sense of recklessness and power. She had a guinea in her little bag and she broke this on a cup of strong coffee in Bewley's coffee house and then she walked to Clery's and bought herself a straw boater trimmed with pink ribbon. When she came into the house wearing this, with her hair put up underneath, mama said: 'Oh, thank God, you have become a woman. Now we shall make something of you.'

A telegram arrived. Daisy took the paper from the boy and scanned it. She could make no sense of it. It seemed to contain news of a death. It was not, as she had assumed, from Cecil Cantwell but from a solicitor in County Meath. 'Regret Elinore Devlin passed away typhus fever Wednesday 7th stop. Under the terms of the will, estate now transfers to Mr Aloysius Grizzard of Canberra, Australia.'

After the funeral the whole house stayed in mourning. Their grief was not just for Lena, whom they had only known for half her lifetime, but for their own lives, for the gift placed in their grasp and then snatched away. Mama could bear it least. 'There can be no worse disappointment in life than this,' she said, and she believed it so. They did not bother to keep the house nor dust the shoes in the parlour nor step outside to breathe the depraved scents of the summer city. They sat around the fire in the kitchen in their dull black dresses, drinking tea. No visitors came, for Lena had known no one except her dead benefactors. When there was finally a knock, none of them wanted to answer it. They crouched in silence and waited for the caller to go away. 'My head!' mama said at last. 'Weenie, go to the door and tell them to stop the banging.'

Weenie came back looking wild with alarm. 'It's a foreigner,' she said amazed. 'It's a man.'

'It is Mr Aloysius Grizzard of Canberra, Australia, come to witness our loss,' said mama. 'Bring him in, do. Let him see what he has achieved.'

The little smouldering room could scarcely stand the brightness of the visitor, his golden skin, his white garments braided in gold. Foggily they gaped at him. 'That's a nice welcome for a bugger back from Bombay,' said Cecil Cantwell. 'Where's Mags? Where's my Daisy?'

Chapter 16

'MARGUERITE?' His voice dropped to a whisper and his eye connected with the long-faced woman who had overtaken his girl.

Five years had turned him into a man and Daisy into a spinster. When she miserably presented herself, he could not hide his disappointment. 'Mags?' He came closer. He looked her over rudely and at leisure, trying to reconcile this plain woman with the bewitchingly concealed girl who had set him on fire. For Daisy the shock was otherwise. His nearness plunged her back into hopeless adoration. She had to scrape her hands behind her back to stop herself from touching him. 'Why have you come?' She tried to rescue her pride.

'Why do you call her Mags?' mama irritably interjected.

'Damn it all, Mags, you were going to do yourself in.'

With this revelation mama began to look more lively. 'We have had a death. I did not know we planned another.'

Daisy was mortified. 'I said I would end it. I meant our affair. I did not wish to see you again.' Mama made an impatient noise and gave herself the more gratifying view of the visitor. 'Do not be ill-at-ease. Make yourself at home. My husband was a working-class man.'

Ba gave her parched laugh. 'No one has asked him to sit down. Sit down, Mr Cantwell. Would you like a cup of tea?' Daisy's misery increased when at last he smiled, for it was not at her but at her teenage sister. 'Thank you, miss, but no. I can't understand you idle bloody lot, huddled in the dark on a day like this. Sun outside would scorch your eyeballs. Come on, Mags. I want to talk to you.'

She was glad of her new straw boater. It hid the shadows on her skin and made up for the stiff black mourning-dress that showed grey in sunlight. Out of doors he looked even more splendid. Passing women admired him and then appraised his mousy partner. Her heart was sore with worship. She felt speechless and despairing. The year's difference in their ages seemed to have turned into a decade. He took her hand. It sat in his grasp, stiff as a claw. 'You don't have to.' Her voice was on the edge of tears.

'It's all right.' His sudden gentleness was hard to bear. 'I've come home. I'll do right by you now.'

'But you don't love me!' she cried up into his blue eyes, darting along the pavement to keep to his pace.

'You needn't go into all that. I won't go back on my word – not now. I thought I was coming home to save your life. Maybe I was and maybe I wasn't. Could be it's you who's saved me.' She had no idea what he was talking about. She kept on scouring him with her little clenched face. 'Why did you hurt me so?' He stopped to look at her. 'You poor bugger!' Right there in the street, amid carts and children and poor shapeless housewives, he swept her into his arms and kissed her. 'Our first kiss, Mags. Forget the past. This is the beginning.'

She began to tremble all over. The warmth of his embrace, the tenderness of his kiss, were two such separate things that they could not be fully appreciated at once. She kept her face lifted to him, wanting it to start again. This time he did not kiss her. He laughed at her. 'You're hot for it, aren't you?' he said in his sharpish voice. 'We'd better get married soon.'

Everyone was pleased except mama. From their first meeting a vigorous confrontation was born between the Englishwoman and the Englishman. Mama said that he was overbearing and uncouth. 'You don't give a bugger a chance,' he laughed. She could feel a sneer behind his mirth and invited him to save his gutter language for his home. He smiled his brilliant smile. 'I feel this is my home since you have all been so kind to me.'

He took lodgings in town while planning his marriage. The city suited him. He had a sharpness lacking in the local males, who were either relaxed or depressed to the point of inertia. The proliferation of beggars in the street and the dismal plight of slum-dwellers distressed him. 'Poor bugger,' he would grumble and empty his pockets of change when he came across a wretched, barefoot mother beset by scrawny offspring. Aside from the surfeit of public misery he liked the smoky sprawl around the Liffey. 'You can smell the sea and see the sky!' He said the city was wide open. Within a week he had a deal going with a man he met in a pub. He had a bit of money saved from the army and planned to establish a superior gentlemen's hairdressing establishment, importing Fred Lewis's Electric Oil, which was guaranteed to produce an immediate growth of hair where other remedies had failed.

'Are you a barber?' Daisy diffidently inquired.

'I'm anything I turn my hand to,' he airily replied. 'I used to cut my brothers' hair at home. And soled their boots!' They were all astounded by his energy. No sooner had he boasted of his intent than he was painting gold lettering on a dark-green shop-front in Westmoreland Street: 'Cantwell and Kilmadden, barber and gentlemen's hair restorer, by appointment to His Royal Highness King George V.' Mama was outraged. 'I suppose you are going to tell us you cut the king's hair along with your brothers'.'

'No,' Cecil Cantwell laughed, 'but if he makes an appointment I will.'

Daisy felt confused. She was at the centre of attention and envied by other women, yet she could not feel secure. She had thought they would be going back to England after their marriage, away from Janey and mama. Instead he was resolved to settle in Dublin. It was as if he was in love with her city and not herself. He kissed her fondly but there wasn't a trace of fire. Sometimes she hated him for his kindness, convinced that he only stayed with her from pity. She saw very little of him. Most of his time was taken up with plans for their future. He was out seeing men on matters of business or looking over houses. He never consulted her. She waited for him, she followed him like a dog, apprehensive of his moods, grateful for any attention. On Sunday mornings they went together to mass. It was odd to discover that he was a Catholic like herself, for she had assumed that all English people were Protestants like mama. He did not take her to the cinema or to musical entertainments. To her surprise he disapproved of such amusements. She longed for him to fill in the years of her abandonment but she was afraid of sounding plaintive. Once it burst out of her. 'Tell me why you left me. Why would you not even write?'

'You'd best leave that subject where you found it,' he said. 'I'm here now, aren't I?'

'Why?' Daisy begged.

'Because I have said it!' he barked. He was sorry when he saw her cringe. 'A man's life is different to a woman's, Mags. It doesn't do for the sexes to be too frank with one another. It's not natural.'

As for her, she was too much in love to be in any way natural. She ought to feel joyful. All she felt was a wild alarm when he looked at any woman, even her. In spite of her petrified state, her future was gathering around her. He had rented a house in Prussia Street, a good address, although close to the cattle market. Beth was sewing a wedding gown of tamboured net with rucking and puffs. Weenie and Ba made a cake which was iced and placed on a table in the shoe shop, out of harm's way. Daisy declined Janey's offer of a wedding party. With even more determination she resisted the proposal of a heart-to-heart concerning the physical side of marriage. Instead she forced her mind on to the practical aspects of her wedding, accepting Ba and Weenie as her bridesmaids, with Janey as matron of honour. Will would give her away and Tom was to act as best man.

The wedding breakfast was in the kitchen at Edward Street. While they ate the cake and drank wine, mama scrubbed the stairs. It was a thing she had never done before but she insisted it would make Mr Cantwell feel at home, as she supposed he had often seen his mother labouring upon her knees. Mr Cantwell was indifferent to her gesture. Exquisite in his white braided uniform, he had eyes only for one woman. He had drunk a lot and his blue eyes were softened with emotion for the girl he toasted as a new member of his family, the most striking woman he had ever met.

'To Janey!'

Daisy shivered inside her ornate gown. Up to now she had kept Janey away from him. From the moment he walked into the church and saw the dark woman in her startling green dress, he could not take his attention from her. The rest of the family looked helpless. Vesty Muldowney lifted his glass in a gesture of arrest. 'To Daisy! God bless the bride. Loveliest girl in Dublin's fair city!' Muldowney was heavily built and his form was menacing. 'You're a lucky man, Cantwell.' Cecil put a defensive arm around his bride and raised his glass again. 'To my wife!' The rasp of his cheek on hers when he kissed her was an unnerving echo of mama's scrubbing brush on the wooden steps of the stairs. She hung on to the word 'wife'. The exhausting years, the dreadful day, were almost at an end. She had achieved the only thing she ever desired. The priest had declared her married, she had papers to confirm it. Still she did not feel it so.

As they were about to depart, mama appeared in a soiled apron belonging to Weenie. Her hair was knotted into an old scarf. With a small, crooked smile she handed Daisy a parcel. 'Your wedding present. A memento! Something useful to start off your new life.' Daisy unfolded the paper and there, disabled by its solitude, was Aunt Ada's primrose slipper. Mama laughed. 'You might as well have it. It is about as much use on its own as you are.' Cecil's jaw grew truculent. He wanted to strike down his mother-in-law, but his baffling bride was smiling, whereas all day, as he had bestowed his life on her, she was the picture of misery. She kissed her mother. There was a momentary sympathy in the glance exchanged between the two traders in her life.

They went to Bray on honeymoon. After a little stroll along the pier, a light supper that neither wanted to eat, they climbed the wide stairs where dust was startled by a steely glint of sea through the landing window. In the room he kissed her and then he went to the bathroom, where he stayed a long time. She remained where she was, looking out of the window. She was thinking of the day she went to the sea with all her brothers and sisters.

When Cecil returned he did not seem so much undressed as resuited. His pyjamas were a fresh regalia. He glanced at her with a mixture of kindness and criticism before climbing into bed alone. In a moment he was asleep. She lay down beside him, clutching the primrose slipper. For her it had always been a symbol of victory – Lord Percy Jermyn dancing with Aunt Ada. When mama gave it to her, she had passed on the baton of success. She studied her husband as he slept and smelled the faint, pleasant male smell of him. At last she felt joy. She need never fear anything again except his unpredictable humours. All the nights of his life were hers and all her life would be used up by him. He was hers to cherish, to touch if she liked. She put out her fingers gingerly to feel the blonde whiskers at his ears. His blue eyes opened suddenly. He smiled on her and stroked her shoulder. 'We'd best get it over with, you poor little bugger,' he said. Her eyes shrank back in alarm although she still smiled. 'It's all right.' He had begun to undo the ribbons of her gown. 'I won't hurt you. This might seem strange to you but I'm your husband and you must do as I say.' He had bared her shoulder and was stamping it with small kisses. Whatever he did she was resolved to endure it. In spite of her fear she was melting to his affection. She allowed her arms to go around him, accepted his head to her breast. He undid the rest of her ribbons and reached down to caress her.

'No!' she screamed.

'Shut up, Mags!' He reeled back. 'I've done nothing. Shut up!'

She silenced herself with a little moan. 'Flesh of my flesh,' he soothed. 'You are mine. I can touch what is mine.' Warily he stroked her.

'No!' she howled. 'No. pa, no!' She shot out of bed and bolted across the room, where she crouched beside the wardrobe. For a moment he was too shocked to move and then he hurtled after her. 'For Jesus Christ's sake, what is it?' She huddled into a ball, her knees to her chin, her face behind her hands. 'My pa!' she wailed. 'He only wanted love. I wouldn't let him. I wished him dead.'

'Your pa?' he said in astonishment. 'Your pa did that?'

'I wished him dead,' she moaned. 'I killed him.'

He stayed beside her until she was calm. Then he carried her back to bed. 'We have to do this, Mags.' He stroked her hair. 'We're man and wife. Otherwise I'd have to go to other women.'

'Pa,' she grieved.

'It's how you get a family, Mags.' He strove to sound reasonable. 'It's got to be done. Lie down now, like a good girl.'

They lay very still side by side in the vague discomfort of their bodies' dampnesses. Outside, the tide upon the shingle beach gave mild applause. He sighed and she turned to him. He had turned blue in the moonlight. 'I can't have you, can I, Mags?'

'Why do you call me Mags?' she said stiffly. 'You promised to call me Marguerite.' In spite of what had happened she was still weak with admiration of him. The curve of his cheek-bones, of his chin and his chest showed extraordinary beauty in the night's deathly glow. He put out his hand and took it back sadly. 'You are pure. Because of what happened to you as a child, you are locked into a child's purity. We're man and wife now. We'll have to get by. But I shall never possess you.'

'No!' She said it before she could think. She had learned without knowing it, from mama, that what can't be endured can be ignored. She had locked him out as her mother, seated in her pretty drawing room had shut out the din of the street and of family life.

'Oh, my love,' he sobbed. 'I worship you.'

She returned from honeymoon a radiant bride. Her husband was tamed and bemused. People smiled, imagining they knew what had happened, but in truth no one knew. Cecil Cantwell could not have said why the morose, prudish girl who excited only his compassion when he came back to her now inflamed his every thought. Daisy had no idea why he had fallen so fervently in love with her. She was childishly proud. There was charm in her childish plaits and old-fashioned garb, for she looked like a girl once more. The best of her beauty came from an inner radiance. Without it she looked dark and sullen. Now she shone with happiness.

In the day she could forget the dread of the nights. In a queer way she came to prize the dismay. There had to be a price for love. She wanted to suffer for him. All the same, she could not believe that this uncomfortable ritual had ensnared him for, as mama had pointed out, men can get their pleasures from other sources. It was only months later that she recalled a phrase from worldly Janey. 'Men want whatever they can't have. You have to hold a part of yourself back.' She could no more have willingly withheld herself from Cecil than flowers can reject the sun, yet without her permission a part of her was shut off from him forever. She rejoiced at this accident. They had to do this thing because they were married, but their love was outside and beyond it. For all her knowledge of life, this was something Janey would not understand.

Midway through their honeymoon there was another surprise. 'I suppose I can leave the business of the house to you,' he said one morning as she was admiring his manly way of spreading marmalade on toast.

'What business?'

'The fancy stuff – curtains, all that! There won't be a lot of money but I can let you have enough for cloths if you could turn your hand to a bit of stitching.' Until that moment it had not fully struck her that she was rid of mama. She would not be returning to Edward Street. She had her own house where she could do as she liked. She smiled at him with such pleasure that he rippled with the gratification of his husbandly role.

They came back to the terraced house that was stark with unoccupation. Cecil had put in a bed and table and some chairs. Beyond that it was yet to be furnished. Daisy went through all its rooms, marvelling at the space – three bedrooms, separate dining and drawing rooms, an indoor lavatory, a small walled garden at the back. At the flick of a switch, the rooms were flooded with electric light. The kitchen was a horror but that would be someone's else's province for her husband had promised her a maid. In addition to a home of her own she had neighbours. Daisy loved showing off her new house and husband to these nice respectable married women who displayed a frank curiosity and good-natured envy of the handsome young couple. As Cecil's temper was unpredictable she worried about his response to an invasion of strangers, but he proved boundlessly hospitable. He made housewives pink and giddy with drink and his attention. He showed a quality of sympathy that induced people to confide in him. At their numerous evenings, he always seemed to be perched on the edge of some man or woman's chair, his blue eyes indignant, his face set in a scowl of sympathy as his mesmerized subject entrusted their most private affairs. Soon Daisy knew all the human secrets of her neighbours and they knew none of hers. Cecil was the youngest householder on the street, but he was deferred to as a man of the world and although she did not have his facility for intimacy, Daisy was respected too. He had given her a position. She resolved in return to give him a setting.

As their house was conveniently adjacent to Sackville Street, she walked in every day for shopping. Her days were spent in a dream of domestic absorption. She appraised the new high-art fabrics in Clery's – Pongee, Chuddah, Mysore – and dove deep into drawers of remnants in the bargain basements. She settled on a décor of pale-green wallpaper with drapes and rugs in dusty pink. Since there was no one left in Edward Street who was interested in needlework, she appropriated the sewing machine and spent her afternoons stitching curtains and cushions and in the evenings she embroidered towels, toilet covers and chair savers. She collected patterned plates and bowls and vases of ruby glass. She warmed her green walls with gilded mirrors and engravings of dogs and children. At last she added little pink lamps, as like as possible to the ones in mama's parlour. The only touch of contrast was the primrose slipper set on a shelf to catch the light.

Cecil tried to introduce his own touches. He had brought back mementoes from India – a tiger skin, a curved sword, some Benares pieces, a trunk with brass fittings. She thought them savage. They reminded her painfully of a life he had lived without her. In the end he put them in the smallest bedroom which became known as the Indian room, and with which she did not concern herself at all. Nor did she bother about the dreadful kitchen, but left it to a poor little girl who came in to do the work.

The little girl, Susan, was one of the few annoyances in Daisy's new life. She was not a proper maid. Cecil had found her in the street and brought her home. 'Look at her, poor little tanner rabbit,' he said to Daisy, who would have rathered not. To her dismay she learned that he meant to give her a home. 'She'll take up no more space than a sprat. She was begging, Mags. We can't let her go back to that. She's a good girl. I'm sure you can find work for her.' Daisy had hoped for a nice girl who would look pleasant in a uniform and be envied by the neighbours. This child had a slovenly look. She kept sniffling. 'I am sure she has a home of her own. Her mother would miss her,' she said as lightly as possible, but Cecil hushed her reproachfully and took her aside to tell her that the child's mother had been a widow who got into debt and killed herself with prussic acid. Whether as a result of this or through her normal nature, she proved difficult to train. The bed was lumpy and trays were set with crumpled linen. Daisy made her a neat little cap and pinafore but she never seemed quite clean. She had the appearance of having slept in her clothes and always looked as if she had been crying. When criticism made her nervous she wiped her nose with the back of her hand.

Cecil would hear no judgement of his find. He even helped her with the housework. 'Can't you be patient, Mags? Poor little bugger's never had a chance.' It irked her to see him carrying trays or a bucket of coal for a servant and she had to tell him so. 'What is the matter with you?' he snapped. It was their first cross word since they had got married. What was the matter with her? She had a home of her own and a husband who adored her, yet suddenly she felt sick with irritation. She could not eat and was repelled by everything, even the air. One day she spotted egg on the spoon that accompanied her tea and had to rush from the room to vomit. When she brought the spoon to the kitchen to remonstrate with Susan, the second sighting of it made her ill again. 'I am sick,' she thought. 'I am dying.' To Cecil she said, 'That child hates me. She is trying to poison me.' He was shocked at her. He said the poor little bugger wouldn't hurt a fly. She was forced to go alone to the doctor. To her astonishment he told her she was pregnant. It was too soon. She had hardly had her husband to herself. Already she resented having to share their house with Susan. Before a year was out there would be someone who would have a share in his devotion too.

Cecil was delighted and impatient. He wanted to know when the boy would be born. When she mentioned a date he shook his head and then winked as if to suggest there were strings he might pull to improve matters. She was glad to please him but could not like what was happening to her body. A little mound replaced her waistline, like a bustle worn back to front. She had a grievous aversion to everything. The sight of quite ordinary things like milk or liver brought on hysterical bouts of retching. At least there was one consolation. Now that she had achieved maternity she was absolved from the act of union that brings it about. Sick and grey, she held herself as still in bed as something filled too full that might spill. When he touched her she made a little warning noise. She was as affronted as a cat when he drew her to him. 'My condition,' she reproached.

He sighed. 'For God's sake, Mags, why must you make a fuss? Why can't you just put up with it like other women?'

'It disgusts me now,' she said softly.

'All right then, be a bloody martyr.' His voice had developed its unpleasant nasal harshness. 'You're my wife. I'm pledged to you and you to me.' He held her down while he exacted his solitary pleasure. She felt a scream rising in her throat but held it there, for she knew she must be sick. She ran to the bathroom. She felt cold and sore. Her legs were trembling. She crouched on the floor a long time waiting for him to come and comfort her but she was left alone. When she returned to their room she did not get back into bed but stood looking down on him, on this man she worshipped, who had turned into a beast. After a time her presence invaded his sleep and he looked up at her. 'Jesus Christ Almighty!' he muttered. She was standing over him, wielding a heavy fire-iron. Her face looked perfectly concentrated. 'You have half killed me and now you are trying to kill my child. If you ever do that to me again while I am in this condition, I will kill you.'

'Jesus Christ Almighty,' he said again, but he stayed away from her after that.

It was a well-known thing that lying-up sometimes affected women in the head. She would never have hurt him. She would have died for him. Had he persisted, she would have endured it, although she would have preferred him to apologize for his need rather than putting her at fault. She was shaken by her own boldness and tried to make up by being tender and submissive. She was even nice to Susan, who rewarded her with an end to her snivelling. To her relief Cecil was not angry. He was too concerned about her maternal state. His suspense was such that she could almost have believed that she withheld his son at will. Propped up in her plump primacy, sucking barley sweets and knitting little coats, she felt like a queen.

Only Susan was not impressed. She continued to be forgetful. It was annoying for Daisy to have to get up from the fire, upsetting all her rugs and cushions, to go downstairs and find out what had happened to her cup of Dr Tibble's Vi-cocoa, for which she had developed a craving. As always, she entered the kitchen with trepidation, antipathetic to its mysteries. She crept in and saw her husband standing at the table. Susan sat on the table, her legs spread like a rag doll. His hands were on her knees and he held them tightly to his hips. His blond head was angled and intent, like a dog with a bone upon the little wasted face. Daisy made no sound. Her eye caught Susan's and Susan's caught hers and they remained locked in panic as his sighs grated on the utter stillness of the air. Daisy backed out silently and returned to her cushions by the fire.

Susan was glad she didn't make a fuss. When Daisy told her to go she said nothing, just looked away as if the subject did not interest her, took her money and left. All day Daisy pondered how to deal with the more serious problem. It was a bitter shock to her that her husband should show interest in another woman, worse, a dirty little urchin. Yet she felt sure she had no rights in the matter. She had rejected him. From what mama had hinted, the physical side of a man's composition was like a diabolical possession. It was without reason or nature. It must be right that a wife should sacrifice herself, should commit herself to this fire and be consumed by it rather than let her husband go astray. In the afternoon, unable to reach any conclusion, she went to confession. The priest confirmed what she feared. She had failed in her duty as a wife. She explained her condition, and how ill and tired she felt. A wife, he reminded her, must not refuse her husband under any circumstance. In doing so, she had sinned. He imposed a penance of four rosaries.

Cecil was late home. She gave herself a drink of whiskey and waited in bed. When she heard him come in, a cloak of fright fell over her. It was the fear of him, the fear of losing him. 'Mags!' he called. He paced around the house and then ran upstairs. 'What the hell's going on?'

'What is it?' Her fingers played in nervous placation. She yearned for a cigarette but he didn't approve of women smoking.

'What's Susan been playing at? Bloody place is like a pigsty.'

'Susan is gone.' She wove the edge of the sheet into a little roll.

'Where is she?'

She looked at him in appeal. 'I had to let her go.'

'You put her out? That poor little buggar! What kind of woman are you?'

'She was not suitable,' Daisy said miserably. 'She left egg on my spoon. She made me ill.'

'You put an orphan on the street because she left egg on your spoon? She's to end up in the Magdalen Institute for fallen women because of a spoon? Is that all you could drum up against her?'

'There is more. You know there is.' She could barely voice the words. She had gone pink with shame.

'I know nothing except that you have gone behind my back.' He paced around the room, pausing to throw her hostile glances. His hands clenched and unclenched. He looked like a tiger and she wished he was one. Then he could have simply torn her to shreds without any malice. 'I saw you last night.' The confession filled her with guilt. 'In the kitchen.' He stopped to gape at her. She had the momentary satisfaction of placing him in the wrong. His blue eyes sparked. 'I gave her a kiss! A poor little child with no one in the world and I gave her a hug and kiss. What are you trying to make of it?' Daisy shrugged in dismal confusion. He seized her shoulders and shook her. 'Don't you ever go against me again. By God, if I had known I married a sneak! You couldn't wait until my back was turned to throw her out. I pay for this house and everything in it. I don't expect gratitude but I want respect. Do you understand?'

'I'm sorry,' she whispered.

He let her go. He sighed, worn out by himself. 'I don't know why you have to get my back up when you know I have a hell of a temper. Things would be sweet if only you wouldn't go against me.' She pawed at him contritely. He bestowed a rueful smile and she took his hand and drew it to her body. 'My God, Mags, you're like a bloody sow,' he laughed. She dropped his hand in consternation. While he undressed she undid the fastenings of her nightgown. She managed a cowardly smile. 'What the . . .? He looked affronted. 'Cover yourself up, girl!'

He slept soundly while she lay awake, stranded beneath her bulk. She had done all she could to keep him and now her woman's body conspired against her. She was six months pregnant and she disgusted him.

Morning had a debris-strewn calm. They tried to smile at one another but the spites and indecencies had been left behind. Daisy felt she had destroyed her marriage. She wasn't sure what she had done wrong but a sense of calamity weighed upon her. That morning she brought him his breakfast, although normally he indulged her condition with a cup of tea in bed. The kipper, which had made her blench to cook it, seemed to restore him fully to good temper. When its hairy spine was stripped upon the plate, he turned to her a face of kindness and concern. 'God, I'm sorry, Mags.' She responded eagerly. 'It's all right. You were not to blame.'

'No, the thing is, you got me on a wrong footing. I was in a hell of a bad humour before I got home. I've packed in the business, Mags.' She tried to smile at him. She could not spoil his humour. 'What happened?'

'It was all a swindle!' His rage was up again. 'Bloody swine should be locked up for life.'

'Who, dear?' She stroked his arm to soothe him.

'Fred Lewis.'

'Fred Lewis?' She tried to accommodate interest and reproach in her voice, having no idea who the swine was.

'His guaranteed hair-restorer left my clients bald as coots. That swine made a monkey of me!'

'This is barbarous,' Daisy said loyally.

To her surprise he let out a snort of laughter. 'Barber-ous! Ha! That's good!' He threw an arm around her and kissed her fondly. 'I love you, girl. You can twist me round your finger. You know that, don't you?'

She nodded uncertainly. 'You can't like me much at the moment.'

'What do you mean?' He drew back from her with an injured look that made her wish she had kept her mouth shut. 'The way I look . . . last night . . .' she said feebly. 'I'm ugly, amn't I?'

'You are beautiful.' He touched her cheek with the tips of his fingers. There's different ways a woman can be beautiful. You're still an innocent girl, aren't you? Ah, you're lovely. You're a fool to put up with me. My worries are no concern of yours. Just look after yourself and the little chap.'

She basked in his affection, in the ordinariness of this married conversation. 'Are you really giving up the business?' He gave her a brisk squeeze. 'I have to. I'm a man of principle, Mags. I try to stand by what is right. Do you know what upsets me most of all? That swine Kilmadden knew all along the blasted treatment was a hoax. He laughed when I told him of my doubts. No, I'm well out of it. We'll find something else.'

'What will we do?' she worried.

'We'll be all right. Maybe it's just as well we don't have to shell out for a domestic any more. Things may be tight. I know it's hard on you in your condition but one of your sisters could help. Do you mind?'

'I'll be all right.' Her heart sank as she thought of the gloomy cavern of the kitchen. In her mind she counted up the sooty grates. 'You're a good wife,' Cecil said. 'I wouldn't have another for all the world.'

She was constantly amazed by him. She wondered if all men were alike or if he was unique. Would she ever learn to anticipate his storms of temper, to master acquaintance with the moth-wing draught that might blow them away? She wondered how he had come to such emphatic acceptance of his married state. Had fate truly drawn them together or were other husbands, corralled after years of difficult pursuit, so swiftly broken to their role? Safely held in his arms, his wrath subsided, she wondered was there any woman in the world more fortunate than she. Others settled for security and companionship but she had held out for all she desired. In spite of their difficulties there was still the reward of perfect happiness when-ever he forgave her.

Often afterwards she wondered about the little girl. She had had no choice in the matter and yet she knew the child was not to blame. Newspapers daily carried stories of poor women who were found dead of cold or starvation in doorways, who died while bearing babies in the street, or fell into the hands of men and were abused and abased for a pittance of money. Cecil never mentioned her again. She felt sure he had forgotten all about her. His impulses of charity were as peremptory as his angers. He could never pass a victim of misfortune without a sympathy so strong that he would shed his overcoat, strip his wallet, offer them his home, yet as soon as he had passed the next corner they ceased, for him, to exist.

Ba came to stay. She still had the air of a stray. She never complained and was grateful for everything. To Daisy's relief she took little notice of Cecil, laughing her same crooked laugh at both his jokes and his tempers. All her attention was for Daisy. It was the first time she had had her to herself since Daisy's entry into the convent and she only wanted to please her. Cecil approved of Ba. The sad death of her fiancé made her a victim and he liked to offer advice and sympathy.

Without mama to repress her, Ba became a comedian and the house took on a festive air. Cecil would open a bottle of wine while she amused them with her mimic's skill, telling scandalous tales from M'Birneys where she worked. On evenings when she went out the house missed her, as a house can complain of the absence of its children. To the newly-weds she was like a family and her presence enhanced their affection for one another. Daisy had never seen Cecil so light-hearted. 'You're a right clown,' he said to Ba. 'You should be in a circus.'

'And you should be in a madhouse,' she'd say with her crooked smile, giving Daisy an anxious moment before Cecil relieved them with his laugh.

The idyll ended when Ba, out gallivanting in her flimsy clothes, took a wetting and caught influenza. She promised to return again as soon as she was better and Daisy, who had only a month to go, agreed to wait. Without Ba to cheer her the last month was tedious beyond endurance. Her back and legs hurt. She could make nothing of her shape. She felt tired and nervous all the time. The ordinary chores of household and shopping exhausted her even by contemplation. Often Cecil would come home to find her weeping amid blackened grates, the breakfast dishes still unwashed. His mind was occupied with a new scheme. He had been in discussion with Mr W. P. Freke of Grafton Street with a view to importing Indian goods for his business of Oriental fabrics and Eastern wares. All the same he felt sorry for Daisy and asked the neighbours to keep an eye on her. 'They're good girls. They wouldn't let a bugger suffer!' This remedy proved so effective that Daisy wondered why she had not thought of it before. The women were enchanted when Cecil confided his wife's helplessness. They competed to help her with the house, to run errands or keep her company by the fire and offer advice about the baby. She was almost sorry when Cecil, very pleased with himself, announced that her troubles were at an end. 'I've got a grand girl to look after you.'

'I meant to say, I have been managing quite well since you spoke to the neighbours.'

He hushed her with a kiss. 'You're only saying that so as not to worry me. I feel ashamed of myself leaving you to struggle on. I promised you I'd look out for someone. Just wait till you see who it is!'

'You mean I know her?'

'She says so,' he laughed.

'Nellie!' she thought. 'But we haven't the money,' she remembered in disappointment.

'That's the beauty of it. This girl won't cost a farthing. She already has work, only she's got no place to live. Anyway, it's too late for argument. I told her to come straight after work, so she'll be here shortly.'

Nellie! She kept her fingers crossed. How had he found her? It was not all that surprising since Nellie was always in trouble and Cecil was always looking for someone to help. Oh, please let it be Nellie.

It was Janey.

'Aren't you going to make your sister welcome?' Cecil was shocked by Daisy's poor response. The cabby came in and filled the hall with leather cases and tapestry bags and a brace of boxes. Daisy looked from one to the other of her handsome relatives. 'Why did you lie to me?' she accused her husband. 'You said it was someone without a home. She has a better home than any of us,' she added woundingly.

'Oh, Day, for God's sake stop making a fuss and give us a drink,' Janey said. 'Cecil was telling the truth. I have nowhere to live.'

'You have a very good home and Vesty is a very good husband,' Daisy said.

Janey and Cecil exchanged glances in which there was pity for Daisy's ignorance, a gratitude for one another's understanding and a brief, amused exploration. 'I've left the oul' eejit,' she said.

Chapter 17

'NO, please, no,' she howled. 'I cannot stand it.' They peered down at her in dismay. She wanted to run away. She tried to scramble free but something held her. Someone slapped her face – no, it was a vinegar-soaked rag which had been slapped on her forehead. The brine ran down into her eyes and made her cry. When she could weep no more and merely whimpered they said she was a good girl and she basked in cowardly relief at their approval.

For a time feeling was suspended. She was inside a tunnel of grey light. Pieces of her were strewn here and there. She saw pa's face and then Bertie. 'I'm dying,' she thought. 'I don't want to go back.' As she began to be cracked and pulled apart again she remembered how she had taken Bertie's pram, had wished pa dead, and she knew she was being punished.

Imagine that I can scream this loud, she thought, and I have always been so quiet. Imagine that mama, who hated any disorder or discomfort, had gone through this ten times.

'How's my good girl?' She opened her eyes and looked at her husband foggily. A healthy pink kiss, perfumed with brandy, roused her from a black sleep. 'How are you? How's the boy? By God, it makes you feel like a man. This is the happiest day of my life. Where is the lad?'

'I don't know,' she said crossly.

'Nurse!' Cecil called. 'Bring us the boy! It is a boy, isn't it?' he checked with Daisy.

'I don't know.' An edge of anxiety crept around her voice. Unwillingly she recalled her disappointment as the nurse asked her if she wanted to hold her daughter.

She watched him unwrap his first child. Disappointment made him look innocent, like a boy who opens the bag of sweets and finds that they are wrapped moth-balls. His eyebrows contracted against the blow and he made a rueful grimace. 'Never mind.' He handed Daisy her ignominious production.

Perversely, he adored the little girl. She felt an odd quake when she saw him bent over the crib crooning into the puzzled pink face, a sense of helplessness, of loss. She put it down to the effects of childbirth – and to Janey who was still in the house.

When she had seen her cases strewn about the hall that day she thought, I can't let this happen. 'It wouldn't work, Janey,' she said quietly. She caught her husband's angry glance and her eyes filled with tears at the effort of going against him. 'Just for tonight, then.'

'Every time I try to do the decent thing!' he stormed past them out of the house, slamming the door. His complaint was muttered through clenched teeth but it caught both the women's breath. It sucked all the air from the house. It swelled and cracked with his fury. Daisy only flinched when the door crashed into its hinges. She was used to it. Soon every door in the house would have ill-fitting catches from his displays of anger.

'You poor oul' herrin'.' Janey led her towards the fire. You're your own worst enemy. You got what you wanted and still you're looking.'

'For what?' Daisy hunched over her maternal deformity. 'For trouble!' Janey thumped a cushion and propped it at her sister's back. 'I'm not!' Daisy shook her head. It was Janey who looked for trouble, fighting with mama, leaving good Vesty Muldowney, barging in where she wasn't wanted. 'What are you doing here? Why aren't you with your husband?'

The actress leaned against the mantelpiece. She looked statuesque, brooding. 'I want to live my own life. He smothered me. He's old.'

Janey was the eldest in this new ménage and she ran the house as if it belonged to her. Meals and ornaments were arranged to her liking. She did not wait to be offered hospitality but poured her own drink. She drank standing up with a hand on one hip. In the evenings she offered Cecil his liquor and he accepted just for the pleasure of watching her.

After his initial outburst he was tamed, mesmerized. He watched Janey's every move. She wore party dresses during the day and did housework in a disdainful, theatrical manner, winding gypsy scarves around her hair, moving about the chores with a faint tinkle as if bells were concealed on her person. If she had left her husband to lead her own life, then clearly this was the life she meant to conduct. She seemed content to sleep in the Indian room and smoke her cheroots and cook and keep the baby quiet. She was a good cook and made a ritual of eating. They no longer called their evening meal tea, but dinner. Janey produced strange foreign dishes. Daisy warned her that Cecil was protective of his stomach and liable to make a fuss, but he loved the spicy food which reminded him of meals he had enjoyed in India. He asked Janey to pass the recipes on to his wife but Daisy knew her hand was too timid to fling hot, earth-coloured powders over her groceries or shower a stew with nuts and raisins like a Christmas pudding. The smell of Janey's cheroots and spices and her perfume invaded the house with languor. They sat about like invalids, listening to gramophone records, tasting glasses of wine. In the evenings candles were lit. The shadows felt around their golden faces seeking the emotions under their grown-up masks – the desires, the cruelties, the fears.

When the baby was born she meant to send Janey away but Ba's influenza turned to pleurisy. She sent Cecil regularly to Edward Street to check on her progress, but he reported that she was very weak. She herself was tired and weak. And she was afraid. The little thing that had come out of her body would some day call her mother. She still wanted her own mother. Several times during her labour she had cried out for her, and afterwards thought how awful, how embarrassing, if mama had come in and found her like that. Mama did visit with Weenie after the baby was born. She examined the child and fortunately made no comment on its sex but observed: 'Well, your life is no longer your own.' This terrified Daisy. Did her life now belong to this strange little toothless creature who had caused her such pain? She was not ready yet. She had not saved herself for an infant girl, but for her husband.

The little girl was named Nan after Cecil's mother. She was a quiet, nice baby. After her first anxieties Daisy liked her. It was pleasant to have a pretty child to wheel out, to dress in dainty things. Although the child rarely cried, she preferred her when she slept. She liked to stroke the soft, translucent hair, to watch her cheeks, succulent with sleep. She enjoyed a prolonged convalescence, surrounded by flowers and greetings sent by neighbours. She rarely had to get up in the night. Janey or Cecil was always willing to see to Nan. When Janey came back from the theatre in the early hours of the morning she went straight to the nursery where she sang to the child and fed her. Cecil, too excited to sleep with his new invention producing unique noises, would pad swiftly down the landing and join Janey in spoiling the girl. Nan did not demand to be fed from the breast. She accepted her father's attention but loved only her mother. No one seemed to blame Daisy for having had a girl. 'Sure you can practise on the female,' said one neighbour. 'Then you'll have the hang of it by the time you have the boy.'

Her figure reclaimed its contours. Sometimes as she stood at the mirror weaving her plait, she caught her husband's tense eye watching her reflection. In his desire for her he looked worried, almost guilty. Of course it was too soon yet. She liked having him at this distance. She could never enjoy the act of marriage but she liked the suspense it engendered.

Nan was born in the early summer and her birth was complemented by the pleasing discovery of more life concealed in the muddy borders of the garden. Little straggling flowers loitered against the wall. The air was innocent with new-born scents. On a mild morning she sat outside, the baby beside her in a basket in the grass, and paused in her knitting of a flimsy garment to take a tray of tea from her husband. He had brought the morning's post. She took his kiss on the cheek while examining the envelope. 'I expect it is from a well-wisher.' She waited until he was gone before picking it open. This was her business. The mirror above the mantelpiece was thatched with cards. Word of birth is winged. She had messages from people she scarcely knew – from nuns, from women in the sweet factory, from old neighbours on Edward Street. There was a fullness in her new role. Mothers love the initiate to birth and Daisy enjoyed this tribal enclosure where women of delicacy acknowledge their power over men.

The letter was on lined notepaper and the writing was like a child's. 'Dear Mrs Cantwell – a member of your family is carrying on with your husband under your nose.' It was signed 'A well-wisher'.

Her first reaction was to seize the child. All the heat went out of the day. She marvelled that the baby stayed so warm while she, marble-fleshed, shuddered against it. Thoughts ran very fast in her head, including murder. She remembered pa's story of Talbot Jutton who purchased soot and arsenic, but that was for a suicide. Absurdly, she recalled pa's joke about using the arsenic to write poison-pen letters. The letter was still in her fingers. She could not let it go. The infant's submissive warmth thawed her. The tiny girl was more than good, she was acquiescent. Already she seemed to know that she was there for her mother, rather than her mother being there for her. 'I love him but I have you,' Daisy said. 'At least I have you.'

Not once did she doubt the truth of the message. She had known from the first moment of their meeting that some day Janey would try to take her husband away from her. 'What will I do? What will I do?' Her cries were hoarse against the baby's little nurturing hand. She remembered nights when both Janey and Cecil had responded to Nan's cries. She realized now that when the baby slept her sister had led him back to the Indian room and done all the things that she promised him in her letters. Perhaps she even told him about the letters. They might both have laughed at her. She could not imagine what things they had done or what she might now do. She was afraid of Janey, afraid to confront her husband too, for she would only provoke his temper and prove herself in the wrong.

Daisy had been holding Nan all morning and there were bright patches of burn on her skin when Janey got back at lunchtime. 'Do you think I should take the baby inside? She looks hot,' Janey said.

'It won't do, Janey.' Daisy had tears in her eyes. 'It just won't do.'

'Oh, for God's sake, Day!' Janey was exasperated. 'What is it this time? I don't meddle with your life. You have no right to interfere in mine.'

'How dare you say you do not interfere in my life!' Daisy held her child like a shield. The patient infant began to grizzle. Janey sighed. 'Do you think I'm a bad influence or what?'

'I think you should go.' Daisy was surprised by the bitter coldness in her voice. 'I want you to leave right now. There is no need to discuss the reason why. You know what I'm talking about.'

'No, let's talk, Daisy. It's time we had a talk. There's things you ought to know.'

Daisy shook her head fiercely. 'Please,' she said. 'Go!'

'Aw, Daisy, have a heart. I will leave. I mean to leave quite soon. But not now – please! You'll ruin everything.'

'Am I to wait until you have ruined everything for me?'

'You oul' pilgarlic! I'd never do anything to hurt you. I know I tease you sometimes, but it's no more than you deserve.'

'I don't deserve it. I want you to leave.'

Janey put out her arms to take the baby but Daisy swept her away as if she might contract a blight from her aunt. The actress allowed her arms to fall in a graceful gesture borrowed from the stage. 'Am I to go right away?'

'Cecil will want to say goodbye.' She would not look at her sister. She wished never to see her again. All the same, she was afraid to face her husband alone.

Janey's look was calm and ironic, while Cecil lamented the wilful obstruction of his charitable impulses, the heartlessness of his own wife to her homeless sister. 'You've put one young girl into the Dublin by Lamplight. Do you want your own sister out on the street as well?' Daisy's face was sunk in her hands. She was unable to argue with him. Janey put a hand on Cecil's arm. The gesture snapped his anger. His gaze lingered hungrily on the lengthy nails. 'It's all right,' she smiled. 'I won't be on the street. I'm going away.'

'Where?' They both looked up in alarm.

'I'm off to America to seek my fortune. The faces of you! How do you like that, now?'

'America?' They seemed never to have heard of such a place.

'It's the new thing. Everyone's going. They are daft for actresses now out there with the moving pictures.'

All the anger and bluster went out of him. He grew callow and unsure. He picked up his knife and fork as if he meant to proceed with his meal but instead he examined them in puzzlement and then very gently laid them down. Daisy had never seen him look so young. 'Why didn't you tell us?' he whispered.

'I was saving up. I didn't mean to go yet.'

'What will you do for money?'

'I went to see Vesty this afternoon. He'll let me have what I need. I'll pay him back when I get work.'

'Stay!' he implored. Janey looked at Daisy, who crimsonly studied her plate. 'There's no point. It's for the best.'

'We shall miss you,' he said stiffly.

'You will, you'll miss me,' she mocked. 'I had yis all spoilt.'

In the morning the hall was once more cluttered with her luggage. She hugged the baby and kissed Daisy's unreceptive cheek. 'Goodbye, herrin'. You watch that oul' savage of yours. He's got a good heart but he's maybe a bit too free with it.'

She went straight to Cobh on the train and booked into a rooming house to wait a week until the world's largest liner docked in the little port and picked up its emigrant quota. None of the family was there to see her off. Somewhere in the chill Atlantic the magnificent White Star liner, *Titanic*, broke in half, disgorging all its passengers into a lumpy broth of ice. Janey's name was not among the survivors. There was no body to bury but they held a funeral service and put her name on a stone in Glasnevin, underneath Lena's and Granny Devlin's, which was carved below pa's.

There was a curious assembly of people in the church, who seemed to have strayed into the wrong venue, for they were dressed as if for a social gathering, with velvet capes and run-down little satin shoes and plumed hats. The women wore make-up. Some of the men too had blackened in around their eyes. They addressed each other in loud voices and seemed very merry but during the service they broke into sobs and the black ran down their faces. Vesty Muldowney and Cecil Cantwell also wept. The family had a bleached and petrified air. Janey's death had taken the excitement as well as the danger out of their lives. Daisy still felt uneasy. There ought to have been a coffin. She should have been able to see for herself that Janey was subdued for all eternity.

As it was she kept thinking of the story her sister had told her when they were children, of the river in Paris that burst its banks and flooded the houses with a cemetery's festering dead. I hear tramp, tramp, tramp. And there's no one there.

The disaster affected Cecil badly. For a long time he remained morose. He did not even seem to notice that Daisy was now beautifully restored and ready to be his wife again. She might have been relieved but for the uneasy notion that his passion had been diminished by the death of its proper object. She prayed fervently, remembering to add a grudging aspiration for the repose of her sister's soul. She tried to reason with her husband. 'Janey was always in trouble. Even as a little girl. She was bound to end up in some bad way. Mama always said so.' He glared at her angrily. 'What is it?' she said in fright. 'Did you prefer her to me?'

'It was entirely different. She gave me confidence. She made me see sense. Janey was one of the few grown-up women I have ever known. I could tell her anything and not be judged. I am entirely responsible for you and Nan and yet sometimes I do not feel a man at all. I am only twenty-six.' This confidence so unnerved Daisy that she went at once to Ba and begged her to come back to help them share the burden of their marriage.

With Ba's return, the house resumed the carefree air that had been damaged by Janey's intervention. The pretence of dinner in the evening was abandoned and they did not have to blind themselves with candlelight but could enjoy the modern luxury of electricity which had come to Daisy with her house. She no longer had to attend to her husband, to lean into his moods, to alert herself to his mystifying plans. Ba took over again with her jokes and stories.

Cecil was wooed by her odd mixture of indulgence and contempt. His face softened and his colour bloomed. Daisy was too good for him, he told Ba. She was a fool to put up with him. Ba smiled her crooked smile. 'She's a fool right enough and I'm an oul' eejit. Nan's the only one around here with a bit of sense.' Daisy picked up the amiable baby and the infant, delighted to placate, coughed up a little laugh. They were safe again. They were once more as they had been, a golden unit, blessed by providence.

As Nan progressed from infant to child, Cecil grew more remote and responsible. He loved Daisy but he did not trouble her very much any more. The apprehension of his nightly onslaughts became a memory of unsure youth. Now she was a matron, serene and respected. Once a month or so, he looked at her with yearning appeal and she looked away from him and removed her garments and her mind while he relieved himself of his necessity.

The thing that astonished Daisy was that Janey had predicted this change. Years ago, when she seduced him with her loathsome letters, she had promised that his interest in such matters would not sustain itself much beyond family life. How did she know? Often afterwards Daisy wished she could have talked to her about the peculiar workings of men's minds, but then she thought that perhaps Janey knew more than was good for her. The girl was dead and all her unusual knowledge had not saved her.

While Daisy and Cecil celebrated their successful domesticity, a family on their street was hacked to death by the man they called husband and father. As far as everyone knew, Dessie Dolan was a quiet, ordinary man, a merchant seaman whose occupation accounted for his long absences from home. It now emerged that the man was the inmate of a lunatic asylum, released on experimental weekends. Up and down the quiet street families hid and fed their secrets and now and then these escaped and gave shocking glimpses of themselves; a respectable dentist had a fondness for little girls, a drunk man pushed his small son in the fire, a widow was battered by her grown-up son. Daisy came to wonder if the street where she lived was especially afflicted by tragedy or if families everywhere were united for the purpose of concealment. She asked her mother, who unnervingly declared: 'Those houses were built on a field of blood. It was the scene of a terrible massacre.'

Sometimes it seemed to Daisy that it was not just her terrace but the whole city that seethed with a barely contained violence. Some vital structure had been undermined. Great Britain Street had changed its name to Parnell Street, after the Home Ruler who died in disgrace following his scandalous marriage. The streets were full of angry, aimless men. Demented-looking women from the workhouse, scrawny from hunger, yet brawny with their occupation of breaking rocks, wheeled dog-carts from door to door seeking slops and left-overs with which the destitute were fed. Unemployed mobs broke into battle and the constabulary subdued them with batons. Listless children hung about in doorways. A massive strike of Dublin workers had been organized by the labour leader Jim Larkin and as the employers hardened and consolidated, families starved and sold off blankets and even beds, and the poor of the city turned into a despairing rabble.

With nothing to do and the pram for protection, Daisy often visited mama and Weenie in Edward Street. It amazed her now to think that she had spent her childhood here in the shadow of the orphanage. In her youth, of course, there had been the drawing room. Mama had never attempted to replace it although her shop afforded her a reasonable living. In spite of the poor living conditions in the city, people still bought buckskin communion boots for their children. Boys of thirteen going to England to look for work were brought by their mothers for stout men's footwear to grow into. This mortifying procedure was borne with a stoic abjection that would serve them well in poorly paid jobs. Wedding shoes and dance shoes were yielded up, years after they had ceased to have any useful function, when a shilling became more tempting than memory. The shop was not attended by anyone. Mama had fitted a bell on a spring and when this alarm sounded she would softly muse, 'Whom shall it be? Beauty or the beast?' Unless she was occupied with housework, Weenie would eagerly respond, for she loved the excitement of having someone to talk to and there was always the hope that it would be a man who would fall in love with her and marry her and take her away from mama. She was equally pleased to see Daisy. She adored Nan. 'Come on along, me oul' segocia,' she'd say, bringing the child into the kitchen to find something sugary for them both to eat. She still dreamed of having children of her own. She was a strange-looking little woman, plump and hopeful, with her long fleece of hair, in which there were now some threads of grey, almost hiding her face. No lover came but customers were glad to see her because she was touched by their stories of hardship or romance and often gave a penny off. Mama was not moved by poor people who scraped halfpennies together to make a necessary purchase or parted with the shoes of a dead husband to pay for the next meal. Fairness, she said, was more than sentiment, and she had never burdened anyone with tales of her luck.

Daisy enjoyed other solitary excursions. She had renewed her old romantic liking for the church and did complicated vigils such as the Novena of the Seven Churches. Arduous worship stilled any prickings of guilt she might have felt at leaving the housework to Ba. All her domestic devotion went into her drawing room, which was her pride and her pleasure. Although there were good rooms up and down the street, they were chilly, unused chambers, uncomfortable to sit in. Daisy's front room was always fresh with nice chintz and pieces of lace.

One day as she returned to her pleasant house her nose puckered upon a reek of poverty. It was from the drawing room. She paused in the hall, afraid that catastrophe might somehow have seeped underneath her door guards, and then she seized her courage and stepped on to her forest of rugs.

'Good day to you, ma'am,' said the vagrant, the tramp, the reeking horror who had been sleeping at full length with his boots upon the sofa and now blearily roused himself to greet her in her own parlour.

'What are you doing here? How did you get in?' she demanded. The smell of his body came through the smell of his clothes. His eyes were bloodshot and a trail of black tobacco juice wandered along the whiskers on his chin. 'Your good man offered me the loan of his key. He said you would give me a bite of dinner.' His tone was querulous now, for he had expected the same rejoicing welcome from the wife as from the man.

'Go down to the kitchen.' Daisy spoke slowly as she wrestled with her dilemma. 'We have eaten dinner but I will get you some bread and cheese.'

'He told me to wait here!' The beggar possessively poked the sofa with a scaly finger. 'He promised me me dinner.'

Daisy took a little silver coin from her purse, grateful for the opportunity to bargain. 'Here! You may go out and buy yourself some dinner.' He took the money and examined it with contempt. 'Where am I going to get me dinner for a bob in the year of 1914?'

'There is a very good shilling fish dinner at Jacob's Temperance Hotel.' She said this pointedly, for she knew he would spend the money on drink. When he saw that he could get no more from her, he departed. Daisy flung open all the windows and congratulated herself on having come to grips with her husband's inconsiderate charity, but the tramp returned in the afternoon, drunk and hungry. 'I am under orders from your husband,' he said belligerently. 'He told me to wait. He said he had something for me.'

Cecil was overjoyed at his subject's loyalty. 'This is a most unusual man,' he told Daisy delightedly. 'I trusted him with my key. He could have made off with all my furniture.'

'I am glad you viewed the situation in all its possibilities,' said Daisy ironically, but Cecil was too pleased to notice. To her embarrassment, he had brought home a friend, an ordinary well-dressed man who might hold her responsible for the invading stench and the occupation of her fireside by a vagabond. She apologized but Cecil said there was no need as his friend, Mr Harvey Critchley, was a man of the world, being a photographer by trade, and that he was here for the express purpose of immortalizing the image of the pauper.

'Take him outside,' Daisy said eagerly, 'while there is still light.'

'He is to be photographed in the drawing room,' Cecil insisted. 'That is vital to my plan.'

The plan was revealed over tea, an uncomfortable meal in which their stretched provisions were rendered surplus by the discouraging aura of squalor. Daisy begged her husband to make the mendicant wash before they sat down but Cecil would only allow him to rinse his hands. It was important, he said, for them all to be familiar with the picture before as well as after. While Ba made signals of comic horror at her sister, Cecil explained that he had found Mr Heffo Lynam languishing in the gutter with the dregs of a bottle of tonic wine and had instantly been blessed by two inspirations. The first was that the man was about the same age as himself and but for the grace of God might have been himself. The second was that even the meanest of circumstances could be reversed by the dispensation of rational alms. 'Rational alms!' he enunciated gravely, pinning them all with his bright blue gaze. It was his intention, he announced, to rehabilitate Mr Lynam into society. 'After this meal Heffo Lynam begins his new life. He will bathe, shave and wash his hair. He will be equipped with a suit of clothes. In the morning he will visit a barber and then he will take lunch at the Shelbourne Hotel.'

By rational alms Cecil meant that although this transformation would improve the lot of a misfortunate, it would also benefit himself. His plan was to make of Mr Lynam a celebrated case. His photographs before and after his improvement would be published in the papers under an advertisement bearing the headline 'Clothes maketh the man!'. Cecil Cantwell revealed his scheme to open a men's clothing store when the case had been proved. If all went according to plan, Mr Lynam would be employed as a clerk in his emporium. 'He is as good as any other man and by noon tomorrow will be seen to be so.'

Watching Mr Lynam imbibing tea from his saucer and eating with his fingers they had doubts to endure, but Cecil patiently instructed his subject in table manners and encouraged him to join in their conversations. 'Dat shaggin' melt tinks I'm rot!' Heffo pointed angrily at Daisy. He belched loudly and added, 'I'm blotto.' Cecil congratulated him on this effort but suggested that a touch of dissimulation was in order for small talk. He might, for example, discuss the weather or items of interest from the newspaper. Mr Lynam, who could not read and had hitherto only employed the newspaper for eating his dinner from, or for keeping out the rain, nevertheless had interests of his own to preserve. 'Give me a "for example"?' he challenged. Cecil read out from the newspaper that the Archduke Francis Ferdinand had been murdered at Sarajevo in Bosnia. They were flabbergasted, not by the crime, but by the hopeless unworldliness of the man upon whom all their fates depended, to imagine that such an incident could have anything to do with ordinary people's lives.

By noon the following day, Heffo Lynam, washed, coiffed and looking surprisingly dashing in a new suit of clothes with patent boots, a hard hat and cane, absconded with twenty pounds of Cecil Cantwell's money in cash. He was the first of many cases of charity, rational and otherwise, whom Daisy would have to endure in her drawing room. It was useless to protest. She burned sulphur flowers, which tarnished her brasses, to get rid of their smell and wiped all surfaces with Jeye's Perfect Purifier, but it grieved her to see both her room and her husband so unworthily absorbed while the family was left to fend for itself.

Ba was almost killed in an incident that came to be known as the Bachelor's Walk Massacre. She was feeling unwell and had gone to see the doctor. Coming back to M'Birney's along Bachelor's Walk she was caught in a hail of gunfire. A troop of the King's Own Scottish Borderers, maddened by the hot summer and unnerved by a blackguard called Erskine Childers, who was running guns to start a revolution, ran amok with their rifles upon an unnerving mob of ragged unemployed. Four people were killed and thirty-seven injured. Ba got home alive, badly shocked and bleeding, not from gunshot but from a wound sustained in the ensuing stampede. Daisy put her to bed and bandaged her cuts but some deeper injury had been inflicted by the shocking sights she had witnessed. A different sort of illness clung to her. She grew gaunt and sullen and would not return to work or resume her household duties. 'Wouldn't it give you the pip,' she said bitterly, 'I'd have to be the one to survive.'

'Thank God for that,' Daisy said. 'We all love you.'

'If you only knew me,' Ba sighed. 'I can't stay here any more. I have to leave.'

Daisy sent Cecil in to talk sense to her but all his attention was for his beggars. When he came out of her room he looked upset but only nodded. 'Yes, she means to leave. She is determined about it. It is probably for the best under the circumstances.'

'What circumstances? She is unwell. Why can't she stay here with us?'

'I don't know.' He looked haunted. 'A change of air, perhaps, will do her good. Leave it be, Daisy. She has made up her mind.'

She went to England to stay with Beth. Her going, as Daisy predicted, took the warmth from the house, and all its comfort too. She had to do the housework on her own and her pleasure in motherhood was thinned by confrontation with its numerous utilities. Cecil, baffled by the sudden lowering of his own mood, diverted his hospitable energies into a diligent campaign of conjugality. After a month of this misery, the whole world erupted into war.

Chapter 18

WHEN war broke out mama took to her bed. Both her boys were gone to fight. 'I have nothing left to live for,' she said, 'nothing but girls.' She erected a large screen around her bed and commenced an occupation that was to absorb the rest of her life, of covering its surface with coloured pictures cut from greeting cards; flowers and little animals and, oddly, little girls. It was strange to walk behind this festive concealment and find her there, an ageing beauty, mad with rage.

Cecil Cantwell was like a child at a sweet-shop window. He longed to put on his uniform again, to get away from his responsibilities, to be a boy among boys and a hero among men. Daisy would not let him go. She said she could not be left alone with a child in a city full of savages. To ease his patriotic conscience he crammed the house with paupers. Every time she stepped into one of her rooms Daisy had to brave the insolent stare of starvation. She could sympathize with her husband's good nature but she could not commend his lack of sense. He gave these wretches his best port and whiskey and entertained them in the drawing room. Her dining room was turned into a soup kitchen for hordes of sly-faced urchins who scrapped over bread while skeletal slatterns unpeeled layer upon layer of filthy rags to produce at table a shrivelled breast for a shrivelled baby. She pointed out that Nan could catch vermin or cholera from their malnourished guests and that she could not be expected to cater single-handed for the city's destitute. 'These are difficult times,' he said. 'We must all make sacrifices.'

She went to mama to ask for Weenie. 'So! He has filled the house with the scum of the city.' Mama sat up in bed to take in this good news. 'He has brought you down to his own level.'

'He is making an effort because of the war,' Daisy argued weakly. 'We must all make sacrifices. 'Let me borrow Weenie until I get some other help.'

'Weenie is here to look after me and to run the shop,' mama said. 'God knows, I did not get much out of ten children. I am left with the fool to look after me. However, she can do nothing about that and nor can I. Heaven made her a fool but you have made a fool of yourself.'

Daisy thought she could have borne the tedium of extra work, the endless peeling potatoes and making pots of stew, if only Cecil had been cheerful and more kind. His depression was not a listless vapour but a volcanic eruption of reddened embers with little spurts of flame. He was lost without Ba to laugh at his humours. The gentleman's suiting emporium had failed. All those who might have had their lives visibly transformed by a suit of clothing were away in Flanders covered in mud. Those who remained were either toffs in military uniform or poor buggers with neither the price of, nor ambition for, a shave.

For the working-class men of Dublin the war represented a favourable turn of fortune. Jim Larkin's strike had been defeated by an employers' lock-out of 25,000 men. Pawn shops fattened on the contents of poor tenement homes. The war represented adventure, money and escape. There was no conscription in Ireland, but half a million men queued up to enlist – one eighth of a population that was mainly made up of children. Forty-nine thousand were to die.

Cecil Cantwell had to close down his outfitting shop. He took a job behind the counter of a cigar store in College Green. Unable to alter the world or come to terms with it, he tracked down the flaws to his own surroundings. 'Why are you not wearing a corset?' he accused his wife one morning as she was making her toilet. 'Why do you never wear a corset? All decent women wear a corset.' Daisy hastily finished her dressing and began to busy herself with her plaits. It was pointless to explain to him that she was not in need of stays. He knew perfectly well that beneath her childish clothes she was as slim as any child. To tell the plain truth, which was that she never wore anything uncomfortable, would have displayed a lack of diplomatic hypocrisy that would have driven him mad with rage. Instead she sought some alibi to placate him, concentrating on her hair until both plaits were woven tight as baskets. He watched her all this time, his arms held tautly to his side, waiting to see what species of excuse would fly from her mouth, and would he have to strike it down. 'Stays are unhealthy,' she said.

'Who says so?' he belligerently demanded.

'The National Health Society. They have published a tract denouncing the constraint of women's clothing. It was in the paper.'

'When? What did it say?' She breathed a sigh of relief as the glare faded from his eyes and interest overtook anger. There had been some such item. She remembered glancing at it as she put the paper away in the brass-bound box where old newsprint was kept for twisting into firelighters. The dissertation praised the construction of the female form, lamenting that this admirable arrangement was 'pinched, squeezed, cribbed, cabined and confined so that the complicated internal organs, which are so wonderfully constructed and so marvellously fitted to their work, are interfered with and pushed out of place. Can it be any wonder that so many women become nervous and hysterical and that trouble and disease are their portion?' Daisy read this out to him as he ate his egg in a fervent silence. For Cecil Cantwell it was pure romance. When she had finished he took the paper and read it out himself. 'How to be Strong and Beautiful!' he repeated the title with admiration. Occasionally he treated his wife to a warning extract.

That evening, when his mendicants had been fed and were tensely crammed into the drawing room, for sometimes there was a sup of porter and sometimes there was not, Cecil recited the remarkable thesis to the entire gathering. 'Women are too much given to pinching themselves up in stays. The stupidity and the wickedness of this custom it is scarcely possible to exaggerate. It not only ruins the health of those who practise it, but it throws a burden upon the next generation and weakens the race.' He gave a searching glance around his assembly, which that evening included an alcoholic man, three exhausted women and their children. It was true that the new generation in this gathering looked feeble, but it was a reasonable bet that none of the ladies present was in stays. 'The heart, lungs and liver cannot possibly act properly if they are deprived of the room which was given to them by Nature,' he rebuked, 'and this is one reason why there is so much indigestion, constipation and flatulence amongst women. Yet, though tight lacing is so harmful, its effect is not lovely. It is the cause of pimples on the face, of a red nose, of faintings, hysteria and nervousness. It produces red blotches in all sorts of unexpected places, and is one of the greatest mistakes ever invented by ignorance.'

Cecil interpreted the eagerness of his audience as approval, although in truth most of them were eager to go on ruining their liver and complexions with something other than stays and it was the prospect of this that kept them alert. 'Stupidity and wickedness!' he repeated. 'And what is to be done about it?'

'Ah, what indeed, sir?' echoed the lazy-minded drunk whose name was Hawkins and who was hoping to encourage a sociable atmosphere.

'On the one hand, to wear a corset is injurious to health, but to wear none is to cast doubt on a woman's respectable status. While the men are away fighting for a better world, women too must maintain a standard. I intend to make it my business that our heroes should return to find their women strong, beautiful and healthily restrained.' He glared at them expectantly. 'Fair play!' growled Hawkins, and he bullied the others into a round of applause. Cecil smiled and nodded happily. 'Thank you. Yes! I have a plan.' Impelled by goodwill he went at once to open the whiskey and signalled Daisy to get the glasses. The paupers brought their drinks to their mouths with such speed as if to quench a fire. 'No!' Cecil said. 'A moment, please! We are to drink a toast.' They held out their emptied glasses and he had to replenish them. 'A toast!' he repeated solemnly.

'To your health, sir!'

'God preserve and keep you!'

'To female fat!' said Hawkins happily. 'Long may it roll!'

'No, friends, no,' Cecil said gently, for he was always kind to his charity cases. 'We are to drink a toast to the Cantwell Corset.'

Cecil set up his factory the following day, employing the three home-less women who were growing addicted to his whiskey. At first he established himself in the drawing room, but when Daisy objected very strongly to this he moved his operation to the Indian room. He bought a white dress-making form and a medical manual and marked out in ink on the figure the position of the human organs – heart, liver, lungs, stomach, uterus. He wanted to ensure that his garment would confine no vital functioning parts. Daisy was sent out to purchase examples of the corsets on the market, from Sparrow's three-and-elevenpenny grey, to their extra strong at half a crown, from Thomson's five-and-elevenpenny Graciosa right up to the Paris corsetry in Switzers costing several guineas. Being the only woman in the household with a figure, she was made to try these on and report on any symptoms of suffering. She also had to perform a number of exercises to see if specific restraints would make her faint or go red in the face. With her arms held over her head, or her body suffocatingly bent to pick up a pin, she attempted to argue that the sort of women who wore such items of torture liked to suffer for fashion and would have no faith in a comfortable corset. He smiled remotely upon her protests and went on with his work. He was happy once more now that he had a mission. All adverse effects were written down on the dress-making form in the specific portion where suffering arose, along with the type and make of stays. The garment was then dissected to identify its punishing aspect. Different fabrics, surgical and fashionable, were purchased, as well as ribbon, lacings and the bones of fishes. Daisy was not involved in the practical construction, for he wanted to surprise her. Instead she was to instruct his poor women in the use of the sewing machine. She did as she was told, although their fingers were not deft nor their concentration excellent. For the last week he locked them into the room for fear of espionage or insobriety, but late at night Daisy could hear loud song, laughter and profanity coming from the factory where they slept on the floor with their children.

When the first Cantwell Corset was completed Daisy was summoned to the Indian room. The state of the place was indescribable. In among Cecil's ferocious swords and skins were heaps of fabric cuttings, piles of unwashed clothing and even dirty cups and dishes. Against this unappetizing background stood a poor woman wearing what looked like a horse's feeding bag suspended from her scrawny shoulders by its harness.

'My God!' Daisy breathed.

'It is a unique garment and quite remarkable,' Cecil agreed. 'As you will see from the replica here, the area of the stomach and kidneys are protected by a lining of alpaca wool.

'Where is the support?' said Daisy. 'How is the figure to be defined?'

'A good question,' he congratulated. 'Josie, come here!' His bedraggled model slouched forward and Cecil took hold of a piece of lacing which hung loose around her waistline. He pulled it hard. At once a drawstring waist appeared and the garment billowed out on its upper and lower portions. The shapeless wretch now seemed to be swollen with unimaginable deformities.

'My God!' Daisy said again.

'I believe that I have revolutionized women's fashion,' proclaimed her husband with satisfaction. 'As you have remarked, dear, certain women seem intent on emphasizing their figures. My corset will be the first-ever convertible model. For modest females, desiring merely to be respectably and warmly covered, the Cantwell will be worn in its original version. To those who wish to advertise their charms, this garment enhances their curves without imposing any pressure.' He seemed not to notice Daisy's shocked expression. 'Do you really mean to go into production with this . . . thing?'

'I have rented a small factory in North Earl Street. We shall be in production within a week.'

'Then we are ruined,' Daisy said faintly.

While she struggled without any help in the house, her husband's staff expanded. The machinists now numbered six and there was a receptionist and sales representative. He took extra mortgage on the house and purchased an expensive cash-register and had a telephone installed. He began to entertain, taking the buyers and fitters from the big stores to lunch in Jammet's or the Dolphin. She knew she had no hope of talking sense into him. She wrote to Beth in London, begging her to contact Ba and send her back to them as soon as possible. She herself had had no word from Ba, except a postcard without any address shortly after her departure. Beth wrote back to say that Ba was doing volunteer nursing with the Red Cross and had asked her to say that she had neither the time to write nor the time to come home.

She appealed to Will, who was fighting somewhere in France. She knew it might be months before he could reply, but it gave her comfort to pour out her heart about her hard life with her foolish, difficult, charitable husband. Within six weeks their money had run out. The sales representative, exhausted and demoralized, had not managed to obtain a single order. Cecil refused to relinquish his dream. He announced his plan to borrow again and to move to a more modest address until they were properly on their feet. 'No!' Daisy protested. 'You cannot take my house away from me. My drawing room!'

'I am an innovator,' he said. 'Men like me were born to change the world. You and Nan mean everything to me but you must not stand in my way.' She felt sorry for him. She believed that he had pushed himself beyond the bounds of reality in order to avoid despair. All the same she could not forgive him. 'The family must come first,' she insisted. So great was her relief when he announced his intention to let go his premises in North Earl Street that she did not immediately absorb the rest of his announcement.

'It is only for the time being,' he apologized as he installed his six machinists, together with their equipment, his fabric stores, his cash-register, dress-making form and receptionist in the dining and draw-ing rooms of their house, with the dividing doors opened out.

'Oh, no!' Daisy begged. 'You must not do this.'

'I think we should remove the sofa and anything breakable to the bedroom,' Cecil advised. 'We shall be very crowded in here.'

'No, oh, please no!' Daisy tried to pull her husband away as he nailed to the front gate a small sign for Cantwell Corsets Ltd.

She retreated to her bedroom and sat on her exiled sofa waiting for the neighbours to complain or for the business to turn them into bankrupts. She could tell from her husband's bright fervour that things were going badly. 'Our world is collapsing,' she confided to her little daughter who had grown into a watchful child of three. Nan studied the bedroom ceiling for cracks and listened to the whine of machinery that drilled its way up through the bedroom floor. She observed uneasily the snow of fluff that drifted up through the house from sheared materials. Beyond their walls, unnoticed by them and of no concern to them, the passenger liner *Lusitania* was torpedoed off the Old Head of Kinsale and 1,198 were drowned, including Sir Hugh Lane who had earlier that year bequeathed to the nation his thirty-nine magnificent French Impressionist paintings. Patrick Pearse and the Irish Volunteers began to plan an armed insurrection against the ruling English government and the whole of Western Europe from Belgium to Switzerland split open into a muddy, blood-soaked gash of trench warfare.

If Daisy thought about the war at all it was because certain foods were in short supply, but even this she ascribed to the extra mouths in her house to feed rather than any external crisis. When Will's letter came at last, she felt a brief resentment of his free and adventur-ous life which mama had facilitated with her savings. She was sorry at once for she saw that he had sent her a present from France. The gift, well wrapped in tissue and protected inside a leather tobacco pouch, was flat and smooth and had the satisfying heaviness of an egg. An enamelled locket, she guessed, but when she unwrapped it she was puzzled to discover that he had sent her something of his own. It was pa's gold watch.

'My little Daisy,' he wrote, 'remember when you used to ask me about things, and I would say, "I'll tell you tomorrow." You always looked so confused when you came back the next day and I told you, "But this is today, I said I'd tell you tomorrow." Only now, twenty-four years later, have I finally resolved that riddle for myself.

'There is no tomorrow. Nothing is more precious than the day in which we live, that is ours to influence, to experience, to spend. I am in a place where a beautiful golden wine is made that explodes in the mouth. This quiet, sunny country town has been turned into a queer sort of permanent hellish night. The sun is blacked out by smoke and the smell is like the Liberties' market with the rotting flesh of dead and living men. Yet even here life is irresistible. Poppies glow out of ditches. Men who are dying grieve to part from life as from the dearest wife or lover.

'Most of the time when we are not fighting we talk about the happy times we had in our lives. Remember the day Janey took us to see *The Waves* – our first moving picture? I was sixteen and I thought my chest would burst with excitement. Then there was the day we all went to the sea and the morning Tom and I bought the Centaur. I realize now that they were the times when we seized a moment and made it ours. Now I am going to take control of my life again. Tonight I mean to go into town with some of my men and drink Champagne. With luck I also hope to go to bed with a girl. Imagine, I am thirty-seven and I have never done more than kiss a girl. I thought it wrong to do so when I had not given any girl my name and yet for the past six months I have been killing men without ever knowing anything about them. I have also decided to send you pa's watch. I do not want it stolen from my corpse by the enemy and I cannot send it to mama because she once made me take it to the pawn. But there is another reason. I used to look at pa's watch when I was a boy and think that the time contained in it was a different and more leisurely time to that on the school clock. But it was only that it was pa's time – pa, who always had time to make each of us feel his favourite. Every time I find you, you are forlorn as a little girl still waiting for tomorrow, but you have a family of your own, you wake each day to the lovely sights and sounds of Dublin. You have life, unlimited in its stretch and prospect. I want you to feel the power of your life, to live each day for me who can only now say how wonderful it all was.'

'Oh, Will,' she breathed. 'You are dead.' She could not bear to open the watch but put it around her neck on its chain. Nan watched the golden disc on her mother's breast with anxiety for she thought it must be very heavy to weigh her down so.

Daisy went to see Sister Cecil. She told her of her fears for Will, of her husband's failure to provide for the family. The nun's imperturbability was both reassuring and disturbing. 'Perhaps your brother is not dead at all,' she commented placidly. 'And if he is, you may be sure he will look after you in heaven. Now what about this corset, Daisy dear? How could one set of stays be much worse than another since they are all such awful garments?'

Daisy reluctantly described the shapeless horror with its lining of alpaca wool. She hated to be disloyal.

'It sounds comfortable,' Sister Cecil reflected. 'It is thoughtful of him to defend the organs against the elements.'

'Yes, but what woman does not care more about her figure than her comfort? Who would wear a corset for health alone, regardless of the fact that it detracted from her shape rather than defining it?'

'Nuns,' Sister Cecil observed, 'would scarcely be swayed by vanity. Convents are very draughty places.'

The matter was put out of Daisy's mind by the arrival of Weenie at her door, bawling, with the telegram in her hand. Will had been killed in action. It was almost a relief. Now she could cry. She could let her husband put his arms around her. Now she could demand that Beth and Ba come home at once.

The news of Will's death affected mama so badly that she would not get out of bed for the funeral. 'I have been killed,' she said. 'All that is dear in life has been taken away from me.'

'There is Tom,' Weenie encouraged, knowing better than to mention the good health of four of her daughters. 'Tom is still alive.' But Tom was in a hospital in Ypres, suffering from wounds, and mama could not believe he would ever return.

Ba came back from London with a little boy called Jack. She was Mrs Pemberton and a war widow. She had met Ernest Pemberton in a café shortly after she arrived in London. Three weeks later he was called up. They got married before he went away. She never saw him again, but she had his son, a pretty baby with Ernest's bright-blue eyes and Ba's fair hair. She was her old self, stoic and ironic. 'I don't think I'll try for romance again.' She gave her wry grin. 'I seem to have a bad effect on men.' Cecil hugged her fervently and told her she was a brave girl. 'No, I'm not.' She pushed him away lightly. 'I hardly knew the man at all. I probably had a lucky escape.' He was shocked by this and Daisy had to point out that it was only Ba's way. She never allowed anyone to know her true feelings. It was a disappointment to Daisy that she could not bring Ba and her baby home with her, but there was no room in the house and soon there would be no house. Ba went back to Edward Street with Beth. She was meek in the company of this older sister who had grown into an imposing woman with her own London fashion salon, Madame Elizabeth. She had a house in Knightsbridge filled with little white dogs. She said she kept in regular touch with Essie through a medium.

On the day after the funeral the four girls took the tram to Howth and slowly walked up the hill. They sat on a grassy bank and Daisy showed Will's letter to Weenie and Beth and Ba. 'He was lucky,' Beth said softly. 'Right to the end, even out there, he held on to his dreams.'

'He should not have died so young,' Daisy protested. 'It was mama's fault for sending him into the army.'

'Will had a lovely life in the army,' Beth said. 'I knew him well in London. He took me to parties when he wasn't in love with some girl. He lived a gentleman's life. Mama did what was right for him. I wonder if any of us know how much we owe mama?'

'How can you say that?' Daisy burst out. 'Will is dead. Essie is dead. If it wasn't for mama, you and Essie could have been together all your lives.'

Beth sighed. 'Poor Essie was always delicate. I would have welcomed the chance to look after her but she would not have lived very long anyway. I like my life. I am content. Will was very good to me and so were mama's relations, the Woods, but most of what I am I owe to mama. We all do. She gave us a sense of style.'

'Mrs Cohen once said that about mama,' Daisy remembered with surprise. 'The Jewish money-lender! She said, "Your mama has something money can't buy – she has style."'

'Yes, and you have it too,' Beth said. 'It is not just a matter of fashion, it is a matter of character and faith in one's own self. You too, Ba! It is a kind of glamour. It saves us all from ever getting ground down.'

'What about me?' Weenie said. 'What have I got?'

Beth put an affectionate arm about her plump and wistful sister. 'You have a great gift for someone if only they could see it. You have sentiment.'

Among the many letters of sympathy was a note from Sister Cecil and an invitation to tea in the convent parlour. Cecil was pleased by this. He approved of nuns and liked to be reminded of Daisy's convent life. Unlike most men who are wary of those women that eschew marriage in favour of God, he found a special appeal in the innocence of women, as in children. 'I shall bring along an example of the Cantwell,' he decided. 'I should like to hear the good ladies' opinion of my design.'

'Oh, no!' Daisy was mortified. 'You are a man. You cannot possibly demonstrate a corset to the nuns.'

'I see nothing to be ashamed of.' He pinned her in the sapphire beam of his gaze until she was ashamed of herself. 'There is no unfit motive here. Modesty is a million miles from prudery.'

The nuns took immediately to Cecil, discovering in him, as Daisy had once done, something of the picture they had given themselves of Christ – the flaming cheeks and radiant hair; the blue eyes burning with inner fire. Whether because of this or through a genuine practicality, the reverend mother placed an order for a Cantwell Corset for each of her sisters. Cecil promised a large charitable donation to the convent and in return the superior granted him the small favour of a testimonial. Armed with this he tackled all the convents of the country, unsettling scores of communities with his charm and his undergarment. He moved his operation to a new, expanding part of the city's suburbs called Sullivan's Cross where a small neighbourhood nestled amid green fields and hills. At last the house was cleared of machines and derelicts. Daisy went to bring Ba back home.

She was worried that Cecil would not wish to bring up another man's child with his own, but in fact he was delighted. He loved children and especially infants and Ba's bright, golden-haired baby was presently more enchanting than his daughter. Nan was a pleasant little girl but she had none of her parents' more dramatic features, rather a dilution of both, having the unfortunate combination of mousy blonde hair and a sallowish skin.

They passed a happy summer. Cecil was in good humour, exhilarated with the reversal of his commercial fortunes and the excitement of having a baby in the house once again. He worshipped little Jack and even got up in the night if he heard him crying. Ba had given up work to look after her son, and she and Daisy spent their days in the garden. Once or twice Daisy suffered a small unworthy stab of jealousy as she watched the boy. He was a blaze of fairness and she felt that the halo of maternal privilege that had once been hers had shifted a little towards her sister. Without meaning to, she sometimes stole from the peace of the moment by a sharpish word or a briskness with her good little daughter.

Nan tried to compensate by being useful. Climbing on a chair, she filled a kettle at the sink and then she moved the chair to place the kettle on the stove. She used the best china, balancing the teapot on the edge of the burner to warm, as Auntie Ba did with the old enamel pot, and measuring in the spoons of tea. As she picked up the seething kettle, the china pot made a tiny crackle as if it meant to hatch something out. Nan peered down and the teapot exploded. Pieces of flowery china sprang apart from the shabby rubble of dead leaves on its base. The surprise of this and fear of her mother's anger at the broken porcelain made her drop the kettle.

When her mother and her aunt ran in she could see from their white faces that what she had done was unforgiveable. They put her away in a strange place, in a large room filled with beds with other children who were being punished. They wrapped her up in bandages and beneath these her skin burned and burned as in the first moment when the kettle fell.

For a long time her mother did not come to see her. 'She cannot stand to see you suffer,' father explained, littering the bed with armloads of presents. 'She feels responsible.' Nan tried to explain that it was her fault, it was she who had dropped the good teapot, but her father shook his head sadly.

'I want Mags,' the little girl whispered.

'You are not to call her Mags.' Her father looked pained. 'She is your mother. You are to call her mother.'

It was ages before her mother came to see her. To Nan's dismay she burst into tears. 'It is my fault,' she said. 'If you are marked I shall never forgive myself.' She sat by the bed and took her little daughter carefully in her arms. 'I have a surprise.' She brought out Uncle Will's watch and opened the case. 'What would you like best in the world?'

Watching the gilded bayonet of the minute hand slice through seconds that were soft with the luxury of her mother's closeness. Nan could think of nothing more than this to want. 'Make a wish,' her mother coaxed. 'Wish for something that would end all foolishness and loneliness and jealousy.'

'That you loved me,' Nan silently wished.

'I have done what your Uncle Will wanted me to do. I have taken control of my life. Nan, my little helper, we need no longer feel that we are second best to Aunt Ba and her dear little Jack. I am going to have another baby.'

Chapter 19

JANEY came home with a new husband and a monkey on a lead. The dismay of her return from the dead would have been enough without these supplementary surprises, and there were more.

Weenie, unable to speak for fright and admiration, led the revenant up to mama and ushered her in behind the screen with its massed collage of human-faced animals and kitten-faced children.

'Janey!' It wasn't a glad cry.

'Eugenia, mama. Eugenia Dubois! That is how I prefer to be addressed.' Janey's deep voice was beautifully accentless. She wore a long cloak of claret-coloured velvet and a big-brimmed hat with lolloping plumes of feather. She said that she was the wife of a banker and asked if there might be an apple for her marmoset, Theodore Roosevelt.

Weenie lurked in the doorway, sprung like a cat with nerves and curiosity. When mama called her she fled from the room, for the imperious summons came out more like a cry for help. 'Weenie! Get Daisy!'

'Janey is back! Janey is back!' Daisy and Ba found Weenie on the doorstep in a state. It was impossible to get any sense out of her. They disturbed Cecil from his tea, bundled up baby Jack and squandered sixpence on a carriage back to Edward Street. When they came into the boot shop there was a man there, trying to control a small monkey with a scalded-looking rump. The animal darted as far as its lead would permit, chewing on leather tongues of shoes, pulling out bootlaces and gnawing on trims and buckles. 'Did you wish to buy a pair of boots?' Ba said. The impeccably dressed visitor looked in dismay at the millipede phalanx. 'I want my wife,' he said. 'I want Eugenia.'

The shop was now all but defunct – a museum or graveyard. In the years of the war it had killed itself by overdose. Women brought in the boots of dead husbands and did not care what they put on their own widowed feet. Dublin Castle had been given over to the Red Cross as a hospital. Unease teased Hiram Wallace's bladder.

The jumble of boots and little dainty ladies' shoes made him think of a massacre. He expected to see false teeth and the golden rims of spectacles poking through. He craved the reassuring hygiene of a bathroom. When the haunted-looking party led him up the stairs he peered around hopefully but he could only see two tiny overstuffed bedrooms and one of these absurdly partitioned by a screen.

'Eugenia!' He called out when the familiar plumes of his wife's hat came into view. She did not emerge from the screen but slowly drew it back like a stage curtain so that Cecil and Ba and Daisy could be amazed.

'Janey!' Cecil's face lit up with pleasure and seemed at once to have robbed all the colour from Daisy's. Mama looked furiously from one to the other of her visitors as if any of them might easily have saved her this distress. 'Why must it be she who comes back from the dead and not my beloved Will?' she complained.

'How come a flower like you grew up in a dump like this?' Hiram Wallace uttered in amazement to his wife.

Janey had not, after all, travelled to America on the *Titanic*. While awaiting its arrival she met a man called Phelim Geraghty in the picture-house in Cobh. They grew fond of each other, and by the time the huge liner lay crouched in the small seaside basin they did not want to be parted. Later, when she was sick of him, she travelled to America on a different liner, paying her passage by entertaining the passengers. Hiram Wallace boasted of her success on the New York stage and added with pride that he had had to send her two dozen roses every day for a month before she would even speak to him. They had married six weeks ago and were now on a honeymoon tour.

'When do you go back?' Daisy asked at once.

'Hiram wants to have a look around,' Janey said. 'He is interested in Ireland. We may settle down here.'

'Where will you stay?' Weenie wondered. 'Will you come and stay with us here in Edward Street?' Mama and Mr Wallace caught each other's eye with equal looks of consternation and Janey said, 'We are presently staying in the Gresham but we are getting tired of hotel life.'

'You can't stay with us,' Daisy said quickly. 'Ba is living with us now, and her little boy.'

'Ba is living with you?' Janey seemed more than surprised. She appeared dismayed. 'What little boy?'

'Ba has been married in England and is a widow,' Daisy told her. 'Her husband was killed in the war. We both of us have children now. The baby is Ba's little boy, Jack. We are all living together very happily.'

'Why did you let this happen?' Janey absurdly accused Cecil. Instead of speaking up for himself he looked guilty and abashed. 'She had nowhere to go. She is part of the family.' Janey took the baby from her sister's arms and studied it critically. 'One big happy family,' she murmured. She raised an eyebrow and handed back the child.

'Yes! That is exactly what we are,' Daisy cried angrily. 'I am expecting another child. We have all been so happy. Oh, Janey, why do you always have to turn up and spoil everything?'

'Daisy!' Cecil was shocked. 'This is a day of celebration. How can you spoil it with your petty spites and jealousies? Janey, please forgive us. We are all so very glad to see you.' Unable to restrain himself he stumbled forwards and took her in his arms. He held on tightly as he kissed her. 'Oh Janey, I am so glad to see you!' Hiram Wallace and his marmoset looked on helplessly while Ba and Janey speechlessly looked away.

In spite of this awkward beginning Cecil got on well with Hiram Wallace and the newly-weds were frequent visitors to his house. Cecil could not speak of business matters to Daisy. She made him feel it was vulgar. Ba was easier to talk to but her teasing manner defied solemnity. Janey had a mind like a man when it came to matters of opportunism and her eyes glowed with eagerness as he spoke of his venture. Hiram watched his wife adoringly and the monkey laid havoc to the fruit bowl and singed its mean little tail in the flame of candles.

Cecil confided to Janey that orders had dropped off since he had equipped all the convents in the country with his corset. 'Then it is time to alter your design,' she said very firmly. He shook his head. 'Great effort has gone into the architecture of the Cantwell. I cannot be a party to the destruction of the female form.'

'Not all societies are as backward as ours,' Janey ventured diplomatically. 'In Paris there are undergarments fashioned to enhance the female body without constricting it. They are made from very soft fabrics such as silk and crêpe de Chine which permit the skin to breathe but are quite draughtproof. They are trimmed with real lace and ribbons of silk or satin.'

175

'Who on earth would go to such trouble with clothes that can never be seen?' said Daisy. 'What are they for?'

'They are for looking at.' Janey smiled mischievously. 'By husbands, of course,' she laughed at their uneasy faces and put a hand on Hiram's knee. 'I assume a husband may have the pleasure of watching his wife undress. This scheme is more practical than it sounds for a housewife can wear a durable wool dress which will not suffer in the streets while her finery is protected underneath.' When they still looked unconvinced, she added: 'Besides, the woman who wears fancy attire out of doors is in danger of attracting the attention of strange men, whereas a modest woman may wear pretty undergarments and appeal to no one but her husband.'

Only her sisters noticed her ironic tone. Hiram regarded her fondly and Cecil with a growing eagerness. 'Look, just suppose there is some sense in what you say, how is a poor bugger like me supposed to design such garments? What do they look like? I couldn't even begin to imagine,' he said wistfully.

'I'll show you,' Janey said slyly.

'No! What are you saying?' Daisy tried to save the hour as she felt the floor beneath her feet grow insubstantial.

'All my undergarments come from Paris. Hiram buys them for me. Don't you, darling?' The use of the term of endearment made them even more uncomfortable. None of the married people they knew made affectionate demonstrations in public. Daisy took advantage of this. 'If these undergarments are, as you say, for your husband's appreciation, then it would be shameful to show them to another woman's husband.' Janey laughed at her. 'Now, aren't you the bad-minded oul' herrin?' Just for a moment her accent skidded back. 'I'm not going to model them. I'm only going to give yis a peek.'

'Oh, do!' Ba begged to Daisy's dismay.

A great heap of the garments fitted into a tiny valise. Daisy had never seen anything so flimsy. There were bloomers, chemises and little waistbands of frills with no other practical function than to support hosiery. Each item seemed to have some deep cut or panel of transparent lace designed to show off the very portion it was meant to cover. Daisy felt doubly mocked. If she had stayed a nun, she thought, she would never have had to acquaint herself with such a side of life. If she were not pregnant, she could have worn these absurd little scraps of fabric to woo her husband away from Janey. Cecil was fingering the items with as much reverence as if they were altar cloths. 'I did not even know such stuff existed,' he marvelled. 'It is softer than skin. Imagine if the volunteers were to come home to such softness. What a welcome that would be for our heroes back from the war. By God, if it wasn't for the war' – he turned on Janey eyes aflame with every sort of passion – 'you and I would go to Paris in the morning and start buying up fabrics.'

Daisy turned despairingly to Ba, but Ba was raptly sifting the flimsy trappings through her fingers. 'How gorgeous,' she sighed. 'Oh, how utterly gorgeous.'

It was not bad enough that Janey should have snared Cecil into her scheme, she even involved Daisy and Ba. After a brief tour of inspection of the factory she declared that the women were not equipped for fine work. Daisy and Ba were to do the hand-stitching, and the rough work could be left to the machinists. She insisted that their number be reduced to three and that the plain-looking receptionist should be replaced by a pretty young girl with a good figure, who could in emergencies model the garments. Daisy protested that she was tired and that Nan needed her at the hospital, but Janey brushed these arguments aside and said the stitching would take her mind off her sickness and was the perfect pursuit for a hospital visitor. Cecil was fuelled by zeal and even Ba was caught up in the excitement. When a small range of sample garments had been copied from Janey's own wardrobe, she took them to show to potential clients. Cecil wanted to go with her but to Daisy's relief she declared that he would only be a hindrance. She returned from her travels triumphantly promising to sell as many garments as they could produce. She had brought a bottle of champagne to celebrate. 'To our new venture, the Cantwell Cancan,' she proposed.

'The Cancan?' Cecil was mystified.

'It is a version of the ballet that has taken Paris by storm. I have decided it is to be the name of our range.'

'To the Cancan!' Cecil solemnly toasted Janey. How splendid they looked together, his fairness and her darkness. All the rest of the assembly, even down to the monkey and the children, looked drab by comparison. Daisy tasted the strange, dangerously fizzing fluid and at once burst into tears. 'What is the matter?' They looked at her with concern and irritation. 'Oh, Will,' she sobbed miserably, thinking that her best-loved brother had died in the place where this odd wine was made, that its teasing bitterness had been his last taste of life and that there was no one left who would help her now.

★

The Cantwell Cancan range enjoyed a mysterious fad – mysterious because in spite of its undoubted success neither Cecil nor Daisy could ever actually encounter a woman who owned one. Cecil bought a motor car and talked of servants and a larger house. New workers were brought into the factory and Daisy and Ba were relieved of the endless stitching. Hiram Wallace was astonished at such good fortune in time of war. 'You men know nothing of human nature,' Janey teased. 'I am surprised that you can ever make any progress in commerce. It is in time of war that people are drawn to that which is frivolous and appealing. It takes their mind off the tragedies of the world.'

To take their own mind off the tragedies of the world Cecil planned an expedition to the seaside resort of Kingstown at Easter in the new motor. Easter Sunday morning was spent at the hospital with Nan, who was recovering well and eager to come home and meet her Aunt Janey's strange pet. The afternoon was passed quietly with mama. She had grown very thin and her mind had begun to ramble. 'I'm afraid I have no time to see you now,' she said. 'I am busy with my children and there are so many of them. The maid will see you out.' She signalled Weenie to perform this ejection and went back to playing with her dolls. When Weenie stood mesmerized as a hen, mama grew impatient. 'That girl is such a dolt she makes me want to vomit. There is no good help to be had nowadays. I believe it is because of the war.' At the mention of the war a cruel lucidity peeled back her fantasy and her face twisted in agony. 'Will! Oh, my Will,' she moaned. She slept a while and when she woke she was relieved of painful awareness. As Weenie passed around cups of tea mama whispered, 'These creatures have not the morals of a hound. Look at the shape of her. I will give you a florin she is *enceinte*.'

Monday morning had a delicate, flower-like quality. A breeze as thin as gauze swept in the salty smell of sea. A small frenzy of bird-song was flung like confetti over cathedral spires and military installations and homes for the destitute. For once the din of commerce – of wheels and hooves and ships and factory horns and motor horns – was stilled by the bank holiday's manufacturing truce. All over the city children were scrubbed and stuffed into uncomfortable frocks or breeches for a coach outing to Lucan or Howth or the Strawberry Beds. Families saved all year for this expedition, which would constitute their annual holiday.

Cecil Cantwell was up at dawn, tensely directing operations and

178

telling his household that the little fledgeling sun, which struggled through a sleepy pillow of sky, would scorch their eyeballs. Ba and Jack were willing recipients of this deception. The baby, with his finely honed instinct for the unexpected, had been unable to sleep. Tense, bleary and speechless with excitement, he was being bullied by Ba into a show of eating breakfast. Cecil, as usual, had dined heartily and was out of doors polishing his motor with a queue of urchins looking enviously on. Only Daisy was still in bed. She felt nervous and unwell. She would have let them go without her but for the worry of exposing her husband to Janey's charms under the liberating influence of the sea air.

'Imagine!' Ba buttoned Jack into a stiff cambric frock with scratchy lace at its cuffs. 'We are to have lunch at the Gresham Hotel with Aunt Janey and Mr Wallace. Only millionaires go there. The knives and forks are made of pure silver. When I was your age we were lucky to get a herring between the ten of us for a treat.'

She left the baby looking starched and mystified and went to rouse Daisy with a cup of tea. 'You'd better get up,' she urged. 'We have to be at the Gresham at twelve and we've to pick up Weenie first. Oh, isn't it grand, Day? It's so long since we had a family outing. Picture us, swanking out in a motor car. I am told Kingstown is lovely. There is a glass pavilion and pleasure-boats.'

'I only wish it was less of a family outing.' Daisy drank her tea. 'Oh, Ba, you have always been so kind to me but Janey will not stop persecuting me until one of us is dead.' She gave a deep sigh, remembering how recently she had been robbed of this reassuring certainty.

'I suppose she'll bring the blasted monkey,' Ba said spitefully. 'Still, if it wasn't for her and her queer notions of underwear, we'd never have a motor car at all – and we certainly wouldn't be going to lunch in the Gresham. Don't let it get you down. We are so often apart, this must be an Easter none of us will ever forget.'

The day opened out beautifully. Driving in the warm air with the wind rustling her hat, Daisy's spirits rose. Everyone was out to enjoy the leisurely day – families with picnics and soldiers walking their girls. People admired the well-dressed occupants of the motor. Cecil was splendid in a navy blazer and straw boater. They rescued Weenie from dark Edward Street and sailed down Summerhill towards Parnell Street and the Gresham.

Midway through luncheon Daisy's good humour began to wane.

The heat of the dining room and the confusion in her head caused by several glasses of wine made her feel unwell. 'I wish we could be out of doors,' she said. 'It is so noisy in here. I wish the hammering would stop.' Her companions interrupted their cheerful conversation to look at her oddly. At other tables polite groups spoke in whispers. The service was so discreet that one never heard the union of spoon and dish. 'What are you on about, you mad oul' herrin'?' Janey said.

'Wait!' Hiram Wallace motioned silence to his wife. 'I hear it too. Hammering, some kind of hammering! No, hang on. Sounds darn like gunfire to me.'

'They are shooting the chicken for our main course,' Ba said merrily. Now that they paid attention they noticed an unease among the serving staff, a whispered communication and occasional glimpses out the window. A dull repetitive clacking brought Cecil to his feet. 'Good God! That is very like machine-gun fire! It sounds as if the city is under siege.'

'Do you suppose the Germans have invaded?' Hiram's eyes were wide with awe.

'Let's go home,' Daisy pleaded.

'We men must make a sortie to see if the coast is clear. We shall take the motor. You ladies are to finish your lunch in peace.' Cecil was clearly enchanted by the prospect of any sort of action. Hiram went less willingly, having understood from the start that a city where washing was at such small premium must always exist on the edge of anarchy.

'They've gone and left us,' Janey said indignantly. 'There's chivalry! Peace and safety, how are you? Come on, girls, let's find out what's going on. It's probably only a few old drunken bowsies taking pot-shots at each other after breaking their Lenten fast.'

'Do you think it's soldiers?' Weenie said wistfully. 'Oh, let's go and see!'

'We should do as we were told.' Daisy looked hopefully at Ba, but Ba's eyes were alight with the prospect of adventure. 'You stay! You ought not take any risks in your condition. Look after the baby for us and Janey and Weenie and I will go and have a gander.'

A waitress brought dishes of chicken and Daisy stared miserably at the plates. With Janey's and Cecil's appetites for adventure there was no telling when either expedition party would return. The rich-looking food made her feel ill. She wanted to lie down but had to keep alert for little Jack. She could sense the waitress's disapproval on her back. 'Well, are you goin' to eat it or did yis only want the satisfaction of seein' the poor brutes die?'

'I don't know when my companions will return. You may take the plates away,' Daisy listlessly waved her hand.

'Would it be more of a sin, do you think,' the waitress reflected as she gathered up the dishes, 'to throw this good food in the bin or to put it in a little bag and take it home to feed me childher?'

Daisy shrugged. 'I see no harm in putting it to good use.'

'That's not what I'm axing. Naturally I'll take it. Only I have been something of an expert on the nature of depravity since the age of ten and I am always in search of clarification on matters concerning me immortal soul and me station in life.'

'All of this is of very little interest to me,' Daisy said coldly. 'At this moment,' she murmured to herself, 'I would trade my immortal soul for a cigarette and a bed to lie on.'

'Wouldn't we all?' The menial emitted a wild cackle which startled Daisy out of her self-pity and made her look around. 'Nellie!' she gasped in great relief.

Chapter 20

THE three sisters had barely set foot in Sackville Street when they got the scent of disaster. There was a smell of cordite in the air and just beyond Nelson's Pillar two horses lay dead. A dirty and bedraggled old woman sat astride one of the animals, swaying drunkenly and singing, 'Boys in khaki, boys in blue, here's the best of jolly good luck to you!'

As they passed the pillar the dainty squeak and crunch of glass beneath their feet enhanced the sense of hazard. Groups of people stood silently around. 'My God!' cried Weenie. 'The GPO! It's in flitters!' Windows were broken and sacks of mail had been hauled about the front of the General Post Office, which was surrounded by a makeshift barricade of barbed wire. There seemed to be a great deal of formless activity. Women pedalled bicycles gingerly across a glittering rubble of glass. Men in uniform and raw youths clambered in and out of broken windows. It reminded Janey of an amateur theatrical production. 'What is happening?' She tugged at the sleeve of a man passing by. 'Has there been an accident?'

'Haven't you heard? The Shinners have taken the city. They have declared themselves a provisional government. Look there at the base of the pillar – a notice proclaiming Ireland a republic!'

'Imagine a day when you could not buy a stamp in the post office!' said a bowler-hatted man in disgust. 'Those boyos, the Volunteers, have killed two Lancers and their beautiful beasts. They want to rule the country, no less.' The easygoing Dubliners had no great desire for independence. They wanted to enjoy their Easter Monday. Janey looked up at the nervous young men on the roof of the post office and the childish flag they had posted there – green and white and orange, like ice-cream and jelly at a children's party. 'They do not look as if they could rule a straight line,' she pronounced. 'It will all be over in half an hour.'

'They have the whole of Dublin under siege,' said someone else, but the shooting had such an improvised look that none of them imagined that hundreds of troops would be injured and killed on that sunny day.

Ba and Weenie were made nervous by the sounds of gunfire. The women crossed over Carlisle Bridge, saluted by shooting from the Four Courts to their right and Liberty Hall to their left. Janey was fearless. 'You're all right as long as you're with me,' she laughed. 'I clearly have nine lives and I have only used up one of them.' Janey was not out for a walk. The others knew that. She was looking for adventure.

All the rest of the Easter parade had now vanished from the street. People lurked in doorways or peered out of windows. 'Let's go back,' Weenie pleaded when they heard guns in Grafton Street, but Janey simply diverted them into Dawson Street. As they drew near to Stephen's Green they heard the whipcrack sound of rifle fire. Groups of men and women and children stood gaping at the railed area of lawn and pond bequeathed to the city by the benevolent Guinness family. The gates were closed and there were men inside with guns on their shoulders. Surrounding houses had had their windows broken and in the centre of the pleasure garden was a barricade of carts and motor cars. Two men with bayonets rushed out of the green and halted a passing motorist. The man and women were ordered to dismount and the car was taken from them and driven, very inexpertly, into the park to reinforce the barricade. A boy with a revolver ran up and down the street. His face was full of fear and rage. Weenie felt sorry for him. He only looked about fifteen. 'What is the matter with you?' she asked him. His eyes were so blank with panic that he seemed scarcely able to focus. 'We are expecting the military at any moment and these people' – with his rifle he indicated the gawking onlookers – 'they won't go home for me.'

'They are sending in the forces,' Weenie squealed as if they were all deaf. 'We have to go back.'

'Yes, yes,' Janey said. 'But I trust they will not lay siege to the Shelbourne Hotel. Let us get a cup of tea. I am parched with so much excitement.'

In the doorway of the Shelbourne they found Cecil and Hiram, very much dismayed. 'What are you girls doing in the street?' Hiram said. 'There is a revolution going on. We thought you were safely back in the Gresham.'

'The Gresham is no more safe than the Shelbourne,' Ba reasoned. 'In any case, what are you two doing here, hanging about like a pair of lounge lizards when you should be racing back to rescue us?'

The men looked gloomy, almost tearful. 'These blackguards have taken my motor to use for their barricade,' Cecil said. 'I shall never see it again.'

An eerie silence had descended as they walked back through Grafton Street. All the expensive stores were exposed to the sunny afternoon through shattered shop fronts. The display models seemed petrified in their new spring fashions. The whole street was paved with glass. Suddenly from lanes and alleys a ragged mob crept out with carts and orange boxes. Silently they began to raid the broken windows. They stole ravenously and indiscriminately, umbrellas, and furs, sweets and fruit, sporting goods, cakes, cigars. Great bunches of bananas were pulled over the broken glass on lengths of rope. Women stood with their skirts held out to catch loot thrown from upper windows. One such accomplice, lowering treasure from an upper storey, was shot in the head by an unseen sniper and fell dead into the street among piles of oranges in winking wrappers of red and silver foil. The crowd silently scurried away until the corpse was picked up and thrown in a cart, and then the looters swarmed back.

In Sackville Street the scenes of plunder were even more audacious. A woman stripped naked in an overturned tram to try on her stolen wardrobe. Some curious inhibition restrained the looters from raiding shops that were not yet damaged and a group of shawlies kept lugubrious patrol outside the pristine window of Clery's with its minks and silks and cashmeres. 'Is Clery's not broke yet?' they lamented. 'Isn't it a great shame that Clery's isn't broke?' From the ruined post office, high-minded rebels urged decent behaviour and fired shots above the pillagers' heads in an effort to maintain order. The decent Dubliners hurled back foul abuse at the patriots and continued with their industrious self-service.

When the exhausted party got back to the Gresham they found Daisy asleep in a seat in the lounge. 'Oh, my poor Mags,' Cecil cried in relief at seeing her. 'Have you been very frightened here all alone? We should not have left you on your own.' Then, realizing that she was indeed alone, he shook her harshly wide awake. 'Mags! Where is Jack?'

Daisy opened her eyes sleepily and gave a wide smile. 'He is with Nellie. We have been very well looked after by my friend Nellie.'

In the middle of a week of shelling and machine-gun and rifle assault, Sackville Street caught fire. It started when a shell hit the Cable Boot Shop, but although that blaze was soon extinguished it set off an epidemic of combustion. On Thursday, first the Metropole Hotel and then the Imperial Hotel sprouted exotic orange blooms under the impact of exploding shells. This spread to Hopkins and Hopkins the jewellers, and smouldering vagrants fled from the inferno, their rags spilling diamonds. Hoyte's the oil works caught fire. Hundreds of oil drums rose into the air and exploded in a blaze of white. The GPO itself was now in flames. The conflagration spread to the beautiful Linen Hall in Henry Street. Across the road a riding school was fired and the cries of burning horses rose with the snap of flames and the crack of gunfire. Blazing horses ran through the streets and troops with megaphones began to clear buildings from Clery's down to the Liffey. All over the city and far out into the suburbs people could see the sinister sight of Nelson's Pillar jerkily animated by a leaping inferno of orange light.

On Friday night Janey arrived with Hiram and Theodore Roosevelt and a very great quantity of luggage. 'I am sorry, Daisy. We went to Edward Street but mama would not let us stay. We can no longer remain in Sackville Street and with so many buildings gone there is not a room to be had in the city.'

Daisy kept the door at an inhospitable angle until Cecil eagerly ushered them in.

Sometime one night she woke. She thought she heard a noise. When she listened there was only silence, so she tried to get back to sleep but alarm was underneath her skin. She felt haunted. She heard it again — a low howl like a banshee. The banshee meant a death. If anything should happen to her little boy! This time it must be a boy. She wished Cecil were there to reassure her but he had moved to the Indian room to let her get some rest, for he talked and ground his teeth in his sleep.

She laughed at herself. She did not believe in ghosts. The sound carved across her smile. It was louder, more protesting. More demanding. She crept out of bed clutching her heavy breasts to stop her heart from leaping out of her body. She had stopped breathing but still little grunts were forced from her mouth as she felt her way along the landing in the dark. Outside the Indian room she paused. The sound came again, but muffled, as if through a scarf. And then she heard a man's voice, a whisper: 'Be quiet, my love. You must be quiet. She will hear.'

★

Hiram Wallace had gone home. After a week of watching the city smoulder he had braved the ruined streets reeking of rotting horses to book a passage from Mr Thomas Cook. He did so stealthily, shrewdly assessing that Janey might be difficult to persuade. When he presented the tickets she refused to leave. 'I have unfinished business here,' she said.

'You're my wife, Eugenia honey,' he pleaded. 'We're on our honeymoon.'

'Stay then,' she shrugged. 'Keep me company.'

Miserably, he declined. Daisy wanted to shake him but she could see that he was as much worn out by his awe of his wife as by dread of the seething city. He took the monkey with him when he left – a bitter frustration for Nan when she was released from hospital shortly afterwards. She was disconcerted too by her mother's lack of response after her long absence. They had been proud of her in the hospital when they took off her bandages and all her scars were gone. She had imagined this would please her mother too, but mother was in an agitated state and seemed scarcely to notice her return. It was some consolation to have two spoiling aunts in the house. They took her for a trip into town and she was astonished to see that it was not just she who had been burnt, but the whole of the city.

To Daisy's dismay Janey would not go home. She told the married couple that she meant to take care of them until the baby was born and the business properly on its feet.

'And I suppose I don't look after them?' Ba made a rare display of bitterness.

'The trouble is, you don't know where to draw the line,' the older sister coolly replied.

Janey was still there in the autumn when the baby began its painful exit. A nursing home had been booked but Daisy refused to go. She would not leave her husband alone with Janey. 'I want to have my baby here,' she said.

'All the arrangements have been made,' Cecil tried to argue. 'There is no provision here for a midwife.'

'Ba can help,' she said grimly. 'I will not leave.' The birth was very bad. Daisy begged Cecil to leave the house and he took Nan into town to see an organ-grinder with a monkey, but Nan was frightened by the miserable little animal. Afterwards they went to a picture-house and ate ice-creams in a café. By the time they returned the baby had been born. It was a boy, fair and blue-eyed, who had

186

lodged awkwardly inside his mother and emerged with the umbilicus tightly wrapped around his neck. He was dead.

Cecil tried to comfort her but she would not be consoled. 'You have no son,' she mourned. 'I could not even give you a son.'

'I have, I have. It's all right,' he lied helplessly.

For weeks she could not face the world. She gulped down sleeping draughts whenever awareness threatened. Day after day she flung herself into a black pit of nightmares that were a kindness compared with her real disappointment. There was nothing she wanted. Ba had to spoon food into her. It seemed as if life could hold no more interest for her, yet one day she woke to a small, grim ambition. 'Janey!' she said. 'I want to see Janey.' She wanted to tell Janey that she had killed her son. She had to make Cecil see it too. Then she could tell her to leave.

Cecil seemed dismayed by her request. He shook his head.

'I want to see Janey.'

'I am sorry, my dear,' he sighed, 'but Janey is not here. She has gone.'

'Gone?' For a moment she felt let down. 'Janey?'

Cecil struck the bed-post with his fist. 'Don't mention that woman's name again!' Cautiously she raised her head from the pillow. 'To think I trusted her!' he scowled. 'She has made a monkey out of me.' Surprise brought a small transfusion to Daisy's veins. 'She has made a monkey of all of us. I dare say she has even made a monkey of her unfortunate monkey. What has she done to you?'

He took Daisy's hand in his. 'You are a decent woman. You do not know the ways of the world.'

'What did she do?' Curiosity, that greatest of human tonics, strengthened an elbow to support her.

'One of her so-called customers called at the factory to place an order. My dear, how can I put this? It was a bawd. She had come with a man who was to sponsor her extravagance. She was dressed indecently and her language was coarse. She insisted that all her friends were in possession of my product and that the Cancan had improved their business even more than my own. My corsetry has not been bought by any ladies. It has been selling exclusively to prostitutes and chorus girls!'

'I don't suppose Janey can be held responsible for your customers.' It was amusement more than fairness that led her to pursue this argument.

'She is directly responsible!' He spoke with vehemence. 'It was she who promoted my merchandise. She would not permit me to go with her. Oh, she knew very well what she was up to.' He sighed and the anger went out of him. He looked forlorn. 'She did not have to go! She deceived me and it was hard to forgive but I would have done if she had shown any remorse. She called me a fool. She said it was time to go back to her husband who was a real man, able to face the facts of life.' He looked abject. 'She said to tell you that whatever has passed between you, she has always loved you.'

For a moment Daisy was tempted to be moved by Janey's speech, but then she thought, she is an actress. When she realized she might never see her again, she could only feel relief.

When next they saw Weenie she was covered in bruises. 'Come quickly,' she begged. 'Mama has got very strange. She is attacking me.' Daisy and Ba and Cecil went with her to Edward Street. Mama was sitting up in bed with her hair tied into bunches with two large ribbon bows. She had grown even thinner but her eyes were very bright and young. She took no notice when Daisy and Ba came around her screen but when Cecil appeared her face lit up and she put out her arms. 'Papa!' she said in a plaintive little voice.

Cecil stepped back as if he had been struck. He fetched Weenie, who was hiding behind the screen. 'This poor creature is black and blue,' he said. 'You must tell us what has passed between you.'

Mama stuck out her lower lip. 'Ada took my doll and I had to punish her. Oh, she is a loathly girl!' She put her head to one side and smiled very coyly at Daisy's husband. 'Have you brought me a present?'

'Mention, Tom,' Ba whispered to Cecil. 'Tell her he is coming home soon. That will surely bring her back to her senses.'

'Your son, Tom,' Cecil spoke loudly and slowly. 'He has been hurt in the war, but he is coming home. Don't you want to see him?'

Mama watched him foxily. 'I do not like boys. I do not like girls either. Most of all I do not like sisters. I only like my papa and I like him best when he has brought me a present.' Cecil reeled out of the stuffy little enclosure. 'She has gone quite mad!'

'Come back, papa!' mama said in a voice that swelled with tantrum. 'If you do not come back you will be sorry.'

'What will you do?' Ba pondered with amusement.

'I shall die!' mama yelled.

She did this with passionate resolve, clamping her jaws furiously, refusing to admit a crumb of food or even a drop of liquid. From time to time her lips parted a fraction but only to call for her papa. Cecil could not be persuaded to enter her eccentric world. When the doctor came and tried to force some nourishment she bit his hand to the bone. She was taken to a private ladies' lunatic asylum in Glasnevin and numbers of the staff were left clawed and bleeding before they finally abandoned her to her ambition.

Weenie, who had been blamed all her life for everything by mama, now blamed herself for her mother's death. 'She didn't know who I was. She wouldn't eat for me. She thought I was trying to poison her.'

'You devoted your life to her,' Daisy said. 'No one could have been kinder.'

'It was not kindness,' Weenie slowly shook her head. 'I was afraid.'

When the funeral was over they brought Weenie back to Edward Street. She did not go into the house but sat behind the counter of the boot shop and wept bitterly. 'You are free now,' her sisters tried to comfort her. 'You can't be sorry. Mama was never nice to you.' Weenie mopped at her tears. 'I'll never be free. This house is full of her. Everything I do, she will be watching me.' The sight of the little hunched figure weeping into her skirt amid the beetling plague of boots was more than they could bear. 'Come home with us,' the sisters said.

This did not please Cecil. He enjoyed sharing his home with the beautiful sisters or with the ugliest strangers but did not wish to be reminded that a graceless little woman was related to his wife. Besides, Weenie's arrival meant that the house was full once more. Already he was regretting his row with Janey and hoped that she might return. If his business gave him ready access to fallen women, he retrospectively reasoned, then it placed him in a perfect position to reform them.

'What hypocrites men are,' Daisy said angrily to Ba.

Ba laughed at her. 'They all want women to be good, but only so good that no other man can get at them except themselves.'

To Cecil's added irritation Weenie's gratitude took the form of devotion. She pursued him with refreshments, put coal on his fire, settled cushions at his back. 'I have not a minute's peace to myself,' he grumbled at Daisy. 'I am afraid to go to sleep in case I find her in my bed.' Daisy, who had lived in mortal dread of Janey's intrusion in her husband's bed, only smiled at this. 'Then you should come back to my bed, for we would scarcely, all three of us, fit.'

'Oh no, my dear,' he said gently. 'You must not mind me. You know I want to but it is far too soon yet. The doctor said you must have rest.'

It was only peaceful for a while. Weenie brought Cecil his breakfast in bed. When she tried to enter his room he leaped from his bed and pushed the door with such violence that he knocked over both bearer and breakfast. 'Why can't you leave me alone?' He stood on the landing in his pyjamas while she sat on the floor covered in tea and egg and bits of broken porcelain. 'I can no longer call my house my own. No wonder you got on your poor mother's nerves, for you have no more discretion than a fly on the wall.'

Weenie ran off and shut herself in her room. Daisy and Ba tried to coax her out but she only answered them once through her sobs. 'He is right. Mama was right. No one could love me, I am ugly and stupid and useless.'

She came down in the evening and let herself out into a cold, wet winter night. When she had not come back by ten o'clock they began to be worried. She had no money of her own, nor any friends. 'Perhaps she has gone back to Edward Street,' Daisy said. 'She never really felt at home here.'

'We'll have to go and see,' Ba decided. 'Weenie isn't capable of looking after herself.'

'It is not convenient without a car,' Cecil complained, as though the comandeering of his motor had been Weenie's fault. 'It is the very devil to get a hackney at this hour of night.'

It was near eleven when the two women arrived at Edward Street. They had left Cecil at home to mind the baby. The curtains were drawn on the little red house and there was a lamp lit inside. 'She is here,' Daisy said in relief. Out of habit and curiosity the two sisters peered in the window before knocking on the door. The cab driver watched their backs stiffen with surprise. The little room had been cleared of boots. Gone were the dusty shelves and misted mirrors. There was a square of cheap linoleum on the floor and this was anchored by a scant few pieces of furniture. A fire burned merrily in the grate. Over the fireplace a picture of the Virgin Mary spread her hands upon an array of homely souvenirs – mugs and photographs and plates painted with mottoes.

'There is a strange family in our house!' Having been robbed of speech for the duration of their witness, the women exploded with indignant chat when they got back to Cecil. 'The boot shop is gone. They have set up house as bold as you like. A man was prodding the fire with a poker and a woman sat knitting in a chair.'

'There were three small children playing with marbles on the floor!'

'What shall we do?' Daisy demanded. 'These people have just walked in and carry on as if they own the place.'

'I dare say it is as much theirs as it was yours.' Cecil confounded them with his calm. 'The house was rented to your mother. It is two months since she passed away and the house has not been occupied by any of you, nor any rent paid. It is not surprising that the landlord has hired it out to new tenants.' In spite of their shock it was a while before they realized the full significance of the loss of 11 Edward Street. Now Weenie was homeless and Ba had no home except her sister's.

Weenie did not return that night. They thought of calling the police but Daisy hated the notion of a scandal in the neighbourhood. She had gone missing overnight before after arguments with mama. 'We think that when she feels unloved she goes into public houses and makes up to strange men,' Daisy told Cecil.

In the morning she was brought back by two policemen. She had been found unconscious on the banks of the canal. She was wet from head to foot and could not stop shivering. 'Where have you been? Have you been with some strange blackguard?' Cecil was incensed. Weenie gave him a devoted smile before she was convulsed with a series of sneezes. 'For God's sake, what does it matter where she's been?' Ba was exasperated. 'Can't you see she's half dead with cold. Get her a drink of whiskey and I'll put her to bed.'

As soon as they had warmed her up with blankets and hot-water bottles she began to burn with a fever. Ba and Daisy sat with her, giving her little sips of hot fluid and cooling her forehead with damp cloths. After a few days she seemed worse. Her skin was bright pink and lacquered with perspiration and her breathing sounded hoarse. The doctor diagnosed pneumonia. For three weeks the fever raged and then at last she grew calm. 'She is getting better,' Ba said to Daisy in relief. But she was strangely inert. Her eyes had a clouded look and she did not want to eat. Daisy came and sat at her bed. 'That night,' Weenie whispered, 'I have to tell you . . .'

'No, my dear,' Daisy squeezed her hand. 'There is nothing you need to say. You have had a very hard life. No matter what you did, God will forgive you.'

'I must tell you before I die.' Daisy had to read her lips, for no more sound came. 'That night, when I left here, I stayed on the canal bank just as I used to do when I went out at night from Edward Street. I know mama thought I was with men but I was all alone. Perhaps I would have been with men but they never seemed to care for me.' After that she slept most of the time and the two sisters stayed by her bed. Once she woke, with her eyes open very wide. 'I am afraid to die,' she said. There seemed no further point in argument. 'You must not be afraid,' Daisy tried to comfort her. 'If you die you will go to heaven.' Weenie began to weep. 'I don't want to go to heaven if mama is there,' she cried.

Tom came home from the war. He had brought with him a young soldier friend, Archie Foster. They were all very pleased to see him. Cecil at once donated the Indian room to the visitors and returned to his wife. Tom was missing an arm and wore a beard to hide the scars on his face. He had gone away a young man. Now he looked old, but he was still their Tom, gentle and full of jokes. He was taking care of the soldier, who had suffered with shell shock. He told them that the loss of an arm was a great advantage, for he had taken to painting with the remaining limb and now called himself an artist.

When Archie was presented to the family he looked as blank as if his name meant no more to him than to them. 'He has lost his memory,' Tom explained. 'Perhaps it is a blessing,' Daisy said as Tom recalled the things they had seen and endured in the war, but Archie seemed to have concentrated all the horrors of his experience into a single nightmare. He scarcely spoke and frequently burst into tears. 'My fiancée has died,' he wept. 'She had such beautiful hair.'

Tom was a gentle and helpful guest, and self-sufficient in spite of his injuries. He played with the baby, painting cartoon pictures for him, and in the evenings held Cecil enthralled with his stories of bloody campaigns. Daisy and Ba hoped that his presence might restore Weenie but she seemed beyond recovery. In the end they sent Archie to sit with her, for he was frightened by their talk and laughter. That evening when he came down to tea he was smiling. Unused to speech, he stuttered: 'She is not dead!'

'Of course not,' Daisy said, alarmed. 'Weenie is very ill but thank God she is not dead.'

'My fiancée.' Archie smiled in triumph. 'You must all come and meet her.' They had to follow him back up the stairs to where Weenie crouched among her pillows, smiling weakly. 'Isn't he gorgeous?' she sighed and blissfully closed her eyes.

When she had regained a little of her strength, Archie helped her downstairs. In the light of a winter sun her hair sizzled around her. During the weeks in bed with scarcely any food she had grown thin. Her green eyes were huge. 'Look at her hair!' Archie demanded. 'Isn't she a beauty?' Even Cecil agreed that she was.

In due course Archie Foster found out that he was a book-keeper and had lodgings in Islington. He did not care that Weenie was his senior by almost a decade, for he had grown shy of life and wanted a mother as well as a wife. Weenie put on weight again soon after their marriage but theirs was an impervious union. They had a stout infant called Prudence and were so overcome with tenderness that they began a campaign against the use of corporal punishment for children. Once they visited Daisy in Dublin. Daisy thought she had never seen any two people so close since Essie and Beth were little girls. Their own small daughter, Prudence, sat inviolate beneath the table and bit the legs of the adults.

When Nellie lost her job in the Gresham she came to Daisy, and Daisy wordlessly and without deference to her husband absorbed her into the household. There was plenty of space. Tom had gone to Cornwall to rent a fisherman's cottage and make his living as a painter. Archie and Weenie were in London. Cecil put up with the intrusion. He enjoyed Nellie's insolent sense of humour although her housekeeping was poor and she would not do as he said. On one occasion he found his shirts ironed so stiffly that he almost had to break the arms in order to enter them. He shook a rigid garment in her face and it snapped and buckled. 'There is enough starch in this to hold up Nelson's Pillar,' he accused her.

'Maybe it isn't only your shirts that could use a bit less stiffening!' She laid down the teapot in a gesture that was dainty with offence.

He swatted her face with the brittle shirt. 'How dare you make a monkey out of me! I'll have you know I took you on when you were thrown out of a job.'

'An' I suppose I don't do my job here?' She put her hands on her hips. 'Looking after you an' your two women an' your two children.'

'They are not my two children,' he said, but the arm that held the

193

brittle shirt had grown limp and his voice took a strange turn that made both Ba and Daisy look at him sharply and then instinctively glance at the little boy, Jack.

'Aye, and the King of England is a Jew,' said Nellie, her small brown eyes grown spiteful. She slammed a heap of dishes on to a tray and walked away, her behind twitching with indignation. 'As plain as the nose on your pikestaff!' she muttered as she left the room.

When Nellie was fired Ba went too, back to England with little Jack. Daisy did not say goodbye to either of them but locked herself in her room and wept a great deal. At first Nan thought it was Auntie Ba mother missed, but she seemed no longer to like her. 'Aunt Ba is not to be spoken of again, nor shall we see her.' She said this to Nan but she was looking at her husband. 'We must forget that she ever existed.'

She spoke with such force that it was like a spell, and whenever golden-haired Aunt Ba appeared in her mind, Nan guiltily drove her out again and in due course the memory of her pale eyes and her crooked smile dwindled away to a teasing spectre in her dreams. In time Daisy came back to herself, but Nan understood that she had to look after her mother now. She learned how to make a cup of tea without mishap and loved to play the spoiling parent to her defence-less elder. 'There, Mags,' she would say in motherly tones, equipping her with biscuits, books and cigarettes.

'Why does she call you Mags?' Cecil irritably inquired. He too had been upset by the upheaval in the household and was moody and critical. 'It is because you have no other children. I shall have to set the example. From now on I shall call you mother.'

Mother reached deep into the pocket of her pinafore for a packet of cigarettes and lit one up, there and then, in front of him. 'I am pregnant,' she said.

This simple formula redeemed them. They smiled at one another. Nan could feel a suffocating cloud begin to drift away from them. For months on end they were held in a chrysalis of hope until mother gave birth to her baby. It was a little girl.

Chapter 21

IN the winter of 1920 Cecil moved the family to the seaside gar-
rison town of Youghal in County Cork. He said it was for their
safety, although Daisy tried to point out that it was he who was at
risk and not them. The patriotic unrest that had begun in 1916 now
manifested itself as a more personal hostility. In a space of twelve
months thirty English civilians had been murdered in Ireland and
148 were burnt out of their homes. In Dublin, slum dwellings
continued to fall down of their own accord. Bewildering to the
average amiable Dubliner, an intense hatred of Britain was asserting
itself and, worse, England was getting tired of Ireland. Winston
Churchill complained that the troops in Ireland were costing the
British taxpayers £860,000 a month. The following year England was
to yield independent government to Ireland, an act which was to
precipitate a civil war and produce the novelty of the first Irish postage
stamp, green, with a white map of Ireland instead of a monarch's head,
and a price of 2d. In the meantime, a law of curfew was imposed and in
the empty streets, a new terror appeared – the Black and Tans. This
dissolute band of ex-soldiers, hastily assembled to reinforce the
beleaguered Irish Constabulary, showed no discrimination in their hostili-
ties. The sound of gunfire in the streets reminded people shut indoors by
curfew of sons and husbands in the Dublin Fusiliers lost at Gallipoli or
Ypres, but mostly it was only bored Black and Tans taking pot-shots at
stray drunks and stray dogs.

Daisy and the children had a frightening train journey to Youghal,
for the rails had been blown up by Sinn Fein rebels. Then they had
to travel from the station in a jaunting car, which was very high off
the ground, and pulled at an aimless gallop by a huge horse. After a
short drive this brought them to a small cottage which was cold and
had no lavatory. Daisy sat at the plain wooden table in the one main
room and wept. 'He wants to get rid of me. He has got some woman
in Dublin and wants me out of the way.'

The cottage was lit with kerosene lamps and for a long time she
seemed unable to rouse herself to the effort of firing them. They sat

in the dark around the table, listening to the squeak of bristly hedges flung against the windows by the sea wind and the howls of creatures unsubdued by civilization. In the dark and with a great shaking sigh Daisy lit a cigarette and then as an afterthought she put a match to the lamp. She could see from the arched shadows over the children's eyes that they were frightened. 'When we were growing up we had no lavatory and no electric light,' she told them. 'You must look on this as a great adventure – a journey into the past.'

Nan succeeded in lighting up the stove, using a lot of sugar. They began to unpack their bags and her mother gave a cry of joy when she discovered that Cecil had packed a bottle of whiskey for her and a box of chocolates. Nan also found a slab of bacon wrapped in greaseproof paper and a loaf of bread and she cut up slices of meat and fried them on the stove. The frying bacon and the smoky stove fuelled by turf soon filled the cottage with comforting smells. They ate their tea and then they said the rosary. Although she was devout this repetitive litany always made Daisy laugh, especially the antics of two-year-old Mary, whose contribution was an egocentric cry in recognition of her name at the start of each 'Hail Mary'. By the third mystery all three of them had their hands on their faces covering their giggles. In compensation for the solitude they went to bed together, the three of them closely bound on a straw mattress which their mother said was sure to be full of fleas. 'We must think of this as a holiday,' she told the children. 'It will not be for long. Soon we will all be back home.' But underneath, already, they were hoping this was not so. Away from their father they knew that Daisy was really theirs. At home they sometimes felt like interlopers in the grown-ups' marriage, but here they were their mother's children. When the lamp was extinguished they felt her soft fingers on their lips as she pressed one more chocolate into their mouths. The straw crunched beneath them and they curled into her, sacrificing any urge to wriggle or scratch to this rare privilege. They were each thinking the same thing. Whatever father was up to, for the moment they did not have to know. And whatever they did, he would not know.

Daisy was cold and cross in the morning but the children were wild with excitement. The smell of salt, the splinters of sea on the biting wind, promised some unknown experience, some catastrophe or phenomenon. They did not think of breakfast or the seeping chill that probed the stone walls of the cottage. Tearing on any clothes they could find, they ran out of doors and down to the sea. Scores of people were already on the beach, advancing on the water with buckets and bowls and pots to reach the leaping chain of silver that had been strung out against the shore. 'What is it? What happened?' The children pushed their way through shawl-clad women and cloth-capped youths to reach the spectacle. ''Tis the miracle,' an elderly countrywoman told them. 'In windy weather Saint Peter do send them out of the water to feed the poor.'

They were dismayed to discover that the miracle was a shoal of mackerel which the high tide had flung on to the sand and which were unable to get back into the water. They touched their beautiful blue-striped backs and found that they were still alive. Immediately they began scooping up the fish into their skirts, racing with them back towards the sea. The country people ran after them and shook them until their sopping skirts spewed up their squirming hoard. 'They'll die!' Nan protested. 'Fish can't breathe out of water!'

'Dublin Jackeens!' one youth contemptuously cried, hearing her accent and delighted to have identified the source of her inadequacy. At once all the others took up the cry, even grown men and women. It was a new and frightening experience to be jeered at by grown-ups. Nan seized Mary's hand and they ran back to the cottage, trembling with cold.

'Where have you been at this hour to get your clothes and your shoes all soaked?' Their mother's normal equanimity had deserted her. 'You will catch your death of cold and there is no one but me to look after you. Nan, I will remind you that there are no servants here. I would expect you at least to light the stove and bring me a cup of tea before you disappear for the day.' Her mood improved when Nan told her about Saint Peter sending the fishes on to the beach and how they had been teased by people of all ages. 'Just remember – ' she savoured her tea and cigarette, huddled into a cardigan while the stove breakfasted voraciously on sods of turf ' – these are country people. City people are more cultivated.'

When the children had changed into dry clothes they all went to explore the town. They discovered a picture theatre and a market selling farm produce. Daisy bargained and bought each of the children an apple for a halfpenny. They were rather bad apples but she paid no attention to this as she herself did not like apples. When the children demurred at eating the freckled, soggy fruit, she gently admonished, 'They are good for you.'

As they passed the town hall they were surprised to hear hearty male voices with English accents applauding them. They saw that all the windows were open and filled with uniformed soldiers. The children were delighted when the soldiers threw sweets to them but Daisy hurried them on, saying that one did not wave to common soldiers. She suffered a pang of disloyalty, thinking of Cecil, but relieved it by entering a little baking shop that smelled beguilingly of jam and cream. As they had no one to cook for them they would have to live on picnic meals, she pointed out, and bought cream cakes and sausage rolls and an apple tart for their tea. After a lunch of cream slices on the wind-seared beach they went to the picture theatre and saw Lilian Gish in *The Paris Hat*. The second feature was a drama about the Ku Klux Klan. Mary, who had slept peacefully through the main feature, now woke up and screamed with fright at the masked horsemen with flaming brands. 'It's all right,' Daisy comforted. 'They are good men coming to rescue a white woman from bad Negroes.' When the black actor was lynched, all the cinema audience cheered.

Although she liked the easygoing life Daisy was cold in the cottage and could not get on with country people. She complained that the local women roared rosaries all day long and then crept into the town hall to consort with soldiers in the evening. She missed her neighbours. She was distraught with concern for her husband, fearing that he lay in some other woman's arms (in this nightmare, even still, it was always Janey's face she saw). There was the alternative terror that he might be murdered in his bed by Republican ruffians and the house burnt down around him, or that he would belligerently break the curfew and be shot in the head by the Black and Tans. When she had prayed and reasoned her way through these anxieties, there remained the dread that he might just abandon them, as he had done with numerous business projects, and start off afresh with another family.

One day when she was staring at the bleak sea while the children went for an ice-cream, a tide of salt water rose in her eyes. She had the hysterical feeling that she was being united with the sea, that she and the children might walk into it and free Cecil Cantwell for whatever he needed to do. A young soldier out for a walk touched her arm and asked if she was all right. 'It's the smoke in my cottage,' she said feebly. 'I'm not used to it. I come from Dublin. It makes the eyes water.' He was dark and handsome but had a bad scar on his cheek. He looked so concerned that a tear fell right down her face.

He took it away with his finger. 'Queer bloody place. Queer bloody world. Wipers to Youghal.' He laid a hand on her shoulder, more weary than inquiring, and she wanted to rest her head on it. The children ran back with their ice-creams. Overcome with pleasure at the accessible male and mother's sense of permission, they hurled themselves at him and clambered on him, flirting and appeasing. He picked Mary up and crouched to whisper something to Nan, winking at her, watching her mother. She croaked with laughter. After he had said goodbye, Nan was still choked with glee. 'Did you hear what he said to me? He asked me, "Are you a mink curtain?"'

'No he didn't,' Daisy laughed, delighted at her daughter's ability to cajole. 'That was his accent. He said, "Are you and me courtin'?" He was asking if you were his girl-friend.' The three of them strolled along the inhospitable shingle, warm with pleasure because of the trivial encounter which was so full of promise and all its promise so readily fulfilled.

Cecil came for the weekend. A curious suspense preceded his arrival. The cottage was cleaned, the children dressed up and a proper meal cooked. Then they waited, unable to move, locked into hope and apprehension. When the jaunting car appeared on the road, their mother flowed from the house like a bird uncaged. Her arms were held out stiffly as if she could no longer bear the burden of their emptiness. Father jumped down from the high cart and the space between them tactfully vanished and they were one person, all the superfluous exterior world cast out. The children watched from the window. Even Mary, who was only two, knew she was no part of this but only a witness, a passive beneficiary. Daisy looked up at him with shining eyes and he bent his head to kiss her. 'You smell of smoke.' He backed away. 'Christ almighty, you smell like a blasted tinker!' Daisy turned into stone. The children crept out slowly to take their share of his anger. 'It's the turf,' Daisy said. 'The cottage is permanently filled with smoke.' He stormed into the little house. He was shocked at the primitive cottage which had been rented through an agency. Immediately he wanted to organize a change of address. Nervously, Daisy declined. 'It is not as if we are going to be here for any length of time,' she pleaded. He turned his attention to Nan, demanding her enrolment in the local school. 'I do not like her running around like a little savage.' To her relief, her mother resisted. 'Nan is very advanced compared with the local children,' she said. 'I cannot be expected to spend whole days here with only an infant for company.'

When he left she wept again. 'Everything I love has been taken away from me.' Nan brushed and stroked her mother's long hair and wondered if she most missed her house or her neighbours or father. She did not say, 'You have us!' She knew mother liked her and Mary and that they loved her, but to their mother love must always be something grand and beautiful and they were small and rather plain.

Daisy did not lack company for long. A young man appeared one morning, stooping to show his face beneath the stunted frame of the cottage door. The rest of him was almost hidden by a huge pile of driftwood he carried. He dropped the wood outside the door and they recognized his uniform. It was the soldier they had met on the beach. 'Lucas Stafford – Lieutenant,' he introduced himself when he had a free hand to offer. 'I found out where you lived. I collected wood on the beach for your fire. It don't smoke as bad as the bloody turf.'

Luke Stafford became Daisy's slave. He carried her shopping, brought wood for her, took the children for walks and bought them sweets. She allowed him to sit at the table drinking tea and whiskey and smoking cigarettes. Once he tried to tell her that he loved her but she subdued him quickly. 'Such talk!' She glanced in the direction of the children as if they might be ruined by it. The children loved Luke and were worried that she would send him away. 'Don't you like him?' Nan begged. Her mother shrugged. 'For me, there has only ever been one man in the world. Apart from your father it is as if the male sex does not exist. That is my nature.' Secretly Nan thought her mother's nature must be perverse to have drawn her to such a difficult member of the species, but she kept her fingers crossed as she said, 'You must like him a bit or you would not let him come here.' 'I'm lonely,' Daisy said. 'He is kind and agreeable. Besides, it is protection to have a man around the place.' In fact the only danger lay in storm and flood. Daisy had another reason. She had held on to Luke Stafford, not for herself but for her husband. She knew he was bored by the small seaside town. He had not turned up the previous weekend. He loved company and she felt sure he would be relieved to have an army man to talk to, after the dangers and restrictions of living in Dublin. She invited Luke to Sunday lunch and wrote immediately to Cecil, urging him to come and meet her friend. He could not resist this enticement. He arrived with presents, with drink and flowers. When Sunday lunchtime came he was spruced up and armed with a corkscrew. 'What does your lady friend drink?' he asked. 'Beer,' Daisy smiled. He was only momentarily disconcerted. 'Ah, well, we're in the country now.' The children squealed with mirth. When Luke arrived and kissed their mother gently on the cheek – a benediction she received as coolly as a queen – father's brow clouded with uncertainty. 'Who the hell are you?' he said.

'Luke Stafford – Lieutenant, sir!' Cecil's expression clarified. As if this was the phrase he had been waiting for all his life to justify his fury, he leaped forward and punched the young man on the jaw. While the boy swayed he boxed him again and reclaimed his advantage until their visitor was stretched out on the stone floor.

'A man!' Cecil nursed his wrist. Like his wife he seemed to believe that there should not be another of the species. Daisy wrung a towel in water and applied it to the unconscious man's forehead. 'Get that swine out of here!' Cecil ordered. For once Daisy made a small show of spirit. 'I cannot carry him on my back,' she said. 'I'm off,' Cecil growled. 'I want him gone by the time I get back. By God, Mags, if I'd known you'd be fooling around in front of my children . . .!'

She did not attempt to justify herself. 'What am I supposed to do for company?' He paused to think about it, his hand gripping the door, ready to slam it. It did not occur to him, no more than to her, that city people might make friends with country people. 'You have the children,' he reasoned. He swept an arm out towards the bleak vista of the small grey town with its acidly churning bay. 'There is scenery.'

'I am not staying,' Daisy said. 'I will not stay one moment longer.' She seized the children loosely as if she meant to fling them in a suitcase. 'I am going home.'

'No, mother!' He paused helplessly. 'You'll have company. I'll send you someone.'

'Who?' They eyed each other with desolation. Between them they had used up all her sisters.

'A lady. I shall find some nice lady.'

'No!' She did not wish to think that he knew any more ladies. They watched indifferently as the young soldier struggled to his feet. He edged past his hosts warily but both of them had lost interest in him. 'I want Nellie,' Daisy said.

'You must be out of your mind!' Cecil came back into the house as if to examine her for signs of madness.

'Nellie!' Daisy lifted pots from the stove and began to serve the meal. 'Are you trying to provoke me?' He slumped at the table, cuffing its wooden edge with his fist. 'I'd as soon swing as have that woman under my roof again.'

'I never try to provoke you.' Daisy placed a plate of food before him. He sighed heavily at the homely meal of bacon and cabbage and then fell upon it and began to eat ravenously, hacking at the tender pink flesh in a manner that made the children cringe. No more mention was made of Daisy's visitor or her outrageous request. After he had eaten he complimented her on the fire, which lapped wholesomely around logs of driftwood. He said how sweet she smelled, of wood-smoke and the sea, and took her in his arms.

'The children!' she warned, both horrified and pleased.

'Off to the sea with you, you idle bloody lot,' he bellowed at the two small girls. 'Sun outside would scorch your eyeballs.' They scampered down to the shore in a sheet of grey rain that cut into them like falling slates.

Nellie had a way of arranging life as if it was tables and chairs, solid but movable. She arrived at the station in Youghal clad in raincoat and sou'wester and carrying a heavy case that was mainly filled with tins of peas and peaches and corned beef and salmon lest country living should impose on her its untamed diet of fresh food. 'Where are your children?' Daisy said. Nellie now had two little girls. 'I expected you to bring them.'

Nellie lit a cigarette. She squinted, as if trying to remember. 'I left them with a friend.' She set about subduing the savage place. She found a chip shop. She located an old gramophone and some dusty recordings so that they had music playing and she kept raging fires burning day and night. Meals became even more disorganized but, as Nellie pointed out, no one need ever go hungry while she was around. There was always bread and jam and a packet of fags on the table. She spoiled Daisy, ordering her to stay in bed in the mornings with her tray of breakfast while she led the children out on voyages of exploration. As they streeled along she told them stories or sang a song:

'A Chinaman came up to me and these are the words he said,
"If you don't marry a Chingchong, you'll have to lose your head."
He painted me all over and put me in a pot to boil,
And while I was a boiling he was singing all the while . . . ooh!'

She waited for the children to join in the chorus:

'Solomon Jingo, my friend Bingo, my friend Sambalingo,
Solomon Jingo, my friend Bingo, my friend Black Man Sam.'

They began each day on the beach and then set off along country lanes. They gathered shells and firewood and nuts and leaves. Sometimes they came across a holy well. These wells, in lonely places, were ornamented with flowers and rosary beads as well as the occasional crutch or surgical boot or dirty bandage, to testify to miraculous cures they had empowered. Nellie told them about a wonderful place called Lourdes in France where the diseased bathed in holy water that was covered in other people's scabs, and were rewarded with what she called 'a merricle'. The children peered down into the wells, hoping to see an angel or a merricle.

One day they saw a farmer pointing a gun at a mongrel which was tied to a tree with a length of string. Heedless of danger they rushed forward to shield the animal.

'Outa me way now.' The farmer waved his weapon. 'That there is a villainous cur that deserves to die.'

'What did he do?' Mary spread her arms in front of the bored-looking creature.

'He ate the arse offa one of me sheep.'

Nellie strode forward and untied the dog. 'I'd like a shilling for every arse you ate off a sheep,' she challenged. When he did not answer she added boldly, 'And every woman too!' The man made no further move to hinder them but watched Nellie with admiration as she led away the cur by its bonds.

They called the dog Tessie. It was hard to believe in the farmer's charge because Tessie was the laziest dog they had ever known. On long excursions it would sit down in protest. Sometimes Nellie had to carry it. It was their mother who pointed out that a change of name might be suitable as Tessie was a male. 'How do you know?' the children asked. 'Because male dogs use the lavatory with one leg in the air,' Daisy produced this surprising knowledge.

'Why did you not tell us it was a boy?' they accused Nellie, feeling let down. 'I did not look,' Nellie said. 'I prefer not to pay attention to that portion of man or beast.'

They changed his name to Teddy, which suited his short tufty orange fur and black eyes and nose. They drew a picture of him and sent it to Uncle Tom asking him what kind of dog he thought it was.

'It is an Ancient Irish Hellhound,' Uncle Tom wrote back. In the evenings, by firelight, Nan made a rapt audience as Nellie and her mother held long conversations in subdued tones. Smoke from their cigarettes rolled around the ceiling, giving the cottage a magical, insubstantial air. Mary usually fell asleep but Nan curled up at the fire with Teddy and absorbed the fleshy resonance of women's talk — of difficult men and easy women, of children born, mystifyingly and sinisterly, on the wrong side of the blanket. They were haphazard about life's dramas, profligate with its catastrophes. They cut out the nugget of life and then pushed it faddily about. Instinctively Nan knew that men never talked like this. Men were coarse in their language but modest in their talk. Like children, men were anxious and wary about life. 'Some day,' she thought, 'I too will be a woman. I will sit and smoke cigarettes and whisper with mother.' On those glowing evenings, with peril so snugly parcelled in warmth and comfort, she could imagine no better ambition.

All through February the biting weather persisted. In March the climate softened and the sky turned a harmless blue, but after only a week the storms began. At first the sea rose up against the town and hurled rocks, tree trunks and the corpse of a man out on to the pier. Shop windows were boarded up and people retired to their houses to listen to the wind howling and branches teasingly clawing at their windows. The waves reared up like the acrobatic horses of picture-house cowboys and fell thundering into the street. Little scummy eddies wandered aimlessly along the road and gurgled into drains. With the next onslaught the puddles collided and choked the drains and retreated in a mad rush towards the houses. Daisy peered out the window in horror and the children waited eagerly for the ocean to enter their house. Nellie counted their stock of tins and cursed. As the waves continued to heave over the sea wall, the rush of water fattened and burst. A little salty finger of sea poked its way under the cottage door and then fled across the floor. The dog's dish lost its purchase and skated over the tiles. 'Jersiful Mayses!' Nellie leaped on to the bed as the flood uprooted chairs and tables and menacingly rattled their store of driftwood. By the following day the water had risen to the level of Nan's knees. The women and dog had confined themselves to the bed, which staggered menacingly in the filthy water. The children waded bravely about with drifting chairs and tables and rooted on the depths of the kitchen floor for sunken treasure.

The flood was beginning to subside when Cecil came for the weekend. He was furious. Why had no one told him, he demanded. Why had Nellie not taken better care? 'We were all marooned here,' Daisy placated. 'We could not leave to send a telegram.'

'The house is destroyed,' he complained, looking at the frieze of mud around the plastered walls, the drowned floor in which smaller pieces of debris were stranded. 'The children could have been killed.'

'What could we do about it?' Daisy pleaded.

'We could leave,' he said.

'Oh yes, oh yes, oh yes,' she breathed over and over. 'Let us go back on the next train. What remains of our possessions can be packed in minutes.'

Instead he removed them to a hotel in the town. It too had been affected by the flood. Carpets had been lifted and a makeshift lounge was established on the first floor. They all looked so wretched after their muddy imprisonment that they had chicken soup sent to their rooms and then took turns having baths in the cavernous bathroom. Nellie brought the children out to inspect the flood damage while their mother and father drank whiskey by the fire and argued. 'You must not treat me like a child,' Daisy said. 'You have to tell me why we may not come home.'

'Why can't you trust me?' he grumbled. 'Other women trust their husbands.' She did not answer this. 'Do you mean ever to have us back? At least tell me if you wish to be rid of us.' Dismayingly, he burst into tears. 'Oh, Mags! Don't you know that I worship you. I have never loved anyone else.'

After he went back to the city they remained in the hotel. It was very comfortable. City people stayed there and there were trained maids to make the beds and bring the meals. Daisy became friendly with other women guests. Nellie, being conscious of the matter of station, tactfully exchanged her mistress's company for that of porters and doormen. Daisy was in the lounge eating tea and fruit cake with her new friend, Mrs Agnes Cambell, when one of the porters delivered a letter.

'It is from my husband,' she said calmly, noting the handwriting which had once affected her so as to deprive her of the use of her legs.

'Bad news, my dear?' Her friend waited patiently for her share of the tidings, but Daisy seemed in a kind of trance.

'My darling,' he had written. 'You are right, of course. Man and wife should not be apart. I have managed to move heaven and earth . . .'

Daisy looked up in dismay as the last piece of fruit cake was taken daintily from the plate. 'He wants me to come home.'

'I see,' said the woman, with a probing emphasis which conveyed that she did not. Her new acquaintance had seemed anxious for home and lonely for her husband, yet her pretty face was full of dread.

'But it's not my home!' Daisy burst into desolate tears. 'It isn't my home at all!'

Chapter 22

A LL the way home the children were held tightly by their mother and seared by the cigarettes which she smoked rapidly, lighting one after the other, crumpling them half-smoked into the little tin ashtray. Every so often they experienced a violent shuddering which came through her body to their own.

'The oul' divil! He done it on spite!' Nellie breathed heavily and comforted herself with a piece of the marble cake she had brought to sustain them on the journey. 'He thinks he's shook me off by moving out to the sticks. Just because I threw a spanner in his capers with your sister.'

'Nellie!' The train entered a tunnel and Daisy's startled eye was masked by blackness. 'Right from the day of my wedding,' she said bitterly, forgetting that they were discussing what must never be mentioned, 'Janey had him under her spell.'

'You've got the wrong end of the handle,' Nellie impudently argued. 'Janey was never after your husband. She saw him as a boy and she liked boys. It was her that kep' him on the straight and narrow, or as straight as he could be. Their friendship was a different class of carry-on. Some kind of a tonic.'

'Platonic.'

'That's the one.'

The train thundered through to daylight, and outside their window a countryside innocent with the first sprinkling of lambs fled past. Instantly, Daisy was roused to indignation. 'Why are you saying all this? None of this should ever have been mentioned again. How dare you talk of such matters in front of the children. Why did Janey come to see you?'

Nellie nodded calmly. 'Little jugs have big lugs.' She handed each of the children a lump of marble cake, as if to wedge their ears. 'She came to see me in the Gresham before she went back to America. She told me what was going on between your husband and your little sister. Asked me to keep an eye on you, like – and on the other one too. She was worried about you. I only mentioned it because of what he's after doin' on you now. I'm laying no blame. That man doesn't know his arse from his antirrhinums. Only you've got to be careful.'

Mary gave her piece of cake to Teddy, who was crouched beneath the table, anchored by a piece of string. She thought of their cottage slapped about by ocean waves and wondered if it had now floated out to sea, past the mackerel that drifted in to land. Nan thought, 'I am eight years of age. In only six more years I will be old enough to go to work and then mother won't have to depend on father any more.'

When first she read the letter Daisy had not noticed anything. He wanted her home. He had moved heaven and earth. His demands and energies exhausted her for she had grown used to the ease of hotel life, but she was glad of his keenness. Then she saw the address. He had written to her from somewhere called Hallinan's Mansions in a newly dug neighbourhood three miles from the city at the foot of the Dublin mountains. The bleak-sounding location had been playfully asterisked and beside it he had scribbled: 'Our new address! I hope you will like it.'

'It is always the meanest addresses that have the highest-sounding names,' Daisy mused bitterly. 'I suppose he thinks we shall be well adapted now for living in a hovel.'

He was at the station. He looked anxious and exhausted. He took the bags from her and then let them down to seize her hands. 'What has become of my house?' Her voice was stark. She held her two hands up stiffly as if there was blood on them.

'Oh, mother, I have had such trouble.' He tried to put his arms around her but her stiff hands were a barrier. 'The business went bust on me. We almost lost everything. I had to send you away because I could not let you see them taking the furniture from the house. I did my best to hang on but the house had to go.'

'My house? You sold my house?'

'It's all right, Mags. I'll make it up to you. Everything will be all right. You'll see.' He tried to smile at her but had to struggle with his shaking mouth. 'I have been so lonely. I have been living in a rooming house and working like a dog, night and day.' He reached for her forgiveness and she beat him back with her raised claws. 'Why can't you get a proper job?' For once he did not lose his temper. He put the luggage into a cab and meekly asked Nellie if they could drop her somewhere. 'Nellie is coming with me,' Daisy said. 'I will not go without her.' Cecil looked unhappy. 'It's a bit off the beaten track. Do we have to take the blasted cur as well?' Nan and Mary quickly hauled Teddy into the cab. Now that the weight of their mother's misery had been lifted off them they began to feel the pulse of a new adventure, the excitement of a new place. Nellie flung out her arms melodramatically. 'I would folly my mistress to the ends of the earth.' Her long face grew thoughtful as she scrambled into the carriage. 'You poor oul' divil. I suppose you'd folly your mistress too, given half a chance.'

When they got to Hallinan's Mansions Daisy cautiously angled her head to the window. She saw two terraces of good red-bricked houses facing one another behind low railings. The houses were not, as she had most deeply feared, in the heart of the country. Nor were they raw with the scars of building. Behind the windows there were curtains. The little lawns in front were small and neat as crustless sandwiches. She arched her neck when a woman with a message-bag banged through one of the gates and with a frowning glance at a privet hedge stabbed her key at the door. A neighbour! She had been shopping. There must be shops nearby. Beyond the houses she could see the spire of a church. She began to wonder about the rooms inside her new house, whether the fireplaces were made of marble or iron, if the ceilings were nice. She drew herself back, remembering her pink and green drawing room.

'They are good houses,' Cecil encouraged. 'Because they are outside the city they are very reasonably priced. In a few years three miles will not be considered a great distance to travel to the centre.' She said nothing. She thought it would be a very long time before she could trust herself to speak to him, although, as his wife, she could not deny him touch. All her old neighbours knew of their disgrace and she had known nothing. She burned with shame, forgetting that it no longer mattered since they were not her neighbours any more.

Their house had a door painted with a wood-grain stain and a nice, bright brass knocker. There was a little porch with red and black tiles in a diamond pattern. Daisy noted with relief that there were green curtains on the drawing-room window. Cecil took the children down from the car and then the bags. Daisy stood aside while he brought the luggage to the porch and opened the door. He came back to lead her through. 'Oh,' she said when he took her in the door, and again when he opened the drawing room. 'Oh, Nellie, look!'

Inside, in this strange setting, her hall and drawing room had been reproduced. Every panel and border, each cloth and cushion, was exactly as it had been. She moved around and touched all her pieces which she had missed so much.

'I could not let them go,' he told her. 'When I knew I would have to sell the house I had all your things put into storage. I vowed that when I got out of that jam you would find every stick and saucer as you had left it.'

'Even the colours are the same. The walls, the paintwork!'

'I worked like a dog,' he admitted.

She did not care about the rest of the house but kept marvelling at this replication of her favourite room. She could not keep herself from smiling. 'Put the children to bed, Nellie,' she said, not wanting the maid to see how easily she could be won.

'The crisis is past,' Cecil told her when Nellie had taken the little girls upstairs. 'While you were away I went to England and introduced the Cantwell to convents there. I have managed to run down existing stocks. I have come to believe that my designs to date were not wholly practical. From now on I shall take a more determined line. Will you stick by me, Mags?'

'Of course.' She looked around at her familiar furnishings. 'I'm your wife.'

'You're a good girl. The best!' Cautiously he put out his arms and she did not defend herself. 'Let me get you a drink.' She nodded, leaning against him. 'Let's have a drink in the dining room,' he said with a sheepish sort of eagerness. 'I am keen for you to see the dining room.' She had had enough surprises for a day. She would have liked to take a glass of whiskey up to bed, to lie there blowing smoke at the ceiling, to let her senses gradually shed their armour of alarm, but he was looking at her as greedily as a child. She could not deny him his praise.

As he opened the dining room the homely scent of cigarette smoke drifted out. The room was full of friendly smoke, filled with her own furniture, crowded with nice, smiling people. They had drinks in their hands. There were cakes on the table. 'Mrs Cantwell!' Cecil presented with quiet pride. He gripped her hand as he led her in.

'Mrs Cantwell! Welcome! Oh, isn't she lovely?' The pleasant people surged forward. Daisy almost wept with pleasure after her months in exile from civilized living. 'The neighbours!' Cecil exclaimed in triumph. 'Mrs Lehane, Mrs Bradish, Mrs Guilfoyle. I arranged a homecoming for you. Mrs Nugent, Mrs Gannon. This is Mrs Martindale. These good people have been waiting here to surprise you. Splendid neighbours! We have become very good friends already.'

'So shall we all be.' Daisy accepted a drink from her husband and timidly inspected the taut curls and loose bosoms, the errant lipstick and counterfeit teeth. They were good women, one could tell at a glance. There was no one here to take her husband.

Mrs Guilfoyle, in a corner, had begun to sing and Cecil, leaning against the sideboard, was extracting a confidence from Mrs Gannon. 'My daughter, Birdie,' she whispered, 'is a nymphomaniac.' The party was in full swing when Nellie returned from settling the children. She entered the dining room and stood glowering in mackintosh and sou'wester until an uneasy silence fell over their mirth. 'Well,' she said. 'This is a nice kettle of affairs. Not even a cup of tea to wet our fiddle and already the house is in uproar.'

'This is Nellie,' Daisy said weakly. 'The maid!'

'Maid by day! Mother by night! So I'll thank you and good evening.' Nellie left the room. Seconds later they heard the front door slam.

'She is good with the children,' Daisy apologized. The silence seemed to swell and spread, suffocating them, until it was tackled by Mrs Lehane. 'Well, aren't you lucky to have her? It's very hard to get a girl after the war.'

'She is something of a charity case,' Cecil explained. 'We took her in when she was down on her luck.'

'Your husband,' said Mrs Lehane to Daisy, 'is a certifiable saint.'

'You arranged all that for me?' At the end of the day they left the chaos of the dining room for Nellie and went upstairs to their room. Cecil took a plait in his hand and slowly began to unravel it. 'Don't you know by now that there is nothing in the world I would not do for you?'

'Now I know it.' She took him in her arms.

'Mags,' he whispered. 'We're starting off fresh. Everything will be different now. There were bad memories in our other house. The things that happened there, I promise you upon the grave of our poor dead little son, they will not happen again.'

'Yes, yes,' Daisy quickly silenced him. 'I am certain you will have better luck with the business now.'

★

In spite of its solid appearance their new house seemed to be made of cardboard. Nan and Mary discovered that you could make a hole in the wall by pushing hard with your finger. A lighted candle, held close to the wall, soon lapped the surface with blue flames. Through the thin partition that isolated their family from the one next door they could hear Birdie Gannon screaming as her father belted her when she came home in the middle of the night – a series of shrill cries like the scavenging birds at the sea in Youghal. 'You feckin' whoor!' he answered her entreaties for mercy. 'I'll splatter you!'

When first they returned from the country their mother and father were so wrapped up in one another that the children and even Nellie left them alone. They missed the sea, so Nellie took them for day-long excursions on the tram, to Sandymount or Dollymount. They wandered up and down the damp sand while Teddy plunged in the meagre waves and Nellie entertained them with stories they could not understand, addressing them as if they were grown-ups like herself. She told them of an old parish priest who used to come in to look at her backside when she was down on her knees scrubbing his floor. 'He used to be fidgetin' under his frock, pretending to say his beads, and once he says to me, polite as pie, "Would you pull my wire, miss?"' After a time Nellie got bored with the children, just as Daisy grew uneasy with her husband's undivided attention, and she went back home, leaving the girls to their own devices.

'Nan Cantwell, Hallinan's Mansions,' Nan recited as she led their expeditions. Her mother had taught her to say this so that if she was lost she could be returned to their address. They found sweet shops close to where they lived, a church, a morgue and a canal. Teddy liked to swim in the canal and often emerged with treasure in his teeth – the inner tube of a bicycle, an old boot or tin can. Once he struggled ashore with a small piece of sacking and dropped it at their feet. When they gingerly undid the string that bound it, they found inside a black kitten. As they stared in shock at the scrap of sodden fur, Teddy began to nudge it gently with his nose. A miniature paw, shrivelled by wetness, poked out in feeble attack. They brought it home to Daisy, who wrapped it in an old black tam-o'-shanter hat to dry. They sat and watched as the angry, rat-like creature fluffed up into a silky, purring ball. 'What shall we call it?' The children eagerly took advantage of their mother's indulgent mood. Daisy blew smoke into its fur. 'Call it Bertie, after my little brother, who was drowned in the canal.' She sighed and walked away from them.

At once the enthralling discovery of the cat was overshadowed by this tragic mystery. Their mother never talked about her family. She had told them that there were ten of them and that they had lived in a house the size of a squirrel's nest. They were left to cope with this curious picture, for they knew that the only person who really interested her was father. Their father loaned them his ancestors to compensate. The walls of their room were crowded with portraits of unknown Cantwells, frowning for the camera. The children were afraid of them, believing that through their scornful glare father could see everything they did.

When they explored their new neighbourhood Teddy came too. He was pleased by city life and particularly the ease of transport. He liked to ride on top of the trams, his long tongue and short ears flapping, his ugly face noble, like a plain man in love. When they went to mass he raised his muzzle to bay solemnly with the organ. At the cinema, he barked at the spectral stampede of silent horses, at mutely hurtling trains. He lowered his lip and growled prudishly at the flashing knees of dancing girls.

He did not know it and nor did Mary, but Nan was growing tired of them. She had discovered girls of her own age in the neighbourhood. They went to school every day and had a womanish confraternity of linked arms and secrets. She was becoming impatient with her low-legged companions who followed her everywhere. Sooner or later either Teddy or Mary got tired and she had to carry them home. She did not want to start her new life handicapped by dependants. She went to her father and asked if she could go to school.

'Aren't you in school yet?' he said in surprise.

When Nan set off in her new green gym-slip and green felt hat, her constant companions tried to follow her. Repulsed, they crouched behind the drawing-room window to await her return. Nellie found them there and dragged them forth, convinced that they were hiding after some misdemeanour. After a grievous interview in which the small girl almost choked on her sobs, Nellie brought her to her mother. 'You should make the most of your childhood,' Daisy told her. 'Your days of freedom will end soon enough.' But Mary's freedom had ended with Nan's departure. She wasn't allowed to go anywhere on her own, and since the grown-ups rarely noticed her they did not take her with them when they went out.

Teddy took to riding the trams alone, travelling on long journeys to the sea, coming home late at night. The outward trip was a simple matter, for he knew the stop the children used and got on the tram as it came. Coming home was complicated by a variety of destinations which attracted vehicles bound for a further assortment of unknown locations. Sometimes he went missing for days on end. He returned home lean and ragged and lay with his face on his paws, moaning with the pounding waves of experience. He developed a dreamer's eye and the abstract demeanour of the romantic.

Mary was now all alone. It was her father who finally took pity on her solitary vigil at the drawing-room window. 'She should have a doll,' he decided. 'Little girls are meant to have a doll.' He gave Daisy a pound. Daisy had never owned a doll. She did not think of them in terms of play but as the stricken bridal party in mama's glass-fronted cabinet. Unwilling to confront the knowing faces of the most glamorous playthings, she steered the disappointed Mary towards a display of rag dolls with black faces and black hair frizzed like Nellie's.

Left with her fierce new playmate, Mary considered her lonely future. The rag doll's outflung arms and devilish grin made her nervous. After a long time she carefully undressed it down to its rag-filled white body and put it away in a drawer. She stuffed Bertie the kitten into the doll's dress and set up her own miniature domestic establishment, with saucers of food and milk. While the kitten prowled amid the debris, its thin tail arched out of the stiffly frilled hem, Mary pushed the stub of a pencil in and out of her mouth and blew imaginary smoke. 'What peace we have,' she said, 'now that the children are at school.'

These pursuits might have sustained them until the passage of time imposed a new order, but they were summoned by a fresh crisis. It concerned Birdie Gannon. Birdie was pregnant. Her father beat her up and she crawled, bruised and bleeding, to the Cantwells' door. Daisy did not like the big morose-looking blonde but Cecil tended her wounds and made her take eggs beaten up with sherry for the baby. He was disappointed when she responded to her mother's pleading by sailing to England to have the baby with charitable nuns. There was a period of peace next door while the nuns extracted the fruit of sin for covert transfer to wholesomer arms, but Cecil had begun to brood. 'There must be something lacking in the home to make a young girl go astray.' He woke Daisy in the small hours to ventilate this theory. Through the thin walls filtered the faint howl of

Mrs Midge Gannon singing tuneless hymns, and her despairing or contemptuous laugh.

'If you ask me, there is something wrong with the whole set-up. Why isn't that woman asleep at this hour?'

'Perhaps she is missing her daughter,' Daisy said doubtfully.

'Missing her, my foot!' The solution struck him in a flash. 'The woman is drinking. A drunken mother and a violent father! Poor little bugger never stood a chance.'

Birdie returned from the nuns thin and ravenous. As though anxious to swiftly replace her stolen child she painted her face every day and went out to stalk strange men. She was indiscriminate in her choice of partner. Nightly, when her father sprang into the back lane that ran behind the houses, he had to sunder her from tradesmen, soldiers, students, solicitors. At length, weary of the bewildering array of opponents, their size and youth, he contented himself with throwing his daughter out in the street. Birdie howled and flung herself at the door. Her father, on the other side loudly detailed an assortment of deaths available to her should she care to step inside. Her mother drank port wine and sang her hymns, pausing for interludes of wretched mirth.

Then there was silence. Up and down the street curtains quivered as neighbours tried to ascertain if the disagreement had ended in death or absolution. In fact, neither was the case. Cecil had removed her from the dangerous influence of her home. He had taken her up to the Indian room to rehabilitate her. Each evening after tea he ascended the stairs to persuade her to mend her ways and Daisy retreated to the kitchen to drink tea with Nellie and wring her hands.

'He needn't expect me to lift hide nor hair for that trollop.' Nellie bashed the fire with a poker. Coal was still rationed after the war but she heaped on sods of turf in defiance of her employer and the kitchen was full of smoke and had the damp, sour smell of their cottage in the country.

'She is a victim of drunkenness and violence.' Daisy tried to defend her foolish spouse. She cleaned her lungs of the smoke of turf with an inhalation of tobacco. 'Given an example of wholesome family life, she will very soon repent.'

Birdie showed no repentance. She came down late to breakfast and sat in a soiled pink satin wrap smoking cigarettes and playing records on the gramophone. She ignored the children and cast hostile glances at Daisy and Nellie, irritably battering the stub of her Woodbine on a saucer. Revived by tea, she would dress up and go out 'with a painted mouth on her like a cut throat', as Nellie put it. In the evening she came back and changed again into Chinese pyjamas and little pink ear-rings shaped like lanterns and went upstairs to wait for her benefactor.

'What can they be doing up there?' Daisy lamented.

'I'm going up to see for myself.' Nellie armed herself with a mop as if it were a sabre.

'Oh, no! You will lose your job. He would never forgive me.' Daisy leaped from the table and wrestled feebly for possession of the floor cleaner.

Nellie reluctantly let go. 'I'm not afraid. I might as well be hung for a sheep as a gander.'

Cecil was cheerful about his campaign. He pointed out as evidence of his success that Birdie no longer went out at night in search of men.

'Why would she when she has my husband up there to entertain her?' Daisy spiritedly argued, although of course she said this to Nellie and not to Cecil. Nellie brooded. The house and its table suffered, for she could not be expected to regulate the contents of the frying pan when her mind was lost in thought.

For a time they were diverted by a smaller controversy. They were getting complaints about Teddy. The mongrel, in his independent life, had developed a liking for religious meetings – not the dull Sunday ceremony which the family attended, but the thunderous street assemblies drawn by the newly fashionable revivalist preachers. The crumbling city in its last days of British rule was ripe for warnings of the world's end and attracted large crowds of both the dissolute poor and the sensation-seeking young. Incensed by bellowed threats of hell, Teddy allegedly sank his fangs into the tender limbs of witnessing women. The family was mystified by this. Apart from the single incident where a farmer had alleged savagery to a sheep, they had never met a lazier or more benign dog.

Nan and Mary decided to follow Teddy. He led them to the tram stop at Sullivan's Cross and there they boarded the vehicle bound for Nelson's Pillar. At the terminus he alighted and ambled with purpose to the part of O'Connell Street by the Hallam Hotel that was known, since the great fire of 1916, as Ruins Corner. A small crowd had gathered around a man in black who stood on an improvised platform, warning about the salary of sin.

The war had propagated a bold new species of woman who perceived the poor lasting qualities of men and managed to incorporate in their appearance both independence and availability. They had shorn their hair to look like boys but wore scandalously short skirts and silk stockings, shiny as scars, to encourage the mating instinct in a population of men depleted and depressed. They were new-born from a world of protected women and, like Nellie when she was a child, they were eager to acquire experience of sin. They were drawn to the revivalist meetings which promised illumination on the perils of the flesh. Groups of these girls with their childish figures and fringed shifts gathered around the advocate who warned of the exquisite tortures set aside for debauchers. At this, three of the girls raised their hems and executed some steps. It was a solemn, elfin little dance, performed with self-conscious care, and involved kicking out their heels and passing their hands across knees that joined and then parted, as though crossing the eyes at the knees. The children were enchanted and mentally planned to try out the dance at home. The men in the audience went wild. The preacher, in a frenzy, roared out that they had sounded hell's knell for Jezebels, and Teddy, impelled beyond his brief span of civilization by some primitive enmity, sailed through the air and launched himself at the shimmering moons of the New Women's knees. The meeting ended in uproar. There were scuffles and screams of 'mad dog', and Nan and Mary grabbed Teddy and ran half-way down O'Connell Street and Marlborough Street until they could hide, tittering in the Pro-Cathedral. 'He thinks they're chorus girls.' Nan wiped tears of mirth from her face. 'He always growls at the dancing girls in the pictures.'

Daisy still fretted about Birdie Gannon. Nellie's long face grew menacing with love and concern as she worried and plotted. At length she brought her mistress a carbonized kipper and the fruit of her reflection. 'Even if you won't say boo to the oul' bastard, at least you can put a flea in the ear of that dirty little faggot.'

'What do you mean, Nellie?'

'Give her the boot, the elbow, the old-heave-ho!' The children giggled behind their hands and the maid sighed heavily at her better's poor grasp of plain language.

'Oh, I couldn't. Mr Cantwell . . . !'

'This is women's business. It's for the good of your marriage.' Provoked out of her apathy by Nellie's elbow, and followed by her and the children at a distance of half an inch, she reluctantly approached the Indian room. Birdie did not ask her in, but stood blocking the door with her broad hips.

'I think it's time you went home now, like a good girl,' Daisy suggested.

'Why should I?' Birdie shook her long yellow hair and nibbled on a fingernail. Daisy cast about for some diplomatic alibi concerning unexpected visitors, but Nellie, who did not waste time on duplicity, shouted over her employer's shoulder, 'Because we don't like you!'

Birdie's brilliant lips shrivelled into a little red knot of ire, 'tight as a fish's arse', Nellie later observed with interest. She banged the door in their faces and they went downstairs to comfort themselves with tea. There the matter seemed to rest, but on a morning shortly after, when Daisy was alone in the house, Birdie came down to see her. 'Now how do you like me?' she said. She stood insolently until Daisy was forced to look on all that soft and hefty pinkness with its startling landmarks of hills and hollows and little foxy beard. Birdie wore no clothes.

Daisy tried to convey this outrage to her husband. 'No clothes?' he echoed in disbelief. 'Naked as the day . . .' Daisy said forlornly. He was furious. 'How could you let this happen? Of course she has no clothes. The poor child was thrown out without a penny. She clearly put her few miserable rags in the wash. Poor bugger must have been mortified. Naked as the day . . .' He gazed with longing at the ceiling. 'I shall deal with it. I shall see that she has whatever cash she needs.'

At this point his plan became effective. Aided by Cecil's money, Birdie began her transformation. Blowsy Birdie, with her heavy hair and floating bosoms, her mean narrow eyes and wide greedy mouth, streeled out one morning a siren and returned that evening a flapper. Her hair had almost gone and most of her eyebrows. Her face looked pale as a pudding beneath the pudding-bowl haircut which, she told them, was called the shingle. Her breasts had mysteriously disappeared and her legs showed the mottled plumpness of a Hafner's sausage beneath an attenuated shift.

They all stared. They stood open-mouthed, the grown-ups, the two children and Teddy the dog. 'The shingles,' Nellie marvelled. Cecil was thunderstruck. 'What have you done to yourself?' he demanded. 'Mother, what has been going on?' Daisy delved deep into the pocket of her dress to make reassuring contact with her cigarettes.

'When I left here this morning,' Cecil complained, 'that girl was an innocent child. I come back to find her looking like some common tart – a consort of sailors.'

Nobody noticed that Teddy, who had been open-mouthed like the rest of them, his tongue draped beguilingly over the armoury of his teeth, had now pulled back the edges of his jaws and was brewing a faint menace in the back of his throat.

'There's nothing wrong with sailors,' Birdie snapped back. 'Sight more life in them than the army.'

Teddy sprang. They were all amazed and the dog looked amazed too. Birdie's scream was that of a woman sawn in half as the animal found purchase with his teeth in her knees. Within minutes both her parents were pounding on the door, demanding to know what was being done to their daughter. Birdie did look a fright. Her little plum-coloured mouth was a gunshot wound in a face the colour of sago. Blood streamed from both her knees and bloody scraps of tattered silk trailed down her legs. 'My stockings!' she wailed. 'He tore my silk stockings.' With a look of loathing at the good neighbour, Gannon led his child away. Nan and Mary crouched behind a chair with Teddy, who unrepentantly slurped salty scarlet from his chops.

Cecil declared that the beast would have to meet its maker. Nellie said the dog should have a medal. Daisy said nothing, but the animal grew fat on cake and pieces of ham with which she rewarded him under the table. Cecil bought a rifle and spent a great deal of time cracking it open and peering down the barrel or poking its insides with a thin rod. This activity made the dog nervous and he went away and chewed on a slipper.

Cecil found his wife weeping in the drawing room. She so rarely let him see her in tears that he was profoundly moved. In her hand she held some limp and sodden thing like a rain-washed rose. 'What is it, my dear?' He stroked and gently kissed her wet face. 'My love, my only love.' In these rare moments it was as if they found each other as they had first found each other at the post-box and for the rest of the time they restlessly sought one another. 'The primrose slipper.' Her voice trembled between grief and relief. 'The dog ate the primrose slipper.'

'I shall kill the blasted cur,' he resolved, needing her to know the violence of his love. 'I shall do it right away.'

'No,' Daisy said weakly, knowing that Teddy had once again

come to her rescue. 'No, don't leave me now.' He went away and put a record on the gramophone, 'Pale Hands I Loved beside the Shalimar'. She sat and smiled out the window while he knelt at her feet and kissed her hands, each finger, each pink and unused pad. The children sensed the aura of homeliness, like a cake in the oven. They crept to the doorway and hovered there, hoping that nothing, not even their own longing, would interrupt the moment. They heard their father swear once more that he would kill the dog and even then they did not intervene, although later, when things were back to normal, they could not help pleading for Teddy's life and driving their volatile parent into a rage.

The controversy went on for weeks, during which time Birdie Gannon, unnoticed, packed her bag and set sail for England and Winston Churchill handed over the rule of Ireland to Michael Collins and the Irish Free State. Teddy too seemed to realize that experience had spilled over this portion of his map and muddied its paths. With the cries and conflicts of family life blooming and wilting on his soft ear, he boarded a tram bound for the sea and was not seen again.